2.

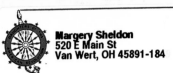

Margery Sheldon
520 E Main St
Van Wert, OH 45891-184

W9-CHI-179

A Warmth in Winter

A Warmth in Winter

LORI COPELAND
and ANGELA HUNT

BOOKSPAN LARGE PRINT EDITION

W PUBLISHING GROUP™

A Division of Thomas Nelson, Inc.

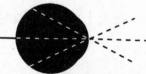

Two people can accomplish more than twice as much as one; they get a better return for their labor.
—ECCLESIASTES 4:9

PROLOGUE

*Oh, distinctly I remember it was in a
     cold December,
And every village member came
     a-knocking at my door—*

I will apologize to Edgar Allan Poe, of course, if I have occasion to see him on one of my excursions into the supernatural realm.

Welcome back. I am Gavriel, captain of the angelic company guarding the small island of Heavenly Daze. I'm delighted, as always, that you could join us for yet another glimpse into the mysterious interactions of God and man.

If you're new to our little island, let me provide the history of this tiny settlement off the coast of Maine. Over two hundred years ago, a retired sea captain called Jacques de Cuvier begged the Father to guard the inhabitants of this place. In answer to Jacques's sincere prayer, the Lord dispatched me and six others of the angelic host. Our mission is simple: We guard and serve those who live in the seven original buildings on the island of Heavenly Daze.

As captain of the heavenly host here, I protect the church and minister to those who serve it—Winslow and Edith Wickam, the pastor and his wife. Since the lighthouse is a relatively modern building, I occasionally peek in from time to time on Salt Gribbon, our light keeper—but only at the Father's command. Unlike the other angels, I rarely find it necessary to don mortal flesh. My brothers, however, live among the people, serving with quiet spirits and humble hearts.

Since the adventures of this most recent November, things have been fairly calm on our island. Birdie Wester, proprietor of the local bakery, did cause a bit of a stir right after Thanksgiving—seems she was using her famous recipe for Nutmeg Shortbread and ran out of the predominant spice. Because the rush order was for the Ogunquit Women's Circle, Bea Coughlin rose to her sister's aid. Taking advantage of her position as postmistress, she used her morning mail run to gather canisters of nutmeg from every kitchen on the island. Birdie baked the shortbread, the Ogunquit women inhaled every last crumb, and the next Sunday Pastor Wickam's sermon extolled the joy of sacrificing to meet a neighbor's need.

The Internet rumor about angels working miracles on the island still brings in letters by the sackful, but Bea and the Women's Circle do their best to answer it all. They say truth is stranger than fiction, and in this case, what the ladies believe to be fiction is truer than they realize. Ah, well. The Father does have a sense of humor, you know.

The days have begun to grow short; the leaves have disappeared from all but the evergreen trees. Soon the winter winds will howl and we'll be blanketed in snow. Winters on Heavenly Daze are not easy.

The other day I overheard Cleta Lansdown laughingly tell Pastor Wickam, "You know, the summer complaints are always saying that we live in God's country. Though it may look like God's country to them, I know he don't spend his winters here!"

Pastor Wickam, who has been yielded enough to speak for the Spirit on several occasions, smiled at his parishioner and truthfully answered, "Yes, he does, Cleta. He's closer than we realize."

Ah, if only Winslow knew the full truth! For God is always near, and ministering angels are but a breath away. Even in the bleak December, when the wind howls and summer tourists are scarcer than buttons on a goose, we remain on this wind-swept island, ready and willing to do the Father's will. For miracles, even in winter, can be found in unexpected places.

Come join me for a very special December in Heavenly Daze.

—Gavriel

CHAPTER ONE

On Saturday morning, Salt Gribbon looked across the expanse of his small home in the lighthouse and thanked God, not for the first time, that the busybody at the yard sale in Wells had insisted on selling the wooden table with its four matching chairs. At the time he'd groused plenty because he only had one bottom and therefore needed only one chair, but the woman wouldn't budge. Even after she agreed to toss in the other three chairs without charge, he had half a mind to leave the excess furniture on the shore, until his Yankee thriftiness rebelled against such waste. So he'd turned the table upside down in his dory, lashed the chairs into position between the legs, and rowed the entire load back to the northern-most point of Heavenly Daze.

Now three of his four chairs were occupied, one by his own weathered behind, and the others by the slender rear ends of his grandchildren, seven-year-old Bobby and six-year-old Brittany. The children, tousle-headed and heavy-eyed with sleep, were munching on molasses cookies, one of their favorite breakfasts.

"Grandfather," Brittany said, breaking one of the cookies with a deft snap, "don't you have Froot Loops? We always had Froot Loops for breakfast when we lived with Daddy."

"We never had Froot Loops." Bobby cast his sister a reproving look. "Sometimes we had cold pizza, but most times we had nothing."

Biting his tongue, Salt scratched his beard and watched his granddaughter. The little girl had a tendency to embroider the truth, especially when the subject had to do with her father, Salt's only son.

Holding her pinkie finger aloft—how'd she learn to do that?—Brittany dunked the end of her cookie into her glass of milk. "I like these cookies better than anything we had at Daddy's 'partment. The pizza was always cold. And we never had milk, only soda pop."

Salt's heart squeezed so tight he could barely draw breath to speak, but he forced words out: "The Good Book teaches us to be grateful for whatever we have. So eat up and get dressed, kids. We have work to do today."

Actually, he had work to do, but he believed young ones should keep themselves busy as well. These two stood in a particular need of structure and discipline. Their father had done almost nothing to teach his children. He'd led a life of waste and drunkenness, leaving these kids to grow up on a diet of television, table scraps, and neglect.

Bobby reached for another cookie at the same moment Brittany extended her hand. Both sets of fingers met on the edges of the last one on the plate.

Bobby spoke first. "I want it."

"It's mine!"

"But I grabbed it before you did."

"Did not!"

"Did too!"

In the ensuing tug of war, their tiny hands knocked over Bobby's glass. As the milk spread over the varnished tabletop, both children dropped the cookie and averted their eyes until Salt stood to reach for a dishcloth. After tossing it into the worst of the puddle, he crossed his arms and stood at the end of the table, waiting.

Two pairs of guilty eyes eventually lifted to meet his.

"You see what happens when you mess around?" he asked, hoping they'd attribute the gruffness in his voice to anger instead of heartbreak. "You waste good milk that you need. You're both too scrawny, and now I'll have to go into town to get more to replace what you spilt."

He lifted his arm, intending to reach for the dishcloth, and winced inwardly when he saw the boy flinch.

What sort of monster had his son been? "Finish your cookies." He lowered his gaze lest they see the shimmer of wetness in his eyes. "Then go pick a book out of the stack. I want you both to read a good bit today."

Without taking another bite, both children slipped silently from the table and moved toward the small TV stand by the fireplace. Bobby plucked *Curious George* from the pile of books on a shelf under the TV; Brittany picked up *Betsy-Tacy and Tib*. Moving like quiet little robots, they sat cross-legged in the vinyl beanbag chairs and opened their books.

Salt shook his head as he wiped up the spilled milk. 'Twas unnatural, the way they responded to rebuke. Though the bruises had faded from their young bodies, the scars on their hearts would take longer to heal.

By the time Salt had washed the dishes, changed out of the long-handled underwear that served as his pajamas, and pulled the quilts over the mattress on his rope bed, the children had finished their reading. Still they sat in the beanbag chairs, apparently waiting permission to move.

"All right, then." Salt sank to the edge of the bed as he regarded them. "You've done a good job of obeyin' and readin'. Now I must ask you to do a good job of something else."

The children watched him, their eyes wide.

Salt pointed toward the lighthouse door. "Alst I ask is that you don't go outside while I'm gone. Stay here in the house. If anybody tries to come inside, you scoot under this bed and lay as quiet as statues until the stranger leaves." He looked from Brittany to Bobby. "Understand?"

As one, the children nodded.

"All right, then." Salt pressed his hands to

his knees, then stood. He hated leaving them alone—he thought the loneliness would remind them too much of the place where they'd lived with their dad. They'd been alone in that filthy apartment when Salt found them, as they'd been left alone countless other days and nights while their father went out drinking.

"Grandfather?"

Salt looked to the girl. "Ayuh?"

Her voice trembled. "Will you bring us some more cookies?"

He would have brought her the world if she'd asked for it.

But what he said was, "If Miss Birdie has molasses cookies, I'll bring 'em."

CHAPTER TWO

Bobby waited until the sound of the grand-father's heavy steps faded into the howling of the wind, then he ran to the door and cracked it. The grandfather's long, dark figure was moving steadily down the graveled path, walking toward the town where they'd been told they must never, ever go.

He closed the door, fastened the latch, then turned to his sister and grinned. "He's gone."

"TV time," Brittany sang out, reaching to turn on the set. The small television received only one channel and all its pictures came in black and white, but Bobby didn't mind. Watching the tiny ghostly images on the screen was something to do, at least. The grandfather didn't want them to watch too much TV, but what else could they do in this place?

At first he'd been excited at the thought of

living in a lighthouse, but after the first day it became obvious that the lighthouse hadn't been built with children in mind. The steep iron staircase circling the tall tower was hard to climb, and wide open spaces separated each step. Though the grandfather climbed the stairs easily, Bobby couldn't help but look at the gap between the stairsteps and notice the long way down. What if he slipped and somehow fell forward between the steps? He was a lot smaller than the grandfather, so he would slip through quick as a flash. There'd be nothing to stop him, either, except the cold stone floor.

The grandfather had warned them not to play on the stairs—not that Bobby wanted to. But it would have been nice to have some place to play.

The grandfather's home had no toys. The circular room had a sink, a stove, and a tiny refrigerator facing a wooden table and chairs. A doorway between the fridge and the fireplace and woodstove led to the unheated bathroom, where the toilet seat always felt like ice. On the day he first showed them around, the grandfather had seemed particularly proud of the fact that he had an indoor toilet.

"I remember the day they dug the water and sewer lines," he told them as he flipped a switch and flooded the tiny bathroom with light. "Electricity and running water—don't ever take them for granted, kids."

Bobby couldn't imagine a house without electricity and water. After all, every apartment they'd shared with their dad had those things. They didn't always have a lot of furniture or food in the kitchen, but Bobby thought everybody had water and light switches. He thought everybody had roaches and rats, too, until the grandfather took them to his house.

Their dad had one thing the grandfather didn't—cable TV. He and Brittany spent hours sitting in front of the set, watching television families with daddies and mommies who went to work, tucked the kids in at night, and slept in the same bed. Those families did a lot of sitting in the living room and talking. Though Daddy never talked much, Bobby figured other daddies did.

He learned his ABCs from watching *Sesame Street*, while *Reading Rainbow* taught him about the beauty of books. His daddy never took him to the library, but when they moved into their last apartment, he'd found a set of old blue books on a shelf in the corner of the living room. When TV got boring, he pored over the books, looking at pictures and sounding out new words.

Slowly, over time, Bobby realized something important—he and Brittany and Daddy weren't like the television families. They had no mommy who went to work, and no butler or nanny or grandfather to pop in and tell stories. Nobody in their house ever sat in the living room telling jokes. Daddy was the only grownup in the house, and he usually slept in the daytime and went out at night after Bobby and Brittany had fallen asleep on the couch. Some mornings Daddy came home with money; sometimes he came home broke. Sometimes he came home stinky, with stains on his shirt, and sometimes he didn't come home until the next afternoon, when he'd stumble in with a few dollars and a bag of groceries.

When Daddy came home with the smell of beer on him, Bobby would help him to bed, then he'd reach under the sink and pull out a rusty can of Lysol he'd found there. From a TV commercial he knew what Lysol did—it cleaned, killed germs, and disinfected, whatever that meant. Bobby had discovered that no matter what else it did, the stuff was great at making stinky things smell better. To help his dad, Bobby cleaned and made sandwiches (when he could find bread and peanut butter) and took out the trash.

After watching *Andy Griffith* reruns, Bobby realized there was a word for his daddy's condition: drunk. When Otis got drunk, Andy and Barney let him sleep it off, and sometimes they laughed about it. Bobby tried to let Daddy sleep it off, too, but he never laughed when Daddy came home that way. Daddy got mean when he drank, and Bobby and Brittany had learned it was better to stay out of his way.

But Daddy wasn't always drunk. Sometimes he managed to clean up real nice. Once or twice a month he would take a shower, comb his hair, and put on a clean shirt and pants. Sometimes he'd read the paper and put big red circles around boxes, then tuck the paper under his arm and practice smiling in the bathroom mirror. On these days, he always pulled Bobby aside before going out the door. "I'm leaving you in charge, Bobby-my-man," he'd say, his blue eyes gleaming. "You take care of your sister and behave yourself. Keep your fingers crossed for me."

When Daddy had gone, Bobby and Brittany would sit in front of the TV with their fingers and legs and toes crossed though they weren't quite sure what sort of wish they were supposed to make.

And then, three months ago, on a cool day in September, Daddy had gone out in a clean shirt and left them alone. As *Sesame Street* was ending, someone knocked on the door. Thinking Daddy had forgotten his keys again, Bobby sprang up.

The man standing in the hall was a Stranger. He was tall like Daddy, and thin, with gray hair and a short gray beard and a gray jacket. Bobby had never seen the man before, but something in his blue eyes seemed familiar.

"Hello there, young fella," the man said, twisting the hat in his hand. "I'm looking for Patrick Gribbon."

Bobby ducked behind the door. He'd been told not to talk to strangers, and he'd get a thrashing for sure if Daddy knew he'd opened the door.

"Are you Bobby?" The tall man stepped forward into the doorway. "I won't hurt you," he said softly, the tips of his fingertips curling around the edge of the door. "I'm your grandfather."

Bobby's mouth opened. He had a grandfather?

He took a step back. The grownups on *Sesame Street* were always warning him not to let strangers in the house, but this man was a grandfather.

Bobby squinted, trying to see him better.

The man came in, closed the door, then bent down and placed his hands on his knees. "You must be what, almost seven years old now?" His voice sounded thick.

Uncertain, Bobby nodded.

"And you have a sister?"

Bobby pointed toward the living room. "In there."

"Will you take me to her?" The man's wide hand reached for his, and Bobby hesitated only a minute before taking it. A grandfather! He smiled as a feeling of happiness bubbled up in his chest. Grandparents were nice; they told stories, they took kids to the zoo, and when kids went to their house, they always got Werther's Originals.

He glanced at the pockets of the man's jeans to see if he could spot a telltale candy bulge. Nothing there, but that was okay. The girl in the commercial didn't get candy from her grandparents until she went to their house.

Brittany looked away from the TV, then her mouth dropped open at the sight of a Stranger holding Bobby's hand.

"Hello there, young lady," the grandfather said, nodding. "You must be Brittany."

Britt glanced at Bobby.

"He's my grandfather," Bobby explained.

"I'm her grandfather, too." Still holding Bobby's hand, the tall man knelt on the rug, lowering himself to Brittany's eye level. "Are you okay, honey?"

Britt glanced at Bobby again, who nodded. Slowly, she mimicked his nod, then put her thumb into her mouth.

The man said nothing, but his free hand reached out and gently lifted Britt's elbow. Bobby tilted his head, watching as the man's big thumb gently traced the bruises on his sister's arm. The grandfather didn't say anything for a moment but made strange noises in his throat.

"Listen." The grandfather turned to Bobby. "I want you and your sister to go into your rooms and pick out your favorite thing.

Then put on your jackets, hats, anything you have that's warm. We're going to take a little trip in my boat."

Bobby blinked. "Are we going to your house?"

The grandfather nodded. "What a bright boy you are. Yes, we're going to take my boat, and you're going to live with me until your father gets the help he needs. You don't have to worry about your dad, because I'm going to write a note and tell him you're with me."

He dropped Bobby's hand. "Okay? You two get ready while I look for paper and a pen."

Without speaking, Bobby led his sister into the tiny bedroom they shared. Brittany paused by the mattress on the floor.

"Who is he?" she whispered, her eyes as shiny as an empty pie pan.

Bobby reached for his jacket. "He's our grandfather."

"What if we don't want to go?"

"It'll be nice, I promise." Bobby picked up Britt's dusty pink sweater from the closet floor. "Grandfathers have candy, remember? Werther's Originals. And they take kids to McDonald's and to the zoo."

Brittany took her sweater, but from the expression on her face Bobby didn't think he'd convinced her. Still, she'd go. She always did whatever he told her to.

They slipped on their shoes, then Bobby helped his sister with her sweater buttons. And that's when he heard it—a slam. The grandfather was still in the living room, but he had just pounded the wall.

Bobby froze, his heart jumping in his chest. None of the grandfathers on TV pounded on the walls. His heart did another jump when he heard another strange sound.

None of the TV grandfathers cried, either.

He peeked through the bedroom doorway. Now the grandfather was sitting on the couch, his elbows on his knees, his hands covering his face. His shoulders were hunched like Daddy's when he came home with bad news.

Bobby was about to pull back and hide, but then the grandfather lifted his head and caught Bobby's eye.

"Are you ready, then?" he asked, his voice rough. He swiped at his eyes with the back of his sleeve, then clasped his hands. "What favorite thing are you bringing, Bob?"

Nobody called him Bob. The name

sounded different and grown up. Maybe that was a special thing for grandfathers. "Bob," Bobby whispered, tasting the sound. He liked it.

The grandfather stood. "What's your favorite toy?"

Bobby's gaze darted toward the dusty volumes on the corner bookshelves. The books had been in the apartment when they moved in, and the landlady said they were fit for nothing but the trash. Still, Bobby liked them.

He pointed toward the shelves. "I want to take a book."

The grandfather peered toward the dusty volumes. "You want to take an encyclopedia?"

Bobby nodded.

"'Tis an awfully big book, don't you think?"

Bobby lifted his chin. "I read them."

"All right, then." Something like a smile flitted in and out of the grandfather's speckled gray beard. "Pick your favorite."

And so Bobby had plucked the *A* volume from the shelf—the one with see-through pictures of human anatomy—while his sister emerged from the bedroom carrying Miranda, the nearly bald doll she slept with every night. Miranda had been in a Christmas basket some church people once brought to one of their other apartments, one a little like this one but bigger and cleaner . . .

Now Bobby looked around his grandfather's lighthouse. The space inside wasn't much bigger than the last apartment they'd shared with Daddy, but it was clean and tidy and warm, especially when the grandfather stoked the woodstove. There'd been no Werther's Originals in his house, but twice a week the grandfather brought them fresh milk, good food, and molasses cookies from the bakery. He also brought them books, so Bobby had new things to read.

And the lighthouse part was pretty cool, Bobby had to admit. The light was automatic, the grandfather had explained, but he still had to keep the lantern glass clean and the generator tuned up. When dark fell over the island, the generator automatically clanked on and started humming, then the brilliant light at the top of the tower began to circle, sending a steady creaking sound spiraling down to those below. And though most of the light beamed out toward the ocean, some of it leaked down into the tower, so the grandfather's house was never completely dark, even in the deepest night.

Britt walked over to the grandfather's narrow rope bed and stretched out on the blanket. Propping her head on her hands, she looked at Bobby. "Do you think we'll ever go back to see Daddy? Or will we live here forever?"

Bobby dropped to his beanbag chair and propped his chin in his hands. The grandfather was an odd man, not at all like Daddy and not like the TV grandfathers, either. But he didn't hit and he didn't yell and he never, ever came home stinking of anything worse than fish.

"I don't know, Britt." He watched the people on the TV, a pair of weathermen who were talking about Portland. "The grandfather said we'd stay until Daddy gets help."

"Who's helping Daddy?" Her voice trembled. "Who's taking care of him?"

Bobby blinked as he considered the question. He'd spent all his life taking care of his father and sister. Until now, he'd never realized that maybe Daddy couldn't get help because there was no one to clean up his messes and help him to bed . . .

"Daddy will have to take care of himself,"

he finally answered, keeping his eyes on the TV.

The answer seemed to satisfy Brittany, who sighed and hugged her doll. But Bobby couldn't forget the question—what if their daddy couldn't get help?

The weather hauses had arrived at Mooseleuk's.

Elezar Smith's smile widened as he held up one of the charming weather houses from Germany's Black Forest. The weather predictors were a favorite with island visitors. When dry weather was expected, the frau came out-of-doors; when ill weather threatened, die frau retreated and der mann of the house came out.

"Vernie?" The store clerk bent over the counter to peer up the winding staircase where the mercantile's living quarters were located: three undersized rooms, a small bath with a shower, sink, and commode, and a kitchenette last remodeled a hundred years ago and in dire need of renovation.

"What is that woman up to now?" Elezar leaned farther on the counter, trying to see up the stairs. Vernie Bidderman, proprietor of Mooseleuk Mercantile, had not been her-self for days. She seemed thoughtful and distant, though Elezar couldn't discover a reason for her preoccupation.

When no answer came, Elezar reached for a box of colorful cross-stitched Christ-mas samplers portraying Saint Nicholas. He frowned as he read: "Saint Nicholas, the bishop of Myra in Asia Minor during the fourth century, was renowned for his gen-erosity and his fondness for children. Dressed in his red-and-white bishop's re-galia, he delivered gifts of fruits, nuts, and small toys to children not on December 25, but on December 6."

Rolling his eyes, Elezar reached for a util-ity knife and slid the blade along the edge of a box of women's chamois nightshirts. The evolution of Saint Nicholas into Santa Claus never failed to amaze him. These earthly folks had bizarre imaginations.

He glanced up the stairs a third time. If Vernie didn't come down soon, he'd have to go up after her. Boxes of merchandise clut-tered the floor, all needing to be unpacked and shelved. He was willing to serve, but he didn't have a clue how she wanted to arrange the newly arrived stock.

He pulled a nightshirt from the box, held it against his chest for a moment, then grinned and set it aside. The other angels would laugh if they saw him holding up a lady's nightshirt, but they'd have to admit the soft beige fabric set off his cocoa-colored skin.

In her bedroom overhead, Vernie Bidderman perched on the side of her mattress and sorted through the contents of a shoebox. Moisture had formed in the corner of her eyes, a reaction, she was certain, having more to do with the dusty objects on her lap than nostalgia.

Carefully she lifted each object and returned it to the shoebox—pressed flowers, a bronze butterfly pin Stanley had given her on their first Christmas together, and Stanley's high-school class ring. She hesitated as she picked up the marriage license with the names Ingrid Veronica Riche and Stanley Bruce Bidderman inscribed in black ink and stamped with the seal of the State of Maine.

Outside the window, a cold wind whistled under the eaves as Vernie's thoughts reluctantly led back to the night she and Stanley had taken the marital plunge. They had not been kids. Stanley was twenty-eight; Vernie trailed him by a year. Her parents, Greta and Rolf Riche, warned her the match would be disastrous. Her father hadn't bothered to pull his verbal punches: "Why, Stanley is meek-mannered, while you, Vernie, have the diplomacy of a bulldozer running on high-octane premium!"

Despite her parents' objections, attraction overruled common sense. Or maybe it was love, Vernie decided a year later when the bloom still fragranced the rose.

Marriage to Stanley wasn't all that bad, and they'd forged a workable relationship. Maybe it wasn't Romeo and Juliet, but what couple did have the perfect marriage? Stanley let her have her way, and she let Stanley join a Thursday night bowling league. When Thursday night rolled around, Stanley would eat a grilled cheese sandwich and a bowl of tomato soup, then put on his turquoise bowling shirt with "Hank's Lube and Tube" silkscreened across the back in red lettering. He'd then pick up his AMF bag containing a pair of white size 10 Dexter shoes and a six-teen-pound blue fingertip Dino-Thane ball Vernie had scrimped for months to buy him.

At exactly six-thirty he'd throw his beloved ball and watch it thump and rattle down the polished alley.

He wasn't the best bowler, but marriage had been a good arrangement.

Dabbing the corners of her eyes, Vernie focused on a yellowed newspaper clipping announcing the Bidderman nuptials. Thirty-nine years had passed since that cold, snowy wedding day. Had Mr. Bidderman elected to come home that night back in '81, they would have celebrated their anniversary on December second. Tomorrow.

The tight knot in Vernie's throat threatened to suffocate her. She inhaled deeply, then heard the door to the mercantile open, followed by Cleta Lansdown's high-pitched warble. "Is Vernie busy?"

Elezar's soft baritone drifted up the staircase. "Vernie? You got a customer down here."

Flushed, Vernie slammed the lid on the shoebox, then shoved it beneath the double bed so suddenly she startled MaGoo. The cat blinked his cone-shaped eyes, gave her a how-dare-you-disturb-me look, then went back to sleep.

Sliding off the bed, Vernie straightened

her dress and repinned a strand of loose hair. Lately she'd been acting like a moon-struck fool. If Cleta knew she was up here pining over some shoebox filled with long-forgotten memories, she'd—well, she'd have a good chuckle.

"Vernie?"

"Coming, Elezar!" Land, a body didn't have time to think around here! After giving the mirror a fleeting glance, she closed the door, firmly leaving the shoebox and its memories behind her.

Cleta Lansdown, manager and co-owner of the Baskahegan Bed and Breakfast, stood chatting with Elezar. Four sets of peppermint pigs sat on the counter in front of her. Vernie eyed the doodads, a Victorian tradition, as she came down the stairs. Those candies were a big favorite with Cleta every year.

"You buying more of those?" Vernie called.

The first lady of the Baskahegan B&B grinned and picked up a set of the hard candy. "Did you know that smashing one of these things is supposed to bring happiness and prosperity throughout the coming year?"

"Good grief, Cleta." The swine sets were cute and gimmicky and sold like maple syrup, but Vernie doubted the pigs produced anything more noteworthy than a cavity. "You don't believe that stuff, do you?"

"Oh, Floyd and Barbara get a kick out of smashing the pigs on New Year's Eve—and you've got to admit the little red velvet bag and steel hammer is as cute as a bug's ear."

As Cleta added another set to her order, Vernie made her way to her desk, refilled her glass of Coke, and took a long swallow. Floyd was Cleta's other half, and Barbara the Lansdowns' only child. Barbara and her husband, lobsterman Russell Higgs, married three years back. Before the ink on the license was dry, Russell moved in with Cleta and Floyd, lock, stock, and barrel. Now Barbara and Russell appeared to have taken root. Talk no longer centered on when Barbara and Russell would move, but *if* Barbara and Russell would move. Cleta didn't seem to mind having her daughter in the house, but Floyd said feeding Russell was like shoveling coal into licking flames. Cleta would get red in the face when he talked like that, and shy Barbara would run, but the Higgses and the Lansdowns hadn't come to blows.

Yet.

Vernie eyed Cleta sourly, then took another long drink. Remembering her manners, she turned and focused an eye on her guest. "Want a Coke?" she mumbled around the rim of the glass.

"No, thanks." Cleta dropped a pair of red fleece earmuffs to the pile of merchandise. "Stopped by to see if you want to go shopping with me over to Ogunquit."

Vernie's glass paused in midair. "Today?"

"Of course." Cleta nodded to Elezar. "That'll do it, Elezar."

After draining her glass, Vernie set it on the counter. "Can't. Promised to help Bea with the angel mail."

Last month someone on the Internet had launched a ridiculous urban legend about angels working miracles on Heavenly Daze. Since then, everybody in town except old Salt Gribbon, the curmudgeonly lighthouse keeper, had been enlisted at one time or another to help answer letters.

Cleta waved Vernie's intentions aside. "Oh, come and go. Bea has plenty of help today. When I passed the bakery a few minutes ago, several of the Smith men were working in there." She fished in her drawstring purse for money to pay her bill. "You haven't got another thing to do and the outing will do you a world of good. I saw this cute tree ornament I want to buy at the drugstore."

"You can buy ornaments from me."

"Not this one—it's a Hallmark."

Vernie glanced out the front window. Hour by hour the clouds grew lower and thicker. For all the world, it looked like Heavenly Daze had been gripped by what might become one of the worst winters in years. Now a stiff wind whipped bare oak branches outside the mercantile, and Vernie shuddered to think of the bone-chilling walk to the ferry. Captain Stroble had already given notice that if foul weather descended, the ferry could close on a moment's notice.

The smiling clerk sacked the order and tied the butcher paper bag with a colorful red ribbon. "Why don't you go, Vernie? You've got a warm coat and mittens. I don't have a thing to do but put the new stock away. I'm assuming you want these things near the front?"

Vernie nodded absently. "Ayuh—anywhere you think best. You have a knack for arranging things."

"Thanks." Elezar shifted his gaze to Cleta. "Once I close up here, I plan to mosey on over to the bakery myself."

Vernie sighed. It had been weeks since she visited the mainland. And her mood wasn't exactly A-1 today.

"Oh, come on," Cleta nudged as Vernie vacillated. "You need to get out, get a little color in your cheeks. We can pick up a few Christmas presents, then eat a bite of lunch. I might even treat us to a movie. Popcorn's on me. Nicolas Cage has a new movie out."

Vernie wasn't in the mood for shopping, popcorn, or a movie, but Cleta was right, she could use a break. Monotony had begun to set in and the worst of winter was yet to come. She glanced at Elezar, who smiled and nodded. "Are you sure?"

"Ayuh." He picked up Vernie's coat, then came out from behind the counter to slip it over her shoulders. After adding her hat, scarf, and an encouraging pat, he slipped his hands into his apron and grinned. "Have a good afternoon, ladies."

The amicable offering barely registered as Vernie's thoughts darted toward the last man who'd slipped a coat over her shoulders.

Stanley the Fink.

Stanley, the skunk who left to go bowling and forgot to come home.

With only a bare nod to Elezar, Vernie followed Cleta out of the store.

CHAPTER THREE

Ogunquit's main street looked sleepy. A few residents hurried from stores to their cars, but for the most part, the town seemed as quiet as a church.

By late afternoon the women were tired of shopping and ready to fortify themselves for the windy ferry ride back to Heavenly Daze. Ducking into a restaurant, they stashed their shopping bags and took off their heavy gloves. The waitress set two glasses of water on the table and smiled. "What'll it be, ladies?"

"Hot tea for me," Vernie said.

Cleta agreed. "With lemon and honey."

"Earl Grey or Lipton?"

"Earl Grey."

"Lipton."

A string of colorful Christmas lights ringed the restaurant's window. One bulb was out and another one flickered, but still the decorations looked pretty. Steam frosted the plate glass so it was just about impossible to see out.

Vernie watched the tops of shoppers' heads bob by.

A white fleece hat.

A bright red woolen scarf.

A battered, snow-encrusted bowler. She cringed. Eugene Fleming.

The old goat that had pursued her for the last six months. As if she'd have the slightest interest in Eugene—or any man, for that matter. When Stanley walked out and vanished twenty years ago, Vernie had washed her hands of men—all men. She wasn't about to fall into that sinkhole again.

Cleta saw the bowler, too. "Look, Vernie." Her voice dropped to a whisper. "There's Eugene."

Carefully folding a paper napkin, Vernie changed the subject. "What are you getting Floyd for Christmas?"

The ploy worked; Cleta sobered instantly. "A lump of coal."

A smile hovered at the corners of Vernie's mouth. Floyd wasn't exactly known for reckless or generous spending. Every year Cleta complained about her Christmas present or her lack of one. One year Floyd bought her a Teflon-coated frying pan, and the day after Christmas he walked around town with a knot on his head the size of a goose egg. He said he'd banged his forehead on an attic rafter, but rumor had it that Cleta had put his gift to appropriate use. No one really knew what had happened, but speculation ran rampant until Floyd finally stood up in church and demanded that the town stop gossipin'. He'd heard more than enough about that frying pan.

Cleta picked up a thread of their former conversation. "So what's wrong with Eugene?"

Vernie consulted her watch. "You got all day?"

Grinning, Cleta smiled at the waitress when she set two pots of hot water on the table, followed by Earl Grey and Lipton tea bags. She stepped away for an instant, then returned with a saucer of lemon wedges. "Anything else I can get you, ladies?"

The women shook their heads in unison. "That'll be all," Cleta announced, dropping the bag of Earl Grey into her cup.

Picking up the stainless steel pot of hot

water, Cleta fixed Vernie with a stern look. "Eugene's a fine man and he's interested in you. Told Sue Ellen Parsons he was. Why do you want to ignore him?"

"I just—"

"It's time you moved on, Vernie Bidderman. It's been, what? Twenty years since Stanley left?" Shaking her head, she poured steaming water into her cup. "You're not so old that love won't find you yet."

Vernie threw her head back and hooted. Love? At her age? With Eugene Fleming?

Diners at a nearby table swiveled in their chairs to discover the source of her amusement.

Vernie dropped her gaze and added a spoonful of honey to her tea. "Do I look like a fool?" she hissed over her cup. "I'm perfectly happy with my life. I don't intend to ever get involved with a man again."

"And why not? Until Stanley walked out he was as good as gold. Why, I remember how you used to talk about him like he was the salt of the earth. You were happy, Vernie; you had a bloom in your cheeks. Don't you want that again?"

Vernie leaned closer and lifted a brow, then frowned.

Cleta dropped her spoon to the saucer. "What are you doing?"

"Looking for the bloom."

"I said your cheeks, Vernie, not mine." Snorting, Cleta took a sip of tea.

Vernie leaned back and relaxed. "I'm perfectly content with my life and I have no intentions of changing it, Cleta. Once Stanley walked out on me, that was it. No more problems of the male persuasion. Elezar's around during the day, and when I close the mercantile, he goes to the carriage house and shuts the door." She took a tentative sip from her cup. "That's the way to keep a man around the house. The only way."

"I still say you're missing a good opportunity to find happiness with Eugene. Why, he may look a little worn, but he's only a few years older than you. Besides, I hear he's made some real money on Wal-Mart stock."

"It would take more than Wal-Mart stock to interest me."

Sighing, Cleta lifted her cup. "You always were hardheaded. No wonder Stanley—"

"I'll thank you to keep your observations to yourself, Cleta Lansdown."

Rolling her eyes, Cleta took a sip, then grinned. "You may change your mind."

"I won't."

"Better to change it now than later . . . when Eugene Fleming's no longer around."

"Cleta, unless you want me to tell your husband you've picked up a new frying pan, you should drop the subject."

And with that, the conversation shifted to holiday worries—how big a turkey should they bake, and how many mincemeat pies?

Vernie was relieved to talk about such trivial things. She'd willingly talk about 'most anything. Except Stanley.

CHAPTER FOUR

Salt shifted his shopping bag from one gloved hand to the other as he walked up the lighthouse path. He'd picked up bread and cookies from Birdie's Bakery, then bought milk, cereal, eggs, and a block of cheese from Elezar at the mercantile. He needed a few other things, too—new toothbrushes for the kids, toothpaste, soap, and laundry detergent—but he'd get those things in Ogunquit when he felt more energetic. The wind seemed to sap his strength today, and he'd begun to perspire under his flannel shirt.

He paused at the row of sand dunes that stood like a barrier between the city and the desolate marsh that covered the northern half of Heavenly Daze. The kids needed clothes, new underwear and sturdy snowsuits. They'd been wearing thrift store castoffs when he brought them home, but he didn't dare buy children's clothing where anyone from Heavenly Daze might see him.

No one could know about the kids. He'd had no choice but to take them, yet the government do-gooders and social workers wouldn't see it that way. They'd say he was seventy and too old to be caring for children, then they'd take Bobby and Brittany and put them in a foster home where perfect strangers would care for his own flesh and blood. Well, that wasn't going to happen. Not as long as Salt had breath. Being a Gribbon meant doing what should be done, and a Gribbon man was supposed to provide for his family. Salt had provided for his wife and son by spending weeks away at sea, and now he would provide for his grandchildren by keeping them close . . . no matter what anybody else said.

He turned his face into the wind and closed his eyes against the icy sting. Ayuh, winter was gathering her strength, no doubt preparin' for a real blast. If his aching bones could be trusted, 'twould be a cold one this year.

Spurred by determination and an undeniable sense of guilt, he pulled his collar to his throat and walked on. He hadn't taken the kids from spite. God above knew he hadn't done that. He'd wished Patrick well; he'd have given anything to know his son was a good father to those young 'uns. But he'd seen the truth with his own eyes. When he arrived at the apartment in Wells, Bobby and Brittany were both as thin as a heron's leg. That apartment hadn't been fit to live in, and when he saw the bruises on the little girl's arm . . .

He'd been right to take them. No social worker could do better for them than he could, and he'd already brought a measure of peace and comfort to their lives. So far they seemed happy to be with him, though they were still a mite shy. Poor things, Patrick had probably told them to keep quiet and out of the way, for they didn't laugh and shout and giggle like ordinary children. In the three months they'd lived in the lighthouse, he couldn't recall them laughing at all.

He couldn't recall many instances of Patrick laughing, either, but he'd spent so little time with the boy when he was young. The sea had called him away, and longliners grew closer to their crew mates than to the family waiting at home.

He struggled to swallow over the lump in

his throat and winced at the pain. Well, no wonder he had a sore throat. He'd been traipsing down to the village more often than usual, and the wind was breezin' up.

"And you're getting along in years," he chided himself, breathing through his mouth as he crossed the final steps to his own front door. "You can't expect to feel fresh in a savagrus month like December."

He hesitated at the door and knocked, then grunted in satisfaction when the boy didn't answer. Yessir, they'd corrected that habit right away. Bobby wasn't to open the door for anyone, not even his grandfather.

He lifted the latch and stepped inside. "I'm home," he called, gratefully pulling off his gloves. Two ash-blond heads appeared from the space beneath his bed. Brittany's gaze darted straight to his shopping bag. "More cookies?"

"More cookies, more milk, and a box of Froot Loops." Salt shrugged out of his coat, then, while the children scrambled to go through his shopping bag, he moved to his rocker by the fireplace.

He needed to sit a minute and catch his breath. Only a minute. That's all he needed.

*   *   *

Safe and warm in Portland, Annie Cuvier signed the last Christmas card with a flourish, then ran her tongue around the edge of the flap. There! Another Christmas obligation dispatched.

After dropping her holiday cards into the outgoing mail basket, she glanced over her desktop and sighed when she saw the stack of research papers. She'd hoped to get out of the office early, but the staggering pile reminded her that tomatoes took precedence over an early dinner and a quick stop at the bookstore.

Reaching for a folder, she opened it and stared at the printed page, willing herself to focus.

Some of the older tried and true ornamentals descend from a collection of Madame Aglae Adanson (1775–1852) and include the rare Tomato Pomme d'Api, which looks like lady apple. Lewis Darby offers more accessible colorful miniatures such as Ochradel, Debbidel, and Chocodel . . .

Yawning, Annie turned the page, ignoring the activity outside her window. Christmas was in full swing at the Southern Maine Technical College. Maintenance men were hanging holly and preparing for the special campus tree lighting scheduled for six o'clock on Sunday evening.

> The lovely pommes d'amour, or "apples of love" as tomatoes were once called, are most succulent when eaten when the sun is high and the weather is hot.

That, Annie conceded, was the honest truth. Her experimental tomatoes, designed to grow in winter, looked more uncertain every day. An early winter had descended upon Heavenly Daze, and the tender plants looked more like starving victims than fruit-bearing plants. Annie had considered uprooting the remaining vegetation and throwing in the trowel, but some persistent and annoying shred of hope prevented her from completely giving up. Her supervisor called her a born optimist, her coworkers called her nuts, but she wouldn't give up until she had no other choice. After all, for a while her experiment had exhibited signs of promise. The spindly seedlings she'd planted on Heavenly Daze had perked up and actually thrived even after her aunt's dog uprooted them. All through October and mid-November Annie clung to hope. But last weekend even she had to admit the plants were teetering on extinction.

Closing the folder, she gently massaged her throbbing temples. Her Aunt Olympia was struggling to hang on, too. Though Uncle Edmund's death had been expected for weeks, the reality of his absence was only beginning to sink in. For the first time in forty years Olympia had no family in the house.

At least she had Caleb. The old butler had served Olympia for as long as Annie could remember. But Caleb couldn't take Edmund's place, and Olympia had only begun to battle the loneliness.

Getting up from the desk, Annie shuffled to the file cabinet. Lately her own disposition hadn't exactly exuded sunshine and mirth. A dark cloud hovered over her heart, ready to devour her. Even though she hadn't been close to Edmund the past few years, she couldn't shake the feeling of loss.

Added all together Edmund's death, the

time she had spent in Heavenly Daze help-ing Olympia tie up odds and ends, and the funeral had thrown Annie hopelessly behind in her work. The extra hours she'd been forced to put in hadn't helped her mood. She hadn't left work before seven a single night this week, and now she was in her of-fice on a Saturday . . . working.

Where was the old Annie?

She'd forgotten how to laugh so hard her side ached.

It had been months since she'd savored the feel of a warm robe fresh out of the dryer.

She missed giggling, the serendipity of finding a forgotten twenty-dollar bill in her coat pocket, and the beauty of a drive on a rural road.

Instead her life had been filled with trudg-ing to work, coming home to a quiet apartment, feeding the cat, and dropping into bed—sometimes too exhausted to eat. Her clothes hung on her, and well-inten-tioned friends had begun to ask if she was bulimic.

Bulimic? Annie Cuvier, who could polish off a Big Mac and fries and go back for a hot apple pie without a moment's hesitation?

Where was the Annie who derived pleasure from something so simple as discovering a no-wait line at the Super Wal-Mart? Or the woman who was delighted to discover a fat-free version of her favorite rocky road ice cream?

She pulled a file from the cabinet, the label blurring as her eyes filled with tears. How had her life become so empty? Her friends had husbands and young children; she had a paycheck and an empty apartment.

Had she missed the boat? She'd been standing on the dock, doing what all the experts suggested. She'd read every book: *How to Find a Mate, Keeping Mr. Right Interested, Living for Love and Loving It, Man Plus Woman: Putting the Two Together*. She had read and studied and taken notes, yet here she was, twenty-eight and still single.

Maybe she should have taken the money she'd spent on those books and put it toward one of those Love Boat cruises—

She glanced up to see her coworker, Melanie Procter, about to tap on her door.

She dashed the tears away. "Come on in, Melanie. What are you doing here on Saturday?"

The petite blonde flashed a dimpled grin.

"Just checking on you. Bought your cruise tickets yet?"

Closing the file drawer, Annie moved back to her desk. "Not yet."

The cruise—she'd pushed it from her mind. The majority of her coworkers were taking a Caribbean cruise over the Christmas holiday, visiting Jamaica, Grand Cayman, Montego Bay, and Cozumel. They were all places she'd love to see, but maybe later, when she was in a more festive mood.

She drew a shuddering sigh.

Melanie frowned. "You are going, aren't you? The deadline for reservations is five o'clock."

Lifting her shoulders briefly, Annie sat down and rearranged a stack of rubber bands. She glanced at her watch. Four forty-five.

"You're not going?" Melanie's blue eyes widened. "You can't be serious. At these prices? When would you ever get a seven-day Caribbean holiday at a bargain basement price? We're talking cheap, Annie. We have a window room—a real window, not a porthole. We can actually look out and see the water. How could you possibly consider not going?"

Annie shrugged. She wanted to go—the price was great. And though it wouldn't be the Love Boat, it could be fun and she could sure use the break.

Venturing into the office, Melanie kicked the door closed, then bent and placed her palms on the desk. "You can't be serious."

"Aunt Olympia—"

"Is grieving. I understand." Bending closer, Melanie's tone gentled. "Invite her to come along. The sea air will be good for her, and getting away from the house where your uncle died will be even better."

"She won't come."

And, if the truth be known, Annie wasn't sure she'd want Olympia along. She loved her aunt and wanted the best for her, but penny-pinching Olympia would be miserable on a cruise, probably groaning the entire time about how much money it cost. And if Olympia was miserable, everyone around her would be miserable, too. Annie closed her eyes, already hearing what her aunt would repeat at least ten times an hour: "That's what's wrong with young people today; they don't know the value of a dollar."

No, she might as well go to Heavenly Daze and spend Christmas in the de Cuvier mausoleum, sitting in the chilly parlor watching paint peel. Her friends would thank her for not bringing Olympia along. And she'd save money.

Caleb would do all he could to inspire a joyful holiday, but Annie knew the effort would be wasted this year. Olympia would immerse herself in grief and Annie would encase herself in self-pity.

Olympia's terrier Tallulah would be the only occupant in the de Cuvier house with any spirit at all.

She looked up and gave Melanie a smile. "I know you'll have a wonderful time. If it wasn't so soon after Uncle Edmund's death, I might reconsider, but I can't do that to Olympia. The holidays are going to be hard for her this year. I need to be there."

"But the price," Melanie argued. "When will you ever get a deal like this? Think about it, Annie—sun-drenched decks, unbelievable food, towels fashioned into cute little animals, being treated like a queen for seven days and six nights. And this boat will have men on it—good-looking men, tanned, muscled, single men. You have to go."

Annie closed her eyes, imagining the strains of Calypso music mingling with the scent of Australian Gold Exotic Blend sun-tan lotion.

Balmy sea breezes.

For seven glorious tomato-free days.

Her eyelids snapped open. "I can't."

Heaving a sigh, Melanie sank into a nearby chair. "You're nuts."

"I know, but I can't, Melanie. And there's no sense in asking Aunt Olympia to go because she won't." Annie's thoughts skipped back to the October day she accompanied her aunt to get a mammogram. That would be a walk in the park compared to getting Olympia aboard a cruise ship.

Melanie wasn't giving up. "How do you know until you ask? She might be more than willing to get away for a few days. Is money a factor?"

Annie smothered a laugh. Money was always a factor with Olympia. She took great pains to portray herself as a woman of means, but Annie knew her airs were only an act. For years Olympia had struggled to maintain the grand old house known as Frenchman's Fairest, but funds had been dangerously tight in the past few months. Edmund's life insurance would provide for Olympia's comfort now, but she couldn't—and wouldn't—be frivolous. A cruise would definitely fall into Olympia's frivolous category, right behind massages and garden statuary.

"Money isn't the point, Melanie. I'd be happy to buy her ticket. But it's too soon after Uncle Edmund's death. I'm sorry. Maybe next time."

Melanie sighed. "Of course I understand, but I wish you would at least ask your aunt. There are always older women on these cruises—your aunt might even make new friends."

Yeah, right. And Mr. Perfect was going to sail through her doorway in the next five minutes.

"Mrs. Oberite in the art department lost her husband last year and she's going," Melanie persisted.

Summoning a smile, Annie repeated, "Maybe next time."

Melanie blew her bangs off her forehead. "Have it your way, then."

As the door closed behind Melanie, Annie stared at the phone. Should she call Olympia? The cruise was such an unbelievable opportunity.

No. She knew what her aunt's answer would be.

But shouldn't her feelings count, too? Olympia was mourning, and such things couldn't be helped. Some women endured widowhood with admirable strength; others took longer to adjust. Olympia had steely fortitude, but she and Uncle Edmund had been so inseparable Annie couldn't begin to predict how her aunt would fare through the coming months. The island women would help, of course. And her aunt's closest friends, Cleta, Birdie, and Bea, would provide emotional and physical support if her aunt would allow them near. But in that lay the problem. Olympia seldom allowed anyone to help her.

Sighing, Annie stood and filed three folders, her mind refusing to dismiss the cruise. She wanted that vacation. She needed a break from the past few hectic months. The tomatoes weren't going to make it; anyone could see that. If she weren't so stubborn, she would have already written her final paper and ended the experiment.

Move on, Annie. Isn't that your mantra? Get on with your life.

Yet she couldn't bring herself to concede defeat . . . and for some crazy reason she couldn't dismiss the desire to take that cruise.

Turning, she absently closed the filing cabinet drawer, her gaze resting on the phone. Melanie's admonition still rang in her ears. *You could at least ask.*

Fascinated, Annie watched her index finger move toward the keypad.

She'll say no. Don't be an idiot. Don't open yourself up for another clash unless you're willing to accept what she says.

Holding the phone to her ear, she heard the melodic tones as her finger tapped the keys, the brief pause, and then the ring.

Hang up. It wasn't too late. And it was a silly cruise. Next year would be different. Olympia would be adjusted to widowhood and Annie could leave without feeling guilty . . .

One ring.

Two rings. Caleb's voice came on the line.

Swallowing, Annie winced. "Caleb?"

"Yes—Annie?"

"Yeah, hi. Is Aunt Olympia around?"

"She is, but she's resting now." She heard silence, then Caleb said, "I gave her a mild sedative. This has been a particularly trying day for Missy, but if you need to speak to her—"

"No." Annie sank to her chair, weak with

relief. "It's not important. Tell her I called. If she wants to, she can call me back."

"I'm sure she'll want to talk to you. She should be awake soon. You'll be home later?"

"No, I'm in the office. I'll be here for quite a while. Thank you, Caleb."

After hanging up the receiver, she propped her head on the back of the chair. Olympia wouldn't go. Even asking was idiotic.

So why had she called?

By six o'clock, after a dinner of cheese sandwiches and chicken noodle soup, Salt felt like he'd been hung out on a mast for four days. His throat burned, his skin felt hot and prickly, and his head buzzed. But still he rolled out the children's bedding before the woodstove, watched them brush their teeth, then settled in the rocker for a quick bed-time story.

At first he'd been horrified and indignant to realize the kids had never attended school, but now he was grateful. Since the children had never been enrolled in the state's public education system, there weren't likely to be any principals, truant officers, or social workers looking for them. And he could teach them. What did six- and seven-year-olds need to know? How to count, how to read, how to share, and how to do a fair day's work. Salt could teach them all that and a lot more they'd never find within the pages of a school-book.

As the overhead lantern whirred, sending an alternating red-and-gold glow over the children's faces, Salt read a chapter of *Black Beauty*, then closed the book and inclined his head toward the bedding on the floor. "Time for you young 'uns to be asleep," he said. "Now don't give me any trouble, but get to bed."

If the truth be known, they'd never given him a minute's trouble, but he figured it wouldn't hurt to let them know he expected it—and wouldn't tolerate it. Bobby moved first, carefully lifting the covers and tucking his feet inside, but Brittany hopped over her bedroll like a frog, her pitiful doll tucked beneath her arm. After much flailing and flapping of her blankets, she tucked herself in and lay still, looking up at Salt with bright eyes.

"Snug as bugs in a couple o' rugs," he

pronounced, standing. The room swam before his eyes, and he reached for the back of
the rocker to steady himself. 'Twouldn't do
to fall in front of the kids . . . but in a minute
he'd be abed, too, and a good night's sleep
would do 'em all good.

Bobby sat up. "You okay, Grandfather?"

"Ayuh." Salt opened his eyes wide and
forced the room to focus. Then, as was his
custom, he made his way to the woodstove,
tossed in another log, then drifted toward
his bed.

He lay atop the blanket, suddenly feeling
too weary to lift it. In a minute he'd catch his
breath, then he'd get up, brush his teeth,
and strip down to his longhandles.

In a minute. When he could find the
strength.

CHAPTER FIVE

Salt wasn't sure how long he'd slept, but sunlight was prying at his eyelids by the time he heard Bobby say, "Grandfather? Are you going to get up?"

With an effort, Salt lifted his heavy lids. Above him, the spiral staircase wound up toward a blinding sky and Bobby's head loomed large and out of focus.

"Grandfather," Bobby repeated. "Are you okay?"

Salt opened his mouth to speak, but no words came. He moistened his tongue and forced a rasp. "Not feeling well. You kids fix yourselves some breakfast. I'll be okay. I need . . . a little sleep."

He closed his eyes and drifted away on a warm tide. The kids would be okay. They hadn't given him a minute's trouble since they'd arrived, and they weren't likely to start now. If he could rest, he'd feel better.

* * *

Bobby frowned as the grandfather's eyes closed. This was not good. The grandfather usually got up before daylight, yet Charles Osgood and *CBS Sunday Morning* had come on and still the man had not moved from his bed.

From her beanbag chair Brittany wailed, "I'm hungry."

"Okay." Bobby turned and pointed to the pile of bedding on the floor. "Let's put away our stuff, then we'll fix something to eat."

Britt made a face. "Why do we have to clean up?"

"We do, that's all." Bobby picked up his quilt and spread it from arm to arm as he'd seen his grandfather do. "He's not feeling good, so we have to let him get over it."

But even as he pretended to have the answers, something didn't make sense. The grandfather wasn't drunk. He didn't smell like beer and smoke, and Bobby hadn't seen him take a drink of anything but milk. Of course, he might have drunk something when he left yesterday morning, but last night he'd read *Black Beauty* without any trouble. Daddy couldn't even sign his name when he was drunk—well, not so Bobby could read it.

But he knew what to do. Long ago he'd learned that when adults stopped leading, kids should keep quiet, keep clean, and wait.

After he'd folded his blankets and stacked them against the wall, he helped Brittany with her bedroll. When the space before the fireplace was picked up and empty, Bobby led the way to the cabinet that served as a pantry.

"He bought Froot Loops, remember?" He opened the door. "And milk. So sit down and let me get us something to eat."

Britt glanced over at the sleeping man on the bed. "Should we fix him something, too?"

Bobby shook his head. "Don't seem like he's much interested in eating now. He'll eat when he's ready."

Bobby pulled two bowls from the dish drainer, then set them on the table with two spoons. He gave Brittany the cereal box to open while he walked to the refrigerator and pulled down the cardboard container of milk.

A sound like spattering raindrops made him turn.

"Uh-oh." Britt stood on the chair with the open box in her hand. An assortment of rainbow-colored cereal circles decorated the table.

Bobby cast a quick glance at his grandfather. The man hadn't moved.

"Just pick them up and eat them," he said, keeping his voice low. "Don't worry about it. You can toss some of them in my bowl."

Brittany nodded, but her eyes widened as she looked toward the refrigerator. "Is that orange juice in there?"

Bobby looked. "Ayuh."

"I love orange juice, Bobby. I had a Florida sunshine tree in my yard when I was a little girl—"

"Stop fibbing; you had no such thing."

Bobby glanced back toward the man on the bed. The grandfather hadn't said they could have the orange juice, but he hadn't said they couldn't have any, either.

"I reckon a little won't hurt," he whispered, setting the milk on the table. "Get the cups, will you? The plastic ones."

While Britt climbed down from her chair, he stood on tiptoe to reach deep inside the old refrigerator. The orange juice was in a big jug, and it was lots heavier than the nearly empty carton of milk. Holding his breath, Bobby hoisted it from the shelf, then heaved it onto the table.

Brittany set two yellow cups before him. "I love orange juice," she repeated, a smile deepening the dimples in her cheeks. "A day without orange juice is like a day without sunshine."

Bobby didn't answer but carefully peeled away the plastic ring on the top of the orange juice jug. Once he'd removed it, he tossed it into the garbage can, then gripped the slick container with both hands.

"Stand back, Britt." His eyes centered on the first cup. "This is heavy."

Brittany took a step back and he lifted, tipping the bottle slightly forward—

The liquid gushed out, splashing the plastic cup with such force that it tipped over, knocking the second cup to the floor. Bobby struggled to catch the slippery container, but it fell against the table. Brittany squealed as juice chugged out of the jug, then Bobby finally gripped it.

By the time he got the gallon jug upright and capped, the tabletop and floor were streaked with rivers of bright orange juice.

Placing her hands on her hips, Britt jerked

her nose skyward. "I am not going to lick that up!"

"Shh!" Ducking, Bobby glanced toward the bed. The grandfather slept on, still in his clothes, still with one hand draped across his chest. He hadn't moved since Bobby woke him.

"You don't have to lick it, just help me clean it." Bobby looked toward the sink. "Where's that rag he used yesterday when we spilled the milk?"

With two fingers, Brittany plucked the dishcloth from the sink and brought it to Bobby. The fabric was cold and sticky against his hand and smelled faintly of sour milk.

He tried swiping the wet cloth through the spill, but the juice only spread over the uneven stone floor. And it smelled! Without even having to look, the grandfather would wake up and know something had happened.

"This isn't working." Bobby handed the dripping cloth back to Brittany, who tossed it in the sink as if it were a disgusting thing. "What else can we use?"

Moving quietly, he opened drawers and cabinets without finding anything useful. Britt found a drawer of clean dishtowels, but if he used one of them, he'd have to leave it dripping in the sink. When he woke up, the grandfather would see it and know about the spill and the wastefulness.

Better to find something else.

Brittany held up an appliance she'd found in a cabinet. "How about this?"

Bobby grinned. "A DustBuster!" He'd seen the commercial a thousand times. On TV the tiny vacuum cleaner picked up dirt, lint, cat hair, and, of course, dust. Why wouldn't it pick up orange juice?

He took the machine from Britt and felt its weight against his palm. He gave the on button a quick push to test the noise, then decided the low rushing sound wouldn't bother the grandfather. If he'd slept through Brittany's squeal and his own splashing, the tiny sound of a DustBuster wasn't going to bother him.

The DustBuster worked—but only for a moment. Then liquid began to spray onto Bobby's hand and face and clothes. Nervously he shut off the machine and set it aside, then took one of the dishtowels to wipe his face. Might as well use the rest of them to clean up the floor. Maybe they could hide the dirty cloths outside . . . and sneak them back into the house. Maybe the grandfather wouldn't notice if they came back one-by-one instead of in a heap.

So he and his sister cleaned up the spill and rinsed the DustBuster and ate their Froot Loops and brushed their teeth and combed their hair and put on clean clothes. They also put five juice-soaked dishtowels into a spare pillowcase, then slipped outside and hid the bundle beneath the grandfather's overturned rowboat.

As they came back inside, Bobby helped Brittany unbutton her sweater, then nodded when she pointed toward the TV.

"Keep it quiet, though," he whispered. "Don't wake up the grandfather."

Things were going pretty well at the lighthouse. Bobby didn't want to rock the boat.

Dust fogged the atmosphere as Vernie whipped a feather duster over the bottles lined in a neat row. She crinkled her nose when particles tickled her nostrils.

"Now, Vernie, what are you doing on that ladder? You're gonna break your neck." Coming from behind the candy counter, Elezar steadied the wooden perch, then peered up at her. "Besides, it's Sunday. You should be resting on a quiet afternoon like this, not working."

"Hold the ladder still. I'm not so tired I can't do a little dusting."

"Didn't say that," Elezar replied. His lips parted as if he'd say something else, but then he must have decided to hold his tongue. Vernie exhaled in relief and kept dusting.

"Shoo, MaGoo." The clerk gently nudged the plump cat away from the ladder. "If she falls she's going to take us with her."

Vernie eyed him disagreeably.

"Plumb crazy," he muttered, not looking at her. "I could get up there and do that."

"Thought you wanted to rest."

"I'm not so tired I can't give you a little help."

The phone jingled, startling Vernie. Her right foot slipped on the rung and Elezar's hand shot out to catch her. Teetering on one leg, she grasped hold of the shelf and righted herself. "Let go of me and answer that! Folks will think we're closed."

"We are closed," Elezar mumbled, but he moved toward the phone.

If not for the grocery needs of her neighbors, Vernie would have had to shut down for the winter. The months of November and December, however, replete as they were with holiday baking occasions, helped keep the Mooseleuk Mercantile profitable even when tourists were as rare as a two-door outhouse.

Keeping an eye trained on Vernie, Elezar edged toward the phone and snatched up the receiver. "Mooseleuk's."

Humming along with the Christmas carols playing in the background, Vernie dusted the jars of maple syrup. Outside, a bright sun glittered on frozen ground. Land, it'd been weeks since they'd seen sunshine, but by the sounds of things, the reprieve was going to be short-lived. Weathermen were predicting a storm to blow through in the latter part of the week. But if you didn't like snow and cold, Maine wasn't a place you'd likely take up residence.

She shoved a couple of pints of maple syrup to the side and dusted around the cans. No one liked bad weather, with the possible exception of Floyd Lansdown. Floyd was taking a ten-week correspondence course in mechanical engineering, so no matter what the weather he was content to sit in front of the fire, his feet propped up on the hearth, and study his lessons. Floyd apparently thought the Heavenly Daze fire engine needed an overhaul. For the life of her, Vernie couldn't see why. Other than Floyd's starting the engine every couple of days to keep the pistons lubed, the truck sat idle. She didn't see how an engine could wear out from that kind of activity.

She glanced over her shoulder when she realized Elezar wasn't talking. He cradled the phone next to his ear, listening, while a frown marked his sober features.

She caught his attention and mouthed, "Who is it?"

Shaking his head, he turned so she couldn't see his expression. Peeved, she stopped dusting. He hesitated a moment and murmured something in a soothing tone, but Vernie couldn't hear a word.

Shimmying down the ladder, she tossed the feather duster on the counter and busied herself filling out the supply order. She needn't worry about Elezar. He'd been her trusted employee for longer than she could remember, and he could handle anything that came up.

She licked the tip of her pencil and studied

her order form. Most of the mercantile's regular stock came from Wagner's, a wholesale grocer located upstate. She was running low on baking supplies and produce, plus she'd promised to order fresh cranberries for Babette. Babette brought the salad each year to the town's annual Christmas party, and the menfolk didn't think the holiday season had arrived until they ate some of Babette's cranberry salad. Then, of course, there wasn't a dash of nutmeg left on the island since every woman had sacrificed her stash to bail Birdie out at the bakery. And yesterday Birdie had mentioned she was running low on sugar, so it wouldn't hurt to order fifty pounds this time.

Pencil poised in midair, Vernie racked her brain to see if she'd forgotten anything. She'd order another bottle of vanilla syrup for her soda pop. Somehow she'd gotten hooked on putting that sugary stuff in her midafternoon pick-me-up. Last month she'd switched to sugar-free syrup, but she still felt a mite self-conscious about the habit. She kept the vanilla bottle under the counter so no one noticed the little shot she indulged in every afternoon. There were worse things than being addicted to vanilla Cokes, but she'd just as soon keep her addiction to herself. She scribbled sugar-free vanilla syrup and sugar on the form.

"Vernie?"

Startled, she looked up to see Elezar holding the receiver in his right hand.

"Who is it?" Probably Cleta calling to inquire when the nutmeg would be in, or Bea wanting help with the angel mail. Land, she didn't have time to work on mail today.

Elezar cleared his throat. "It's for you."

"Can't you handle it? I'm filling out the Wagner's order. Got to get it faxed in this afternoon."

The man's face gentled as his eyes shone with compassion. "I'm afraid you'll have to handle this one."

Puzzled, Vernie dropped her pencil. Elezar could handle anything having to do with the business, so who could be calling? She had no children and no siblings. Ma and Pa had been dead for years. Anybody from Heavenly Daze would just tell Elezar to holler at her.

She lifted the phone to her ear. "Ayuh?"

"Vernie?"

"Yes."

"It's Stanley."

Blood drained from Vernie's head.

Stanley.

The Stanley?

Stanley Bidderman, the rat who'd gone bowling and kept on traveling? The fellow who hadn't called or written or sent her so much as a Christmas card in twenty years?

"Stanley who?" she asked, hoping against hope it wasn't Stanley Bidderman. Surely even Stanley Bidderman wouldn't have the gall to call out of a clear blue sky after all these years.

"Stanley . . . your husband. I called to wish you a happy anniversary."

Bitterness swelled to the back of Vernie's throat. As blood pounded in her ears, she grasped the side of the counter and struggled to stay on her feet. The soft sounds of the Christmas carols faded into a buzz, then she heard herself saying, "I don't have a husband."

"I expected you to say that." The voice on the other end sounded very old, very tired. "I don't blame you for feeling that way, but I really want to talk to you."

Swallowing, Vernie glanced helplessly at Elezar, who stood at a discreet distance. His eyes sent a private, supportive message, as if he understood the cyclone swirling in her head. Her hand rose to her throat.

"Vernie?" Stanley's voice came over the line. "Have you fainted?"

Stiffening, Vernie fixed her eyes on the Wagner order form. "I don't faint, Stanley Bidderman, and if I had, I wouldn't be talking to you now, would I?"

A pause, then a soft chuckle. "Same old Vernie."

The suggestion brought heat to her cheeks. "No, Stanley," she calmly corrected. "I'm not the same old Vernie—not by a long shot. Now, is that all you wanted? I'm busy."

Nervously she tapped her pencil on the order blank. Her thoughts were whirring so madly she couldn't think straight, but Stanley couldn't know that. She only had to hold together long enough to tell him to stay wherever he'd been all these years and leave her alone. For whatever reason he had called—and she didn't believe he'd called to wish her a happy anniversary, not for a minute—she was going to play it as cool as if they had talked every day for the past twenty years.

As if he hadn't walked out on her and left her alone, bewildered, and hurt. She'd waited for weeks, jumping at every ring of the phone, starting at the sound of every cart on the gravel road. She'd called the police, fearing a car had flattened him and he was lying in the hospital unable to speak and/or suffering from amnesia. A quick check of police records on the night of his disappearance produced no accident reports and no hospitalized John Does.

For weeks Vernie kept a vigil, clinging to the fading hope that he'd fallen and hit his head and didn't know who he was. Perhaps he had wandered off in a daze, searching for his home, his family, his wife.

But that idea proved to be sheer fantasy. The police had tried to cushion the blow; they told her men sometimes needed a little breathing space. They told her not to worry, that he'd call soon.

So Vernie had waited by the phone, scorning anyone who suggested Stanley had left of his own volition. Why, that was crazy! She and Stanley had a good marriage—maybe not the fireworks kind portrayed in books and movies, but they were comfortable together. When the islanders teased Stanley about Vernie wearing the pants in the family, he would smile and say, "Yes, I reckon she does." He wasn't concerned that she was more practical-minded, that she could run the store, handle the books, and paint the woodwork better than he could. Stanley wasn't handy around the house, but he didn't seem to care. He was content to remain in the background, bowl on Thursday nights, and occasionally, when asked, vacuum the carpets when Vernie was too busy to clean.

She knew they had a good life. And she had thought Stanley would be the last person on earth to abandon his wife.

But he had.

And now he was on the telephone and she didn't know what to say to him. She didn't have anything to say to him.

His voice brought her back to the present. "I wondered if we might talk."

"Talk?"

"Talk," he repeated quietly. "You have every reason to deny me, but I need to speak to you, Vernie."

"Ha." She slammed the receiver down, startling MaGoo. The cat jumped, then landed on all four feet, his hair standing straight up.

Silence as thick as wool filled the mercantile as Elezar quietly returned to the register. Outside, a cloud moved in front of the sun, filling the room with gloom. The carols drifting from the radio suddenly lost their poignancy.

Vernie focused on the ticking clock over the doorway and struggled to regain her composure. She felt numb.

Sick at heart.

Puzzled.

Furious.

Happy anniversary? Where had that come from? And why, after twenty years, did Stanley finally want to talk? Did he think she actually cared where or who or how he was?

A chiding voice rose from her conscience: *Where's your human kindness, Vernie? Maybe he's sick and has only a few weeks to live. Maybe he wants to apologize before he meets his Maker. He's human, and humans make mistakes. You've made a few in your time.*

Ayuh, but she didn't walk out on her spouse. She didn't leave without a word of explanation. She didn't leave the one she loved worrying and wondering what had happened. And she hadn't left him in a pool of fear and guilt, wondering what he'd done to make her want to leave . . .

Maybe he wants to tell you.

"But maybe he needs money and pity and a place to stay until he checks out."

She didn't realize she'd spoken the hateful words aloud until Elezar looked up. Shoving the Wagner's order under the counter, she pulled her coat from the peg near the door, then shrugged her way into it and yanked a stocking cap over her hair.

"I'm going out for a while," she told Elezar. A long, cold walk would clear her head. A brisk, windy walk would remind her that folks in her family didn't easily forget wrongs. They had memories like elephants. Her father kept a list of those who'd wronged him. "Fool me once, shame on you," he'd often told Birdie. "Fool me twice, shame on me. If you let someone hurt you again, you're nothing but an idiot."

Elezar crossed his arms and leaned against the counter. "Bundle up," he said softly. "It's cold out there."

Vernie left, closing the mercantile door behind her. Elezar didn't ask where she was going, and that was good. Because she had no idea.

She didn't know where she was going, what Stanley wanted, or where he'd been for the last twenty years. He could take a flying leap at a galloping goose as far as she was concerned.

She no longer cared.

By the time Salt opened his eyes again, shadows had begun to lengthen in the room. He turned his head and saw Bobby and Brittany sitting before the TV, their faces bathed in a gray glow.

"Hey," he rasped, feebly waving in their direction. "Did you get something to eat?"

"Yes, sir." With all the seriousness of a five-star general, Bobby stood and came to his side. "We ate cheese and bread and Froot Loops. Would you like something?"

Suddenly grateful for the boy's precocious independence, Salt closed his eyes. "Just wanted to be sure you were okay. Let me sleep, and I'll be right as rain in the morning . . ."

As his concentration dissipated in a fever-fed mist, he slipped away.

Bobby watched the grandfather's eyes close. Stepping forward, he cautiously extended his hand, then pressed it to the man's lined forehead.

Hot. Burning hot.

"He's sick." Bobby turned to Brittany. "What should we do?"

Without taking her eyes from the TV screen, Britt said, "Four out of five doctors recommend Tylenol for their patients with fever."

Frowning, Bobby walked into the bathroom and shivered in the cold space. His teeth chattering, he lowered the toilet seat and stood on it, then reached for the door of the medicine cabinet. Inside, neatly arranged on three glass shelves, he saw a can of shaving cream, a silver razor, a comb, a bottle of cough medicine, and a bottle that said "Aspirin."

His frown deepened. No Tylenol.

Biting his lip, he hopped down from the toilet and left the bathroom, closing the door firmly behind him.

"No Tylenol," he told Brittany, moving toward the bedrolls against the wall. "We should get ready for bed. Maybe he'll be better in the morning."

"I know something we can do." Giving Bobby a confident smile, Britt went to the sink, took the last clean dishcloth from the drawer, then held it under the water. As Bobby watched in fascination, she folded the wet cloth into a palm-sized rectangle, then walked toward the grandfather. Holding the rectangle between two fingers on each hand, she gingerly placed it on his forehead.

The grandfather didn't respond.

"What does that do?" Bobby asked.

Brittany lifted her hands in an I-don't-know pose. "I saw the mother do it on *Little House on the Prairie* when Half-Pint was sick."

Bobby tilted his head, watching for some response from the old man, but nothing happened. So he and his sister pulled out their bedrolls, spread them on the floor, then went into the bathroom and quickly brushed their teeth.

Leaning against each other, they sat in front of the TV far into the night, long past the time they were usually allowed to watch.

But no one told them to go to sleep.

Salt dreamed that he struggled to handle the dory on a rough, rollicking sea. The oars danced and jerked in his hands, tossed by impact with high swells that looked like rolling hills.

Huddled in the bow, Bobby and Brittany rode with him, their faces drawn and pinched and pale as death. He tried to smile at them, but they weren't looking at him. Their eyes focused on the sea swells as their thin arms hugged their shivering bodies.

"Don't worry," Salt cried, his voice only a hoarse croak above the howling wind. "We're going to be fine."

But neither his words nor his tone seemed to assure the children. They kept their faces turned toward the distant shore, their bodies melded together, their manner distant. He had risked his life to perform this rescue, yet they seemed to have no idea who he was or why he cared.

The oars rebelled in his hands, pushing against his palms when he wanted to pull, pulling away when he tried to push. When he finally felt the oars yield to his will, his arms trembled with weakness, having spent all their strength in the struggle.

CHAPTER SIX

When Bobby woke the next morning, he thrust his head out from under the covers and blew out a frosty breath. The fire had died during the night.

"I'm freeeeeeezing!" Brittany said, her teeth chattering. She peeked out through a crack between her pillow and her blankets. "It's as cold as a dead man's tongue in here!"

Bobby shushed her. The grandfather said that all the time, but it didn't sound nice, especially not when he was lying over there so sick and still.

Sitting up, Bobby glanced at the man in the bed. He must have gotten up during the night, for now he lay under a blanket. He was curled up in a knot, an odd position for a man so long and tall.

Bobby shivered as a rush of cold air hit the parts of his body that had been warmed by the covers. He drew the quilts about his shoulders, then realized that the grandfather had only one thin blanket over him.

With his covers trailing behind, Bobby stood and walked to the rocker, then pulled the knitted afghan off the back of the chair. Walking slowly, he crossed the room and dropped his own quilts, then quickly draped the afghan over the grandfather's spare figure. When the grandfather was covered, he dove back into his quilts, then crawled to Brittany's bedroll and huddled against her.

Her head reappeared from beneath the blankets. "Is it morning?" she asked, shivering.

"Yeah."

"It's cold."

"I know."

"Colder than an igloo." Her head vanished beneath the blanket again, and he knew she wouldn't come out unless he did something to warm the room.

But what? He'd never started a fire before. The apartment had a furnace, and Daddy had been really strict about the thermostat on the wall. Bobby hadn't been allowed to touch it no matter how cold the room became because heat cost money and money was something they didn't have.

But grandfather's stove burned wood, and Bobby knew a stack of split logs stood right outside the front door. It would only take a minute to bring in a couple of logs, shove them into the stove, and toss in a match. Then he would shut the door before he or anything in the house had a chance to catch fire.

He looked again at the sleeping man, hoping for some sign of life, but the grandfather seemed as sleepy today as he had yesterday.

Taking a deep breath, Bobby wrapped his quilt tighter around his neck, gripped it with one hand, then tiptoed across the cold stone floor. A bitter burst of wind blew into the house when he opened the door, ruffling the pages of the newspapers stacked against the wall. Dropping his quilt, he twice darted in and out, bringing in a short log each time. Shivering without his covers, he carried the logs, one at a time, to the wood-stove.

The polished handle was heavy and the latch tight, but Bobby finally managed to get the door open. A few red embers glowed in the coal dust, and he took that as a good sign. He shoved the logs into the narrow firebox, then looked about for something to start the fire.

A matchbox lay on the mantel above the fireplace, and a few sticks of pine fatwood stood in a bucket on the stone hearth. He'd watched his grandfather light the fire several times, so he thought he could do it.

He had to do it.

With fingers trembling from cold and nervousness, Bobby lit the match, then held it to the end of a piece of fatwood. After a moment the stick began to blacken and burn.

From within her woolen cocoon Britt called, "Be careful!"

Bobby swallowed his anxiety and tried to act as though his heart weren't pounding.

When the flame burned steadily, he thrust the fatwood into the stove, making sure it landed beneath the logs. For good measure, he tossed in a couple of other sticks, then shut the door and latched it tight.

Brittany's blue eyes were wide. "How'd you learn how to do that?"

Bobby shrugged. "Nothing to it, really."

He looked at his bed. The temptation to

curl beneath the covers was strong, but something told him he couldn't afford to go back to sleep. Grown men should not lie in bed for more than a day without eating or drinking water. The grandfather needed help.

Serious help.

Bobby stood, then ran his fingers through his hair as he moved toward the bathroom. "Get yourself dressed," he said, keeping his voice low. "We're going out today. The grandfather needs us."

"But we're not supposed to—"

"We'll be careful. But the grandfather needs us to go because we don't have any Tylenol."

After stuffing down a quick breakfast of bread, cheese, and molasses cookies, Bobby led Brittany outside. They'd walked along the beach a few times before, but always with the grandfather keeping watch from the window halfway up the lighthouse, where he could see anyone coming. They knew Puffin Cove, where the grandfather kept his rowboat, and the rocky shore bordering the north end of the island. They also knew the graveled road and had been expressly forbidden to follow it.

"What do you suppose is over that way?" Bobby pointed toward a wind-swept field stretching from the lighthouse to a series of sand dunes.

"Don't know." Britt lifted her hand to shade her eyes from a bright morning sun. "Hills."

"But what's behind the hills?"

"Don't know."

Bobby moved forward, his chin lifting. "Why don't we find out?"

His eyes scanned the field as they moved over the gravelly path toward the dunes. No trees stood here, but tall silvery gray grasses stirred as the wind blew over the sand. The grasses whispered to themselves as they walked toward the town, saying, "Shh! Shh!"

Bobby felt like walking on tiptoe.

A few minutes later they lay on the cold sand, the dampness of the earth seeping through the thin fabric of his jacket. From where they lay against the dune he could see a street bordered by pretty houses, a restaurant, a small brick building, and a white church with a tall steeple.

Brittany pointed toward the church. "Does God live there?"

"Don't know." Bobby frowned as a man stepped out of the church, locked the front door, then moved across the lawn to a blue house. "Maybe. But why would they lock him in?"

"Look at that." Britt pointed toward the tall house across the street from the church. A small, puffy figure stepped off the front porch, followed by a tiny white dog. To their amazement, the child—for that's what the puffy thing was—began to walk in their direction, the dog running ahead, straight toward . . . them.

Brittany's round eyes focused on the animal. "Should we hide?"

Bobby considered. Ordinarily he'd say yes, but they needed help. And somehow it seemed safer to talk to another kid than to a grownup. Surely the grandfather would agree.

Making what he was certain was the most important decision of his life, Bobby stood, climbed to the top of the dune, then waved both hands over his head, catching the other kid's attention.

As the puffy child drew nearer, Bobby saw

that the kid was a boy about Britt's age, pink-cheeked and plump, with a tangle of brown curls escaping from the hood of his padded snowsuit. He stared at Bobby and Brittany with eyes as wide as saucers, then grinned.

"Hey," he called, running toward them with the dog. "You been up to Puffin Cove?"

Bobby nodded. "Ayuh. We've been there. But there aren't any puffins around today."

"No?" As the little white dog licked Brittany's fingers, the boy stopped and looked Bobby up and down, then pointed at Britt. "Who's she?"

"She's my sister Brittany." Bobby thumped his chest. "And I'm Bob."

"I'm Georgie Graham." The boy did a spin on the toes of his sneakers. "And this dog is Tallulah. I live there"—he pointed toward the tall house where they'd first seen him—"but she lives at the fancy house down by the dock." He paused, then bent to pet the dog. "Are you from away?"

Bobby nodded. "Ayuh. But we're here now. Until."

"Oh." Georgie looked puzzled for a moment, then grinned. "Lots of kids from away come here, then they go. But not many come in the winter."

Brittany crossed her arms in a rare display of defiance. "Well, we're here."

Bobby slipped his cold hands into his jeans pockets. "We're living in the lighthouse. But the grandfather is sick."

"Really sick," Brittany echoed. "And hot. Burning hot."

"Old Cap'n Gribbon?" Georgie's face wrinkled for a moment, then brightened. "Maybe he has the mumps. My dad had the mumps a few years ago and he got to stay home and eat ice cream. Mom said they made his face all puffy, like he had acorns in his cheeks."

Bobby shook his head. "It's not the mumps."

"Measles?" Georgie grinned again. "Does he have spots all over? I haven't had 'em, but my mom told me they can make you really sick."

"No spots," said Brittany.

Georgie put his mittens to his mouth for a moment, then slapped his hands to his cheeks. "Chicken pops? I had the chicken pops last year when some kids from away brought them to the island. I wasn't too sick, but Miss Birdie caught them and scratched and itched something awful—"

"No pops," Bobby interrupted, strengthening his voice. "He's hot. And he doesn't move. He's been lying in the bed for two days without eating anything."

"He needs Tylenol." Britt nodded wisely. "Four out of five doctors recommend it for their patients with fever. Because ibuprofen can cause stomach distress."

Turning, Georgie pointed toward the road. "We have Tylenols. My mom takes them every night when Dad gives her a headache."

Bobby lifted his head as hope sprang up in his heart. "Could you bring us some? I think I could get him to swallow some if you can get them."

Georgie flashed a confident grin. "Sure. I'll be right back."

He sprinted away then, the little dog prancing alongside his pounding sneakers.

"Bobby," Brittany began, a note of warning in her voice. "We're not supposed to let anyone see us."

"We won't." Taking her hand, Bobby led her back down the dune, out of sight. "But we got someone to bring us medicine, right? So we'll hide until Georgie comes back, and then we'll give the grandfather the Tylenols. Then he'll be okay."

"But what if Georgie tells someone about us?"

Bobby shrugged. "Won't matter. Nobody listens to little kids."

Birdie Wester smiled as she put the last éclair into a bag and folded down the top. "That'll be five twenty-five," she said, smiling at Babette Graham. "I think you'll enjoy these. Abner's done something special with the filling."

"Almond flavoring," Abner called from the counter where he was working. "One extra drop. I think you'll find the difference almost . . . heavenly."

Babette moved to the counter and opened her purse. "I'm sure I'd like anything you make."

At that moment the door blew open, propelled by a gust of wind and the outstretched arm of an almost-six-year-old. Georgie Graham, encased in an insulated coat that made him look like a Pillsbury doughboy, waddled into the room and peered at his mother through the tight oval opening in the coat's drawstring hood.

"Mom," he tugged at Babette's sleeve,

"we gotta take some Tylenols to old Cap'n Gribbon. He's sick, but it's not mumps or chicken pops."

"Salt's sick?" Birdie's heart did a strange double beat in her chest. She and Salt weren't courting, exactly, but they'd taken a walk or two in the last couple of weeks . . . walks they didn't exactly have to take.

Babette shot Birdie a not-so-fast look. "George Louis Graham," she cupped her son's chin, "you know I've told you not to go near the lighthouse. Cap'n Gribbon doesn't take kindly to visitors. The man likes his privacy."

"I didn't go up there, Mom." Georgie's face squinched in earnestness. "She told me he was really hot."

An unexpected dart of jealousy pierced Birdie's heart. "And which she would this be?"

Georgie turned toward her, his nose crinkling. "Brittle-knees. She was playing up near the dunes and she said old Cap'n Gribbon was hot and needed Tylenol, and then Bob said she was right and did we have any, 'cause old Salt needs help and they don't know what to do with him 'cause he won't eat or move or anything."

Birdie and Babette looked at each other, and, as was fittin', the boy's mother reacted first. "And who's Bob?"

"Brittle-knees's brother, I think. Or maybe cousin. I forget. But they asked me to bring them some Tylenol 'cause four out of five doctors recommend it for their patients with fever."

Babette drew a deep breath, then blew out her cheeks. "Son, I want you to go stand by the door while I pay Miss Birdie. Don't go outside; don't leave the bakery. You and I will walk home together."

She pushed at the back of the boy's puffed jacket as he turned to glance over his shoulder. "But what about old Cap'n Gribbon? He needs help."

"Don't worry, Cap'n Gribbon is a grown man. He can take care of himself."

Babette gave Birdie a rueful smile as she dropped a quarter on the counter, then opened her wallet. "Honestly, that child's imagination is going to be the death of me," she whispered, counting out five dollar bills. "But I don't have the heart to be too hard on him. With no other children on the island at this time of year, I can't really blame him for creating imaginary friends."

Birdie laughed as she took the money. "You gotta give his imaginary friends credit for stamina if they're playing outside on a day like today. Captain Stroble was in an hour ago, and he said the wind was blowin' so hard his chicken had to lay the same egg five times!"

Babette chuckled. "Well, Georgie is always keeping me guessing. So I'll think I'll take him home and fix his lunch. Food ought to keep him occupied for a while."

"You're a good mother, Babette." Birdie slid the bag of éclairs over the counter. "At least you give the boy a chance to run and play instead of plopping him down in front of the television all day."

"Well—he does watch a bit of TV," Babette said, turning away, "but only enough to help me keep my sanity."

Reaching her son, Babette spread her hand and gripped his neck—rather firmly, Birdie noticed. She grinned as the two exited beneath the jangling door, then she picked up a towel and began to wipe the counter.

Odd, that Georgie would say Cap'n Gribbon was ill. Men like Salt never seemed to get sick. The former swordfish boat captain was as tough as shoe leather and as independent as a gypsy. She couldn't imagine him lying abed up at the lighthouse, but . . .

Had the light shone last night? She didn't know whether the light was on some kind of automatic switch or whether Salt had to activate it manually. And last night she and her sister had retired to the cozy keeping room behind the bakery, with Birdie spending the night knitting in her rocker while Bea read and sorted angel letters. She hadn't looked out the window to check on the lighthouse.

She made a mental note to call the Ogunquit Memorial Library where she used to work. Faye Lewiston, the head librarian, was an old friend and would be happy to pull a book or two on lighthouses and send them over on the ferry. The next time Salt came 'round for a chat, Birdie could impress him with her knowledge of lighthouses and lanterns and whatever made them go 'round and 'round.

"Strange that we haven't seen the captain today," Abner volunteered from the mixing counter. "He should be ready for more cookies by now."

Birdie shook her head. "He came in day

before yesterday for his usual cookies and bread."

"Ayuh, but I remember thinking that he looked a little pale." Abner paused, his hand gripping a wooden spoon. "He didn't stick around to talk, remember?"

A creeping uneasiness began to rise from the bottom of Birdie's heart. What if Georgie was telling the truth? What if Salt was lying abed and the lighthouse wouldn't shine tonight? Theirs was a tiny island with a rugged shore, and any small craft could crash into the rocks once the sun went down . . .

Untying her apron, she turned to Abner. "I think I might ride up to the lighthouse and see what set Georgie off," she said, ignoring the knowing smile that crossed Abner's face. "Do we have any soup left in the Crockpot? It wouldn't hurt to take that, I suppose, in case Salt is doin' poorly. Who knows? He's probably as healthy as a horse; the boy only thought it odd when Salt didn't holler at him for playing too near the lighthouse. Anyway, it won't hurt to drive up and have a look, will it?"

Abner grinned. "No, ma'am, it won't."

*   *   *

Next door at the mercantile, Vernie faced her first customer of the day with bad news.

"No nutmeg?" Edith Wickam lightly fingered the string of imitation pearls at her neck. "Oh, dear. Winslow was hoping for an early pumpkin pie."

Vernie smiled, hoping to allay the pastor's wife's fears. "It will be in Wednesday afternoon, Edith. Don't worry. Deliveries are running behind because of the weather. The moment the shipment gets in, I'll have Elezar personally deliver the nutmeg to you."

"There's no need of that." Edith smiled pleasantly and added a tin of baking powder to her order. "Winslow needs to be watching his cholesterol these days, but I've found this skim pumpkin pie recipe that uses Egg Beaters and low-fat milk. I figure one or two slices aren't going to send him to an early grave."

The front door opened and Cleta and Barbara Higgs came in on a rush of cold air. The women exchanged pleasantries, commenting on how they would all be glad to see spring when it finally got there.

"Winter doesn't officially arrive until the twenty-first," Vernie reminded them. She gave Cleta a warning look when the bed and breakfast proprietor took a napkin out of her coat pocket and began to feed MaGoo the remains of a sausage biscuit. "Stop that. He won't be able to get through the doorway if you keep feeding him breakfast leftovers."

Cleta grinned and offered MaGoo a piece of sausage that had fallen to the floor. "Oh, a little taste won't hurt him. Can't let Maine's Heaviest Living Cat lose his title, can we?"

MaGoo purred, lacing in and out of Cleta's legs.

Vernie shifted her attention to Cleta's daughter, Barbara, who was browsing the cosmetics aisle. Barbara had always been a shy child, hanging in the background and turning beet red whenever anyone dared to ask her a direct question. She'd stammer, shuffling her feet and sometimes taking as long as five minutes to come up with an answer.

Barbara looked pale and washed out this morning, Vernie decided. Why didn't girls like her try a little harder to fix themselves up? She wasn't a beauty, but she wasn't unattractive, either. And her husband, Russell, was a downright handsome boy, so they didn't exactly go together like doughnuts and coffee. But Barbara had a heart as big as Texas. Too bad in the looks department she was a floor short of lingerie.

The phone rang and Vernie snatched it up with a free hand. "Mooseleuk's." She listened, then sighed. "No need to worry, Babette, this weather's slowed everything down. The cranberries will be here in plenty of time for you to make the salad. If you bought them in Ogunquit, they wouldn't be fresh for the Christmas party. Just hold your horses. The party is ten days away yet."

She held up a finger as Cleta approached. "I promise, the moment they come in I'll send Elezar with your cranberries. You say hello to Charles for me, okay?"

She hung up, then turned to Cleta. "Babette's worrying her head off about cranberries."

"Well, the Christmas party wouldn't be complete without Babette's cranberry salad," Cleta said. Her eyes followed Barbara, who was engrossed in a lipstick display across the room.

Noting Cleta's distraction, Vernie smiled. "A new cosmetics company sent me some samples. They're trying to get women to sell their product." She raised her voice. "Maybe that's something you'd be interested in, Barbara—selling cosmetics. They say they pay their sales representatives real well. If you sell enough lipstick and such, they'll give you a blue Cadillac."

Barbara shrugged and picked up a lipstick. "I don't drive."

Vernie blew out her cheeks. Sometimes that rule about no non-emergency motor vehicles on the island was a blessing, but now it was a downright annoyance. She forced a smile. "Well, selling cosmetics still might be something to consider."

Barbara replaced the lid on a tube of Papaya Pink. "I don't think so."

Vernie gave up. She rolled her eyes at Cleta, who giggled softly. "Nice try, Vernie. Now—how about a pound of that fresh ground coffee behind you?"

Vernie scooped up a pound of coffee, then poured it in a bag. "Anything else?"

"No, that should do it. You're sure that nutmeg will be here Wednesday afternoon?"

"Nutmeg, sugar, and cranberries. I ordered extra so we'd be sure to have enough to go around."

"You're sure?"

"Do I look addled?"

"No, but it would be a terrible shame if we got snowed in and couldn't get nutmeg and cranberries." Cleta peered out the window at the lowering clouds. "A real shame."

Vernie grimaced as she totaled Cleta's order. A Christmas grocery shortage would be more than a shame; it would cause an insurrection among the menfolk. Winslow Wickam could out eat every man on the island when it came to Babette's cranberry salad. At the last community Christmas party she'd had to make two punch bowls of the stuff just to keep the preacher happy.

Twice more the phone rang—the first caller was Abner, inquiring about the supplies and reminding her that the bakery was running low on sugar, the second was Dr. Marc, who planned to host a gathering at his house after the Christmas Eve service.

"I need nutmeg for the eggnog," he said. "It's my own special recipe. I can't take shortcuts this year because my son, Alex, will be here."

"Unless there's an emergency," Vernie reminded the doctor. Unfortunately, she'd heard him say the same thing for the last several years, and the good doctor's neurologist son had yet to make a Christmas appearance. At least Dr. Marc realized that folks didn't schedule car accidents or cerebral aneurysms in order to disrupt their physician's holiday plans.

"Not to worry, Dr. Marc," she told him. "The nutmeg is on its way."

CHAPTER SEVEN

Bundled in her down coat, boots, gloves, and hat, Birdie unzipped the cover of her golf cart, then situated herself on the hard fiberglass bench. The clear vinyl cart cover had been designed for sunny golf courses in Florida and California, but it did a fairly decent job of keeping out the cold in Maine—as long as she remembered to put the vehicle away. One night last winter she forgot to put the cart in the garage, and in the morning the vinyl was as brittle as glass.

She rubbed her hands together, gave the cover zipper a downward yank, then pushed the button to start the electric engine. Within a few moments she was powering her way up Ferry Road, a Crockpot on the floor and a bag of Salt's favorite rye bread in her lap.

While the soup was warming, she'd had time to reflect upon the last time she saw Salt. He had seemed a mite streak-ed on

Saturday, and he hadn't lingered to talk like he often did. She'd asked about the books she gave him, and he'd replied that they were fine stories, all of 'em.

At this, Birdie had winked at him. She had a strong suspicion the man couldn't read, but apparently he was trying to remedy the situation by applying himself to simple children's books. Last month she'd visited the Ogunquit library and bought several volumes from their clearance room. Salt seemed to appreciate the gift—well, as much as he appreciated anything. The man was as obstinate as a cross-eyed mule and about as conversational. But at least he seemed willing to better himself, and though Birdie couldn't understand how he intended to learn how to read, at least he was willing to take a stab at it. And she was willing to help . . . if he ever got around to asking.

Babette Graham was checking her mailbox as Birdie zoomed by the gallery, and Edith Wickam stood hunched at her gate, her hands tucked under her arms. She and Babette were probably doin' a bit of neighborin', and Birdie knew they'd undoubtedly wonder where she was going in such a hurry. The only inhabited building past the

Graham Gallery and the parsonage was Salt's lighthouse . . . well, if they wanted to talk, she'd let them.

Birdie drew a deep breath, inhaling the scents of beef barley soup and rye bread. Sick or well, Salt would have to appreciate her friendly offering. Though he hadn't been what anyone would call an ardent suitor, he had given her a smile or two and taken her on walks, which was more than he'd done for any other female on Heavenly Daze. Given Salt's crusty personality, such overtures were tantamount to a declaration of strong Liking.

The road curved beyond the Lobster Pot, closed now for the winter. Birdie kept both hands on the steering wheel as the cart advanced from cobblestones to gravel—the road was apt to be bumpy up here, and she didn't want to upset the Crockpot. To her left, the wind moved over the marshy reeds, bending them like waves in a storm.

The thought of a storm renewed her sense of urgency, so she pressed harder on the pedal. Finally, like an exclamation point at the northern tip of the island, the lighthouse appeared. Birdie urged the cart forward.

A few moments later she stood with the bread balanced on the Crockpot and the crockpot on her hip. Tentatively, she knocked at the bright red door, then waited, listening to the strident call of a sea gull.

No movement from within, but perhaps she'd caught Salt on the tall staircase. She knocked again, louder this time.

Content to wait, she turned. Sometimes Salt walked along the beach, and sometimes he fished in his small dory. Though the shore was rough and rocky up here, a sand bar protected a shallow inlet known as Puffin Cove, making it relatively easy for a man to launch a boat from this point. But no—the dory lay upside down on the beach, so Salt wasn't out on the water.

"Salt?" Gathering her courage, Birdie tried the latch. To her surprise, the door opened easily.

She stepped into the circular room. Captain Gribbon had taken up residence in the historic lighthouse about the time Bea had returned to the island. Though she'd heard rumors that Salt had remodeled the old monument into comfortable living quarters, none of the other townspeople had been allowed to venture inside. Except for his regular visits to the bakery and an occa- sional stop at the mercantile, the lightkeeper kept to himself.

Now she looked at a tidy room, ade- quately if oddly furnished. To her immediate left the circular wrought-iron staircase spi- raled up and away to the lamp at the top of the tower. Birdie felt dizzy looking up, so she lowered her eyes to more familiar territory. Beyond the staircase, a sink, stove, and re- frigerator lined the curving stone wall. A solid table, gleaming with some sort of mot- tled veneer, stood within arm's reach of the sink, and four chairs—four!—sat around the table.

She smiled at the sight of the chairs. Why, for all she knew Salt Gribbon might play cards every night with a bunch of lobster- men. Wouldn't that be something if the town recluse turned out to be a party animal?

Just past the refrigerator, a door had been cut into the stone wall, and Birdie knew the room beyond it housed a modern toilet, shower, and sink. There'd been a bit of a brouhaha years ago when Salt petitioned the city council to install his plumbing. Vernie Bidderman had insisted that if the former lighthouse keepers could make do with an outhouse and/or chamber pot, Salt Gribbon should be able to do the same. But Salt had stared at the town committee with those frosty blue eyes and replied that his house was no more historic than any of theirs. If he had to make do with an outhouse, so should they.

Birdie suppressed a smile as her gaze moved past the bathroom door. Just beyond the doorway stood the fireplace, flanked by an old wooden rocker and two vinyl beanbag chairs, one red, one orange.

She wrinkled her brow. Men were peculiar creatures, to be sure, but beanbag chairs? What did he do, settle his backside in one and prop his feet in another as he relaxed in front of the woodstove?

A tiny television with rabbit ears sat on a stand beyond the fireplace, and a dark wooden bed stood next to the TV. The bed traversed the rest of the circle, with its footboard less than a yard from where she stood—

She jumped as the mound of blankets on the bed shifted. "Oh, my." She hesitated, then leaned forward. "Salt?"

She heard only the rasp of labored breathing.

After placing the Crockpot and bread on the table, she rushed to the side of the narrow bed. Salt lay upon a thin mattress, his body covered by a faded quilt and an afghan, his face pale and shiny with perspiration. The stale odor of sweat rose from the bed.

Bending, Birdie placed her hand upon his forehead. Still hot, but the perspiration was a good sign. At least he hadn't completely dehydrated.

Without hesitation, she crossed to the sink, then crinkled her nose at the mess there. A half-dozen cups lay in the basin, along with a handful of silverware, a pair of bowls, and a DustBuster.

Salt obviously had not felt up to cleaning up.

She pulled a clean glass from a dish drainer, gave it a perfunctory swipe with a dishtowel she saw on the counter, then drew a tall glass of water from the faucet. Before taking it to him, however, she stepped into the bathroom, shivered in the frigid air, and flung open the medicine cabinet.

Aspirin. She took the bottle and shook two tablets into the palm of her hand even as a memory rose in her brain. *He needs Tylenol.*

She glanced at the other items in the medicine cabinet. Georgie was right, Salt had no Tylenol, though aspirin would work just as well for fever. But Georgie might not know that.

She left the bathroom, then frowned as another thought struck her—how had Georgie known that Salt had no Tylenol? As bold as the little urchin was, she doubted he'd have the nerve to invade Salt's bathroom and inventory the medicine chest.

"No time to worry about that," she muttered, crossing the room. Kneeling on the stone floor, she slipped one hand behind Salt's heavy head. "Cap'n Gribbon, you must drink some of this water and take this aspirin. Come on, now, drink."

Somehow, he heard. As his lips parted she brought the glass to them, struggling to lift his head. Her hand tangled in his wiry hair and his eyes never opened as she sloshed water over his neck and chest and bedclothes, but he swallowed, and that was good.

The medicine would begin its healing work.

*   *   *

Salt clung to the warm darkness as long as he could, but a soft voice persisted in calling his name. "Captain? Drink some more. Come on, only a little more."

He lifted his heavy lids and blinked as the world shifted dizzily before his eyeballs. Birdie Wester's face hovered inches above his, her eyes shining with concern, her lips pursed. "Ah, Salt." A smile spread across her narrow face. "So you've decided to join the land of the living. It's good to see you."

He blinked again and felt the pain of hot skin bending over his eyelids.

"Tarnation," he whispered, dropping his head back to the pillow. He felt like saying something worse, a sailor's word not fit for the ears of women or children—

The children!

Alarm rippled along his spine. Where were the children?

Resisting the shooting pains that raced along every nerve, he forced himself up on his elbows, his eyes darting left and right. A fire crackled in the woodstove; a lamp burned at the window over the sink. Through the odors of wood smoke he could smell the aroma of warm and hearty food—

But the lighthouse lantern mechanism

creaked overhead, so the sun had set. And Bobby and Brittany weren't in their beanbag chairs, at the table, or curled up on the floor before the TV.

His eyes met Birdie's. "Where are the kids?" he asked, his voice coming out in a rough croak.

"Kids?" Birdie cackled a laugh. "Oh, I expect Georgie's home with his mom and dad." Her strong, thin hands caught hold of his shoulders. "Now you lay back down and rest, Salt. I'll admit I was wondering how Georgie knew about your medicine chest, and Babette's going to read him the riot act when she hears he's been up here bothering you. But don't you worry, Georgie won't come around again—"

"No." Salt struggled against her grip, unable to believe that a mere one-hundred-pound woman could hold him, even push him, down to his bed. He drew a breath, felt the burning of his lungs, and wheezed out two more words: "My kids!"

Her eyes blazing with determination, Birdie forced him to lie still. When he saw that she would not relent and he could not overpower her, he stopped struggling.

Gradually, she relaxed her grip. "My

goodness, Salt, I thought you were over the worst of it. But if you're hallucinating, maybe you shouldn't be sitting up just yet."

He shook his head from side to side, steeling himself against the pounding at his temples. "No," he rasped.

Her finger fell across his lips. "You hush while I think this through. I knew fever could make a person delirious, but I never knew it could make a person . . ."

A line formed between her brows, a harbinger of worry. "My stars," she whispered, "I wonder if you're coming down with old-timer's disease."

Salt lifted his arm, trying to throw her off, but she gripped his shoulders again. He struggled, but her thin iron strength held until his will diminished like the flames of a dying fire, then faded into darkness.

Outside the lighthouse, Bobby thrust his hands deeper into his jacket pockets, threatening to rip the lining. Beside him, Britt huddled against his back, her clattering teeth sounding like the skittering of cockroaches from their last apartment.

"Bobbbbby," she wailed, genuine anguish

in her voice now, "I'm freezing! We have to go in!"

"Not yet." Shivering, Bobby glanced at the red door of the lighthouse. The woman had been inside all afternoon, so surely she'd come out soon and go home. When she did, he and Brittany could go inside. But until then, they'd wait. The grandfather had told them to never, ever let an adult from the town see them. That would bring certain danger, and none of them could risk it.

Still—Bobby didn't think he'd ever been so cold. A cloud of vapor rose with every breath he exhaled, and his feet were so numb they felt like weights at the bottom of his legs. The wind off the ocean had water in it, too, like an angry monster spitting at them with frigid breath.

He looked around the beach. With the tide coming in there'd be no shelter on the rocks where they'd been sitting, but the grandfather's boat lay on the sand, ghostly in the moonlight.

"Come on." He gripped Britt's hand. "We're going to find shelter."

He took her freezing fingers in his, then together they ran to the boat.

"Bobbbbby," she cried, balking. "I can't

crawl under there. It's dark. What if there's a crab, or a lobster . . . or an alien?"

"You've been watching too many *X-Files*, Britt. There's nothing under there." Bobby squatted near the narrow opening to be sure. "And I'll go first to prove it. But you've got to come in, too, or you'll freeze your fingers off tonight."

Kneeling, he lifted the boat slightly, felt it rock on the point of the bow, then lowered himself to his knees and elbows and crawled inside. The deep darkness beneath the boat smelled of fish and seaweed, but the wind didn't roar in his ears here, nor did the spray sting him through the thin fabric of his jacket.

He scooted closer to the side to make room for Brittany, then froze when his foot encountered a soft lump. For an instant icicles coursed through his blood, then he caught a whiff of stale orange juice and remembered the dishtowels. He and Britt had tossed them here, to hide them from the grandfather.

He thrust his head toward the opening. "Come on, Britt; it's fine. You'll be warmer under here, and we can watch the house through this crack."

Reluctantly, Brittany knelt and inched her way into the darkness. When she had curled next to him, Bobby rocked the boat back to its resting position, then put his arms around his little sister. "We'll wait here until we hear the golf cart leave." He drew a deep breath to ease his shivering. "Then we'll go inside by the fire. It'll be okay. After all, we wanted someone to come help the grandfather. Once she leaves, everything will be better."

Britt kept shivering. "Do—do you suppose that lady is Georgie's mother?"

Bobby shrugged. "I dunno. Maybe."

They huddled in silence, listening to the distant pounding of the surf and the howling of the wind. Bobby felt the wet from the sand begin to seep through his jeans, then his underwear. He might have a cold bottom by the time they could go back inside, but at least the yapping wind couldn't nip at him here.

Time passed. Bobby's eyelids had begun to grow heavy when the boat rocked and the noise of the wind abruptly increased. He opened his eyes. A man stood on the sand, one hand supporting the boat, the other extended. His hair, skin, and coat gleamed like the moon in the night sky.

"Bobby," the man's voice was gentle, "you and Brittany need to come with me. Come now, before you get much colder."

Bobby didn't hesitate. He nudged Britt, whose sleep-heavy head lay pressed against his chest, then pushed her toward the man. Smiling, the man pulled her from beneath the boat, then lifted her into his arms. He waited until Bobby stood beside him, then he took Bobby's hand. Carrying the still-sleeping Brittany with one powerful arm, the man led Bobby down the road toward the village.

Though his mind buzzed with questions, Bobby didn't speak. He didn't want to seem rude, and he was so cold. This man knew his name, so he had to be okay. Only the grandfather and the boy, Georgie, knew his name, so either the grandfather or Georgie must have sent this man. He didn't understand how the grandfather could have sent anyone, but still, he must have done something.

Bobby didn't care anymore. Even though the cold wind still howled over the island with spit in its breath, his teeth were no longer chattering and he could breathe without shivering.

They passed the brick building with a sign that said "Public Rest Rooms" and the dark restaurant with a picture of a lobster above the door. They walked silently past Georgie's house, then they turned up the path leading to the church.

Bobby gaped at the building, his eyes lifting to the tall steeple. "You live in the church?"

The man's mouth split into a smile that lit his dark eyes like the sun sparkling on the waves. "Yes, I do."

Bobby swallowed to bring his heart down from his throat. "Are you God?"

"No." Again, the sparkling smile. "Only one of his servants. And I'm going to make certain you and your sister are safe and warm tonight."

Then the man reached out and opened the same door Bobby had seen the pastor lock. Through the church they walked, then they moved down a wide wooden staircase into a bright basement room where a furnace glowed and filled the room with heat.

Brittany stirred and lifted her head. She looked first at Bobby, then at the room, then at the man who held her. "Hello," she said, placing her hands against his chest. Her voice seemed small in the open space. "Who are you?"

"I am called Gavriel." The man lowered Britt to the floor. "But you can call me Gabe. That's easier to say, isn't it?"

Nodding, Brittany took a cautious step forward. The place wasn't fancy. Lots of metal folding chairs clustered around a few long tables, but at the back of the room, behind a counter, Bobby could see a kitchen—a sink, a stove, and what looked like an old refrigerator.

Gabe must have read his mind . . . or heard Bobby's stomach growling.

"I think I can find something for you to eat," Gabe said, moving toward the kitchen with long strides. "How about some peanut butter sandwiches, potato chips, and hot cocoa?"

"Yum!" Britt sank into a chair, then rested her arms on the table and dropped her chin to her hands. "Sounds like a picnic!"

Puzzled, Bobby watched the stranger. The guy walked without making a sound, almost as if his feet glided over the floor without touching it. What was he wearing, special sneakers?

Gabe laughed, his musical laughter

warming the room as well as the rumbling furnace. "A picnic—what a good idea."

Bobby sank into a chair, too, swinging his legs back and forth as he looked around. Overhead he could see pipes and wires and dark beams. Beyond that lay more wood, probably the floor of the big room above. The walls here were painted block, and the floor was yellow tile, scuffed with black shoe marks. It wasn't the prettiest place to spend the night, but it was definitely better than sleeping under a boat.

"Do you have a TV?" Brittany asked, looking around. "If it's seven o'clock, it must be time for *Perfect Families*."

"It's past seven," Gabe called, pulling a pot from a cabinet. "And there's no television in the church. There's no need for one. People come here to learn about God, not to watch someone else's idea of a perfect family."

Britt's lower lip edged forward in a pout. "I like that show. It has funny stories."

"Does it?" Gabe sloshed milk from a jug into the pot. "Well, I know stories, too, some pretty good ones. While you're eating, I might be willing to tell a story or two."

"Really?" Bobby felt his spirits rise. He

had enjoyed learning to read the books at the lighthouse, and if he could hear a story without even having to read it—well, the night might not turn out so bad.

"I might even be willing to tell you a story now, while the milk warms." Gavriel put the pan on the stove, then smiled at them over the counter as he pulled bread out of a plastic bag. "Which would you rather hear—a story about love or war?"

Brittany straightened in her chair. "Love!"

Bobby glared at his sister. "I don't want to hear anything with kissy parts."

Gabe laughed. "Okay. Maybe I can think of a story with a little bit of love and war. Let me think . . ."

"I hate war stories." Britt slumped, supporting her head with one hand. "One night we watched war movies all night long—at least Bobby did. I fell asleep."

"That's probably a good thing," Gabe said, spreading peanut butter upon slices of bread. "Was it one of the nights your daddy didn't come home?"

Bobby glanced at his sister. Nobody, not even the grandfather, knew about all the nights Daddy went out and didn't come home until the next day. Once he stayed gone for two nights, then staggered home and slept on the couch for another full day.

Tilting her head, Brittany gave Gabe a questioning look. "You know our daddy?"

"I know about him," Gabe said. "I also know about your grandfather. He's a gruff fellow, and most of the islanders tend to leave him alone. But he loves you very much."

Bobby sat taller in the folding chair, then pulled his knees to his chest and hugged them. People on TV talked about love all the time, but he'd never heard the word in real-life conversation. Until now.

Britt hadn't seemed to notice the word. "You know our grandfather's sick," she said, her eyes following Gabe's hands as he sliced the peanut butter sandwiches into triangles. "That's why we were waiting outside. We tried to get help, and then we heard that lady coming up the road. We ran outside when we heard her coming 'cause we're not supposed to let anyone see us."

"I know." Gabe pulled two paper plates from a plastic bag, then set the bread triangles on them. He then opened a huge can and sprinkled a handful of potato chips beside each sandwich.

Bobby had never seen more beautiful food in his entire life.

"You two come on and grab a plate while I pour the cocoa," Gabe said, turning toward the stove. "And while you're eating, I'll tell you the story I promised."

They scrambled out of their chairs and took the plates from the counter, then settled into places at the table and began to eat. Gabe came out from the kitchen with two steaming mugs of chocolate milk, complete with tiny marshmallows on top.

Bobby swallowed a bite of the sandwich, then inhaled the warm, chocolaty steam. Gabe had to be a friend of the grandfather's. No one else would want to take care of them.

Brittany lifted a potato chip with her fingers, then carefully snapped it in half. "Okay, tell your story," she said, commanding Gabe as if he were her servant.

The man seemed to take no offense. He settled into a seat at the end of the table, propped one white sneaker on a rung of Britt's chair, then folded his hands at his waist.

"All right, here's my story, and it's true. Once upon a time, while the people of God were living at a place called Rephidim, the warriors of fierce King Amalek came to fight against them. Moses, the leader of the Israelites, commanded his assistant Joshua and said, 'Call the Israelites to arms, and fight the army of Amalek. Tomorrow I will stand at the top of the hill with the staff of God in my hand.'"

"What's the staff of God?" Bobby lifted his mug. "His assistants?"

Gabe chuckled. "His staff did assist him, but this staff was a tall stick. He used it to help him walk through the desert. Moses was an old man at the time."

Bobby nodded as the picture focused in his mind. The grandfather often walked slow and hunched over when he first woke up in the morning. A walking stick might help him, too.

"Anyway," Gabe went on, "Joshua did what Moses had commanded. He led his men out to fight the army of Amalek while Moses, Aaron, and Hur went to the top of a nearby hill. As long as Moses held up the staff of God with his hands, the Israelites fought well. But whenever he grew tired and lowered his hands, the Amalekites began to win. Moses finally grew too tired to hold up the staff any longer. So Aaron and Hur found a stone for him to sit on. Then they stood on each side, holding up his hands until sunset. As a result, Joshua and his fighting men were able to defeat the army of Amalek."

Silence fell over the room as Gabe finished, the stillness broken only by the sound of Brittany's potato-chip crunching.

"So," Bobby began, knowing there had to be a lesson in the story. "If we're ever in a fight, should we have somebody hold up a stick?"

"Not exactly." Smiling, Gabe leaned forward and rested his arms on his knees. "I told you the story so you'd see the power of cooperation. You and Brittany are a team. Bobby, you've always been the leader, and you've done a fine job of taking care of your daddy and your little sister. But seven-year-old boys shouldn't have to carry so much. Now it's time for you to let someone take care of you."

Bobby blinked. "The grandfather?"

Gabe's smile deepened. "Yes—and other people, too. You can trust the folks on this island. They're good, God-fearing people, and they'll learn to love you . . . when they learn you're here."

Britt's face clouded. "Will they love my daddy?"

Still smiling, Gabe's gentle glance passed over her. "God loves your daddy, sweetheart, just as he loves your mommy. Your grandfather loves your parents, too. But sometimes people let other feelings get in the way of love."

Propping his head on his hand, Bobby stared at his empty plate. The sandwich and warm milk now sloshed in his belly, and waves of tiredness rippled through him. He lowered his head to the table and felt the coolness of the hard surface beneath his cheek.

"You're tired." Gabe stood. "Come with me, both of you. I think I can make you more comfortable."

Obeying, Bobby stood and followed Gabe to the corner where the furnace belched and blew a current of warm air into the room. A padded pallet lay on the floor.

"I found this in a storage closet," Gabe explained, sinking onto the thin plastic pallet. "It's nothing plush, but I think we can be warm and comfortable for the rest of the night." Without seeming to care if he got his white clothes dirty, he sat with his back pressed to the wall, then stretched out his long legs. "Come on, you two. Sit beside me, and let me tell you another story."

Brittany bounded to Gabe's side, settling beneath his arm like an affectionate puppy. Bobby followed a little more cautiously. Gabe placed his arms around each of their shoulders, then in his deep voice he began to tell another tale:

"In the beginning Jesus the Word already existed. He was with God, and he was God. He was in the beginning with God. He created everything there is. Nothing exists that he didn't make. Life itself was in him, and this life gives light to everyone. The light shines through the darkness, and the darkness can never extinguish it."

"Like a lighthouse," Britt murmured, her voice soft with sleep.

Gabe chuckled. "Yes, like a lighthouse. And the light had a helper, a man as independent as your grandfather. He was called John the Baptist, and God sent him to tell everyone about the light so that everyone might believe. John himself was not the light; he was only to tell people that the one who is the true light, who gives light to everyone, was going to come into the world."

"The Guiding Light?" Though his eyelids were heavy, Bobby forced himself to look up. "Like the TV show?"

Gabe shook his head. "He is a guiding light, but not many people know him that way. You see, although the world was made through him, the world didn't recognize him when he came. Even in his own land and among his own people, he was not accepted. But to all who believed him and accepted him, he gave the right to become children of God."

Nodding drowsily, Bobby listened, the words of the story coming steadily until he fell asleep.

CHAPTER EIGHT

Salt opened his eyes in the time of half-light, before color filled the morning and night fled away. The gray air lay still and cool against his face; the heaviness of dark quilts covered his body. The woodstove had ceased its crackle and hiss; the only sound touching his ear was a quiet snoring from somewhere off to his right.

He closed his eyes and shuddered in relief. The children were safe and sound. Bobby snored like that, especially in the morning when his sinuses were stuffed from the night.

He'd had a terrible dream. Birdie Wester had been tending him, and the little woman had held him in his bed while he tried to tell her there were children about, two kids who must be fed and warmed and sheltered . . .

Weariness clung to him like a shroud, but still he managed a wry smile. His mind must have been playing tricks on him, conjuring up terrors and trials as his fever staged one last stand against the healing touch of time.

Shifting his weight under the heavy quilts, Salt rolled onto his side and opened his eyes. Silvery light from the approaching sun filled the room, bathing the kitchen table in a cool patina. Shadow pools filled the crevices of the beanbag chairs and the floor, but in a moment or two the room would brighten a bit more and he'd see his dear little snorer . . .

The wooden creak of the rocker broke the steady rhythm, and Salt frowned. He adjusted his gaze, saw a form curled in the chair, a blanket draped about the chest and shoulders. Why would Bobby sleep in the rocker? He had a perfectly comfortable bedroll against the wall.

Salt lifted his head as his eyes adjusted to the semigloom. The shape in the chair seemed wrong; it was too long and too sprawled, with one bony arm draped over the side and extended toward him. The hand at the end of that arm was long-fingered, with a gold ring gleaming above polished nails.

Bobby didn't wear jewelry or nail polish.

Adrenaline pulsed through Salt's bloodstream, fueling him with the strength to shove away a mountain of blankets and sit up. Driven by a fear he could not name, he placed his stockinged feet on the floor and squinted at the body in the chair, half-expecting to discover the form of some sea witch from the mariner's stories he'd heard as a child.

No—as the light brightened he recognized the shape of the head, the graying hair pulled back with a wide barrette. His visitor was Birdie Wester.

So it hadn't been a dream. And the children—

Bending to peer under his bed, he lost his balance and pitched forward. He cried out as his hand hit the stone floor, then closed his eyes as Birdie squeaked, "Salt! What on earth are you doing on the floor?"

Opening his eyes, he turned his head to look under the bed. He could see nothing in the dark space—no forms, not even the semblance of shadow. He stretched his hand to search the space, hoping his eyes and ears had turned traitor and refused to reveal the children's presence. But his fingers closed on dust and empty air.

"Salt Gribbon, you're going to kill yourself if you don't get back in bed."

Birdie Wester knelt beside him now, her iron fingers prying into the space under his arms. "I'm going to try to lift you, but you'll have to help me."

Salt could not answer. He curled his dusty fist, empty and helpless, into his mouth and wept.

"Salt?" Alarmed by the sound of his dry, racking sobs, Birdie bent over the prostrate man. His fever had broken; his skin was cool to the touch. But every trace of the fiercely independent curmudgeon had vanished.

"The kids," he choked out the words. "I told 'em not to come in if anyone else was about. And they're good kids, so they've got to be outside." Still weeping, he pressed his hands to the floor and pushed himself up to a sitting position. "I've gotta go out and find 'em."

Birdie's breath caught in her lungs. This wasn't a man given to delirium. "What kids do you mean, Salt?"

"My grandkids." He turned to her, his eyes glassy and wet. "Bobby and Brittany live with me now. They must be outside."

The startling confession brought another

thought to her mind, with a chill that struck deep in the pit of her stomach. "Salt, they couldn't be, no one could—" Her voice broke in midsentence. The truth was unthinkable. The temperature had been well below freezing for most of the night.

She stood, the truth slamming into her as she reached for her coat. Georgie had said he was playing with two children. His friends weren't imaginary, after all.

"I'll find them, Salt." She dove into her coat, then pushed him back toward the bed. "You're in no condition to go out. Get in bed, and when I come back with the children, I'll fix you all a warm bowl of soup."

His eyes blazing, he caught her hand. "You've killed my grandchildren, woman." The words echoed in the empty silence of the tower. "You came here to meddle, and my kids did what they'd been told and hid away. And now they're out there somewhere, frozen and cold as the grave."

Birdie drew a breath, then closed her eyes and jerked her hand free of his grasp. He might well be right, but she could still hope . . . and pray.

"Please, Lord," she whispered, tears stinging her eyes as she opened the door and left Salt struggling to get dressed. "Let those children be all right."

Salt cursed as his fingers refused to hook the zipper on his coat. Abandoning the effort, he pulled open the front door—when had it grown so heavy?—and stepped out into the cold. The gray grass around the lighthouse gleamed with frost; even his dory shone with an icy glaze. The night had been a cold one.

"Bobby!" He stepped forward and grimaced as the bawling winds caught his voice and tossed it away. He hadn't the strength to yell louder, but he'd have to. Victims of hypothermia usually fell asleep, which meant he might have to wake Bobby and Brittany in order to save them.

He stumped toward the boat, struggling against the wind. The old dory offered the only shelter against the damp weather, and Bobby was bright enough to figure that out. The kids would have been cold passing the night here, but at least they'd have been somewhat protected.

He gripped the edge of the vessel and struggled to lift it. Summoning strength that refused to come, he groaned, tugging with arms that felt as limp and powerless as noodles. Then another pair of hands joined his. The boat rocked, then rolled over onto its spine.

He and Birdie stood side by side, staring at a patch of sand littered with seaweed and rags.

"What's that?" Birdie pointed to a pile of cloth.

Salt stared, then knelt and gingerly lifted one of the corners. "Why—it's one of my pillowcases." Turning the case upside down, he stared in amazement as a half-dozen stiff dishtowels tumbled out onto the sand.

He shook his head. "They must have spilled something . . . and were afraid I'd scold 'em." He glanced up at Birdie, whose mouth had pursed in a disapproving expression. "I wouldn't have, you know. Because of their daddy. He beat those kids, so now they're afraid to make a peep."

He wanted to lower his head into his hands and die on the spot, but Birdie wouldn't leave him alone. "Come on." She nudged his arm. "We can walk along the beach. Maybe the kids are sheltering in the rocks."

Not knowing what else to do, Salt plodded after her while shame and despair rose within his heart. If Bobby and Brittany died, he'd be the one to blame, not Birdie. If he hadn't tried to keep the world at arm's length, those kids would never have left the shelter of the lighthouse. He'd killed the two children he meant to protect with his life. He'd driven them away when it was the world he meant to shut out.

Tears clouded his gaze, obscuring his vision, but Salt lumbered on, not caring if the wind and the day sapped the last of his strength and left him a wasted shell of a man.

The children weren't on the beach. One quick glance assured Birdie that the meager cover offered no place for them to hide, no shelter at all. Besides, the wind was colder and wetter here, and even a child would know to come out of the storm.

That left the dunes. They might have headed toward the marsh and the sand dunes, but the piled sand would have offered little protection from the cold and wind.

She pressed her hand to Salt's shoulder and turned him toward the lighthouse. "You go back inside and turn up the heat on the Crockpot," she said, shouting to be heard above the pounding surf. "I'm going to take my cart and follow the road. If the kids are hiding anywhere about, I'll find 'em."

Salt looked at her, dazed and obviously weak, but he moved toward the lighthouse, his shoulders slumped and his bare hands swinging limply at his side.

Her hair flying, Birdie ran to her cart, unzipped the vinyl cover, and pressed the starter button. The engine clicked, but the cart wouldn't start. Probably too cold.

Hunkering inside her coat, Birdie stared at the road ahead. Nothing moved in the emptiness, warmed now by the first genuine rays of morning sunlight. A half-mile up, Edith Wickam and Babette Graham were undoubtedly rousing their households, setting up coffee makers, and popping frozen waffles into toasters. Georgie Graham probably lay sleeping in his bed, his feet twitching with restless energy as the radiators hissed and clanged, filling his room with life-sustaining heat . . .

Her eyes widened. Of course! Georgie had

met Bobby and Brittany, and maybe the children knew where he lived. If they couldn't go into the lighthouse, perhaps they had gone to the Graham Gallery. They might have even approached the little cottage behind the main house where Zuriel the potter lived.

Birdie stepped out of the golf cart and began jogging down the road, her hands in her pockets and her breath frosting with every step. Her mind kept returning to the sight and sound of Salt blaming her for the death of his grandchildren, and her blood ran thick with guilt. But how could she have known?

As she ran, other pieces of the puzzle began to fall into place—Salt's asking her about children's books, his obvious delight that she'd brought so many, his gruffness and discourtesy when she once tried to surprise him with a visit. Why, he'd been hiding those children for weeks, and nary a soul had spied them!

A dozen questions leaped into her mind—where had they come from, why had they come, and how had Salt managed to get them onto the island? Birdie hadn't known that Salt had a son. Come to think of it, she knew very little about the man at all, even after being his neighbor for nearly fifteen years.

Tears, unbidden and unchecked, flowed down her cheeks, stinging her cold skin. "Bobby?" she called, craning her neck as she approached the municipal building. The place was locked, but perhaps he and Brittany had managed to jimmy open a window. The brick structure housed the mayor's office, a single jail cell, and two public restrooms, which the kids might have needed at some point during the day and night.

Walking as fast as her panting lungs would allow, Birdie skirted the building and tested the windows. All were closed tight, and the door wouldn't budge. Floyd Lansdown had locked the building on Columbus Day, the official end of the tourist season, and wouldn't open the place again until April.

She glanced across the road to the Lobster Pot. The restaurant's painted sign swung forlornly in the wind, a testament to its emptiness now that the last tourists had departed, but the children might have sought shelter there. There were no windows, but she thought there might be a back door . . .

"Please Lord," she whispered, thrusting

her hands into her pockets as she lengthened her stride and crossed the windblown street. "Let me find those kids in a safe and warm place."

"Bobby?"

Bobby's eyes flew open as the voice shattered his dream. He looked up to see the man called Gabe looking down at him. "We have to go now," Gabe said.

Bobby straightened, a little embarrassed to realize that he'd slept all night against Gabe's chest. Brittany looked natural curled up against this strong man, but boys should be able to take care of themselves.

Gabe's eyes crinkled as he smiled. "You've done a fine job of taking care of your family. I don't think any boy in Maine could do better."

Bobby felt the corner of his mouth lift. "Really?"

"Really." Gabe looked down and gently shook Brittany awake. "Britt, honey, it's time to wake up. It's morning, and your grandfather's worried about you."

Brittany yawned, then her big blue eyes opened. She lifted her head, and Bobby saw a small circle on her cheek—the imprint of Gabe's shirt pocket button.

She looked toward the kitchen. "Is there any breakfast?"

"Miss Birdie will have breakfast for you." Gabe stood and stretched, his long arms seeming to fill the space above Bobby's head. "So hop up, both of you, and button those jackets. Miss Birdie's outside and coming this way, and we don't want her to worry any more than necessary."

Bobby wanted to ask how Gabe knew about Miss Birdie, but the man seemed to have something on his mind as he reached down to pull them up. Once he'd stood them on their feet, his big hands smoothed Brittany's tangled hair, then he gave both kids a push toward the rest rooms. "Freshen up, and splash a little water on your face," he called, bending to fold up the vinyl pallet they'd slept on. "And be quick. We don't have time to waste."

Bobby slowed his steps as he approached the door of the rest room labeled GENTLEMEN. "How does he know so much?" he whispered to his sister.

Britt shrugged and pushed on the door marked LADIES. "I like him. He's nice."

Five minutes later, with his hair smoothed and his jacket zipped, Bobby followed Gabe and his sister up the wooden staircase. As they walked through the silent church, Brittany gaped at the windows. Tall and narrow, and made of bits of multicolored glass, they held pictures of trees, ships, and crosses. In the biggest picture, the one right behind the wooden box on the stage, a man with long brown hair carried a little lamb.

Bobby thought the windows were cool, but he didn't want to say anything. They had never been inside a church in their lives, but saying so probably wasn't a good idea—especially since this man lived in one.

They left the big room, then Gabe led them into a small space lined with wooden paneling. Two oil paintings hung above a table—an old-fashioned picture of a man in uniform holding a feathered hat, and another portrait of an ordinary-looking bald man.

Bobby slipped his hands into his jeans pockets and nodded toward the paintings. "Who are they?"

Gabe glanced over his shoulder. "Sea captain Jacques de Cuvier, the founder of the town, and Winslow Wickam, the current pastor." He winked at Bobby. "You'll be meeting Pastor Wickam soon, I think."

"I don't know." Britt looked down at her hands. "We don't go to church."

"Perhaps that will soon change." Still smiling, Gabe opened one of the double doors. The wind rushed in, flapping the papers on the long table.

"Go on, now," Gabe said, holding the door open. "By the time you reach the end of the walkway, you'll see Miss Birdie coming out from behind the Lobster Pot. Go to her right away, and she'll take you to your grandfather."

Nodding soberly, Bobby gripped Brittany's shoulder and steered her out of the building and down the sidewalk. And though he distinctly heard the door close behind them, he had a strong feeling that Gabe was watching long after they reached the street, waved to Miss Birdie, and saw her come running toward them with tears in her eyes and a wide smile on her bright red face.

"My goodness!" Her heart singing with delight, Birdie embraced the little girl, then hugged the boy a second time. "Bobby and Brittany! I'm so glad you're all right!"

Bobby pulled out of her frantic grasp. "Is the grandfather okay?"

Birdie lowered her head to smile at him. "Yes. Your grandfather is much better this morning, though he's terribly worried about you. Come, let me walk you back." Placing a hand at each of their necks, Birdie herded the children toward the north end of the island.

"Where did you sleep last night?" she asked, trying to keep a nagging note from her voice. "We were so worried."

"We slept in the church." Brittany looked up, her eyes as wide and blue as the sky. "Gabe let us in and fed us peanut butter sandwiches."

"Gabe?" Birdie tilted her head. She'd never heard of a Gabe even visiting Heavenly Daze. "Are you sure his name wasn't Pastor Wickam?"

"No, ma'am." Bobby answered this time, his eyes meeting his sister's. "We saw the pastor's picture in the little front room. Gabe doesn't look anything like that."

"Really." Birdie pasted on a casual smile. "Well, what does Gabe look like?"

Brittany lifted her arm high over her head.

"He's very tall. Taller than the grandfather, probably. And he has white hair."

"Lots of white hair," Bobby added. "Like I said, he doesn't look anything like the men in the pictures."

If the children had seen the portraits in the vestibule, there was no doubting they had been inside the church. But how? Pastor Wickam kept the building locked when there were no scheduled activities. Even if they had found a way to slip into the building, the place would be dreadfully cold on a week night. The old furnace barely performed well enough to heat the place for Sunday services.

"A tall man with white hair . . . named Gabe." Dismissing the thought, Birdie hooked her fingers into the collar of each child's coat. Children with imaginations this vivid might be tempted to soar away on the wings of fancy.

"That's his nickname," Brittany added. "His real name was Gallabelle."

Bobby lifted his chin. "No, it wasn't. It was—Gab—well, it was something else. But it didn't have any bells in it."

"Really." Quickening her stride, Birdie hurried her charges along, more than ready to get inside and warm her hands by the fire. She and Salt could solve the riddle of the children's whereabouts later.

The day had brightened along with her mood. The sky swept over them, cozy with cloud, but backlit with brilliant sunshine. The kiss of sunrise had summoned a rosy flush to the gleaming lighthouse in the distance, and Birdie felt her heart lift at the sight.

They hurried forward, her long shadow flanked by two smaller ones, and as they rounded the curve they saw Salt standing on the shore, his hands in his pockets, his shoulders hunched. He faced the sea, a picture of dejection.

"Grandfather!" Bobby cried, his voice catching as if he were unused to the word.

Salt turned at the sound of the boy's call, then his eyes widened. For a moment he seemed to sway on his feet, then he staggered forward, his arms lifting. The children sprinted to meet him, and they met at a place where a tumble of blueberry vines clung tenaciously to the soil, unbroken by the wind and as yet unbowed by the cold.

CHAPTER NINE

Back in the lighthouse, where a freshly laid fire blazed in the stove and the children sat at the table with warm oatmeal in their bowls (Birdie had been horrified to learn that he'd been feeding them cookies for breakfast), Salt reclined on his bed, wrapped in a warm bunting of relief. Birdie had ordered him to rest, and now she seemed intent upon fortifying him with a bowl of barley soup, extrastrong now that it had simmered in the Crockpot for nearly twenty-four hours. He willingly obeyed her, his heart softened by gratitude for the children's safe return.

"You haven't told me," he said between force-fed spoonfuls, "where you found them."

"They were on the road," Birdie said, tucking her feet beneath the edge of a lap blanket covering her legs. She leaned forward in the rocker, pushing soup toward him. "Walking along as if they hadn't a care in the world."

"So where"—he slurped the spoon nudging against his lower lip—"did they sleep?"

"In the church," Bobby called, looking up from his oatmeal. "With Gabe."

Salt narrowed his eyes at Birdie. "What on earth is the little dickens talking about?"

"I'm not sure," she answered, her voice as smooth as the shiny skin on the back of her hands, "but apparently someone let them into the church, fed them, and watched over them. So don't go getting your feathers ruffled, Cap'n Gribbon. You should be thanking the good Lord that someone was willing to look out after these children."

Feeling the sting of rebuke in her words, Salt lowered his eyes. Ayuh, he was grateful, to her and to whomever had taken the kids in last night.

"Maybe they got turned around in the dark," he finally said, pausing to accept another spoonful of soup. "Maybe they ended up at Zuriel Smith's cottage. He's got that long hair and a beard, and maybe it looked white in the lights or something—"

"Or maybe your two grandchildren have vivid imaginations."

He shifted his gaze to Brittany, who was licking the back of her spoon with great relish. "The little one does have a tendency to embellish a story."

Apparently satisfied that he'd finished the soup, Birdie dropped the spoon into the bowl and lowered it to her lap. "They seem like bright kids, Salt. They must take after their grandpa."

Without warning, tears stung his eyes. Salt looked away and lowered his voice. "Their dad was bright enough when he was young." He felt a flush burn his face. "But then he started drinking, and I think his brain's turned to mush. I went over to Wells a couple of months ago, thinkin' I'd pay him a visit, but he wasn't home. Instead, I found these two, lookin' as though they hadn't seen the inside of a bathtub in weeks."

Lowering his voice to a whisper, he struggled to push the words over the boulder in his throat. "They were bruised, too, even the little girl. I haven't talked to them about it, but I know he wasn't a fit parent."

Birdie didn't answer for a moment, but when he looked at her again, he saw that her eyes were shiny. "So you took them and brought them here."

"Ayuh. I left a note telling Patrick that I had 'em and said he could come see me after he'd gotten some help."

"Has he come?"

"No."

"Called?"

Salt shook his head.

"So—you're determined to keep them until your son gets his act together? That could take a long time."

He frowned, amazed at the unspoken objection in her voice. "Why wouldn't I keep 'em? They're my own flesh and blood. No one has any more right or responsibility than I do."

"Perhaps." She tilted her head, then glanced over her shoulder at the children, who were talking over their bowls of oatmeal. She lowered her voice a degree. "I applaud your concern, but you can't expect to take care of two young children without help. They'll need to go to school; they need the company of other kids and other people."

"They weren't in school when I found 'em. They've never been to school a day in their lives, but Bobby can read almost any book you put in his hand. You know what he wanted to bring from his old place? An encyclopedia! The kid's a budding genius!"

"Still," Birdie leaned closer, "the three of you are likely to go stir-crazy if you winter up here all alone."

"I ain't never minded bein' alone."

Her eyes sparked. "You're not an impressionable child. And look at you—flat on your back, weak as a baby, and about to wizzle away to nothing. Admit it, Salt—those children would have been lost last night if they hadn't stumbled into the church. What's going to happen the next time you're sick?"

"I won't get sick again." With an effort, Salt pulled himself off his pillows and sat straight up. "I don't get the flu often; after this I'll be good for another five years or so—"

"You'll be lucky if God decides to grant you another five years."

She was hissing at him now, her face only inches from his, and Salt could do nothing but stare at her. Birdie Wester had more gumption than he'd thought, and her arguments were more reasonable than he wanted to admit. But what more could he do? If the townspeople found out about the children, it'd only be a matter of time before the news slipped out to the mainland. Cleta Lansdown at the B&B was the coordinator of gossip central; tell a story to that basket and it'd be leaked all over town in an hour. And even if the news didn't travel to Ogunquit and the county beyond, some do-gooder like Dana Klackenbush or Edith Wickam was bound to get it into her head to call social services. And if someone called in bureaucrats from the State of Maine, the children would be taken away, pure and simple.

"Birdie Wester." Leaning over, Salt gripped her wrist with every ounce of strength he could muster. "You know my secret—it couldn't be helped, and I'm grateful for what you did today. But you've got to keep quiet about these children. The state will take 'em away, as sure as the sun will rise tomorrow. They won't think a man of my age"—he paused for effect, knowing that Birdie wasn't too many years behind him—"could take care of youngsters. They think we're old and twitterpated, but no one, I tell you, is better qualified to take care of kids than the man who loves 'em."

She pulled away from him, but her piercing blue eyes never left his face. "Why, Salt Gribbon," she whispered, "I believe you do love these children."

Salt swallowed, anger and indignation rising inside him. Why should she find that hard to believe? He was an independent man, not a misanthrope, and he could love as well as anybody. He'd loved his wife while she lived, God rest her, and he'd loved Patrick with every breath he drew. He still loved Patrick, wherever he was, but his love for his son had long since ceased to be blind.

An idea formed in his mind then, a strategy he'd often used in his marriage and with the crew of his ship. He hadn't been much around people, though, and even the best of tools could grow rusty if you didn't use them.

"'Course I love 'em," he whispered, his voice hoarse. "What's not to love? They're good kids, and they'll be fine here with me . . . as long as we've got you to help us."

He lowered his lids, then lifted his head to look at her through the slit between his lashes. Most women could recognize flattery a mile off, and Birdie Wester was no fool, but she'd have to be warmed by the compliment . . . and by his willingness to confide in her.

"You're the only one I trust," he went on, hoping she wouldn't realize he had no choice in the matter. "The kids know you now, and it's obvious they like you. In fact," he widened his eyes to smile at her, "I thought you knew about the kids a long time ago. When you started bringing me those children's books, I was certain you'd found out."

"The books?" A blush warmed her pale face. "Why, I brought you those books because I thought you were illiterate. I was sure you were trying to teach yourself to read."

He looked at her and blinked hard, then grinned in the first moment of pure mirth he'd felt in days.

"Birdie Wester," he said, not resisting as she pushed him down and pulled the covers to his chin, "you're a right opinionated gal."

"A woman has a right to her opinions," she answered, her voice light as she smoothed the blanket over his chest. "And I'm of the opinion that I'll keep your little secret—at least until you come to your senses and get well enough to be out of this bed. I don't think you're firing on all four cylinders, so to speak, so you lay back and rest. Don't worry about a thing. I'll be here with the kids, and we'll all be fine."

And, as he closed his eyes to surrender,

Salt smiled in the certainty that Birdie was absolutely right.

As Salt slept, Birdie helped Bobby and Brittany clean up the kitchen, then clean themselves. She found herself delighted by their chatter, and she was amazed by the children's independence. Salt was right— though the kids assured her they'd never been to school, they seemed to know quite a bit about a lot of different things.

For one thing, they'd been amazed to learn that Salt had no Werther's Originals tucked someplace inside his house. After all, Brittany explained, the grandmother on TV always gave her granddaughter that candy when she came for a visit.

"I finally told her it's because he's a grandfather, not a grandmother," Bobby explained. "Maybe only grandmothers have 'em."

Birdie was a little surprised to hear them talk openly about their father. For children who had been abused—and she didn't doubt Salt's story, not for a moment—they referred to their dad more often than she would have expected.

"My daddy likes to fish," Brittany said as she helped Birdie wash out the soiled dishtowels they'd hidden on the beach. "He doesn't do it often, though. He's too busy looking for a job."

Birdie glanced at Bobby, but the boy only pressed his lips together and grunted as he wrung out one of the wet towels.

"When Daddy's not out or sleeping, he watches TV with us," Brittany went on, apparently oblivious to her brother's silence. "He likes football. He likes the Steelers. He said he's going to take us to a game, so we'll go next year when they win the Super Bowl."

"The Steelers aren't going to win the Super Bowl," Bobby said, icy contempt flashing in his eyes. "And Daddy's not going to take us anywhere. Daddy hasn't even come to see us. Daddy doesn't care!"

Birdie felt the noise in the room abruptly cease. She placed her hand over her heart, uncertain how to answer in the unnatural silence, then Brittany bent into the sink and began to slosh another dirty towel in the hot soapy water.

"Miranda is my doll," she said, not looking at Birdie. "She sleeps with me every night, no matter where I am."

And so the afternoon had passed, with Birdie listening more than talking.

Now Bobby grinned at her as he wiped a plate with a dishcloth. "Did you know, Miss Birdie—" (since they'd come to know each other so well after meeting almost at death's door, she'd thought it fittin' to allow them to call her by her given name), "that an aardvark can grow to be five feet long? They are the color of sand and have short hair."

Birdie made a face. "Goodness! I wouldn't want to run into one of those in the dark."

"You wouldn't find them here," Bobby answered, his countenance falling. "They're only in Africa. So I suppose I won't ever see one."

"I saw one on TV," Brittany said, turning from the table she'd wiped. Birdie glanced at the tabletop—gleaming wet streaks indicated that Brittany had done an admirable job of wiping the edges, but her short arms hadn't touched the center of the table where a few bread crumbs and two pink cereal loops remained.

Brittany dropped the wet cloth into the sink. "The aardvark has a long nose and eats ants. They said you can find them in America."

Bobby glared at his sister. "Can not."

"Can, too!"

"Can not! They're only in Africa! The encyclopedia says so!"

"Can too! You can find one in a zoo, smarty!"

Unnerved by the argument, Birdie threw up her hands. "Children! Why don't we find something quiet to do? Your grandfather needs his sleep. It's too cold to play outside, so perhaps we can play an indoor game."

"Really?" Her eyes alight, Brittany bounced on her tiptoes. "What kind of game?"

Birdie tried not to frown. "Perhaps, um . . . Simon Says?"

Bobby and Brittany shared a quizzical glance, then Bobby looked at Birdie. "We don't know how to play that."

Birdie searched her memory. "London Bridge?"

Bobby shook his head.

"Um . . . Hide and Seek? Though this isn't the best location for it—"

"We've never played that." Brittany spoke this time, her voice dripping with regret.

"Red Rover? Duck, Duck, Goose? Ring around the Rosey?"

The children stared at each other again, then Bobby shrugged. "I reckon we could learn something."

Birdie sighed. She was too tired for squatting and running, and she wasn't about to climb the iron staircase in what could be a dangerous game of Hide and Seek.

"Why don't we forget games right now." She bent forward and pressed her hands to her knees. "What do you like to do?"

"Watch TV." Without another word, Brittany moved toward the tiny set next to Salt's fireplace.

Bobby pointed toward the thick blue volume on the fourth chair at the kitchen table. "I like to read. I'm reading through the As. That's how I learned about the aardvark."

"Okay, then." Birdie watched helplessly as Brittany turned on the TV and Bobby picked up his book. Without knowing what else to do, she moved toward the rocking chair and slowly lowered herself into it.

What was she doing? She knew absolutely nothing about taking care of children. Neither she nor her sister Bea had been blessed with the privilege of motherhood, and the only children Birdie ever talked to were the kids who came into the bakery during tourist season—and Georgie Graham, of course. But she rarely said more than hello and good-bye to Georgie; most of her conversations about him were directed at his mother.

Leaning her head back, she sighed and relaxed, breathing in time to the rocker's steady creak. She'd stepped into a mess this time, one she didn't know how to handle. Salt Gribbon was some kind of devil, bringing her up here—

She hesitated, correcting herself. Okay, Salt hadn't brought her up here. She'd come on an errand of mercy, drawn by Georgie's insistence that Cap'n Gribbon was sick. And he was sick, and Birdie had been of help, but she'd encountered far more than she'd bargained for.

Two kids! One in love with the television, another married to an encyclopedia. And both of them given to telling fibs, for there was no one fitting Gabe's description on the island.

Closing her eyes, she made a mental note to speak to Pastor Wickam. She wouldn't mention the children, in deference to her promise to Salt, but she'd suggest that the pastor take a careful look around the church to be sure the kids hadn't damaged anything. The good Lord knew something in that building broke or sprang a leak nearly every week. If anything had gone amiss while the children were inside, she and Bea would cover the expense of repairs.

After all, she was glad they'd found shelter. And it seemed fitting, somehow, that they'd found it in Heavenly Daze Community Church.

The watery sun floating overhead did little to combat the wind blowing off the ocean. Annie huddled deeper into her down coat, clamping her teeth together to keep them from chattering. Sometimes, safe in Portland, she forgot how chilling the Heavenly Daze wind could be, but ever since driving down to visit Olympia for a surprise midweek visit, she'd been mercilessly reminded.

Now she stared at her tomato plants— holocaust survivors. The stems leaned to one side, whipped by the punishing wind.

"Time to put you out of your misery," she murmured.

Weeks, months, and endless nights of

burning the midnight oil had failed to produce the results she'd hoped for. She'd designed a hybrid that would be pollinated by the wind, not insects, and thus could survive even in winter. She'd dreamed of thick slices of tender red tomato resting on burgers. She'd hoped to produce a tomato that'd make an unbeatable salsa, delicately flavored with cilantro, lime, and garlic. Her visions of a potential BLT garnish producer now lay gasping for breath, begging for mercy. A succession of swift yanks, and the experiment would be over.

As she knelt, her hand involuntarily moved toward the plants. "This will hurt me more than it hurts you," she whispered, closing her eyes before the compassionate final act.

"Hot cocoa?"

Annie's eyes flew open. She spun on the balls of her feet and saw Dr. Marc extending a steaming cup toward her. Rising, she gratefully accepted the warmth, cradling the stainless steel in her gloved hands. "Thank you. It's freezing out here."

The two stood for a moment, sipping the cocoa and staring at the plants. Neither said anything until the silence stretched uncomfortably.

"Sad, isn't it?" Annie heaved a sigh.

"Not at all." The older man shook his head. "Actually, I'm impressed. The plants are still alive, and—" He paused, stooping to examine a tiny green orb dangling in the wind. "Why, by Jove, they're actually producing fruit!"

He had no sooner spoken the words when the baby tomato dropped to the ground with a soft plop.

"Oh, dear." He reached for it, then set the tiny green button in the center of his palm. Too upset to look at the misbegotten fruit, Annie focused on the doctor's hands. You could tell a lot about a man by his hands. Dr. Marc's were large, with smooth nails neatly trimmed. A surgeon's hands.

"My father used to grow tomatoes," he said. A distant look entered his eyes. "Early Girls, he called them. Mother used to can quarts and quarts of produce and make gallons of tomato juice. We'd drink it on special occasions like Christmas afternoon. Nothing quite hit the spot after a large dinner like a glass of tomato juice."

Perhaps intuiting that tomatoes might be a sore subject, Dr. Marc dropped the fruit, then slipped his hands into his pockets.

"Dad had the biggest garden on the block and supplied the whole town with string beans, zucchini, and sweet corn. In the fall the pumpkins would come on and we'd help scrape the innards. Mother would boil them and pack them in quart jars to make pumpkin pies during the winter."

Annie smiled, watching reminiscences play across the doctor's face. He obviously had pleasant, happy recollections of his childhood. She didn't have those kinds of memories. Her mom and dad had died in a plane crash, leaving her a seven-year-old orphan. That had been a rough time, even after she'd come to live with her Aunt Olympia and Uncle Edmund at Frenchman's Fairest. Yet though she'd known struggle and pain, she still had fond memories of golden autumn afternoons in Heavenly Daze with the smell of wood smoke in the air, Caleb calling her to supper as bronze shadows filtered through the branches of oaks decked out in variegated yellows, reds, and russets . . .

"Pinch off the top blossom," Dr. Marc said.

Annie frowned. "Pardon?"

"Top blossom. You have to pinch it off if

you want a good crop. That's what Dad always said. Pinch off that top blossom."

Apparently still focused on the plants, the
doctor took a sip of cocoa. As tired of tomatoes as she was, Annie still felt a moment of
gratitude, for in the instant the doctor di-
verted his thoughts from the tomatoes he'd
doubtless mention his son, the single, eligi-
ble neurosurgeon, the Catch-of-New-York.
In the short time Annie had known Dr. Marc,
she'd learned that the man was a match-
maker at heart, a born romantic.

No thanks. Anyone who needed this much
strong-armed help in the romance department wasn't for her. Couldn't the guy get a
date without his father's influence? She shivered as another thought struck her—merciful
heavens, was the good doctor as broad in
his hints with his son as he was with her?
Had Dr. Alex Hayes heard two dozen reports
on Annie Cuvier from Heavenly Daze, the Girl
who was Desperate for a Date?

She glanced around for something else to
talk about. Any minute now, the well-inten-
tioned doctor would say, "Have I mentioned
my son is coming home for Christmas?"

She glanced back at the house. She
could talk about Uncle Edmund—but that

dear man's death was too fresh to be discussed with anything but reserved sorrow. Ditto for Aunt Olympia and Caleb. She could talk about the weather, but she'd sound like an inarticulate fool, babbling on about wind and chill factors and mud—

Dr. Marc had mentioned his son every weekend Annie came home this fall. They'd been supposed to meet at Thanksgiving, but an emergency had come up and Alex had canceled his visit at the last moment. Annie knew Dr. Marc had been disappointed, but he understood the demands a doctor faced. Some things simply couldn't be helped.

His gaze shifted to her face. "I reckon you'll be here for the holidays, then?"

Uncomfortable, Annie shifted her stance, huddling deeper into her coat as she remembered Olympia's reaction to the suggestion of a cruise. When Olympia finally returned Annie's call, she'd listened to Annie's proposal in frosty silence, then flown into a temper, saying she couldn't go sailing across the ocean with Edmund barely cold in his grave. Smothering her resentment, Annie had reminded her aunt that the cruise was only a suggestion. They could just as easily spend Christmas at Frenchman's Fairest.

But two tickets for the cruise ship *Glorious* lay in Annie's desk drawer—she'd beaten the reservation deadline with only two minutes to spare. The ship would embark from Miami the afternoon of Christmas Day and return on New Year's. Annie was clinging to the hope that Olympia's indignation would cool and the saving grace of second thought would persuade her to change her mind.

Swallowing her frustration, she lifted her chin. "I suppose I'll be here—at least that's the plan right now."

Dr. Marc sipped from his cup. "Have I mentioned that my son, Alex, is coming for Christmas?"

"Really?" Annie gave him a polite smile. "How nice for you."

"Yes. I'd love for the two of you to meet—Alex's a real catch, you know."

"I imagine so."

Ready to change the subject, Annie looked away toward the ocean. The wind had begun to pick up; dark clouds scudded across the waters. She couldn't stand out here a moment longer. She either had to pull up the plants or let them struggle another day. The weather was growing more miserable by the minute.

"Leave them," Dr. Marc advised as her eyes returned to the struggling vegetation. "It's a shame to destroy a living thing, and the plants are holding on. If they don't make it, at least they'll die from natural causes."

Because the doctor had seen more than his share of life and death, Annie knew he offered good advice. This experiment, like so many in her life, had gone awry, but nothing required her to end it today. Or tomorrow, for that matter. The world would survive without winter tomatoes, and their demise certainly wouldn't hamper modern civilization.

Dr. Marc fell into step beside her as she walked back to her aunt's house. "Olympia is going through a difficult time right now. Edmund's death is only beginning to sink in."

"But he was sick for so long—"

"Unfortunately, most people believe they're prepared for death, but they rarely are when it actually happens. Your aunt spent most of her adult life with Edmund, so a part of her died along with him. It will take time, Annie. Time and patience for her to come to the point where she'll want to live again." He gave her a dazzling smile. "I'm so pleased you're willing to help Olympia through the holidays. Your coming home reveals what a generous and unselfish person you are."

Swallowing a knot of guilt, Annie thought of the tickets in her desk drawer. Going on a cruise wouldn't mean she didn't care about Olympia. The cruise was three weeks away—maybe Olympia would start to feel better by then. And the holiday was a time of joy, so maybe the spirit of the season would brighten her aunt's outlook. The women on the island would help Olympia through the sad days that lay ahead, so Annie didn't really need to be here. Her tired presence would do little to cheer her aunt, and the cruise would do wonders for Annie's sagging spirits . . .

"So," Dr. Marc opened the back door, then reached for her empty cup. "Can I count on you coming to my Christmas Eve party?"

She forced a grin. "Better put me down as tentative. If the weather's bad and I can't cross on the ferry—"

"The Lord wouldn't keep you from home

on Christmas Eve. I'm praying for good weather and fair seas." His eyes sobered. "You are coming, aren't you? You and Alex would hit it off."

"We'll see. I'll try my best." That wasn't exactly a lie. Even if she did go on the cruise, she could still spend Christmas Eve with her aunt—as long as she reached the airport before 6 P.M.

"Thank you." The older man beamed, his hand clasping her shoulder. "Merry Christmas, Annie."

"The same to you, Dr. Marc." After patting his hand, she stepped into the warmth of Frenchman's Fairest. The smell of roasting meat filled her nose. Caleb was preparing her favorite supper: roast beef, mashed potatoes, and brown gravy.

Caleb turned from the stove as she came into the kitchen. "Annie! You must be near frozen."

Annie warmed her hands over the hissing radiator pipes. "They're not going to make it, Caleb."

His silver-laced brow lifted slightly. "The tomatoes?"

Annie nodded. "I was about to rip them out when Dr. Marc interrupted."

"Pity," Caleb murmured. "I know they look rather worn but perhaps—"

"No perhaps." Annie might be a dreamer, but she knew when she'd been beaten. The experiment was over. Her tomato hybrid could not survive a harsh Maine winter. Whatever had made her think they could?

Hot water bubbled from a pan on the stove. Caleb poured a cupful of steaming liquid into a cup, then added a tea bag and a generous dollop of honey. "Missy likes honey better than sweetener," he said. "Care for a cup?"

"I had hot chocolate earlier, but—" She smiled when he pressed the cup into her gloved hand. "God bless you," she murmured, sipping the scalding brew.

The old man's mouth lifted in a smile. "Oh, he does. Every day." Turning back to his work, he asked, "What did Dr. Marc have to say?"

"Not much. He invited me to his Christmas Eve party." Annie set her teacup on the kitchen table, then removed her gloves. "Is Aunt Olympia going?"

Lifting the lid of a pot of boiling potatoes, Caleb shook his head. "I hope she will agree to attend this year. The outing would be good for her."

"It would, but it's hard for her to see that right now."

Annie dropped her gloves to the table, then slipped out of her coat and sat down. The kitchen was always bright, no matter the weather. The room had been Annie's second-favorite in the ornate two-story house, surpassed only by the attic room overlooking the sea. During her youth she had spent endless hours in the attic room, dreaming up numerous gadgets and inventions.

Come to think of it, she had passed a pleasant childhood on Heavenly Daze, and even now she enjoyed visits home—once she got over dreading the effort. Occasionally her aunt came up with wry observations that tickled Annie's funny bone. On one of their fifteen-mile excursions to Sanford, home of the nearest Wal-Mart, Olympia had been a regular laugh riot.

"Impulse spending," she'd snorted as she tossed yet another item in her cart. "This store is chock-full of stuff I had no idea I needed until I saw it."

That was Annie's life: chock-full of stuff she didn't know she needed until she received it. Like a cup of Caleb's soothing hot tea. And Dr. Marc's kind observations. And the warm, welcoming embrace of this cozy kitchen.

These things made the long trip from Portland worthwhile.

Caleb sat down, pleasure creasing his features as he stretched his legs beneath the table. "Any luck talking your aunt into that cruise?"

"None. Zilch. Nada." When they last spoke on the phone, Annie had pleaded until she was breathless, but to no avail. Now the subject of the cruise was off limits; Olympia would probably burst into tears at the mere thought of leaving Frenchman's Fairest on Christmas Day.

"Edmund and I always celebrated the birth of Christ in our home," she had stated unequivocally. "This year will be no different."

Whether Olympia accepted it or not, however, this year would be different. Only Olympia, Annie, and Caleb would light the advent candle and fill the four stockings hanging in the parlor: Olympia's, Annie's, Caleb's, and Tallulah's. Festivities would be forced and dismal.

Caleb's features softened as he reached out to cover Annie's hand with his own. "I'm sorry, honey. You're caught in a dilemma, aren't you? Your aunt needs you desperately, but perhaps you need something for yourself, too. Something neither Missy nor I can give you . . . for we would, you know." His eyes shone with love. "We would give you the moon if the Father would loan it."

Annie fought back tears. Even when she was a child, Caleb always seemed to know her deepest thoughts. But she was a woman now, and tears wouldn't change her circumstances . . . or make her feel better about them.

She needed to forget the cruise. Big deal. She could always go to the Caribbean next year.

Drawing a deep breath, she thought of the tickets in her desk and negotiated a mental truce with her yearning heart. At least she'd had the foresight to purchase travel insurance, so she wouldn't lose much money.

"I'll be okay, Caleb." She managed a trembling smile. "You don't need to worry about me . . . but I'm glad you do."

He squeezed her hand. "So—do you plan to attend Dr. Marc's party?"

She gave the old caretaker a wry look. "Honestly? No."

He frowned. "The doctor will be disappointed—why, he gives a fine party, Annie. Folks talk about it for weeks afterward. The man makes a scrumptious eggnog." Caleb closed his eyes and pressed his lips together. "My, my. I can taste it already."

Annie drained the last of the tea, then set the cup on the table and grinned at the old butler. "Come on, Caleb. He's only trying to set me up with his son."

"And would that be so bad?" Caleb leaned over to wipe Annie's upper lip. Embarrassed, she snatched the napkin and finished wiping a smear of honey from her mouth.

"From what I hear," Caleb continued, "the young man is talented and intelligent. He's one of the finest doctors in New York City."

"And probably just as adverse to being set up with a complete stranger as I am." Annie shoved away from the table, then stood. If Alex Hayes was all she'd heard, he wouldn't need his father to find him a wife, of that Annie was certain. That was quite possibly the only thing she was certain of these days—that, and the fact that her tomatoes had gone kaput. She moved toward the hall, then paused in the doorway. "Is Aunt Olympia resting?"

"I'm not sure. She stays in her room a lot these days."

"I'll go up and say good-bye." Annie glanced at her watch. She still had a two-hour drive back to Portland.

Alarm crossed Caleb's features. "What about dinner? It's almost ready."

Annie sighed, thinking of the long trip ahead. If she left now, it'd be at least seven before she arrived home, and she didn't like driving in the dark. But Caleb had prepared all her favorites.

"I'll have a quick plate. And maybe I can talk Aunt Olympia into coming down for a bite."

"That'd be good."

Annie turned to leave, then had a sudden thought. "Caleb—do me a favor?"

"Anything."

"Destroy the plants sometime this week. I'm not into mercy killing." Stepping forward, she dropped an absent kiss on his forehead, then reached for her gloves and moved into the hall.

She hadn't yet reached the staircase when the old butler's gravelly voice met her ears.

"Father—" He was praying. Annie knew

he prayed often, for her and for Aunt Olympia. Caught by curiosity, she paused in midstep.

"She's a good girl," Caleb said. "Ease her pain, and help her to know the true meaning of Christmas is not found in the doing, but in the giving."

Drawing another deep breath, Annie moved up the stairs. She was giving all she had to give. What more did they expect of her?

By suppertime, Birdie had a pot of stew on the stove (concocted from a thorough gleaning of Salt's pantry and refrigerator) and three places set at the table. She'd swept the floor, dusted the few surfaces in the house, and scrubbed the bathroom, including the floor and shower stall. Salt was sitting up in the bed, apparently well on his way to full recovery, and the two children were staring at her as if she'd suddenly sprouted a halo and wings.

"I have to leave you three now," she said, slipping into her coat, "but I'll be back tomorrow to check on things." She sent a wink winging toward Salt. "I'll bring some of that rye bread and the molasses cookies you're so fond of. I noticed there isn't a cookie crumb left in this house."

A six-year-old body suddenly wrapped itself around her left leg. "Can't you stay?" This from Brittany, whose pixie face looked positively woebegone.

"I'm afraid not, darlin'." Birdie bent to pat the child's face. "I have a sister, you see, and she's bound to be worried. If I don't go, she'll have half the town up here searching for me."

"She has to go," Salt boomed from the bed, ending all debate.

Birdie made a wry face, then moved to caress Bobby's cheek, too. "You be a good boy, help your grandfather, and I'll see if I can't find something else for you to read. The encyclopedia is a very interesting book, but not really designed for children. I'm sure I can find something more fittin' for you."

Buttoning her coat, she moved to the foot of Salt's bed, then looked up and met the sea captain's eye. "I don't know a blessed thing about children," she told him, "but I know how to cook and converse and give a hug when it's needed"—she felt herself blushing—"to the kids, I mean. Seems to me they need a lot of hugging."

Salt grumbled in his throat, then pressed his hands to the bed and pushed himself into a standing position. "Get on with you then," he said, reaching for his robe, "and we'll be seeing you tomorrow."

Birdie exhaled slowly. What had she expected, hugs and thank-you kisses? Not likely from a man like Salt Gribbon.

Pulling her knitted cap upon her head, she tied the string under her chin, then gave the children a parting wave. As she put her gloved hand on the doorknob, Salt's crusty voice stopped her in midstep: "Thank you, Birdie. For everything."

Blinking back unexpected tears, she gave him a nod, then opened the door and stepped out into the biting cold.

"Saints have mercy, where have you been?" Bea stopped in the kitchen and dropped her gloves onto the table as Birdie came through the back door. "I was about to call Vernie and ask her to ride with me up to the lighthouse. I'd have gone myself, but I'm a little afraid of old Cap'n Gribbon."

Birdie pulled off her gloves, then moved to the roaring fire and held up her hands.

"Georgie Graham was right—Salt was really sick, too sick to even get out of bed. He was delirious with fever when I arrived, but he's better now."

Bea sank into a chair with an audible thump. "You mean you spent the night up there? I thought you came in late and left early, but I had no idea—"

"Good grief, sister, be reasonable. He was a sick man, and in no condition to carry on in any sort of improper fashion. My reputation is more than safe."

"Your reputation?" Bea snorted softly. "I think folks would be more concerned about Cap'n Gribbon shooting you than seducing you. Why, the way he threatens tourists with that rifle—"

"There wasn't a gun in sight, and he didn't even growl—well, he only growled once." Birdie unbuttoned her coat, then slipped it off and hung it on the rack by the door. "Brr, it's cold. I'm starving and frozen to the bone."

Bea lifted a brow. "Didn't Cap'n Gribbon offer you any supper?"

"Salt Gribbon," Birdie answered, moving toward the kitchen area at the back of their cozy keeping room, "has little to spare, so I threw a light supper together and left it for him." She lifted the lid of a pot on the stove and inhaled the scents of lobster chowder. "Bea, this smells wonderful."

"Abner made it. He was concerned and would have gone off looking for you himself if I hadn't told him to stay here and mind the bakery."

Birdie opened the cupboard and pulled out a bowl. "How was the store today? Busy?"

"Not too. Edith Wickam came by for some almond croissants, and Olympia wants a chocolate log for Christmas. Apparently Annie and Dr. Marc's son are planning to come in . . . at least, Olympia and Dr. Marc hope they are." She shook her head. "Young people! Never can seem to make up their minds these days!"

"Tell me about it," Birdie murmured, thinking about the debate she'd enjoyed with the children at lunch. Brittany had wanted a Domino's Pizza (inspired, no doubt, by the pizza commercials that sang out from the television every five minutes), while Bobby had expressed a yearning for hot dogs. In the end, however, they had to settle for Froot Loops, milk, and a few squares of processed cheese Birdie found in the fridge.

"It's okay," Brittany had said, nibbling on her cheese like a mouse. "Velveeta is versatile."

Now Birdie tilted her head, trying to remember when the company used that slogan as a jingle.

"So"—Bea shifted in her chair as Birdie ladled out a bowl of chowder—"what'd you do all day up at the lighthouse?"

Birdie shrugged. "I took care of a sick man. Fed him crackers, made him drink lots of water, and made sure he took aspirin. His fever broke this morning, so I tried to get some food into him."

"Pretty boring work, that kind of nursing." Bea wore a bemused expression. "I mean, you're an active woman, Birdie. What'd you do, sit in a chair and stare at the man while he slept?"

"There was plenty to do up there." Birdie took her bowl to the table, sat down, and bowed her head for a quick prayer of thanks. When she lifted her eyes, Bea was staring at her with a gaze sharp as a needle.

Birdie stared back. "What?"

"Is he a slob, then?"

"Not at all. He's a tidy man, I think, but the place still needed a bit of cleaning up. I swept and dusted, then started a stew." She laughed softly as she spooned up a bite of the rich chowder. "I had to use my imagination. He didn't have much in his pantry."

Bea leaned her elbow on the table. "Did you have to do anything with the light?"

Birdie frowned. "What light?"

"Sister!" Bea rapped her knuckles on the tabletop. "For heaven's sake, it's a lighthouse."

"Oh, of course. No, I didn't have anything to do with it. I think it's automated." Birdie swallowed a bite of the chowder, then dropped her jaw and reached for her water. The soup was hotter than she'd thought.

She drank and lowered her glass, then looked toward the window, where the sun had disappeared. Outside, over the roof of Abner's cottage, stars spangled the heavens in glorious abandon. Soon the lighthouse would send out its beam, and she would never again see it without thinking of the man who lived beneath it.

"Going to be a clear and cold night," Bea said. "Cold last night, too."

Lowering her gaze to her bowl, Birdie stirred her soup. "Ayuh."

"Bad night to be sick. Worse night to be alone."

"Salt doesn't seem to mind. He's a solitary sort by nature."

Bea folded her arms on the table and leaned closer. "For a loner, he's been seeking out your company plenty these days. Why, last month he asked you out for a walk up to the point, didn't he? And now you've gone up there and not come home for a night—"

"Why, Bea Coughlin!" Birdie pasted on an appropriately horrified expression. "What are you insinuating?"

Bea puckered her lips into a tiny rosette, then unpuckered enough to whisper, "I was married, Birdie. I know about love . . . and men."

"I can assure you there's nothing going on between me and Cap'n Gribbon." Birdie straightened her shoulders. "We're friends, that's all. High time the man made some friends on the island; we've been scared of him for too long. But he's a nice man, a little shy—"

"Not too shy to shoot rock salt at people who go up there!"

Birdie lifted a brow. "Maybe he has his reasons. Maybe the tourists were pesterin' him, or in danger of damaging the lighthouse. He's not an unreasonable fellow."

Bea leaned back, her thin mouth curving into a slow smile. "Why, Birdie, I think you're a little infatuated with that old hermit."

"You're jealous."

"Of that old codger? I wouldn't have him if he were the last man on earth."

Birdie harrumphed and went back to eating her soup.

"You are infatuated." Bea fairly sang the words. "Little sister's got a crush on Cap'n Gribbon."

"I'm not your little sister, not anymore," Birdie said, keeping her gaze lowered. "And if you say one word about this, or make even a peep to Vernie about my visit to the lighthouse, I think you'll find I can still wrestle you to the ground." She looked up and smiled when she saw Bea's lips part in a silent gasp. "Yessir, and Daddy's not around to pull me off you, either, so don't you be forgetting that. Leave me be, sister, and we'll both be better off."

With that said, Birdie stood, wiped her mouth on a paper napkin, then turned on her heel and left the room with what she hoped was a regal toss of her head.

CHAPTER TEN

The next morning, Birdie dressed with her usual efficiency, moved into the bakery to check on Abner's plans for the day, then sat down at the counter to make a grocery list. Salt desperately needed a few things from the mercantile, and for a few days he wouldn't be in any condition to venture into town.

When Abner paused at her elbow, Birdie reflexively brought up her left hand to cover her scrawlings.

"How's the captain?" he asked, balancing a tray of blueberry tarts on his open palm.

"He's fine—well, he's doin' a little poorly, if you want to know the truth. He was really sick, but I think he's mending." She folded the list, tucked it in her pocket, and shifted to face her assistant. "I was thinking about picking up a few things for him at the mercantile and taking them up to the lighthouse this afternoon—unless you think I'll be needed here."

Abner, bless his heart, pretended to act as though he actually needed her help. "Nobody makes those filled cookies like you," he said, glancing at the freshly filled display case. "But I think we're set for now. It's been fairly slow on account of the windy weather. Most folks are holed up inside to keep warm."

"Don't bake too much, then." She glanced at the filled display case again, half-worried about what she'd do with so many pastries. Business was always slow during the off-season, but it could come to a virtual stop if a spell of really bad weather hit. And there was nothing quite so unpopular as a stale doughnut.

"I was thinking you could take some day-old pastries up to Captain Gribbon," Abner suggested, pointing to a row of paper bags he had taped shut. "I filled them with molasses cookies, gingerbread men, and those nice brioches with the sugar sprinkles on top. And I included a couple of loaves of rye bread, since the captain likes them so much."

Birdie stared at the row of sealed bags.

Gingerbread men and brioches? Why, the children would love those! But though Salt had often expressed a liking for her rye bread and molasses cookies, as far as she knew he'd never bought a brioche or gingerbread man in his life.

She squinted toward Abner, wondering if he could possibly know Salt's secret. But the stout baker turned back to his work, humming "Joy to the World" as he transferred the blueberry tarts from the baking sheet to a doily-lined tray.

"Thanks, Abner." She reached for her stout basket. "I know Cap'n Gribbon will appreciate these things. Considerate of you to think of him."

She narrowed her eyes again, searching for any sign of knowledge or conspiracy, but his guileless face seemed as carefree and innocent as a baby's.

Shrugging, Birdie arranged the bags of day-olds in her basket, then moved toward the back of the building to find her coat, hat, and gloves.

"Give the captain my best when you see him," Abner called. "And tell him I've been experimenting with a recipe for a butterscotch candy just like Werther's Originals.

Next time you go up, I'll send a batch along."

Too surprised to do more than nod, Birdie stumbled through the hallway, wondering how much Abner knew and how he'd come to know it.

With her shopping bag on her arm, Birdie ducked into the mercantile in time to see MaGoo roll over, treating her to a rare glimpse of his expansive belly.

He blinked in the blast of cold air that accompanied her, then narrowed his eyes to slits as she called a greeting. "How be you, MaGoo?" She peered over the candy counter to see if Vernie had noticed her entrance. "Do you know if your mistress has any Werther's Originals on hand?"

If the cat knew, he wasn't saying. He settled onto his haunches and took a deep breath, inflating himself like an oversized black-and-white pincushion, then tucked his paws beneath his chest and closed his eyes.

"That you, Birdie?" The voice was Olympia's, and it came from behind the apothecary aisle where Vernie sold Carmichael's Imperial Cuticle Cream, Bag Balm, and mutton tallow. (Vernie was fond of reminding customers that mutton tallow, used for treating dry skin, psoriasis, and eczema, had been standard issue in every GI's first-aid kit in both world wars.)

"It's me." Sighing in resignation, Birdie stepped out from the candy and confronted Olympia among the pharmaceuticals. She wouldn't be away from the mercantile as quickly as she'd hoped if she had to stop and chat with every neighbor she met.

Remembering her manners, Birdie reached out and took Olympia's thin hand. "How are you all getting on over at Frenchman's Fairest? I've been thinking about you and Caleb and Annie. I know things can't be easy since Edmund passed on."

"I miss him." The forthright statement caught Birdie off guard. This was a new Olympia—the old one would have mumbled a few polite niceties and pasted on a stiff upper lip, never admitting that she missed her dear husband. But this—Birdie leaned forward slightly and peered into Olympia's faded blue eyes. The experience of Edmund's death had changed the woman; the crust of her stiff shell seemed to have softened.

Birdie squeezed Olympia's hand. "Why don't you stop in tonight for tea? Bea and I always have a cup after supper, and you're welcome to come and join us."

"I don't like to go out after dark." Olympia offered a small smile. "The sidewalk is so slippery, and I daren't risk a fall—well, you know how it is. Our bones can't handle upsets like they used to."

"I suppose you're right." Birdie considered asking Olympia for supper, but she wasn't certain she'd be back from the lighthouse at a decent hour. Salt might need her, and heaven above knew the children would need entertaining.

"Tomorrow, then." Birdie smiled. "I've got to run some things up to Cap'n Gribbon at the lighthouse, but I'll make a point of being home early tomorrow so you can come to supper."

"Did I hear mention of Salt Gribbon?" A deep voice cut through their genteel conversation like a foghorn. Birdie shifted her gaze in time to see Vernie step out from behind the counter. Wiping her rawboned hands on her apron, she smiled a sly, secret smile.

Edith Wickam appeared from another

aisle, her shopping basket bulging with scented candles—Christmas gifts, no doubt. "Good morning, Birdie," she called, her eyes gleaming with curiosity. "How be you this morning?"

Birdie was about to answer Edith when Vernie interrupted. "I heard about your going up to check on Salt," she said, folding her arms across her chest as she entered the circle of conversation. "I heard you spent the night up there."

Birdie bit her lip as a blush burned her cheek. Honestly, what didn't these people know?

"The captain was sick." Birdie glanced at Olympia. "Too sick to get out of bed, in fact, with a raging fever. I stayed with him until the fever broke."

"My stars." Olympia's hand went to the lace at her throat. "What did he have?"

"The flu, I think." Birdie shifted her shopping bag from one arm to the other. "I'm going to pick up a few things for him and tote them up there—"

"Seems to me you coulda called Dr. Marc," Vernie interrupted, one corner of her mouth lifting in a wry half-smile. "After all, he's a little more qualified to deal with influenza than you, Birdie. What did you do, feed him doughnuts and cookies?"

"I gave him aspirin and water." Birdie could feel heat rising in her neck. "The man was helpless; he couldn't even get out of bed. He was also delirious; he kept talking nonsense about . . . things."

She bit her lip, realizing she'd go too far if she wasn't careful. Besides, for all she knew Salt's secret had already leaked out. The kids might have met someone when they slipped into the church, and Abner certainly seemed to know more than he was saying . . .

At least the news hadn't reached this henhouse.

"If Salt needs a pastoral visit, I'd be happy to tell Winslow," Edith offered. "Maybe we women could take turns carrying casseroles up there. Or maybe Cleta and Floyd would take the captain in at the bed and breakfast. He has to be awful lonesome up there all by himself—"

"He's all right, and he seems to like the solitude," Birdie cut in. "I've offered all kinds of help, but he's a right gormy old fellow. Terribly independent."

"Mind you watch yourself around that man." Olympia pressed her hand to her chest. "He's always frightened me a little. He's so big and so . . . gruff."

Birdie nodded. "Ayuh, that he is, no doubt. But I've a suspicion his heart's in the right place."

She nodded a polite "excuse me" and slipped past Olympia, but not before she heard Vernie's braying laugh. "His heart—now the truth comes out," she called, her voice echoing over the assembled toiletries. "Birdie's interested in love at last."

As a furious blush burned her cheekbones, Birdie ducked and hurried forward, intent upon her shopping list.

Feeling only a little weak and empty-headed, Salt placed two cereal bowls on the kitchen table, then braced himself against the counter as the children began their breakfast.

"These are yummy, Grandfather," Brittany said, crunching the Froot Loops. She dropped her jaw, giving him a direct view of pink, blue, green, and orange goop, then snapped her mouth shut and grinned. "Know what that is? Seafood."

From the end of the table, Bobby snorted.

"She saw that on *Leave It to Beaver*. Eddie Haskell did it."

"Not very good manners for a little lady." Salt crossed his arms. "You ask Miss Birdie when she comes. She'll tell you about manners."

A mocking voice from within rose to chastise him: *Birdie could teach her lots of things, if you'd allow it. Face it, man, you're not equipped to teach a girl . . .*

Well, maybe not a young woman. But Brittany was only six, and hardly in the market for womanly things. He could handle a six-year-old.

A knock at the door interrupted his musings. Bobby and Brittany both froze at the sound, then turned to him with questions on their faces. Pressing a finger to his lips, Salt went to the door. He lifted one hand toward the children, ready to point them toward the bathroom, but a glance through the peephole revealed Birdie Wester standing outside.

He sighed in relief, then opened the door. Shivering like a wet hen, Birdie stepped across the threshold and sent a smile winging toward the children.

"Well," her bright voice warmed the room,

"aren't we the slugabeds this morning? I've been up and about for hours!"

Was she calling him lazy? Salt opened his mouth to protest, then saw the twinkle in her eye.

"Glad you're up and on your feet," she said, shrugging out of her coat. "I could use a hand with some things out in my cart. I stopped by the mercantile this morning."

Salt glanced out at her golf cart, parked outside the door. A wooden basket sat on the passenger seat, and a canvas bag bulged on the floor.

"Did she bring cookies?" Brittany's bright voice piped up at Salt's elbow.

Birdie laughed. "I brought all kinds of goodies, plus I picked up a few things." She shifted her gaze to Salt. "I got cold medicine for you and some Children's Tylenol in case the kids catch whatever you had."

A tremor scooted up the back of Salt's neck. "You bought children's medicine from Vernie Bidderman? What were you thinking, woman?"

"Relax." Birdie grinned as she pulled off her gloves. "Your secret is still safe from Vernie. When she remarked on it, I told her I thought you'd like the taste." She lifted a brow. "Won't you?" She turned to the children. "I have good things in my bag, but first I want a hug from each of you."

Grinning, the children ran into her arms. Feeling a bit overwhelmed, Salt stepped out the door and hauled in the groceries.

By the time he returned, Birdie had moved to the table, swept up the empty cereal bowls, and carried them to the sink. As efficient as a company supervisor, she began ordering them around. "Bobby, why don't you get those bedrolls put away so we have room to walk? Brittany, if you promise not to splash, you can help me wash the dishes. But first turn off the television. And when we're done with our morning chores, I have a little something special for you. Abner made us some delicious treats."

Salt felt his stomach sway. While the children scrambled to do her bidding, he turned, his jaw tightening. "What did you tell Abner?"

"I didn't tell him anything." Birdie twisted the faucet and held her fingers in the water, waiting for it to warm. "He's an odd one, though, and sometimes he seems to sense things. I don't think he knows about the children, but he must know something's up. But don't you worry, Abner's as loyal as they come. He won't say a word to anybody."

Salt carried his heavy thoughts to the table, then sank into a chair. What he had to do next wouldn't be easy, and might be interpreted as ingratitude. But it had to be done.

"Birdie," he began, not daring to meet her eyes, "I don't want you to think I don't appreciate your gentle care of me and the kids these last couple of days. If the truth be known, I don't know what we'd have done if you hadn't come along. But I'm much better now, and the kids are okay. So I was thinking . . ."

She turned and bent to meet his gaze, then held it. "What were you thinking?"

He took a deep breath. "I was thinkin' that maybe you shouldn't be coming up here every day. Once a week is plenty and would keep me from having to go into town so much and leavin' the children alone. As soon as I get my strength back, I'm going over to Ogunquit and layin' in a store for the winter. The kids need heavier coats and shoes and socks and things."

Birdie gave him the kind of smile you'd give a temperamental child. "And why shouldn't I come up here?"

"Because . . . people might talk."

She stared at him a full ten seconds without changing her expression, then she tipped her head back and exploded in laughter. "Salt Gribbon," she turned to plug the sink, "you are a silly! Why, people are already talking! Just this morning I had to run the gauntlet at the mercantile, and last night I had to endure a thousand questions from Beatrice. But you'd be proud of me—I answered as best I could, I told the truth, and I didn't let your secret slip."

"But if you'll leave us be, you won't have to worry about anything."

Shaking her head, she bent to open the cupboard beneath the sink, then pulled out a bottle of dishwashing liquid and squirted a stream into the water. "You need to understand," she went on, "that I'm a grown woman and I can take care of myself. And this is a free country, last time I checked, so I aim to come up here as often as I like." She turned and her eyes softened. "As long as I have an invitation, that is."

Though his head spun in bewilderment, Salt forced a smile. She was barely five foot two and couldn't weigh more than a hundred pounds, but when Birdie Wester got her wind up, he felt like a little dinghy, helpless before a gale.

A tremor touched her lips. "You wouldn't be denying me an open invitation, would you?"

Slowly, Salt shook his head. "No, ma'am." He lifted a hand and feebly waved it as the children ran toward the sink, their giggles filling the air like an exotic sweet scent. "Right now I couldn't deny you anything."

Vernie stepped over MaGoo and looked out the window. She'd been scouring the Internet for deals, and the morning had flown by.

A biting wind rattled the green-and-white striped awning outside, but she could see nothing but gray skies, wet leaves, and the detritus of winter. Her eyes scanned the deserted road to the ferry. Captain Stroble's boat had docked, but she didn't see anyone with a dolly coming up the hill. Just Buddy dragging a large sack of mail.

Scratching her head, she called out to Elezar in the storeroom. "Shouldn't those deliveries be here by now?"

The clerk poked his head around the corner, a pencil propped behind his right ear. "I'd think so. What time is it?"

Vernie glanced at the clock. "Twelve-thirty."

"Hmmm—the ferry must be running late today."

"The ferry's here." Vernie returned to the window, lifting the curtain. With her sleeve, Vernie wiped moisture off the thermal windowpane. The deliveryman rarely ran late, but with the holidays approaching she supposed she could forgive a single slip-up.

Speaking of slip-ups—her thoughts suddenly shifted to Stanley and his phone call. Why had he called? It couldn't have been the anniversary because he'd let twenty of those slip by without so much as a how-do-you-do. So if it wasn't the anniversary, and if he wasn't dying, then he must have called because . . . he wanted a divorce.

Vernie's pulse thrummed. That was it; the old geezer had found another woman and now he wanted his freedom.

Straightening, she turned from the window. Neither she nor Stanley had bothered to dissolve their marriage. She wasn't about to spend good money on a divorce lawyer, and Stanley had never notified her of any proceedings on his part. Legally, they were as much married as they'd ever been.

She lifted her chin. The Riche family did not condone divorce; the Good Book allowed few grounds and until today Vernie hadn't considered the possibility of adultery. Stan had his failures, but *adultery*?

She shook the image of Stanley and another woman out of her head. If Stanley wanted a divorce, he was going to have to come to Heavenly Daze and face her like a man. And when he left, he could have not only his divorce, but his clothes, his spare bowling ball, and his stuffed moose head. She'd kept that stuff far too long, and it'd be nice to have extra room in her storage closet.

She shuddered as she remembered the day Stanley brought the stupid moose head home and hung it in the mercantile. He hadn't shot the moose; Stanley didn't know beans about hunting. He'd bought the smelly old head at a flea market. Said he'd always wanted one and this one begged him to find it a home. He said he liked the look in the animal's glass eyes, that it looked content.

"You'd be content, too, if you were deader than a doornail!" Vernie had shouted, then promptly draped a scarf over the animal's face.

Now she wished she could drape a scarf over her own face. Her head had begun to throb, and she needed an Excedrin Migraine pill.

"I think I'm going upstairs now," she called to Elezar. "Can you handle things down here?"

"Yes, ma'am, you run along. Watch those stairs; they're real steep."

Vernie's day wouldn't be complete without hearing at least a half-dozen of Elezar's loving admonitions: *Watch those stairs, now. Bundle up tight; it's cold out. Stay cool now, you hear?*

At least Elezar was concerned about her welfare. She didn't know what she would have done without him all these years.

Stepping to the window a final time, she scanned the road. Georgie Graham was using a hockey stick to scoot a tennis ball down the street while Tallulah and Butch, the Klackenbushes' bulldog, tried to intercept it. But she saw no sign of a deliveryman.

Oh, well. Christmas was still weeks away.

Turning toward the stairway, she hesitated and reached under the counter, holding one hand to her throbbing temple. Caffeine helped a headache, didn't it? Pouring Coke into her favorite glass, she looked up with a furtive glance, then reached for the bottle of vanilla syrup and unscrewed the lid. After adding a generous shot of the sweet stuff, she shoved the bottle back into her private drawer and took a long swig from her glass.

Ah. The tastes were a delicious combination, nectar for the soul. Just what she needed on a trying day.

CHAPTER ELEVEN

"Elezar! Will you please get that phone! It's ringing off the hook today."

Vernie glanced down the stairs, then grumbled under her breath and returned to her desk in the spare bedroom. She didn't need to be told who was calling on a Saturday. Either Cleta or Babette would be on the line, doubtless in a blind panic because the nutmeg and cranberries hadn't yet arrived.

She signed off her AOL account, then sat silently as the mechanical man took his leave with a musical "good-bye." The shrill ringing of the phone had distracted her so much she'd forgotten to check her Microsoft stock and visit her bridge loop. The holidays left little time for Web surfing and she would be glad when the hoopla was over. Too many folks forgot the true meaning of Christmas. They got all caught up in things like cranberries and nutmeg . . .

"No ma'am, Cleta," Elezar was saying as she came down the stairs and entered the mercantile. "We haven't seen a thing of the deliveryman, but he'll be here, don't you fret. You need to watch that blood pressure. We can't have you sick during the holidays."

After saying good-bye, the clerk hung up the receiver, his eyes swiveling to Vernie. She waved at him in a who-cares gesture and stared at her candy display. Someone— probably Georgie Graham—had mixed all the green peppermint sticks in with the red ones, and the sixteen saltwater taffy flavors had been completely confused.

She began to straighten out the mess, then snorted and walked away. She had enough on her mind these days. Why should she worry about candy? With that strange phone call from Stanley and the wholesaler being slow to deliver her order, she hadn't slept much the past few nights. If the nutmeg didn't come today, Cleta was threatening to buy her baking supplies in Ogunquit. Ordinarily Vernie wouldn't care, but in the off-season she needed every bit of business she could get.

Stepping to the window, she peered out. Nothing moved on Main Street but feathery lines of soft snow pushed by the cold wind. The ferry sat at the dock, tethered by heavy rope lines, but there'd been no sign of a deliveryman.

Where was that order? She could only restrain Cleta and Babette for so long. Even Dr. Marc was getting frustrated. If he'd reminded her once, he'd reminded her thirty times that eggnog without nutmeg might as well be milk.

Behind her, Elezar had busied himself stocking canned goods he'd brought up from the basement. Though he was as worried as Vernie about that delivery, she appreciated him for having the good sense to keep quiet. Yessir, Elezar Smith was good as gold and kept his opinions to himself unless she asked for them. The world could use more men like Elezar.

As the front door opened, Buddy Franklin came in, tracking mud on Vernie's spotless floor. He paused before the candy display, eagerly scanning the selection as if something new might have materialized, but it offered the usual fare: Skybars, Mallo Cups, nonpareils, Necco Wafers, Heath Bars, and Fralinger's saltwater taffy in every imaginable hue.

Wiping her hands on her apron, Vernie smiled at her customer. She liked Buddy Franklin, though the boy had about as much sense as a tick on a dead dog.

"What can I do for you, Buddy?"

He looked up, a sly grin creasing the corners of his mouth. "Whatever." His eyes focused on the box of Necco Wafers. "Does them have a marshmallow taste to 'em?"

"No, no marshmallow."

His eyes moved from the Necco Wafers to the Mallo Cups. "Reckon I'll have a Mallo, then."

Vernie handed him the candy, then took his dollar. "Seen anything of a deliveryman out there?"

Buddy ripped the wrapper, then took a big bite of chocolate-covered marshmallow. "No, ma'am," he mumbled.

Vernie shook her head as she moved to the register for his change. "I don't understand it. I sent that order in over a week ago." She pressed a quarter into his palm. "Would you mind running down to the ferry and asking Captain Stroble if he has a box marked for the mercantile?"

Buddy nodded as he slipped the quarter into his pocket, then took another huge bite of candy. As he closed his eyes, savoring the taste, Vernie crossed her arms and watched him chew. After a long moment she said, "Today, Buddy?"

His eyes flew open and a flush crept up his neck. "Um. Sure."

Elezar stepped away from the shelves to look out the front window. "Ferry's just pulling away, Vernie. And there's no sign of anything on the dock."

"Shoot." Vernie bit her lip. Now she was going to have to call Cleta and Babette and Dr. Marc and beg for an extension.

"I don't understand," she fretted, pulling her ledger from under the counter. "I know I placed that order."

She opened the large book, then felt her heart stop. The order lay inside the cover, half-completed and unsubmitted.

Great day in the morning, she hadn't placed the order! How could she make such a mistake? She always faxed the order the first Sunday of the month. She'd done the same thing this month, working with Elezar in the quiet of a blustery Sunday afternoon. She clearly remembered ordering extra nutmeg, cranberries, sugar, chocolate chips, baking powder, candied fruit—

Powdered sugar and eggs.

Stanley.

Her eyes narrowed. She'd been in the process of filling out the order when the louse called and got her all flustered.

"Anything wrong, Vernie?"

Elezar's voice jarred her from her thoughts. Clearing her throat, she abruptly folded the order and slipped it into her sweater pocket. Forgetting an order wasn't the end of the world; she could fax it into the wholesalers this afternoon and they would deliver by midweek.

Taking a deep breath, she avoided her clerk's eyes. "Not a thing, Elezar. I think I'll do a little bookwork upstairs. Will you be all right here for a few minutes?"

The clerk turned to study the nearly empty store. Buddy Franklin, the sole customer, stood at the magazine rack reading a Blues Clues comic.

Elezar grinned at Vernie. "I believe I can handle it."

"Good," Vernie murmured, moving toward the stairs. "If Cleta or Babette calls again, tell them our supplies will be here no later than Wednesday. Guaranteed."

Elezar's face brightened. "You've heard from the wholesaler?"

"Kind of." Guilt climbed the steps with her, but it would vanish as soon as she faxed the order in.

Upstairs, Vernie stepped into her bedroom and sat down on the bed, then saw that her hands were shaking. Never, not once in her entire life, had she failed to complete her order. Closing her eyes, she sucked in air. She still had time. She didn't need to panic. Keeping Cleta and Babette and Dr. Marc at bay without revealing what she'd done might be tricky, but she could do it.

She could hear what Cleta would say if she knew the truth: "You forgot to order? What's happened, deary, are you getting senile?"

Not hardly. Vernie Bidderman was as solid as the Rock of Gibraltar. Stanley's call had knocked her a little silly, but what woman wouldn't be upset by such a thing? Blast that Stanley's hide! He'd always brought her nothing but trouble. She thought that particular thorn in her side was long gone, but here he was again, back to plague her after twenty long Stanley-free years.

She jumped when the bedside phone shrilled.

Jerking up the receiver, she barked, "What is it?"

Silence hummed on the line, followed by a soft apology. "I'm sorry. I was calling the Mooseleuk Mercantile."

Vernie tempered her tone. "This is Mooseleuk's."

"Vernie?"

Her heart plunged when recognition washed over her. "Stanley?"

"Hello, sweetums."

Cupping her hand to the receiver, Vernie lowered her voice. "Don't you dare call me that, Stanley Bidderman."

"You used to love it when I called you that."

She sharpened her tone. "You're a swine."

After a brief hesitation, Stanley continued: "Just because something is true doesn't mean it needs to be said."

Vernie closed her eyes. "What do you want?"

"Conversation, sweetie. Simple conversation. Is that too much to ask from one's wife?"

"Yes, it is. After twenty years of not knowing if you were alive or dead? Yes. Conversation is too much to ask. So I'm going to hang up now, Stanley, because it takes two to have a conversation and one of us is leaving."

She dropped the receiver back into the cradle, then stared out the window. Ships passed in the distance, plowing through the icy Atlantic.

Vernie's heart felt as cold as that water. If Pastor Wickam were here, he would remind her that she needed to turn to God for comfort, that the world was full of troubles not necessarily of the Lord's making. Perhaps that was true, but the Lord hadn't been much help when Stanley walked out on her. He hadn't seemed to care when she was left shamefaced to explain to her neighbors why a married man would up and run off and never come back.

Heat flushed her cheeks as pain she thought she'd given up long ago came back in a hurtful rush.

She drew a shuddering breath and held it, fighting off the assault. The townsfolk had tried to be kind. Floyd had mowed her back lawn for two years afterward, and Edmund de Cuvier had done her taxes every year since. Yet she'd felt the pressure of curious eyes on her back whenever she entered a room, eyes that silently asked what she had done to make her husband leave without a word. She'd borne those glances for so many years her skin felt calloused from the pressure of so many prying eyes.

And now that mole wanted to share a conversation with her?

She reached for a tissue and swiped at her eyes. To make matters worse, she couldn't help feeling guilty about hanging up on Stanley a second time. He had never been persistent, so that last call would likely be the end of his attempts to reach her. Though Vernie was glad to be rid of the nuisance, something in her churned in discomfort . . .

No. She'd done the right thing. Now she could concentrate on work instead of dwelling on the past. She had a business to run and nobody was going to do it for her.

Still—Stanley had called. Twice. Whatever had possessed the man?

Lying back on the bed, she closed her eyes and refused to open them until she heard Elezar closing up for the night.

Thankfully, the phone did not ring again.

*   *   *

Watching from the sofa in the Lansdowns' front room, Vernie dropped a handful of popcorn into her mouth and wished she had begged off the Lansdowns' annual tree-trimming ritual. Micah Smith, the gardener at the B&B, had stopped by to remind her of the event that afternoon, promising that he'd picked out the best Christmas tree ever.

Vernie had to admit the tree was nice. The nine-foot blue spruce in front of the Lansdowns' front window now sparkled with multicolored lights and silvery tinsel. "Didn't I tell you?" Cleta Lansdown took a step back to enjoy the women's handiwork. "It's the prettiest tree we've ever had."

"You say that every year," Floyd grumbled. Stocking-footed, Cleta's husband pored over his mail-order mechanics course before a snapping fire. Cleta complained that he spent more time on his schoolwork than municipal matters, and his studies kept him underfoot and in her way. Last month she'd embroidered a sampler that now hung over Floyd's leather Berkliner: "I've got one nerve left and you're stepping on it."

"More red balls, Mom." Teetering on a stepladder, Barbara extended her hand for more ornaments.

Vernie munched on popcorn and tried not to think of her own barren living quarters. She couldn't seem to summon the energy to put up a tree, so she'd hauled a tiny desktop model down from the attic and stuck it in the middle of her kitchen table.

She couldn't summon much enthusiasm for anything these days. After Stanley's second call, the wind had gone out of her sails. She hadn't checked her computer after supper, and she never let her e-mail pile up. She didn't get a lot of personal messages, but her AOL mailbox regularly filled with advertisements for cheap airfare and new diet products guaranteed to take off twenty pounds overnight (as if she would believe any of that foolishness). The only time she'd fallen prey to a similar come-on she ordered a bottle of grapefruit pills that nearly burned a hole in her stomach before she realized her heartburn was due to an overload of acid in her system. She'd thrown the pills away and deleted all subsequent messages about losing weight. Occasionally she engaged in chitchat with folks on the loops she'd joined, but it seemed the same people exchanged most of the ideas and she could never think of anything to say. Someone had shared a good fruitcake recipe earlier in the week, but she didn't care for fruitcake. Stanley used to say—

She clamped the thought off in midstream. That phone call had her bumfuzzled.

"Don't fall, Barb." Cleta hovered near the base of the stepladder, ready to steady her daughter.

From his spot by the fire, Floyd cleared his throat. "Says here rubber wears out if it sits too long—gets dry rot."

Cleta turned to eye him. "So?"

"So." Floyd eyed her back. "That means the engine could use a new set of rubber."

Shaking her head, Cleta handed Barbara a star for the top of the tree. "You and that silly fire truck. The tires on that engine are perfectly good—why, it's not used twice a year."

"Tell me about it! That's why it needs new rubber, Cleta. What happens if a fire breaks out and we discover a bad case of dry rot? The whole town'd burn down before we could change a tire. Ayuh, I reckon I'll warn folks at the next town meeting. Dry rot ain't to be messed with, not if we want dependable fire protection."

Vernie picked up a popcorn kernel that

had fallen between the sofa cushions. "Barb, where's Russell tonight?"

A rosy flush invaded Barbara's cheeks at the mention of her husband. "Out."

Vernie chewed the popcorn, thinking. Where could Russell have gone "out" on the island? The Lobster Pot had closed in October, and other than the bakery where almost any time of day you could find someone sorting angel mail, there wasn't anywhere to be "out" in Heavenly Daze. On a blustery night like this, no one in his right mind would want to be out. Why, it was blowin' fit to make a rabbit cry.

"He's at the dock working on his boat," Cleta volunteered. She stood on tiptoe and pointed at the tree. "Needs more tinsel in the left-hand corner."

Barbara glared at her mother. "You want this job?"

"Of course not, deary. You're doing fine— but the tree needs a little more tinsel." Cleta jerked her chin in Vernie's direction. "You seen Birdie today?"

"Dry rot," Floyd interjected before Vernie could answer. "Nothing to be messed with, ladies. Tires might not seem like a big deal to you, but you'd better hope you don't need fire services anytime soon. And with all these electric lights and dry Christmas trees—"

"Haven't seen her," Vernie answered. "She called this morning about sugar, though. She's anxious to make her Saint James Puddings once the supplies arrive."

Cleta paused, absently studying the tree. "Have you noticed she's acting a mite strange these days?"

"Birdie?"

"Dry rot," Floyd growled. "You ever see a good case of dry rot?" He shook his head. "Ugly."

"I need more tinsel, Mom."

"You've got too much on that side."

"Do not."

"Do, too."

Their voices faded as Vernie's thoughts drifted from the family scene. She had helped decorate the Lansdowns' tree for the past twenty years—ever since Stanley left her without a tree-trimming partner. She'd only missed one holiday with the Lansdowns, the year she came down with the swine flu. Floyd and Cleta treated her like family, but she didn't feel like family tonight. She felt old and alone. Other than Elezar and MaGoo, she had no one.

Twenty years ago she'd been young enough to start over, but she hadn't because she thought Stanley would return any day. When it became clear he wasn't coming back, anger and resentment embittered her until she vowed she'd never marry again. But no matter how well her friends treated her, the holidays were a lonely time.

She made a mental note to stop by and visit Olympia one day next week. Until she experienced loss, she'd had no idea of how painful simple family acts like decorating a tree could be.

From his recliner, Floyd picked up the television remote and punched the power button. A helmet-haired weatherman from Portland stood before the camera and gestured to the map at his back.

"—nor'easter due late next week. The center is still forming off Virginia, but this one could be a doozy, folks. Meanwhile, our Accu-weather forecast calls for a high tomorrow of twenty-eight, low, seventeen. Tuesday will be windy with a chance of possible sleet; high, forty-three, low, twenty-one. Not a pretty picture, Lisa."

The attractive newscaster pretended to

shiver. "Brrr. Thanks, Bill. I can't wait till spring. This is Lisa Littleton, WPXT. Stay tuned for sports with Stone MacKenzie."

"Don't like the sound of that weather," Floyd said, closing his notebook.

"Me either." Cleta threw Vernie a worried look. "Maybe I ought to send Floyd to Ogunquit if the ferry's running tomorrow. Why, Christmas without my pumpkin pie wouldn't be Christmas. The men would be in a snit for sure."

"Christmas is still over two weeks away," Vernie pointed out. "No reason to panic."

"But what if we get snowed in?"

Vernie rolled her eyes. "I swan, Cleta. Have I ever failed you?"

Her word was good as gold, and Cleta certainly ought to know that by now. Vernie might have fallen short in the marriage department, but her business was to look after her neighbors and that meant keeping them well-stocked with cooking supplies. Why, she'd faxed—no, wait. She'd mailed—

She bit her lip. No. She hadn't mailed the order; she'd have remembered walking out to the mailbox. So she must have e-mailed it. That was it. She had e-mailed the order.

Or had she?

No. She hadn't checked her e-mail after supper.

She felt suddenly lightheaded. She'd been sitting on the bed, about to finish filling out the order form when the phone rang. Stanley again . . .

Forgetting about the popcorn in her lap, she bolted up from the sofa. The plastic bowl flew across the room, spraying Floyd and his easy chair in a salty white snow. He sprang out of the Berkliner, arms flailing, and accidentally knocked Barbara on the ladder. She teetered and toppled sideways onto her mother, who caught her in a half-hearted embrace before both women fell to the carpeted floor.

As Cleta and Barbara filled the air with an assortment of squeals and shrieks, Floyd eyed Vernie as if she'd suddenly sprouted a third head. "Dad blame, woman! What's wrong with you?"

"Nothing. I have to go."

"Go?" Cleta echoed, brushing herself off as she stood. "Why, we haven't had our wassail and cookies yet!"

"It's breezin' up—I really need to go. Elezar will be worried."

"But the Smith men are having some sort of meeting at the church."

Vernie was in no mood to explain. Snatching her coat from the hall peg, she shrugged into it, then wound her wool scarf around her neck.

Cleta fretted aloud as she yanked the front door open and Vernie sailed by. "You're going to break your fool neck running home in the dark like this!"

Floyd ventured out on the porch, wrapping his button-down sweater closer. He peered into the darkness. "Vernie, let me walk you home."

"I've walked myself home for twenty-odd years and haven't broke a bone yet." Her foot slipped on a patch of ice. "Whoops!" Catching herself, she latched onto the porch railing and carefully worked her way down the steps. She had to get home and find that order . . .

"You're gonna break your leg," Cleta called. "Jumping up like a scalded cat and taking off. For heaven's sake, Vernie, we've got a bathroom you could use!"

Trudging across the frozen sidewalk, Vernie gritted her teeth and ignored Cleta's yelping.

"Just remember," Floyd yelled, obviously straining to pitch his voice above the wail of the wind. "If you've never seen a good case of dry rot, you can't appreciate the value of new rubber."

Bursting into the mercantile, Vernie rooted through stacks of magazines and papers on the counter, frantically searching for the order form. Nothing. She paused, scanning her memory. She'd found the order here, but then she'd gone upstairs to her office. That's where she'd been distracted.

Thumping upstairs, she flew into her bedroom. She searched the floor and looked under the bed, then pulled the spread off and tossed pillows across the room. In desperation she stripped the sheets and shook them out, hoping for a glimpse of the ink-scrawled order form . . . but there was nothing.

After she'd talked to Stanley, she'd been still for a while, then she'd gone back down to see Elezar.

Thudding back downstairs, she ripped ledgers out of drawers and shook spiral note-books. Nothing. She raced back upstairs to her bedroom, overturning table lamps and peeking under lace doilies. Nothing.

Where was that confounded order? She'd eaten dinner, then slipped out of her sweater and work apron to put on a fleecy red jacket, something in keeping with the spirit of the holiday—

Her gaze fell upon the sleeve of her brown sweater, a forlorn lump under a discarded bedsheet. Vernie picked it up and swatted it, listening for the telltale crackle of paper— there! In the pocket, where she'd slipped it to conceal her mistake from Elezar.

Unfolding the order, she spread it flat on the desk and picked up the phone. She'd call Wagner's and explain things, tell them to put a rush on her order.

Three rings later an answering machine came on the line: "Wagner's Wholesalers. The office is now closed. Our hours are from 8 A.M. until 5 P.M., Monday through Friday. If you know your party's extension, dial it now, or stay on the line and record a message at the beep—"

Vernie hung up and swallowed against a dry throat. She wouldn't panic. The Heavenly Daze Christmas party was still a week away. She'd fax the order tonight. She'd request an overnight delivery and pay extra. No problem.

A strong gust of wind rattled the old house, reminding her of the inclement weather brewing somewhere out in the ocean. All right, then. If her plans went astray, she'd send Elezar over to Ogunquit for supplies. He could keep a secret. But it wouldn't come to that. First thing Monday morning she would call the wholesaler to make sure they'd picked up the fax. The other women would never know she'd failed to place the order.

Her pulse thrummed. Failure wasn't a thing often associated with Vernie Bidderman. She prided herself on her self-sufficiency. Why, she'd never forgotten to do anything in her whole life! And even this wasn't her fault, it was Stanley's. He had her so unnerved it was a wonder she could remember her own name.

Sinking to the floor, she held her head with both hands. Dear Lord, what was happening to her? When her hot flashes receded, she'd assumed the worst of the change was over, but obviously nature had other tricks up her sleeve. Now her mind was taunting her, as it had when she started into the change—

She heard the sharp click of the key turning in the front door lock. Elezar. She sat up straighter. He would have seen the downstairs light and was probably stopping by to see if she needed anything . . . because she was supposed to be at the Lansdowns'.

Crawling on her hands and knees, she scooted into her closet, then dragged herself over shoes and boots and slippers to the very back. Heavy footfalls thudded across the mercantile floor, then creaked the stairs. The steps paused before her closed bedroom door.

"Vernie?"

Holding her breath, Vernie remained quiet.

She heard a hesitant tap. "You okay?"

She gasped when she looked up to discover a pair of puzzled sea green eyes peering at her in the darkness. MaGoo. Her hand shot over to cover the cat's mouth when it meowed.

"Vernie? You in there?" The door squeaked open.

MaGoo squirmed, breaking free of her grip. The cat darted away, throwing a final resentful look over his shoulder before he disappeared into the closet darkness.

Vernie heard the click of the light switch, saw the beam of light disappear from the bottom of the closet door. She pressed her hand to her mouth, wondering if she'd lost her mind. Why was she hiding from Elezar? He wouldn't know what happened unless she told him, and she wasn't going to tell him. She wasn't going to tell anybody what she'd done. And listen to them laugh? No, thank you. She was smart enough to stall the island women for another couple of days. Vernie Bidderman would not be the Grinch who stole Heavenly Daze's Christmas, not this year. By Wednesday morning Mooseleuk would have more nutmeg, cranberries, and sugar than Kroger carried in their entire chain.

She sat for another fifteen minutes until she was certain that Elezar had locked up and moved on out to his cottage.

Pulling herself out of a pair of flattened shoeboxes, she winced, listening to her bones crack.

She hated getting old.

Really hated it.

After going downstairs, she poured herself a tall glass of Coke, added a splash of vanilla syrup, then took a long, cold drink. The sweetness and bubbles helped.

Tomorrow will be better, she promised herself. All she had to do was think of a logical explanation for why her bedroom looked as though a cyclone had ripped through it.

The phone rang, but Vernie ignored it. She was, as far as most people knew, still at the Lansdowns', enjoying their wassail and cookies on tree-trimming night.

After the third ring, the machine picked up the call. A moment later, Stanley's voice rumbled over the line: "Vernie, please. We need to talk. It's Christmas, sweetums. Can't you find it in your heart to—"

Her hand slapped the delete key. Hard.

She dumped another shot of vanilla in her Coke, then carried the glass upstairs, nearly tripping over MaGoo in the hallway.

The fax machine sat on her desk, ready and waiting for her order, and this time nothing was going to stop her from sending it.

CHAPTER TWELVE

Christmas carols floated through the restaurant speaker:

Deck the halls with boughs of holly, fa la la la la la la la la.

Threading her way through coworkers, Annie smiled at Dean Witsell and his wife, Luella. "You look lovely tonight," she said, complimenting Mrs. Witsell as she paused to greet the elderly couple. She would have stayed for more polite conversation, but another man stepped forward to take Mrs. Witsell's hand—a fellow with more political pull than Annie.

Excusing herself, she worked her way through the crowd, smiling and calling "happy holidays" to coworkers she passed. She doubted her smile fooled many people—she hated office Christmas parties. They were boring and hot and an uninspired extension of an already long workday. If it weren't for Melanie's insistence that she put in at least a brief appearance, Annie would now be on her way to a hot bath and a rented Mel Gibson video.

She was on her way to greet Melanie when Hank Walters grabbed her. Dangling a sprig of mistletoe over his head, he flashed a set of expensive caps. "Merry Christmas, Annie." As the megabucks dental detail came in for a landing, Annie turned her head at the last instant and redirected his smooch to her cheek, the only respectable place where she could entertain a kiss from a married man.

Hank was every woman's nightmare. He hung around the water cooler making lewd remarks for cheap laughs. His wife, a shy sort, stood near the wall nursing a glass of punch, a pained expression on her thin face.

"Merry Christmas, Hank," Annie called over her shoulder as she moved away. "I hope Santa doesn't forget where you live."

She sighed in relief when she finally reached Melanie. "This is awful," she murmured, crossing her arms. "I hate these parties."

Melanie brightened her smile. "Guess who's here?"

Annie accepted a glass of punch from a waitress wearing blinking reindeer antlers. "I don't know. Old Saint Nick?"

"Better."

"Three kings bearing gold, frankincense, and myrrh? For me?"

"Wrong again." Melanie giggled. "A. J."

Pausing with her glass halfway to her mouth, Annie frowned. "Who?"

"A. J. The guy I've been telling you about."

Annie scanned the crowd. "Which one is he?"

"He's over there, the guy talking to Professor Blight." Hugging Annie's arm, Melanie shivered. "Now is that a man or is that a *man*?"

"A man," Annie agreed. Melanie had definitely found herself a handsome, suave-looking guy somewhere between thirty and thirty-five, a fellow who wore his slacks and blazer like a model for *GQ*. Melanie had suddenly developed a case of Good Taste; she was usually attracted to the *Popular Mechanics* type who wore ponytails and sported grease stains beneath their fingernails.

"Nice." Annie shifted her gaze to search for the buffet line. "I'm starved. Let's eat."

"Nice? That's all you can say about a hunk like A. J.? That he's nice?"

Annie gave the subject another quick once-over. Charcoal sport jacket, black collarless shirt, light gray slacks. "Okay, very nice. I hope there's shrimp on the bar—"

"Very nice? Are you nuts?" Leaning in closer, Melanie tightened her grip on Annie's arm. "Look at him." She rolled her eyes. "He's to die for. I'm trying to talk him into joining us on the cruise."

Annie gaped at her friend. "You're kidding, right? How many dates have you had?"

Melanie giggled. "Counting tonight, two. But when lightning strikes, it takes out anything in its path, including caution. He's the one, Annie. The one."

Giving her friend a careful smile, Annie took Melanie's arm and steered her toward the buffet line. Melanie needed food—energy for the brain. But as they were making their way across the floor, the hunk turned and spotted the two women. Melanie pranced on her toes, waving and causing a spectacle. "A. J.! Over here!"

Annie groaned and lowered her gaze. Threesomes were always a drag. She'd nod at the introduction, eat a bite of shrimp, and be on her way.

Mr. Right casually excused himself and sauntered toward them. Peeking from beneath her lashes, Annie noted dark eyes, curly black hair, and a signet ring on his left hand. So, Mr. Wonderful was a college boy. Smooth. Cultured. And incredibly handsome.

For a moment she felt a surge of adrenaline, a moment of alertness, and something rose to the tip of her tongue . . . then disappeared. Whatever she'd remembered was gone. As he came closer she lifted her head and studied him head-on. She was sure she had never met the man, but she'd known plenty like him. Most were jerks, pretty boys with more flash than character.

"Honey," Melanie looped her arm through his, "I want you to meet my friend, Annie. Annie, this is A. J."

Mr. Right gave her the slow, easy kind of smile that made a woman smile back. "Annie." He extended a hand. The faint scent of expensive cologne teased her senses.

She gave him a brief smile. "A. J."

Melanie squeezed his bicep. "I was just

telling Annie that if we asked real nice, you might take us up to see the lights of the city."

Annie blinked. How had she missed that?

"Tonight?" The easy smile remained in place though surprise flickered briefly across his face. Melanie squeezed his arm again, then turned back to Annie. "A. J.'s a pilot. He owns his own plane—unless you're afraid to fly? I know you lost your parents in a plane crash."

"It's okay." Annie cleared her throat. She had too much of her pilot father in her to fear flying. Sometimes at takeoff she developed butterflies in her stomach for a few minutes, but by the time the plane leveled her fears always subsided.

"The plane's small," Melanie's man warned, still smiling. "A 182 Cessna."

"A small four-seater," Melanie teased. "Like we all have a plane. Wouldn't that be fun, Annie, to view Christmas lights from the air?"

"I don't know." Annie cast about for an excuse. She hated to be a fifth wheel—or, in this case, a third party.

"Come on," Melanie pressed. "How often do you get a chance to fly in a private plane with such a competent pilot?" She tilted her head and cast a dazzling smile at Mr. Right.

Annie frowned. How did Melanie know this man was a competent pilot? For all she knew he could be a crazed psychopath who preyed on starry-eyed women. But, she decided, looking him over, he seemed perfectly sane and fairly comfortable with the suggestion. Melanie might be impulsive and change men as often as Annie changed shoes, but she had a sound intuition about people.

"Come on, spoil sport." Melanie made a playful moue. "A. J.'s a real doll to ask."

A. J. hadn't asked; Melanie had coerced him. But Annie adored flying, and a Christmas-lit Portland by air would be spectacular.

Before she could think of a reason to protest, she found herself in the backseat of Mr. Right's metallic gray Lexus.

"Nice car," she said, getting in.

"Belongs to the company." He tossed the answer casually over his shoulder.

"Nice company," she answered. "Any openings for a frustrated botanist?"

In answer, he grinned at her in the rearview mirror.

Half an hour later, he drove into a private hangar belonging to "the company I work for." A very wealthy company, Annie surmised when they entered a building that contained not one but two sleek Lear jets.

Melanie had hit the jackpot with this one.

Behind the jets squatted a small green-and-white Cessna, gleaming in the hangar lights. Delirious with joy, Melanie squeezed Annie's arm several times after A. J. left them to file his flight plan. "Isn't he wonderful?" she whispered.

"Yeah," Annie answered, sinking her hands in her pockets. She might not have a boyfriend to keep her warm, but at least she had a nice heavy coat.

Half an hour later they were taxiing to the runway. Wearing headphones that would prevent them from having to shout above the roar of the engine, they talked. A. J. patiently answered Melanie's questions about aeronautics and his flight experience.

Annie couldn't help being impressed. The man proved masterful behind the controls; the takeoff was picture-perfect. Climbing to his assigned altitude, A. J. consulted charts, flipped levers, and talked with the tower until the plane was soaring above Portland.

In the backseat, Annie pressed her nose against the window and drank in the twinkling landscape below. The smell of leather surrounded her, mixed with the faint, exotic hint of Mr. Right's cologne. With A. J.'s help, she and Melanie were able to pick out a few landmarks below.

While Melanie babbled in the front, Annie stared out the window and kept her thoughts to herself. How lucky could Melanie get? She was a great friend, and Annie was happy for her, but still a gremlin of envy rose whenever she thought of Melanie's good fortune. Where were the A. J.s when Annie was looking for a good man?

"Down there," A. J. turned his head to address her, and his strong baritone sent delicious shivers up her spine. "That's your home territory."

"Southern Maine Tech?" Annie peered at the dotted lights below.

"It looks so small from up here," Melanie yelled.

Small, but beautiful. White lights dotted the campus, and in the surrounding neighborhood colorful Christmas displays winked up at them. It was a perfect night for flying: light wind, great visibility. Celestial stars twinkled overhead as man-made stars glittered below.

Annie sat back and hugged herself, the warmth of the cockpit enveloping her. She didn't care if this flight never ended.

They flew for over an hour, and in the darkness ahead Annie recognized the familiar outline of Heavenly Daze. She leaned forward, tapped A. J.'s shoulder, and pointed to the lights below. "Look," she called, "see how the streetlights form a cross?"

"It's an island," A. J. answered, glancing over his left shoulder.

"Believe me, I know," Annie whispered, sinking back into her seat. All of the important events in her life had centered around that island. She'd been raised there, loved and taught there, and she'd grieved there. She'd cried and dreamed and learned to face disappointment and elation there. Uncle Edmund lay buried there, and in the biggest house on the highest point, Aunt Olympia was almost certainly sitting alone in her room, awash in tears . . .

"Look!" Melanie squealed, diverting her attention. "Over there—isn't that a ship? Wonder if it's like the ship we'll be taking on the cruise?"

Annie sighed. Melanie hadn't yet convinced A. J. to sail away with her to a sunnier clime, but the girl deserved an A for effort.

The hour of eleven had come and gone when the lights of the Portland Jetport finally reappeared. The plane dropped, glided smoothly on the approach, then the wheels lightly touched the runway. They taxied to the hangar, and Annie closed her eyes, hating for the adventure to end.

Later, A. J. drove Melanie and Annie back to the restaurant where she'd left her car. While Melanie babbled on about how wonderful, kind, and thoughtful A. J. was to take them for a flight, Annie sat alone in the back, lost in her thoughts.

She snapped out of her reverie when A. J. got out and opened her door.

"You didn't have to do that," she said, feeling heat on her cheeks. "You could have just dropped me on the corner."

"Door-to-door service is my specialty." His smile gleamed in the starlit darkness. "If I can't see you home, at least I can see you to your car."

She led the way, feeling a little foolish as he followed her through the parking lot.

"Melanie will be wondering what's keeping you," she said, slipping her keys into the lock.

"Melanie will understand."

Feeling more flustered than she wanted to admit, Annie opened the door and got in, then hesitated. "Thanks. I had a wonderful time." She felt a jolt when their eyes met. An electric, knock-your-socks-off kind of jolt that unnerved her.

If he felt the electricity, he didn't show it. But a man like A. J. probably wouldn't. He reached in and flipped the lock on her car door, his eyes still fixed on her. "Drive carefully, lovely lady."

Nodding, Annie took a deep breath. She'd never felt this lightheaded, this giddy around a man. She must be coming down with something—altitude sickness?

She reached out to close the door and he stepped into the narrow space and caught her hand. He smiled. "I'd like to have dinner with you some night. Is that possible?"

Alarm slapped at her. Maybe she had mistaken a smooth male predator for a gentleman. "I can't—there's Melanie."

His brow flickered. "What about Melanie?"

"You and her—I mean, she and you—"

Chuckling, he released her hand and stepped back. "Forgive me if I'm speaking out of turn, Annie." He bent closer and his warm breath touched her face. "But I've only dated Melanie once. Tonight. Twice if you count the night I met her among a group of friends."

Unable to find her voice, Annie nodded.

"So—can I call you sometime?"

"Better not," she murmured. Melanie was a good friend, and Annie knew she viewed the situation in a different light.

"Maybe another time," he said quietly.

As she drove off she risked a final glance in the rearview mirror. Mr. Right stood in the parking lot, watching her taillights. Had he felt it, too? She closed her eyes, breathing in the lingering scent of his aftershave.

She'd felt the power.

The breathless, once-in-a-lifetime connection.

Magic. Just like in the movies.

Pure magic.

CHAPTER THIRTEEN

On Wednesday afternoon Vernie cupped the receiver and turned her back to Elezar. Lowering her voice, she whispered into the phone: "What do you mean, a dock strike?"

"A strike, lady." The rep from Wagner's Wholesalers sounded impatient. "Teamsters' dispute. The men walked off the job late Monday afternoon."

"What about my order?" She tightened her grip on the mouthpiece. "What about my cranberries and nutmeg?"

The man on the phone let out an audible sigh. "When did you place the order?"

"Faxed it in Saturday night. The eighth."

"Saturday—let's see. That would have sat in the fax till Monday, and—uh-oh."

The last thing Vernie wanted to hear was an uh-oh. "What's wrong?"

The man sighed again. "We're doing all we can to keep business flowing, but I gotta tell you, lady, it don't look good. You'll have to wait your turn."

Shaken, Vernie hung up. She didn't have time to wait her turn. The island Christmas party was Saturday night and there wasn't a dash of nutmeg on the island. Nor a single cranberry, so Babette wouldn't be able to make her holiday salad. Vernie's inattention would ruin everybody's Christmas, and they wouldn't be quick to forget.

Fumbling beneath the counter, she pulled out a plastic bottle of Coke and refilled her glass. This was awful. She'd go into Ogunquit and pay retail for supplies, but gale force winds were keeping them all island-bound. The ferry hadn't run in two days, but perhaps that was a blessing in disguise. At least she hadn't had to think up lame excuses about why her order had not been delivered.

Leaning down, she pulled out the slender bottle of vanilla syrup, then splashed a liberal shot into the icy Coke. At that moment Bea Coughlin pecked on the front window, startling Vernie. She looked up in time to see Bea frowning at the bottle, so Vernie shoved it under the counter and pasted on a smile.

Pressing her fingertips to the window,

Beatrice yelled, "I'm going to ask Annie to bring sugar when she comes for the party this weekend. The bakery's getting low."

Vernie shook her head. "No need to do that—"

Wait a minute. What was she thinking? There was a need—a strong need. And Annie was the answer! She could e-mail Annie and have her bring nutmeg, cranberries, and sugar when she came this weekend. Surely the weather would let up enough for Captain Stroble to bring the ferry across by then. The weather channel was still calling for a nor'easter by Sunday or Monday, but Annie would have come and gone by that time.

Rushing to the door on a tide of relief, she jerked it open and smiled at Bea. "That's a good idea, Beatrice. I've just heard that the wholesalers are on strike, and who knows when they'll get that order to us? So I'll e-mail Annie and ask her to pick up the things we need. Maybe she can get here by early Saturday afternoon and we'll have plenty of time to prepare for the party that night."

Bea slapped a mittened hand to her cheek. "On strike! I was afraid something like that would happen. We should have gone to Ogunquit last week and picked up those supplies."

Vernie forced a smile. "I know, I know. But no harm done."

Feeling drained, she closed the door, then leaned against it. If Annie brought the supplies, no one would have to know about her incompetence. She ignored a prick of conscience. Why did anyone need to know?

Like a scratchy record, Stanley's voice echoed in her ear: *You can't admit your mistakes, can you, Vernie?*

She lifted her chin and spoke to the memory. "Of course I make mistakes. I'm not perfect."

Without warning, Elezar stepped around the corner, a dustcloth in his hand. He shot her a questioning look. "Everything all right?"

"Everything's fine. I'm going to ask Annie to bring our supplies since the strike is holding everything up."

His expression sobered. "A strike? Is that the problem?"

"It is today—that and the weather. The wholesalers don't know when they'll be able to deliver, so Annie will have to help us out. Everything's going to be fine."

The man's eyes darkened, and a hint of a smile played at the corners of his mouth. "Yes, ma'am."

Feeling more confident than she had in days, Vernie picked up her glass and moved toward the stairs. "I'll have Annie pick up some cat food, too. MaGoo's gained five pounds on table scraps this week."

Elezar nodded, then pointed toward the door. "I was thinking about going out for a walk. Will you be okay if I leave for a while?"

Vernie snorted. "It's not like anyone's beating down our door. Go on, I'll be back down in a few minutes."

She tackled the stairs with spring in her step and climbed them in record time. In five minutes she'd be logged onto AOL, and then her problems would be solved.

The wind tugged at Elezar's hat, but he held it firmly in place as he strode toward the church. A breath of snow was in the air, but a thin sun drifted in and out of the threatening clouds. Dirty patches of half-melted slush bordered the cobblestone road and sidewalks. His breath formed a frosty vapor as he walked and thought about the humans he had been assigned to serve.

He ached when Vernie made bad choices, and she'd made several lately.

Lifting his gaze to the sky and the invisible realm beyond, Elezar addressed the Lord: "Father, what must I do? Pride is a crippling thing. We all saw what it did to Lucifer. Now Vernie has allowed pride to come between her and those she loves, and I don't think she's aware of her mistake."

He paused at the churchyard, trying to identify the lone bent figure by a snowbank between the church and the Lansdowns' bed and breakfast. The man wasn't Winslow Wickam. This fellow was larger, with long white hair flowing over a white coat . . .

Elezar grinned. Gavriel had decided to materialize.

As Elezar drew nearer, the angel captain turned. "Brother! You're just in time." He gestured to the pan in his hand, which contained something white.

Puzzled, Elezar walked on.

"I've heard the women talking about snow cream and I thought I might try some." Gavriel extended the pan for Elezar's inspection. "Will you join me?"

Falling into step with his brother angel, Elezar lifted a brow. "Are Salt Gribbon's grandchildren doing well?"

"The children are happy." Gavriel dropped his voice as they entered the church through a side door, then descended the steep staircase to the basement. "Now, let's see if the kitchen has what we need."

Bemused, Elezar watched as Gavriel set the pan on the counter, then rummaged among canisters and jars in the cabinets. "Sugar and vanilla extract, I believe I heard them mention. Milk. An egg, and a dash of salt."

Elezar eyed the pan skeptically. "With snow."

Gavriel flashed a grin over his shoulder. "They say it's quite tasty."

"Some mortals say liver and onions are tasty, too, but I have never agreed."

Gavriel laughed, then splashed ingredients into the bowl. He stirred and tasted, made a face, then shrugged and dumped more sugar into the mixture. "Now," he said, looking up. "Where shall we enjoy our treat?"

Elezar frowned. "We eat it like that?" Gavriel's concoction looked nothing like ice cream. Ice cream was smooth and firm. And it wasn't sprinkled with specks of dirt.

Draping an arm around his fellow angel's shoulder, Gavriel pointed toward the staircase. "Some of the women are due to arrive here soon for a cleaning session, so we'd best clear out. But I know where we can go."

He picked up the pan and led the way up the stairs and out the side door. Elezar followed wordlessly as his leader led the way to the cemetery. Looking around at the barren spot, he huddled deeper into his coat. Gavriel was right—not many mortals were likely to come out here in this kind of weather.

"Now, this is nice," Gavriel said, perching on a marble slab. "We don't do this often enough."

Elezar cast a worried glance toward Ferry Road. The citizens of Heavenly Daze were going about their work as usual, completely unaware of the angelic activity around them. Bea's mail cart sat in front of the Graham Gallery. Babette stood on her front porch, scattering rock salt on her steps and sidewalk.

Pulling two plastic spoons from his coat pocket, Gavriel dipped one into the pan of snow cream and offered Elezar the first bite.

Elezar took a tentative taste, then smiled. "It's good."

Gavriel took a heaping spoonful. "Ayuh. Scrumptious."

They ate in silence until the pan was empty. Elezar shivered, chilled now from inside and out.

Gavriel wiped his mouth with his fingertips. "Did you have something you wanted to talk about, brother?"

"Ayuh. Vernie."

"I thought so." Dropping the empty pan to the brown grass, the angel captain sighed. "Her pride again?"

"It's stronger than ever. She forgot to order supplies at the beginning of the month. But instead of confessing the truth, she's hedged and dodged the other women's requests for sugar, cranberries, and nutmeg. Now the wholesaler can't deliver because of a strike, so there will be no eggnog, cranberry salad, or pumpkin pie at the Heavenly Daze Christmas party . . . all because Vernie can't admit she made a mistake."

"Sad."

"That's not the worst of it. Stanley Bidderman called. You know—the snake."

Gavriel lifted a brow. "After all these years?"

"He wants to talk to her, but she refuses. She can be so hardheaded."

"What could he want?"

"I was hoping you could tell me. Have you received instruction from the Lord about this?"

Gavriel shifted his gaze to the breakers crashing on the beach. "Sorry, Elezar, but I've heard nothing. I suppose this is one of those occasions where people exercise free will and we wait to see how we may strengthen them . . . or help them up after they fall."

His eyes, lit by the sun, glittered with concern. "Why do humans cling so strongly to their pride? Vernie's mistake was a simple one, easily corrected. Now the townspeople will be inconvenienced, but she will suffer a far worse fate. Pride leads to alienation. Just look what it did to Lucifer."

Elezar spread his hands, driven to defend his charge. "But that's what she fears! I believe Vernie's afraid the women will abandon her. She values their friendship and feels that they look upon her as the epitome of self-reliance. She's convinced herself that she doesn't need anyone—no other humans, at least. I don't think she's hardened her heart toward the Father."

Gavriel thought for a moment. "And forgiveness comes hard for her."

"Very hard. She can't forgive herself for something like forgetting to order nutmeg and cranberries. So how is she supposed to forgive Stanley?"

The angels sat in silence, listening to the wind hooting among the tombstones.

"What does Vernie plan to do next?" Gavriel asked.

Elezar sighed. "She's e-mailing Annie and asking her to bring the supplies when she comes this weekend."

"But—"

"I know." Elezar closed his eyes. "The forecast called for a nor'easter, and the storm might prevent Annie from coming."

He blew out his cheeks. If it did, Vernie wasn't going to be the most popular woman on the island.

*   *   *

Hi, Annie,

Will you please bring twenty-five pounds of sugar, five pounds of fresh cranberries, and twenty tins of nutmeg when you come this weekend? Cat food, too, if you remember it. MaGoo likes the kind in the little pouches.

Thanks!
Vernie

Frowning, Annie clicked on her next e-mail, this one from Beatrice Coughlin.

Annie,

Honey, can you bring us some sugar and nutmeg when you come Saturday? We're afraid to wait any longer for Vernie. She says she's going to e-mail you and ask you to bring supplies, but I'm afraid to trust anything she says these days. She's been promising supplies for two weeks now and we've not gotten them yet. She's been acting downright weird lately and I suspect that she's drinking. I don't know for certain, but I've caught her pouring something into her Coke on occasion.

I know that's a shocker but I don't know any other reason for her state of mind of late. Maybe you could pop in and ask Elezar what's going on. If I send Abner or Birdie she'll know something's up. (Birdie's been acting strange, too, but that's another story.) Anyway, if you can bring the sugar and nutmeg we sure would appreciate it. Thanks, sweetie.

Beatrice

Vernie Bidderman, the poster child for the Women's Temperance Union, drinking? What was going on in Heavenly Daze?

A rap on the door broke into her thoughts. Annie looked up to see Melanie standing in the doorway, a pleased grin on her face. "Isn't he everything I said he was?"

Annie blinked. "Who?"

"Who, my foot." Melanie moved into the office and kicked the door closed with her heel. "A. J. Don't you think he could be"— she wiggled her index fingers—"Mr. Right?"

Annie didn't know what to say. He might be Mr. Right for someone, but he certainly didn't seem to share Melanie's warm and fuzzy feelings. If he did, why had he invited Annie to dinner?

Propping her chin on her hand, she studied her friend. "Is he going on the cruise?"

Melanie's face fell. "No. He's spending Christmas with family."

Annie felt a sudden rush of mingled guilt and relief.

Popping the lid off a carton of yogurt, Melanie sat in the guest chair across from Annie's desk. "We'll have to do without him—but we'll still have fun."

Annie drew a deep breath. "About that cruise, Melanie. I won't be going."

Melanie's spoon hovered in midair. "You're kidding—you bought tickets already."

"I know." Annie stood. "But I bought insurance, so I won't lose all the money."

Melanie's face contorted in despair. "Annieeee! You can't back out on me now!"

"I'm sorry." Throwing up her hands, Annie began to pace. "I should have been honest with you, and myself. I thought I could go, but I can't. Aunt Olympia needs me, so I have to spend Christmas in Heavenly Daze."

The admission pained her more than she wanted to admit, but it wouldn't do any good to dwell on thoughts of sun-bleached beaches, handsome men, and tropical seas. Her only option was to ignore the disappointment that grew stronger and deeper with every passing day . . .

"Well, that stinks." Melanie scooped a spoonful of yogurt and narrowed her eyes.

Annie shrugged. "Nancy and Becky will be there."

"Yeah, I know, but that makes the cabin arrangements awkward. I'll either have to stay by myself or share with them—three girls using one teeny, tiny bathroom." She rolled her eyes.

"You won't be in your room that much."

Her face brightened. "That's true. Maybe I'll get lucky and meet someone who'll keep me dancing all night."

Easing back into her chair, Annie frowned. "What about Mr. Perfect?"

"A. J.? What about him?" Melanie's eyes narrowed further as she licked her spoon. "We've only dated twice—just once, actually, 'cause we met on that first night." Grinning, she scooped up another spoonful of yogurt. "Hey, don't get me wrong, A. J.'s wonderful. And if I don't find anybody better on the cruise, I'll be on him like white on rice.

But on a cruise all prospects are put on hold. There could be a better Mr. Perfect just beyond the lido deck."

Annie rolled her eyes. Amazing how Mr. Perfect could evolve into Mr. Possibility in a heartbeat.

Thank goodness she had no man in her life. She didn't need those kinds of complications.

CHAPTER FOURTEEN

On Saturday morning, Annie bundled up and left her apartment at nine-thirty, planning to stop by the well-stocked Hannaford Brothers grocery for sugar, cranberries, cat food, and nutmeg before she made the two-hour drive to Ogunquit. To her chagrin, she discovered that the store didn't have twenty cans of nutmeg. She would have to swing by her local grocery store to complete Bea's and Vernie's wish lists.

Grumbling at the inconvenience, she parked in the second wet parking lot of the day, pulled her collar up to her ears, and trudged into the grocery store.

After yanking a cart from the line of buggies, she pushed it toward the spice aisle. Rounding the corner in a rush, she collided with a fellow shopper's cart, jolting her from stem to stern. The corner of her buggy swung wide, knocking over a display of thirty-two ounce bottles of Mountain Dew. Plastic bottles toppled and hit the ground, several exploding in pressurized yellow streams as unsuspecting shoppers slipped and slid through the sticky assault.

By the time she'd righted the bottles, helped an older woman up from the floor, and tried to explain the collision to a nervous store manager, Annie was drenched. Holding her sticky blouse away from her chest, she looked at the damage to her clothing and muttered, "Good grief."

A rumbling baritone chuckle answered her wry observation. She glanced up to see A. J. grinning at her, the front of his blue shirt, silk tie, and leather jacket saturated in soda pop.

Her pulse rate kicked into overdrive. "What—what are you doing here?"

"Picking up some soda?"

Annie burst out laughing as a clerk approached with a mop.

"I'm so sorry," Annie apologized, bending to help pick up the ruptured plastic bottles.

"No problem, ma'am, please be careful. Stand back."

Like a knight in soaking armor, A. J. took Annie's arm and pulled her away from the carnage. Beside a bin of broccoli she dabbed at her blouse with a paper towel, aware that a pink flush now dominated her face. Of all people to run into—literally—she had to soak Mr. Perfect.

Her thoughts abruptly shifted. What was A. J. doing here?

She lifted her gaze to meet his warm brown eyes. "Did you know I live near here?"

He stopped wiping his jacket long enough to give her a smooth smile. "How would I know that?"

"Maybe Melanie told you?" She didn't want to believe he'd found out where she lived and was haunting the grocery store in order to meet her—or did she? Maybe she did, but then she'd be a traitor. Melanie might be as fickle as the wind, but she was a friend.

Mr. Perfect's smile hadn't faded. "The subject of where you live and shop could have come up the one time I was out with Melanie—or two, if you insist on counting the night I met her."

Annie grinned, dropping her head when her cheeks burned hotter. "Okay. So what are you doing here?"

"Looking for you."

Half her heart thrilled at his words, the

other half wished he wouldn't tease. There was no way he could have known she would be in this store at this hour.

Reason won out. "I wish you wouldn't say things like that," she said.

"Okay," he conceded. "I'm following you."

"You are not." She tossed her crumpled paper towels into a trash can, then reached over to retrieve her dripping cart. Conversation like this would get them nowhere.

His smile deepened. "Like I said, I came in for a soft drink and a deli sandwich. I had a consultation in Portland earlier this morning, and now I'm on my way to the airport."

Of course, Annie thought. The airport was only fifteen minutes from here. This would be a logical stop if he wanted to pick up something for lunch.

She lowered her gaze, afraid he'd think she was intent upon grilling him. What did his schedule matter to her? They were barely friends. Mere acquaintances.

He fell into step beside her as she pushed her cart toward the cash register. His eyes widened when he saw what she was buying—eight tins of nutmeg.

She laughed. "It isn't for me. I'm doing friends a favor."

"You had me worried. I thought maybe you had a nutmeg addiction."

He flashed a million-dollar smile, then stepped away to get his sandwich and soda. As Annie pushed her cart through the checkout line, a wave of resentment washed over her. Why should Melanie have this man? She didn't deserve him—well, maybe nobody did. So why should Annie feel guilty for feeling attracted to him? Something would be wrong with any woman who wasn't attracted to this guy.

But Melanie, no matter what her faults, was a friend. And friends didn't steal other friends' boyfriends.

So Mr. Perfect was taken.

After she paid for her purchases, she walked slowly to the door, then smiled when he caught up with her.

"Express lane?" she asked, nodding toward his single grocery bag.

"Always." He grinned. "Life's too short to stand in line."

They walked out to her car, which he seemed to remember.

"On your way home?" he asked, holding the door open after she unlocked the car.

"No, I'm off to visit my aunt for the weekend." She paused, studying the lowering sky. The clouds looked bruised and swollen. "Do you know if they're predicting snow?"

"I hope not; I still have to fly to New York." A. J. ducked as his pager went off. Checking the number, he said, "I have to go."

"Me too." She slipped behind the wheel and he held the door a moment longer. Their eyes met.

"You will let me know?"

"Know what?"

"When I can take you to dinner."

She dropped her gaze. "I think that will be up to Melanie."

"The girl I dated only one time, two if you count—"

"The night you met." She nodded. "That would be the one."

He grinned as she turned the key in the ignition and looked up at him. "You're a mess, you know it?" she said.

"Maybe I need a good woman to clean up my act."

His eyes held hers and it was there again. Magic.

As she drove out of the parking lot, he followed in the Lexus, but at the first traffic light, he turned and headed toward the airport.

Sighing, she turned on the radio and hummed along with Bing Crosby who was dreaming of a white Christmas. And though she knew she shouldn't, she took a few small liberties with the lyrics.

She was dreaming of a sweet A. J.

Such a silly, harmless thing to sing.

By the time Annie pulled into Ogunquit's Perkins Cove, sleet was pelting her windshield. Ice had built up on the wipers, causing them to thump noisily against the glass.

After parking near the dock, she climbed out of the car and sprinted to the white clapboard office. The ferry was still moored to the dock, but by her watch Captain Stroble should have been halfway into his noon run by now.

Maybe she'd gotten lucky.

Breathless, she pulled the door open and greeted the captain with a smile.

"Well, look who decided to come home," he said, tipping back his cap to grin at her. "I was beginning to think we wouldn't see you this weekend."

"Sorry I'm late." She held her hands up to

the small space heater in the corner. "But I'm glad you haven't left yet. Got room for one more?"

The captain gave her a rueful smile. "Sorry." He inclined his head to look out the window. "The storm's moved in faster than they predicted. I don't think we'll be going out at all today."

Annie's heart sank. Vernie and the women at the bakery would be disappointed that she couldn't bring their cranberries, sugar, and nutmeg, but Annie had a far more pressing problem. In weather like this, she didn't dare start back to Portland.

Outside, waves rocked the channel and the dozens of boats anchored there. "I reckon I'll have to find a room here tonight."

"Ayuh." The captain tugged at his beard. "The Williams at the Puffin's Nest might put you up. They're not really open for business, but since you're a local gal and all . . ."

"Thanks, Captain. I'll drive over there."

The Williams did take pity on Annie, welcoming her to their bed and breakfast even though they'd officially closed for the season. After settling into her room, Annie called Frenchman's Fairest and explained the situation. "I'm sorry, Aunt Olympia. Maybe the weather will clear by tomorrow."

As she disconnected the call, she heard the weatherman's voice from the television downstairs. "This is going to be one for the record books, folks."

Annie sighed. She had another call to make, one she dreaded even worse than the call to Olympia. If Vernie really was nipping at the bottle, news like this might really drive her over the brink.

"Vernie?"

Vernie broke into a relieved grin when she heard Annie's voice on the line. "You made it!"

"Afraid not. I'm stuck in Ogunquit. The ferry's not running 'cause of the storm. I'm sorry, Vernie."

Vernie slumped against the counter and glanced at her watch. One o'clock. The town Christmas party started at six. So she had ruined the festivities and the islanders' annual celebration.

The phone buzzed in her ear. "Vernie? Are you still there?"

Heaving a resigned sigh, Vernie stared at

the sleet peppering the mercantile's front window. "I'm here. Thanks, Annie, for trying." She paused, aware that she was being self-centered. "Are you all right over there?"

"I'm fine; I'm spending the night at the Puffin's Nest. But I'm worried about you."

Vernie frowned. "About me?"

"Ayuh. I just want you to know that we love you, Vernie. You don't have to look for answers, you know, in chemicals. And after Christmas, maybe you should check into one of those, um, support groups."

Vernie listened in bewilderment. What in blazes was the girl talking about? Chemicals? Support groups? Must have something to do with the menopause program Annie'd been urging Olympia to join. Olympia had come into the mercantile with a long list of herbs and vitamins she wanted Vernie to order, saying they were all-natural and the best way to keep a woman's hormones under control.

Vernie hadn't bought into those claims. She'd learned her lesson from the grapefruit diet pills.

"Annie," she forced a laugh, "sometimes you just have to get through things as best you can. Sometimes I still feel a little tingly in my hands and feet, but my mind's all together. Most of the time."

"Oh." Annie's voice softened. "Well, okay. But let's talk the next time I'm home, okay? And maybe tomorrow the weather will ease up enough for me to get the supplies to you."

Tomorrow would be too late, but that wasn't Annie's problem. It was Vernie's, and now she would have to face up to it. She thanked Annie again and hung up, then dialed the bakery's number.

Birdie sounded more resigned than angry when she heard the news. "Well, I reckon we're not going to die without pumpkin pies at the party."

"I'm sorry." Vernie twisted the phone cord. "Reckon I should have let you buy the nutmeg while we could."

The call to the Graham Gallery wasn't any easier. Frustration tinged Babette's tone, but at least she understood. "I guess the storm caught us all off guard."

"Well, you know," Vernie offered lamely. "Maine weather. Who can predict it?"

"Okay." Babette fell silent for a moment, then added, "Don't worry. I have a can of fruit cocktail on hand, so I'll add it to the Jell-O for my salad."

Fruit cocktail? Dejected, Vernie hung up and placed other calls to Cleta and Dr. Marc.

By six o'clock, candles and greenery festooned the drab basement of Heavenly Daze Community Church. Winslow Wickam, Floyd Lansdown, and Mike Klackenbush tried their best to hide their disillusionment when the meal began, but Vernie couldn't help but notice their eyes searching the table for a miracle. Babette's famous cranberry salad, now reduced to red gelatin spotted with chunks of glutinous grapes, pineapple, and peaches, did little to lift their spirits. With a wan smile on her pretty face, Babette offered the bowl to Floyd, who obediently dropped a teaspoonful onto his plate.

Abner had come up with a gooseberry pie in lieu of pumpkin, and as he placed his offering on the dessert table he explained that the bakery was down to its last canister of sugar so the gooseberry pie only contained one cup of sweetening. "I hope that's good news for any of you who are watching your weight," he added with a hopeful smile.

The occupants of Vernie's table received

the gooseberry news silently, then their lips involuntarily puckered.

Spirits improved as Pastor Wickam led them in prayer, reminding the islanders they had much to be grateful for this Christmas—good health, family, and food on the table. Vernie sliced into the turkey (which, thank heaven, had been delivered in November) and listened to her neighbors laugh and visit as they ate, their hearts warming the room even as the wind whistled around the eaves outside. They were all present, she noticed, except poor Annie, stuck in Ogunquit, and old Cap'n Gribbon, reclusin' away up in his lighthouse.

"Things could be worse," Cleta pointed out, scooping another helping of sweet potatoes for Buddy Franklin's plate. "We could be homeless and out on the street. We're being mighty ungrateful if we fret too much about missing cranberries, sugar, and nutmeg."

"Ayuh," the men halfheartedly agreed.

Birdie took a bite of the gooseberry pie, pursed her lips as tight as a persimmon, then unpursed them enough to tell Abner, "Sugar would have helped."

"We all eat too much sugar," Bea corrected. "It's not good for us." She took another helping of turkey from the platter. "Think about all that angel mail we get from people with dire needs. It makes our wants seem petty, doesn't it?" She leaned over to spoon another helping of string bean casserole onto Olympia's plate. "You need to eat, hon. Just try a taste. This year I used one can of mushroom soup instead of two."

They all agreed the fuss over the missing traditions did make them look unappreciative. "Awful petty," Mike Klackenbush echoed, which Buddy Franklin seconded with a "Whatever."

Elezar, for one, seemed positively overjoyed to be part of the celebration. He made a point of mentioning the Lord's goodness and how fortunate they all were to share the annual celebration with friends—good friends. The more he talked, the heavier Vernie's guilt grew. Everyone around her seemed to be going out of his or her way to make light of the situation, but she knew what they were thinking behind those friendly facades. She'd known these people too long; they couldn't fool her.

She couldn't deny the truth. She was responsible for the lackluster dinner. She and her pride. If she had told the women that she'd forgotten to send the order, they could have picked up their baking supplies in Ogunquit . . . and Russell Higgs wouldn't have such a sour look on his face.

Winslow Wickam caught her eye and winked. "Always got a little indigestion after I ate all that dessert. This year I won't be up drinking soda water in the middle of the night."

"You will if you eat that gooseberry pie," Birdie warned in a stage whisper.

Edith, the pastor's wife, shook her head. "I don't know how you stand that soda water."

Winslow grinned. "If it was good enough for my parents, it's good enough for me."

"That Alkey Seltzer stuff ain't bad," Floyd called from the end of the table. He extended his plate toward Vernie and gestured at the meat platter. "More ham, Vernie, if you please."

She speared a slice, then dropped it into the sea of melted red gelatin on his plate.

"Well, ladies." Charles Graham pushed back from the table and patted his stomach. "You've certainly outdone yourself, cranberries or no cranberries." He smiled at Babette. "Going to have to loosen the belt a notch, honey."

Their son Georgie piped up, "We can have us a cranberry party after Christmas!"

"That's a good idea, Georgie." Cleta beamed. "Why, there's still plenty of time to get our things in before Christmas. And even if the storm doesn't let up until New Year's, pumpkin pie will taste as good in January as it does in—"

"Oh, all right!" Vernie's fist slammed to the table, rattling the silverware. A dozen pairs of eyes snapped toward her.

"It's my fault that you don't have cranberries and pumpkin pie, okay?" She whirled to confront Cleta. "I forgot to place the order—okay? I forgot. Twice." Her face flamed. "So there. Hang me."

Tossing her napkin on the table, she stood and bolted toward the kitchen, bawling like a fool.

Two minutes later Birdie and Babette found her slumped in a chair by the stove, weeping into a soggy handkerchief. "I'm an old fool," Vernie mumbled between sobs. "And the dinner was ruined because of me."

Babette knelt beside her. "Goodness, Vernie, who said the dinner was ruined? Everyone's had a wonderful time."

"Land, if I had a nickel for every time I forgot to do something," Birdie added, "I'd be rich as Bill Gates."

As Babette slipped her arm around Vernie's shoulders, the other women came through the doorway—Cleta and Barbara, Bea, Edith, Olympia, and Dana. Forming a circle, they surrounded Vernie, their love engulfing and overwhelming her.

"Is that what's been worrying you—your silly order?" Cleta asked. "Why, deary, you should have told me. Together we could have figured out some way to get the things you needed."

Babette patted her shoulder. "Did you honestly think a few cranberries could come between friends?"

Speechless, Vernie covered her mouth with her handkerchief, unable to talk around the lump growing in her throat. But they needed to know the entire truth.

"It's all Stanley's fault," she finally blurted out.

Curious looks shot back and forth. Eyes widened while eight sets of feminine brows lifted.

Dana timidly raised her hand. "Are we talking about *your* Stanley?"

274 Lori Copeland and Angela Hunt

Vernie dropped her handkerchief. "He's not my Stanley."

Birdie pressed her hand to her throat. "Did he write you?"

"I don't want to talk about it." Burying her face in the cloth, Vernie bawled again. "I'm sorry," she said when she could speak. "I've been nothing but thoughtless and scatter-brained these last few days—and I've always been proud of being so dependable. But pride can be a bad thing, can't it?"

Bright tears formed in Olympia's eyes. Stepping forward, she reached for Vernie's hand. "You can't teach me a thing about pride. I'm the queen of self-importance, but lately I've been learning that folks will over-look pride and even blind bullheadedness if you ask them to." A tear spilled and rolled down her cheek as her eyes moved slowly around the circle. "It's not easy, but there's something sweet in asking folks you love to overlook your mistakes." A smile trembled on her lips. "It's the season for forgiveness."

"Ayuh," the women whispered.

"The Lord forgives us when we ask," Edith added in a hushed tone. "If he is faithful to forgive our shortcomings, we can surely forgive a sugar shortage."

"And cranberries," Babette added.

"And nutmeg," Cleta finished.

Then the women did what most women do when the tie that binds them is strong and sweet and perfect in the love of Christ— they threw their arms around each other and boohooed together.

CHAPTER FIFTEEN

"Floyd? This call's for you."

As Winslow carried the cordless phone to the table, Floyd dropped his fork. "Who could be calling me here?" he asked the others. For an instant his blood surged, then calmed. It couldn't be an emergency; every resident on the island was present and accounted for with the exception of old Salt Gribbon.

Taking the phone from the pastor, he grunted a greeting: "Ayuh?"

"Floyd?"

"Ayuh."

"It's Stanley."

Floyd blinked in astonished silence.

"Did you hear me? It's Stan."

"Stanley Bidderman?" Somehow Floyd found his voice. "Great day in the morning, man. Are you kidding? Is this really you?"

A hoarse cough rattled over the line, then Stanley said, "I need a favor, Floyd. Please."

Floyd's gaze darted toward the kitchen. Through the opening above the counter he could see the women clustered around Vernie. His eyes shifted to the men sitting at the table, their attention now focused on him.

Looking away, Floyd lowered his voice. "We didn't know if you were dead or alive."

"Right now I feel mostly dead," Stanley admitted.

"Where are you?"

"Standing at the side door of the church. Calling on a cell phone."

Floyd took a quick, sharp breath, then met Pastor Wickam's curious gaze. "Heavenly Daze Church?"

"That would be the one." Floyd flinched when Stanley's words were punctuated by an explosive sneeze.

"Stanley Bidderman?" Winslow leaned closer. "Vernie's husband? I never met him."

Cupping his hand over the receiver, Floyd whispered, "Stanley says he's here, at the side door."

"Impossible," Charles Graham concluded, thumping the table. "The ferry isn't running."

"Impossible," Russell echoed the sentiment. "It's dark out there."

"Someone's playing a joke on you," Charles added.

Lifting the phone back to his ear, Floyd said, "How'd you get here? The ferry isn't running."

Another violent sneeze exploded, then: "I hired a guy to bring me across. That nutty lobsterman."

Floyd lowered the phone and relayed the information. "He hired Crazy Odell to bring 'im across."

The other men rolled their eyes and nodded in unison. Odell Butcher was the only human within sixty miles desperate enough to risk roiling Atlantic waters for a twenty dollar bill.

"If he's really outside," Pastor Wickam said, "why doesn't he come in?"

Floyd turned back to the phone. "Why don't you come in? You'd have to be crazier than a backhouse rat to stay out when you could come in and get warm—"

"Vernie's there, isn't she?"

Floyd glanced toward the kitchen again. "Ayuh, she's here. In the kitchen with the other womenfolk."

"Then I ain't so crazy. I can't have her see me, not yet. She's still all fussed up about us."

"Hold your horses, then. I'll be out directly."

Floyd punched the power button, then handed the phone to Winslow. "I better get him inside before he freezes."

"I wouldn't tell Vernie just yet," Winslow whispered, looking toward the weepy women. "We better break this to her gently."

Floyd nodded, then made his way through the fellowship hall. He took the steps double-time and hurried to the side door. Sure enough, Stanley Bidderman sat slumped on the steps, his face flushed, his eyes bright and watery in the porch light. He looked every day of twenty years older, but there was no mistaking Stanley's slight form and round face.

"In heaven's name, Stan. What's going on?" Kneeling, Floyd felt the ailing man's damp forehead. "You're burning up."

"Don't tell Vernie," Stanley whispered, his hand coming up to grasp Floyd's coat. "Promise me, Floyd? She'll throw my carcass off the island if she finds out I'm here before I'm ready."

"Vernie wouldn't do that."

"She would. You don't know my sweetums like I do."

"I don't think I care to know her that well. I got enough headaches with Cleta." Floyd grunted as he helped his old friend to his feet, then picked up his battered suitcase.

"Can you give me a room for the night? I'm sorry to put you to any trouble, but this fever came on me this morning. If you'll give me a room, I'm sure I'll feel better tomorrow."

"You're not putting me to any trouble." Supporting Stanley's slight frame, Floyd led his unexpected guest toward the back porch of the bed and breakfast. Wind buffeted them as sleet stung their faces.

Floyd chided his friend as they walked through the deepening darkness. "Why in the world would you try to come here in your condition? This weather's a beast!"

Stanley drew a breath that dissolved in a coughing fit. "Had to talk to Vernie, and you know Odell—" He coughed again, then squeaked, "He's fearless."

"He's batty. You're lucky you made it in one piece." Floyd helped Stanley up the slippery stairs and onto the ice-covered porch. After turning the skeleton key in the lock, he hurried the sick man inside, shivering as a cocoon of warm air enveloped him.

"Come on in here." Floyd led Stanley toward the front room. "You sit on the sofa and relax while I chuck a couple more logs on the fire." He turned on a lamp, then reached for a log and asked, "You had anything to eat?"

Waving the question aside, Stanley shivered. "What about it? Can I have that bed for the night?"

Floyd straightened. "Cleta will be in big trouble if Vernie hears about it."

Stan's fever-bright eyes pleaded his case. "I have nowhere else to go."

"Man, I don't know. After all these years . . . Cleta will skin me alive."

Stanley fell back on the sofa and lifted a feeble hand. "Please."

Floyd stood for a moment, running the toe of his shoe over a pattern in the worn carpet. After a while, he sighed and shrugged. "Sure. There's a bedroom in the attic we sometimes use for overflow in the summer. It's cold as a well digger's ankles up there, but I'll get a couple more blankets and a heater from the storeroom." He grinned. "Cleta doesn't have to know you're up there either, at least, not for a while."

"Thank you, Floyd." The two men's eyes

met, and Stanley's shone with gratitude. "Vernie refuses to talk to me. I thought if I came to see her she'd have to listen."

"She's not going to be happy about you barging in at Christmastime."

Stanley broke into another coughing spell, then croaked, "I know."

"What you did to her was rough." Floyd sat in his easy chair and reached for his pipe. "You broke her heart. She walked around like one of those mechanical robots for months afterward and couldn't seem to hold her head up."

Stanley lowered his eyes. "I'm not proud of what I did."

Straightening, Floyd confronted him head-on. "Why, man? What would make you do such a thing?"

Stanley shook his head, then pressed his hand to his mouth as another coughing fit seized him. When the attack subsided, he dropped his head to the back of the sofa. "It was the most despisable thing I've ever done."

The phone rang, and Floyd reached for the receiver. "Ayuh?" He listened, his eyes centered on Stanley. "I'll be over in a minute, hon. I needed to put some wood on the fire."

As he hung up the phone, he glanced at his guest. "I gotta get back. If I don't go over there and help Cleta tote her dishes home, she'll be over here dragging me out by the collar." His tone softened as he stared at the sick man. "Come on, Stan. Let me get you tucked into a warm bed. Things are gonna be okay, you wait and see."

A few moments later he had settled Stanley between musty smelling sheets. As he tossed a third blanket over the bed, he frowned. "You ought to see Dr. Marc."

"I'll . . . be . . . fine," Stanley assured him through clattering teeth. "God b-bless you, F-floyd."

"Well—" Floyd hesitated, his hands in his pockets. "At least let me fix you a cup of something hot before I go."

"Maybe . . . tea would . . . be nice."

Ten minutes later, as Floyd crossed the darkened lawn to return to the church, he glanced over his shoulder to look up at the attic window. Darkness had covered the island like a velvet cloak, but as long as Stanley didn't turn on a light, no one would know he'd arrived . . . none of the women, anyway, and the men would never tell. Of course, he'd have to tell Cleta soon, and she'd give him the very Jesse when she learned he'd slipped Stanley Bidderman into their spare guest room and tucked him beneath her mother's comforter.

Should he tell Vernie about his unexpected visitor? Years ago the two couples had shared a close friendship. When Stanley ran off, Cleta vowed to shoot him straight between the eyes if he ever stepped foot on the island again. She wouldn't, of course. The Good Book didn't hold with killing; and if Cleta was anything, she was a God-fearing woman. She liked to blow off steam every now and then, yet she was true blue when it came to Vernie. So the odds of her welcoming Stanley were slim to none.

But Stanley had been Floyd's friend. And though he didn't understand how any man could up and leave a woman without discussing his feelings, he reckoned there were a lot of things he didn't know about the Biddermans' past problems. What Stanley did wasn't right, not at all, but a man could change and after all these years maybe Stanley had seen the error of his ways. Why else would a sick man risk his life crossing a gale-tossed sea on a night not fit for man nor beast? People didn't do such things on a whim. They only took such risks if the matter concerned life and death—

Floyd halted in midstep, his mouth going dry. Was Stanley dying?

That had to be why he'd come back—Stan had a terminal illness. That's why he looked so thin and pale, and that was why he'd been begging Vernie to talk to him. He was trying to settle his earthly accounts before he coiled his ropes and stepped onto a heavenly shore.

Floyd sank to the concrete steps at the church's side door, his gut twisting. How could Stan be dying? They were about the same age. Though sometimes Floyd felt as though he'd just begun to live, they were all of an age now when anything could happen. Was it cancer? His heart? Floyd frowned, trying to remember Stanley's family history. The elder Mr. Bidderman, Stan's father, might have been but a young man when he died of heart problems—or was it the sea that got him?

Slipping through the church doorway, Floyd clutched his middle, realizing that either the gooseberry pie or the thought of Stanley's illness had soured his stomach. Probably the latter. But, sour stomach or not, he had to do something to help. You couldn't turn a dying man out into the cold, no matter how furiously your wife might protest his presence.

Another thought flitted through his mind then, one that had nothing to do with the dinner or Cleta. Over two thousand years ago, maybe on a cold night like this one, another man had sought shelter . . . for himself and his pregnant wife.

And he'd been given not an attic, but a stable.

Floyd lifted his chin, convinced he'd done the right thing. But, like the infant Jesus, Stanley might face the wrath of a ruler in a very short time. Cleta and Vernie didn't have the power of King Herod, but they might have power enough to make Stanley yearn to meet his Maker.

CHAPTER SIXTEEN

Hoarfrost fogged the north kitchen window-panes on Sunday morning. Despite a sour sensation in his stomach and aching muscles, Floyd rose with the sun, hoping to fix Stanley a breakfast tray before Cleta caught the scent of his secret.

He wasn't fast enough.

"Mornin', Floyd." Cleta wandered into the kitchen, scratching her chin and yawning. Curlers sprouted from her head like pink bean pods.

Floyd whirled from the microwave, hot water splashing from his mug onto his hand. "Good grief, woman! What'd you mean, sneaking up on me like that?"

Giving him a dour look, his wife plugged in the percolator. "Since when does coming into the kitchen constitute sneaking up on you?"

"You scared the willies out of me." Setting

the cup on the table, Floyd dropped in a tea bag, then stirred in three heaping teaspoons of sugar. Vernie watched, her eyes as wide as boiled eggs.

"Why are you drinking tea, Floyd?"

"No special reason." Floyd dropped the spoon as heat crept up his neck. "Just had a notion for a cup of hot tea. Is that a crime?"

Her eyes narrowed. "Tea's not, but using that much sugar might well be. You know there's a sugar shortage on the island—" Her jaw dropped, then snapped shut. "Why, the only man I ever knew to take three teaspoons of sugar in his tea was Stanley Bidderman. If you start acting like him—"

"I won't, Cleta. My stomach's a little tense, so I thought I'd try tea instead of coffee. So get breakfast on the table and leave me be."

Cleta snorted, then tossed her head and moved toward the pantry, her slippers flip-flopping against the linoleum.

Floyd glanced at the clock. He'd stopped into Stanley's room only to find that the man's temperature had risen to 102. If he didn't get some food in Stan, he'd never have the strength to face Vernie. And he had to face her, and soon, because Floyd couldn't keep him hidden away forever.

What would be good for a sick man? Something bland, maybe, and warm . . .

Lifting his chin, he called to Cleta. "I want cream of wheat this morning."

Cleta stepped backward out of the pantry, sleepily eyeing him over her shoulder. "You detest cream of wheat."

"Confound it, woman; I want cream of wheat!"

Their eyes met in a silent duel, then Cleta spoke in a clipped voice: "I don't have cream of wheat. I never buy it because you never eat it. How about oatmeal?"

"I reckon that'd do."

Snorting again, she stepped back into the pantry, mumbling loud enough for him to hear: "The man's got rocks in his head. Cream of wheat? Whatever's gotten into him?"

She fell silent as she came out of the pantry, then knelt to rattle pans in a cabinet. Finally she tossed a saucepan onto the stove and stood. "I'll have to do dishes before church, looks like. Vernie's coming over after the service to make candy, and that'll use every pan in the house."

Floyd froze. Vernie, here? World War III would break out if she discovered that Floyd

had offered Stanley amnesty. Without thinking, he blurted out, "You can't bring Vernie
over here."

Filling the pot with water, Cleta glanced
over her shoulder. "And why not?"

"Because . . . it's your turn to go over
there."

She gave him The Look.

"I mean it. It's Vernie's turn to host the
candy making. You two get to cackling and
I can't think . . . and I need quiet today. I'm
not feeling so good and I have to study for
finals."

Cleta spun the dial on the stove. "Finals,
my foot. That's a home correspondence
course, so you can take that test anytime."

"I can not! I need to have it in by January
fifteenth." He absently lifted the cup of tea to
his mouth and took a sip, then struggled to
keep a straight face. Man, how could anyone drink this syrup?

Lowering the cup, he trained his eyes on
his wife. "I need quiet today, that's all. I want
to be finished with my studies before Christmas, so I'll have free time to do family things."
He grinned. That should make her happy.

But a warning cloud had settled on his
wife's features. "There's no rush, Floyd, so

drink your tea and let me cook in peace. Russell and Barbara will be down any minute wanting their breakfast. I'll call you when the oatmeal is ready."

Picking up the mug of tea, he stood and moved to his wife's side. "You go on over to Vernie's and make that candy." He kept his voice low and level, the voice of a man who meant business. "I mean it, Cleta. I need peace and quiet this afternoon. I'm into the chapter on pistons, and as the feller says, they ain't easy to learn."

Carrying his mug, he stomped up the back stairs, hoping Cleta would assume he was going to sip his tea while getting dressed. He'd tiptoe up to the attic and leave it with Stanley, then come back and sneak the oatmeal up to the sick man, too. And then, after church—he sighed heavily as he stepped onto the landing and nodded good morning to his son-in-law. He had to get Cleta out of the house and Stanley back to good health before feathers hit the fan.

Across the street, in Frenchman's Fairest, Caleb was also preparing tea, but he served his in an heirloom silver service. His charge,

Olympia de Cuvier, stood at the window of the living room. Though she wore her best church dress, her thoughts seemed a long way from Sunday worship.

Stepping into the parlor with the tread of an aging mortal, Caleb set the tea tray down on a table. "Come away from the window, Missy," he said, lifting the delicate china cup and saucer. "Annie's most likely on her way back to Portland. You know she has to work tomorrow."

Sighing, Olympia dropped the lace curtain. She moved to the sofa and sat down, then accepted the cup of tea Caleb had poured. "So she isn't coming."

"Not today," Caleb said softly. "But for Christmas."

Olympia released a dignified huff. "Probably not—with my luck, the weather will stop her again. I might as well prepare myself." Her eyes moved to the lace-covered window. "We will be all alone this year."

Caleb offered her the sugar bowl. "Luck has nothing to do with it, Missy. And you're never alone. You have the Lord with you. And me." He softened his voice. "We'll be fine."

He glanced out the window. "The weather

is a bit windy. Would you like to take the carriage to church this morning?"

Olympia sighed as she spooned up a sugar cube. "No need for that. I'll walk." Her eyes grew wistful. "I was so hoping—"

"Don't borrow trouble; today has enough of its own." Dropping the lid on the sugar bowl, he smiled at her. "Miracles happen all the time. Why, just this morning I found two new blooms on Annie's tomato plants. Imagine that." He drew a deep breath as wind whistled down the fireplace chimney. "Two healthy blooms, surviving even a gale like this one." He smiled. "You see, Missy? Miracles happen when we least expect them."

"I need a miracle, Caleb." After only a perfunctory sip, Olympia set the cup aside and left the room.

An hour later, Vernie stepped through the doorway of the mercantile and blinked in the sting of the wind. The walk to church would be frigid, but there was no way she was going to get all sissified and drive a cart whenever the temperature dropped below forty degrees. She usually rode her scooter around town, but the church was only a five-minute walk and she could handle it without any problem, thank you very much. After all, she had a coat and scarf and hat to keep her warm.

She walked to the end of the porch, then paused for a glance at the ferry dock. The big boat was absent, as she'd feared it would be, but a solitary figure stood on the dock, dark against the mist rising off the waters. Olympia.

Vernie felt her heart twist. Olympia had always seemed like the original iron maiden, but with her husband just passed and Annie unable to come for the town's party . . .

Olympia might find this a difficult Christmas.

And so might Dr. Marc. His son hadn't made it to the party, either. The doc had put on a brave face, saying that Alex had been called away on an emergency, but Vernie hadn't missed the glimmer of regret in the doctor's eyes.

Life sure had a way of fouling things up. If it wasn't cranberries missing the boat, it was people.

She leaned against a porch post, wondering how long Olympia would stand on the wind-swept dock. She might be on her way to church, too, and if she came soon Vernie would offer to keep her company.

"There's no sense in standing there wishin'," Vernie whispered to the solitary figure in the distance. "The ferry's not coming, and wishin' won't change anything. The good Lord knows I'd done plenty of wishin' in my time, and none of it did me a bit of good."

Stuffing her hands in her pockets, she studied the frozen ground around the porch. Mud season would be upon them before they knew it, and the bitter cold of winter would fade into dim memories. Olympia's pain would fade, too, but there was no sense in telling her that now. When a body was shivering, tales of warm beaches and summer days weren't worth a flip.

Her own bitter memories had faded, though sometimes they crept up on her and caught her by surprise. She'd been caught when Stanley called the other day—the sound of his voice had grated across her nerves like nails across a chalkboard. Her pulse had begun to pound, and every coherent thought had stood up and marched right out of her brain . . .

Maybe Olympia was battling similar memories. One of Edmund's belongings, his voice on the answering machine, his scent in an old sweater—any of these things could have chased her out to the dock to be alone with her thoughts.

Vernie waited until her teeth began to chatter, then she stepped off the porch and walked to the church with brisk steps. Olympia would be okay in a little while. She would spend Christmas day with Caleb, doing her best to cope with memories too fresh to be of comfort and too sweet for tears.

Vernie grinned and waved as Elezar stepped out of the carriage house and began his own trek to the church. She would spend Christmas with him and MaGoo. If in the hubbub of celebration she found time for a quiet moment, she might allow herself to wonder why Stanley had called.

And why her dreams were haunted by a man for whom she no longer cared.

After Sunday supper, quiet filled the mercantile like a soothing fog. In the back room, Vernie relaxed in her chair, skimming the latest Vermont Country Store catalog. MaGoo curled next to the fire, soft snores resonating from the mound of fur. Elezar had gone off to church for his regular Sunday night meeting with the other Smith men. Vernie didn't know what the meetings were for, exactly, but she suspected pizza filled a major part of the agenda. Lately Abner Smith had taken to baking a huge one in the church basement every Sunday night.

Rows and rows of chocolate candies filled sheets of waxed paper in her kitchen, the results of her afternoon of candy making with Cleta. Come morning, she'd wrap the chocolates and put them into decorated tins as she did every year, and come Christmas Eve, she'd deliver a tin to every household in Heavenly Daze.

And, if things went well, the weather would let up sometime this week—enough for her to get over to Ogunquit and fetch the sugar, nutmeg, and cranberries the town needed for a proper celebration. Christmas wouldn't seem like Christmas without one of Birdie's traditional Saint James Puddings under her tree.

Outside the window, a mixture of snow and rain dripped from the eaves. Earlier she'd phoned Olympia and invited her over for a bowl of soup, but the widow declined, saying she wasn't feeling well. She added that Annie had given up and gone back to Portland. The two-hour trip had taken five because of worsening road conditions.

Despite Olympia's attempt to sound casual, Vernie knew she was upset. "It'll be okay," she said.

The statement didn't seem to register. "Spent all that money on a room this weekend," Olympia went on. "That's the trouble with young people these days; they never think twice about wasting good money."

Now Vernie had Andy Rooney for company, and he was well on his way to wrapping up *60 Minutes*. She liked Andy. Seemed like a down-to-earth sort of fella.

The phone jangled.

Stirring, she fumbled for the receiver. "Mooseleuk's."

"Vernie?" Cleta's voice came over the wire. "I'm on my way over for Pepto-Bismol and Advil. Floyd's sick as a dog."

Vernie sat up straighter, trying to clear her drowsy brain. "Sure, come right on. What's wrong with him?"

"Flu, I suspect. Woke up from his nap with a high fever and he's chilling."

Vernie hung up, then shoved herself out of her chair with a groan. This cold was murder on old bones.

Padding downstairs, she pulled bottles of Pepto-Bismol and Advil from the shelf and dropped them in a bag. Unlocking the door a few minutes later, she handed the items to Cleta.

Wind whistled through the crack, penetrating her thin sweater. "Thanks," Cleta said, her teeth chattering. "Add it to our tab, will you?"

"Sure. And let me know if I can do anything to help."

"Ayuh." Cleta turned and hurried back across the street, hunching into the wind.

By eight o'clock Vernie was sitting with a bowl of popcorn, ready for the CBS Sunday night movie, a feature starring James Garner and Julie Andrews. The phone jangled again.

She reached for the receiver. "Mooseleuk's."

Cleta's worried voice met her ears. "Vernie, I hate to ask but Floyd's awful sick and I'm afraid to leave him. Can you bring me a box of Epsom salts? I need to get him in the tub and bring his fever down."

Vernie cast a longing glance at the television. Jim and Julie would have to wait. "I'll be right over." After hanging up, she set the VCR to record and punched the button. Five minutes later, after layering on sweater, coat, hat, gloves, and boots, she left the mercantile and trudged toward the bed and breakfast with a box of Epsom salts.

Cleta was waiting by the back door to let her in. "I've never seen Floyd so sick," she said.

"You want me to fetch Dr. Marc?"

"Floyd insists it isn't necessary, but if the salts don't bring the fever down, I'm going to have to call him. You want to come in and warm up before you go back?"

Vernie hedged. The last thing she wanted was a case of flu. Once the flu got started, it would tear through the island like greased lightning. Maybe it already had begun—after all, Birdie had been in to buy Tylenol or something for Salt up at the lighthouse . . .

"Cleeeeeeta." Floyd's weak voice echoed down the stairway. "I neeeed youuuuuu."

Reaching for Vernie's arm, Cleta pulled her into the warm kitchen. "Stay here a minute. I'll see what he wants." Then she was off, muttering something about sick men being such babies . . .

Vernie shifted her weight from foot to foot, listening to the television blaring from the parlor. Someone was watching the Sunday night movie.

She moved closer to the doorway, aiming to sneak a peek. Russell and Barbara sat on the sofa with their backs to her, while on the television James Garner sat wedged in the front seat of a sports car with Julie Andrews behind the wheel. Oh, this was going to be good! If Cleta didn't need her she would go on back—

Cleta appeared, tight-lipped. "Pigheaded man," she said, stomping down the stairs. "Care for a cup of coffee while you're here?"

Vernie pointed toward the door. "I'll get on back. I kinda wanted to watch the movie."

Again Floyd's voice rolled down the staircase. "Cleeeeeta. Can you get me a glass of juiccccce?"

The women's eyes met. "I'm going to kill him," Cleta said.

"He's sick," Vernie reminded her. "Remember when you had that gallbladder attack last summer? Floyd went all the way to Boston to get that brand of vanilla ice cream you wanted." She nudged Cleta toward the stairs. "I'll get the juice; you take care of your man."

A few moments later Vernie walked past Barbara and Russell—who remained oblivious—and carried a glass of orange juice up the stairs. Pausing in front of Cleta's bedroom door, she called, "I have the juice."

Cleta thrust her head through the doorway and took the glass. "Can you bring me some extra blankets? They're up in the spare attic bedroom."

"No problem." As Vernie turned toward the seldom-used attic stairs, she heard Cleta yell, "Floyd! Get back in that tub! What's gotten into you?"

Searching for blankets, Vernie walked into the attic bedroom and headed immediately for the closet. Two blankets sat on the top shelf, but they were on the thin side, and a person with fever could get terribly chilled, especially in weather like this. May as well take the comforter from the bed, too.

She dropped the folded blankets into a guest chair, then turned and frowned at the rumpled bed. Lumpy and bumpy, it looked for all the world like neither Barbara nor Cleta had found time to clean since their last guest. She sniffed. The air was stale, too, and a tray of dirty dishes sat on the floor near the door.

"My, my," she murmured, bending to grasp the edge of the comforter. "Cleta must be slipping a little." She gave a yank, pulling in one smooth movement, and in that instant a body shot up from the bed, hair waving atop its head, shrunken chest looking like that of a dead man, and blue boxer shorts—

A man!

Vernie screamed and closed her eyes, unable to bear the sight. This intruder must have sneaked into the house while Floyd and Cleta were at church, and he was hiding out in this room—

"Heavenly days!" a voice croaked. "Can't a man get some sleep in this place?"

Vernie halted in midscreech. Opening one eye, she peered at the apparition and shuddered when she realized the apparition was peering back.

Oh, my. This was no intruder—it was Stanley Bidderman. Older, thinner, and balder, but unmistakably the rat.

Time froze as Vernie collided with her past. For a long moment she stared, then her anger rose in a full-throttled rush.

"Floyd Lansdown," she shrieked, dropping the comforter to the floor. Without missing a step, she trotted down the attic stairs and burst headlong into Floyd's sickroom. Cleta nearly dropped the glass of orange juice she was force-feeding her robe-wrapped husband. "Why do you have that man in your house?"

Stanley followed a few minutes later, his eyes as dark as two burnt holes in a blanket.

Forgetting Floyd, Vernie turned on her long-lost husband. "What are you doing here, Stanley Bidderman?"

Stanley lifted his hands in a don't-shoot pose. "Now listen, Vernie, I can explain—"

"Floyd!" Cleta exploded. "Did you know Stanley was in the attic bedroom? How long have you had him hidden up there?"

Floyd rolled over in bed and covered his head with both arms. "I'm siiiiick, Cleta. Have mercy."

"Behind my back, you brought that—that—" Running out of words, Cleta thumped out of the room and down the stairs. While Vernie sputtered and turned her fury upon Stanley, Cleta returned a moment later with Floyd's grandpa's ten-gauge shotgun. At the sight of the weapon, Floyd struggled out of bed and began to wrestle with his wife.

"Cleta Lansdown, have you lost your mind? Give me that!"

"Don't you touch this gun, Floyd! I took a vow, and Stanley has this coming!"

As Vernie yelled and shook her fist at her bewildered husband, Russell entered the room and demanded, "Where's the fire?" Barbara hovered in the hallway, timidly peering around her husband's frame.

Russell snapped his suspenders into place. "Mom, put the shotgun away. You could hurt someone!"

"I'm gonna put the fear of God in him!"

"Sweetums, you have to listen, ah-ah-achoo!"

"Cleeeeeta! Be reasonable!"

"You're sick, Floyd! Be quiet! Stanley, get over here and take your medicine like a man!"

And while the Lansdown household wrestled and yelled and thundered over the floor, Vernie separated herself from the commotion and stared at the scene, then shook her head.

For this she was missing the Sunday night movie? Sighing, she turned and left the room, then took the stairs one slow step at a time.

She had some serious thinking to do.

"There, now. That ought to hold you awhile." Elezar gave MaGoo an affectionate pat as he watched the cat lick a bowl of cream. The pudgy feline purred, leaving the treat long enough to affectionately rub the length of the man's leg.

"Yes, you're a good ol' kitty—"

Elezar shot straight up when the front door opened and slammed so hard the percussion toppled a display of cardboard Christmas trees standing on the counter.

MaGoo hissed, his four legs stiffening as his fur stood on end.

Vernie filled the doorway, her cap perched unevenly on the top her head, her earflaps hanging lopsided. Steam rolled out of the wool plaid collar.

Eyes widening, Elezar dropped the can of cream, splattering the sticky contents over the floor and MaGoo's back.

"My goodness . . . Vernie?" Elezar took a tentative step forward. "Is something wrong?"

"Wrong?" Snatching the hat off her head, Vernie marched through the store, shoving displays out of her way. Cans of tomatoes and tuna crashed to the floor. An apple barrel overturned. MaGoo bolted for cover.

Muttering under her breath, Vernie shrugged off her coat and threw it in the general direction of the closet. She peeled off her galoshes, and then stomped back to the counter where she uncapped a thirty-two-ounce bottle of Coke and poured a tall glass, adding a splash of vanilla. She took a long, deliberate swig, lowered the glass, then added another dash. While Elezar held his breath, she drank the heavily-laced Coke and drummed her fingers on the counter as if she could drive her nails through the pine.

Elezar stood by, uncertain. Vernie was upset, but why? A simple errand of mercy shouldn't have aroused this kind of irritation.

Vernie took another long drink, her throat bobbing with each swallow. After a deep gulp, her gaze fixed on him. "Do you know who's sleeping in the Lansdowns' attic?"

Elezar felt a frown creep onto his face. "Do Floyd and Cleta have guests?"

"Do they!" Vernie eyed him, tossing down another swallow. When she finished, she belched, then wiped her mouth with the corner of her sleeve.

Expectancy hovered on Elezar's face as he waited for her to continue. She'd been in a good mood earlier—watching TV and relaxing. What could have lit her fuse?

"Vernie?" he prompted.

"What?"

"Do the Lansdowns have a guest?"

Vernie slammed her glass down on the counter. "There I was, minding my own business and getting extra blankets for Floyd who's sick as a goose that's eaten ripe peaches. I was doing the Christian thing, pitching in when somebody's down and out."

Elezar nodded. "Stomach flu?"

"Head, stomach, you name it." Vernie picked up the soda bottle and refilled her glass. "Judas!" she yelled. The clerk jumped when she slammed the bottle to the counter. His eyes scanned the room for a suspect. Judas? What had gotten into her?

"Judas!" she reiterated, splashing more syrup into her drink.

Elezar inched forward. "Excuse me, Vernie . . . have I done something to upset you?"

"Not you. Him." Vernie sputtered (highly irregular for Vernie). Now Elezar noticed that she was shaking, her hand unsteady as she lifted the glass back to her mouth. Crossing the floor, he took her by the shoulders and gently steered her to a nearby bench. She sat down with a stunned look on her face, and then her tongue loosened.

"There he was, Elezar. Big as life, hunched under the covers, feverish and talking out of his head. After all these years—can you imagine? I should have known he'd try something like this—but how did he get here?" Vernie's eyes darted to the front window where sleet pelted the pane. "The Devil himself couldn't get across in this kind of weather."

The woman wasn't making a lick of sense. "Who?" Elezar asked, sinking to the bench beside her. "Who was under the covers feverish and talking out of his mind?"

The fight suddenly drained out of her. She slumped, and Elezar caught her, holding her tightly for a moment. Whatever was wrong was bad wrong, he decided. Trivial matters didn't upset Vernie.

"What is it?" he asked softly. "What has you so distressed?"

Emotion clogged her voice. "Stanley. Stanley's at the Lansdowns'." She looked up, tears rolling from her eyes. "Did you know, Elezar? Did you know Floyd invited Stanley into his home?"

Elezar's heart ached. "I knew."

Hurt shone from Vernie's red-rimmed eyes. "And you didn't warn me?"

"No, I didn't."

"Why?"

Elezar shook his head. "It wasn't my place to warn you, Vernie. But you have to face him. Whether tonight or tomorrow or the day after. This is a matter only you can settle."

Shrugging out of his hold, Vernie crossed her arms. "Why is he here?"

"You would have to ask Mr. Bidderman."

"Oh, I know why." Vernie tipped her head back and took a deep breath. "He's here to beg my forgiveness."

Elezar let the words echo in the empty store a moment, then he whispered, "You don't know that."

"Oh, I do know that." She drummed her fingers on her knee. "He thinks I'm angry, but I'm not angry."

Elezar kept quiet. Unacknowledged and suppressed emotion often hindered the ability to forgive. And Vernie had harbored a horde of pain and hurt for years.

"I'll tell you one thing—I can't forget. He can't expect me to just smile and say hello as if nothing had ever happened."

The clerk nodded.

"And someone has to pay," she murmured.

Elezar scratched his head. Who had to pay? Stanley? Vernie? Elezar longed to remind her that every argument had two sides. But he remained silent. He was not there to judge, but to minister.

She shoved up from the bench. "If Stanley is here to ask forgiveness, he doesn't know me. He doesn't understand how a woman's need for justice differs from a man's need for . . . whatever."

"Men and women aren't so different," Elezar pointed out. "Everyone seeks justice. And everyone needs forgiveness."

"There is no justice in this situation. Stanley walked out on me. Period. I didn't walk out on him. I'm living with the memories, not him. I can't forgive myself for being such a fool. I shouldn't even try."

"Is forgiveness not an option?"

Vernie shrugged the suggestion aside. "I'm not the forgiving kind."

Elezar closed his eyes a moment, seeking direction from the Spirit. "Forgiving someone who violated your trust doesn't mean pretending nothing ever happened." He worked gently now.

"If I forgave him, God forbid, he would only walk out again. I know his kind."

"Yet he was a trusted husband and your confidant for years, wasn't he?"

"Until he decided to go out and forget he ever knew me." She walked to the counter and pounded it with her fist. "Not one word—all these years, not one word! And now I find him in my best friend's house, cozy as a bug in a rug in their attic bedroom, and not one person thought to inform me the rat was back in his nest."

Elezar tilted his head. "I understand Stanley is very ill."

"My sentiments exactly."

"Physically ill," Elezar said, a note of reproach in his voice.

"He's going to be more than physically ill when I get my hands on him." Straightening, she pushed her empty glass aside.

"Then you do plan to see him?"

"Certainly not. I wouldn't waste the time of day on that man."

"How will you know what he wants if you refuse to talk to him?"

Vernie whirled on him with a flash of defensive spirit. "I know what he wants. He wants what all men want after their little midlife fling. Forgiveness from the dutiful wife. Well, let me tell you something, Elezar Smith. Forgiveness is a journey; the deeper the wound, the longer the journey. My wounds are so deep it would take an angel and a Ditch Witch to unearth them. Stanley can't just waltz in here after all these years and pretend all is forgiven. Life doesn't work that way."

"But, Vernie! His purpose for coming may be something entirely different—"

Her features hardened. "I know one thing—I'll never speak to Floyd Lansdown again. He's responsible for this fiasco, and I'm going to find out what part Cleta's played in the whole mess, too!"

Whirling, she stomped toward the stairway, leaving Elezar to wearily view her ascent.

Oh, Vernie, he pleaded silently. *When humans forgive, they set a prisoner free . . . and the one released is not the forgiven, but the one who forgives.*

CHAPTER SEVENTEEN

On Wednesday morning, Salt slipped another log into the woodstove, then latched the iron door and slowly rose from his knees. The lighthouse seemed preternaturally silent without the children—in the past few months, he'd grown used to their laughter and arguments, even the quiet sounds of their breathing at night. He'd intended to keep them only until Patrick got help, but how could he adjust to the silence if they left?

On the other hand, what if Patrick never got his act together? The boy could be sitting over in that filthy apartment right now, a full bottle in his hand and an empty heart in his chest. Salt loved the children, but Birdie Wester had been right about one thing—he was seventy years old. Though he felt strong and capable, every day his aching body and weakening eyes reminded him that man's days are numbered, his strength a finite thing . . .

After moving to the kitchen sink, he washed the soot off his hands and stared out the window at a snowy landscape. The children were playing in front of the light-house, just as he'd told them. Bobby wore the puffy blue snowsuit Birdie had found at a yard sale in Ogunquit; Brittany's was the color of a ripe orange and made her look like a pumpkin. But both outfits were down-filled and certain to keep the kids warm.

In the past week and a half, Birdie had become Salt's lifeline. Before the weather stopped the ferry, she'd gone over to the mainland and picked up what he needed for the children, and she'd been careful, she assured him, to buy things from folks who didn't know her. Now nearly every day she brought something nice for him or the kids— new books, something tasty from the bakery, a couple of boxes of medicated tissues when Brittany got the sniffles.

She'd even begun to read up on light-houses. The Heavenly Daze lighthouse, she informed Salt, had been built in 1898 and immediately fitted with a Fresnel lens and electricity. "That's the best kind of lens in the world," she told him, lifting her chin, "and I happen to know that this one uses a thousand-watt bulb—that's equal to the brightness of 449,000 candles."

Salt laughed. "What are you trying to do, woman, impress me?"

Twin stains of scarlet appeared on her cheeks. "Maybe," she'd said, smiling. "Just a little."

Salt shut off the water and wiped his hands on a dishtowel, then leaned on the counter and smiled at the children's antics. Bobby was trying to build a snowman, but the ball he'd rolled looked more like an egg than a sphere. In an effort to help, Brittany was packing snow onto the top, caking the white stuff into her knitted mittens. Tallulah and Butch, the bulldog that lived in town, were barking and biting the snow.

Salt bit his lip. He'd told the kids they could play outside for half an hour, no more. Though he could well understand how active children could go stir-crazy living in a one-room house, the weather was too cold and the risk of discovery too great to allow them outside much longer.

Still, it did them good to play like this, and it did his heart good to see them having fun.

Tomorrow he'd give them some pointers on how to shape a snowball, maybe even dig out an old scarf and corncob pipe. Working together, the three of them could build a perfectly lovely snowman—

He swallowed. No, they couldn't. Though the townspeople didn't often come up to Puffin Cove in the winter, he never knew when one of them might take a notion to walk up and stand by the rocks or look for puffins on the shore. And if they saw a snowman in front of the lighthouse, they'd think the lightkeeper had gone daffy.

Movement from the south caught his eye. Salt drew nearer to the window, pressing his hand against the glass as he struggled to see around the corner. A golf cart was slowly spinning up the snow-covered path, its vinyl cover glaring in the sun.

It might be Birdie. Then again, it might not.

Salt pounded on the glass, but the children didn't hear. For an instant he thought about raising the sash, but the storm window beyond that had a tendency to stick.

He sprinted toward the door, his heart pounding. "Bob! Brittany!" He stepped out into the crisp cold and waved for their attention. "Quick! Come inside!"

Without hesitation the children moved away from the mounded snow and lumbered toward him, two padded figures in bright colors. Bobby turned to see who was coming, but Salt threw an arm around the boy's shoulder, pulled him into the house, and slammed the door.

"What if it's Miss Birdie?" Bobby asked, a note of wistfulness in his voice. "She might be bringing us some more gingerbread."

"Or some Werther's Originals," Brittany added, a flicker of longing in her eyes.

"I'm not expecting Birdie today," Salt said, motioning toward the bathroom. "Now, both of you, go in there and take off your wet things."

"But if it's Miss Birdie—," Brittany began.

"If it's Miss Birdie, you can come out. But if it's not, you'll stay put. Go, now."

Like little soldiers they marched into the bathroom while Salt pressed his ear to the wooden door. The golf cart had crunched to a halt outside, the two dogs were barking, and someone was taking their sweet time about coming up to knock.

Salt reached for his rifle. This past summer, right after the children arrived, two yuppie couples from Manhattan had pulled up in a rented golf cart and demanded to tour the lighthouse. They seemed to think it was a public building and theirs for the taking. Salt hadn't hesitated to blast the ground in front of their toes. The horrified look on their faces had been worth the $7.69 it cost him for rock salt and lima beans.

Good thing he'd repacked the rifle. Through the peephole he could see Floyd Lansdown and Winslow Wickam, the persistent preacher, unzipping themselves from the cart. They seemed to be having trouble getting clear of the dogs.

"You kids stay in that bathroom," Salt barked, then he opened the door.

The wintry wind hit him like a fist, or perhaps it was fear shriveling the flesh around his belly. He brought the rifle up and held it in both hands, his trigger finger resting lightly at the point where the stock met the firing mechanism. Only a fool could misread his intention, but Lansdown and Wickam kept coming, their heads encased in caps and earflaps, their faces red above their neck scarves.

"Morning, Cap'n," Floyd called, clapping his gloved hands together as he approached.

"Heard you'd been sick. I was poorly, too, and this is my first day outta bed."

Salt didn't answer but shifted his jaw as he chewed the soft flesh inside his mouth.

"I hope you're feeling better," the preacher called, coming up from the other side of the cart. The bulldog followed at his heels. "We came out to see if we could offer some assistance."

Salt bit down hard, catching a flap of skin between his teeth and causing blood to flow. He waited until the men drew closer, then worked up a good spit and let them have it. The bloody glob landed on the snow at Lansdown's feet, stopping him as neatly as any blast of salt-and-limas.

"Good heavens, man!" Lansdown cried, staring at the mess in the snow. "Are you coughing up blood?"

"Let me call the paramedics," Wickam said, coming closer. "Let's get you inside, and we'll fetch you some help—"

"Stop right there." Salt brought the gun down, level with the preacher's quilted jacket. "I'm not sick and I don't need your help. Don't have a phone, and I don't want anybody meddlin' up here."

Blanching, Floyd took a half-step back. "Put that gun away, Salt, what are you tryin' to do? As mayor and caretaker of all municipal property, I thought it was my responsibility to come up here and make certain the lighthouse is functioning properly. After all, if you've been ailin'—"

"The light is fine," Salt drawled, "not that you'd know anything about it."

Stiffening, Floyd took another step back. "I happen to be quite mechanical. I'm taking a correspondence course—"

"Salt didn't mean any insult, Floyd," the pastor interrupted, his voice dry.

Floyd's chin jutted forward. "Don't care. Birdie said you were almost human these days, but apparently she's as psycho as you are. How anybody could expect the town lunatic to change is beyond me."

Turning, he tromped back toward the cart, but Winslow Wickam was not as easily dissuaded. Pressing his hands together like a child saying prayers, he gave Salt a soft-eyed smile. "Cap'n Gribbon, I know this life must sometimes be unbearably lonely for you. Won't you let us come in? You might discover that you've missed having regular companionship with other human beings. And certainly the Lord longs to fellowship with you—"

"God and I are already on speaking terms, thank you very much." Salt shifted the barrel of the rifle toward the pastor. "So good day, Reverend. Now you'd better hurry and get in that cart, 'cause the walk back to town is a fairly good piece."

Wickam turned, and his mouth opened when he saw that Lansdown had already put the golf cart in reverse. The minister ran toward the vehicle, waving one hand and shouting, while Tallulah and Butch nipped at his heels. Salt kept the rifle trained on his visitors until they had rounded the corner and were lost to his sight.

Sighing, he stepped back into the lighthouse and propped the rifle in the corner. Rock salt and lima beans wouldn't pack a lethal punch, especially on a man dressed in layers of winter padding. But it could sure sting exposed flesh, and the sound of the blast could rattle a body's nerves . . .

And quite possibly scare a child.

Salt latched the door behind him, safe with his secret and relieved he hadn't had to fire the weapon. No sense in spoiling a perfect winter day.

*   *   *

Vernie sat in her bedroom window and watched the snow fall. Three days ago she had been mad enough to spit at Stanley Bidderman. Now her anger had cooled and melancholy had set in—a deep ache for things that might have been. Perhaps she was wrong in refusing to see Stanley. Cleta had sent word that Stanley was slowly improving, and could Vernie find it in her heart to hear him out?

Vernie could not. Not yet. Maybe never.

Then again, maybe Elezar was right. Maybe she ought to at least hear what he had to say, even though she wasn't the slightest bit interested. Their years together had been good for the most part. She smiled when she recalled the two-pound box of Fannie Mae's they'd eaten on a dare one evening. Stanley claimed he could eat more chocolate than her, and she'd said, "In a pig's eye." After polishing off the entire box, they hadn't been able to look a chocolate in the eye for years afterward.

They both liked thin crust pizza with Canadian bacon and green peppers.

Dagwood and Blondie had been their

comic strip of choice—they fought over the funnies every Sunday morning.

They each took three teaspoons of sugar in their coffee, followed by a dollop of cream.

They favored vinegar and mustard in potato salad, celery stuffed with peanut butter, and cutesy cards as opposed to gushy ones. Guests and backyard cookouts were frequently enjoyed at the mercantile in their early days. Vernie would bake for a week getting ready for Saturday night open house. Friday nights, weather permitting, they played Monopoly and Rook with a couple in Ogunquit, and then later with Floyd and Cleta and Olympia and Edmund—before Olympia got so uppity.

Vernie closed her bleary eyes, resting her forearm on her forehead. Those had been good years. Why did things have to change? Why couldn't life stay good? Most of all, why hadn't Stanley remembered all the good times when he decided to leave?

Why couldn't she eat a Fannie Mae chocolate without getting the sniffles?

A headache pounded at the base of her skull, threatening to batter her brain. She massaged the tender spot, wondering where she'd put the Advil. The unrelenting cold made every bone in her body ache, and the older she got, the worse it seemed to affect her . . .

A soft knock interrupted her musings. "Yes?"

"Are you all right, Vernie?" Elezar's inquiry penetrated the heavy wood. "You're usually downstairs by now."

"I'm not feeling up to par this morning. We're not busy, are we?"

"Nary a customer yet. You rest for a while. I'll call you if you're needed."

"Thank you, Elezar."

"Can I get you anything? Hot tea? Juice?"

"A new body." She was too old for her own good.

She heard Elezar's chuckle on the other side of the door. "In due time, Vernie. In due time."

Vernie stretched out across the bed and pulled a crocheted afghan up to her neck. Elezar was so good to her. What would she do without him? His capacity for human kindness and forgiveness far exceeded hers.

She shivered as a sudden chill set her teeth to chattering. The bedroom was as cold as Pharaoh's tomb this morning. As goose bumps welled, she sat up and turned the electric mattress pad up to 14. Crawling between the sheets she'd left an hour earlier, she reached for a book on the nightstand and read a random devotional thought: "We do not forgive because we are supposed to; we forgive when we are ready to be healed."

Sighing, she dropped the book. Was she ready to forgive? Not now, surely, but maybe when she felt a little stronger.

Right now she felt as though she needed to sleep for a nice, long time—like maybe a week.

CHAPTER EIGHTEEN

As a black-and-white puffin flew overhead, Bobby squinted, then gasped as the bird dove into the water, as fearless as an Olympic diver. Eager to see if the puffin would surface, Bobby ran to the rocks, ignoring Brittany's breathless cries to wait.

From here, at the northernmost point of the island, he could see cream-colored lines of surf rolling in across the rocky beach. The grandfather said they could not swim here even in summer, for the rocks were sharp and the currents treacherous. That's why the lighthouse stood atop the hill, to warn sailors away. "Don't you be thinking about getting into the water anywhere," the grandfather told him right after he and Britt arrived on Heavenly Daze. "I'm not as young as I once was, and I can't be jumpin' in to save you all the livelong day."

Shading his eyes with his hand, Bobby

scanned the sea, hoping for a sign of the diving puffin. Several of the small birds bobbed on the surface, apparently at ease in the cold water. They didn't worry about rocks or currents.

For a moment Bobby wished he were a puffin. They were funny little birds, but good swimmers as well as fliers. If he were a puffin, he could fly home to his daddy and make sure everything was okay, then he could swim back to the lighthouse so the grandfather wouldn't be lonely. He'd spend Mondays and Wednesdays and Fridays with his daddy, and live at the lighthouse on Tuesdays and Thursdays and Saturdays—

He stopped to count on his fingers. What to do with Sunday?

Brittany clambered over the rocks and stood below him, her nose making a funny little squeak with each breath.

"Grandfather will be mad if he sees you up there," she warned. Her nose whistled as she inhaled. "He'll make us come in. If you make him mad, you might get smacked."

"The grandfather doesn't smack."

"Well, then . . . he might send us back."

Bobby froze, his outstretched hand before his eyes. This was another of Brittany's fibs; she was just talking. But what would happen if the grandfather got mad? Would he send them back? Bobby didn't want to go—at least, not to stay. He wanted to check on Daddy, that was all.

But if climbing on the rocks could make the grandfather mad enough to send them back—

"I'll come down," he said, squatting. He sat on his bottom, then slid over the ice-glazed rock, feeling the cold through the slick surface of his snowsuit.

He landed smoothly, his sneakers hitting the sand with a soft thud, and when he lifted his eyes, he saw that they were no longer alone. Britt turned, peering out of her hood, then she saw, too. "Oh," she said. "It's you."

Though a powder blue snowsuit encased the boy standing before them from head to toe, it wasn't hard to recognize Georgie Graham's round cheeks and sparkling brown eyes. The grin, too, was familiar, except now a gap appeared in what had been a perfect row of stumpy white teeth.

Brittany noticed the difference right away. "You lost a tooth," she said, pointing to the space in Georgie's smile.

"I know." Georgie's grin widened. "Got a quarter for it from the tooth angel."

Britt giggled. "The tooth angel? That's silly. It's a tooth fairy! I see him on TV all the time."

Georgie shook his head. "Uh-uh. Zuriel told me all about the tooth angel who lives on Heavenly Daze. Since God knows when even a puffin falls to the ground, he certainly knows when a boy loses a tooth. So at night, when a boy is fast asleep, the tooth angel will slip in and leave a quarter under his pillow."

"That's not right." Brittany spoke in a matter-of-fact tone. "I saw the tooth fairy on TV. He's a little man with a bald head, and he wears a tutu and walks around telling people they aren't brushing good enough—"

"Hush, Britt." For no reason he could name, Bobby lost patience with his sister. "That's TV, and TV is not real life. Heavenly Daze is real, so if Georgie says there's a tooth angel, there must be."

"I gots the quarter to prove it." Georgie's mittened hand reached into his pocket, then extracted a shiny coin.

Bobby and Brittany stepped closer and stared at the money, then Bobby nodded.

"That's proof, all right. I believe you." He looked at his sister. "I never got nothing from the tooth fairy."

Britt pointed to the backpack hanging from Georgie's shoulders. "Whatcha got in the sack?"

"My paints." Georgie shifted the bag and held it before his chest. "I have a tablet, watercolors, some brushes, and some crackers. Goldfish."

Brittany gave Georgie a smile that proved she'd forgiven him for being right about the tooth angel. "I love goldfish crackers."

Georgie nodded. "We can sit somewhere and eat while we paint. But not here—it's too cold."

He turned and looked toward the lighthouse, but Bobby shook his head. "We're not supposed to bring anybody inside."

Georgie pointed toward the town. "Then there."

Britt shook her head. "We're not supposed to go into town, either. We're a secret."

"You don't have to go into town." Georgie hefted his backpack across his shoulder and took a confident step forward. "There's the bathroom, and no one ever goes there in the winter. But there's a place to sit on the sidewalk, and a roof, and no one will bother us."

Bobby looked at Brittany for a moment. He remembered the brick building that housed the public rest rooms. It stood right next to the lobster restaurant and across from the fire station. But there were no fires, and the restaurant was closed, so even though the bathrooms were in town, they were still far enough out that the grandfather shouldn't mind . . .

"Let's go," Bobby said, leading the way.

CHAPTER NINETEEN

"Jooooooy to the worrrrrrld, the Lord is cooooooome."

Birdie made a face as she poured flour into the mixing bowl. Abner's song might be a joyful noise, but it was still noise. The baker couldn't carry a tune in the proverbial bucket.

"Abner," she called, checking her recipe book. "Did we use up that entire tin of nutmeg already? I'm making Saint James Puddings for Christmas gifts, but I'll need nutmeg."

Abner stopped singing long enough to give her a frown. "I thought we got plenty when Vernie's order finally came in."

"Well, the new tin is empty, and I'm almost out of cloves, too. Better call Vernie and tell her we need more—I'm going to need allspice, too, for these puddings."

Birdie blew her bangs out of her eyes and

wiped her hand on her apron. The recipe for Saint James Pudding came straight from the 1896 *Fannie Farmer Cookbook*, and she'd been gifting her neighbors with the traditional puddings, neatly packaged in buttered one-pound baking-powder boxes, for nearly thirty years. She'd thought her troubles were over when Vernie's supplies came in on Wednesday, but apparently she hadn't ordered enough. Either that, or Abner had gone spice-happy in the last few days.

"Joy to Vernie Bidderman," she muttered, closing the recipe book with an emphatic snap. "This time the spices had better come quick, or nobody on Heavenly Daze is going to get their Christmas pudding from Birdie's Bakery."

Abner opened his mouth, probably about to utter one of his consistently optimistic proverbs, but the jangling of the bell cut him off. Birdie walked toward the counter, grateful for the interruption. Sometimes she didn't feel like being optimistic and cheery. Today she felt more like Scrooge—one who'd be happy to steal some nutmeg, if she could only find it.

Babette Graham had entered the store, and she greeted Birdie with a worried frown.

"How be you," she said, setting her macramé purse on the counter. "I'm glad you're in."

"We're always in when the weather's this cold," Abner joked, energetically rolling out a piecrust.

Birdie ignored him. "Are you wanting some doughnuts, Babette? Wait—I think we have some of those fried apple pies your Charles is so fond of."

"I'll take a couple," Babette said offhandedly, her pretty mouth set in a frown. "But I really wanted to talk to you."

Her tone sent a tremor up Birdie's spine. "Nothing wrong at your house, I hope?"

Babette tilted her head. "That's what I'd like to know. I'm a little worried."

Birdie glanced at Abner, who winked and lifted his hands from the rolling pin long enough to make a go-on motion. Birdie nodded.

"Let me pour us both a cup of cider," she said, moving toward the stove where a saucepan simmered. "Abner keeps a pot warm for occasions like this. We'll sit out there at the chairs and you can tell me all about it."

Babette sighed and moved toward one of

the tables at the front of the store, shedding her coat as she went. Birdie ladled cider into two china teacups, then placed them on saucers and carried them out to the table.

Babette had pulled a sheaf of folded papers from her purse. Now she stared at them as if the source of the world's trouble lay revealed on those pages.

Slipping into the chair across from Babette, Birdie eyed the papers. "What do you have there? The mortgage?"

Babette smiled and shook her head. "Nothing so grown up, I'm afraid. Look at these—they're paintings of Georgie's."

Bemused, Birdie took the pictures and unfolded them. The tempura paint cracked as she bent the page, and the mingled scents of paint and paper reminded her of long-ago mornings in Sunday school, when she and Bea had painted pictures of Calvary and Sunshine Mountain . . .

These paintings, she noticed, were of puffins. That was nothing unusual, because Georgie had always displayed a fondness for the birds. So why was Babette disturbed?

Birdie lay the three sheets on the table, then spread her hands over them to keep the bent pages from returning to their folded shape. "Three puffin paintings," she said, wondering what Babette had seen in them. "So—Georgie's exhibiting a penchant for puffins again?" She lowered her head to meet Babette's troubled gaze. "Is that bad news? I know the boy gave you fits last month, but I thought you all were past that trouble by now."

"It's not the paintings that concern me— well, not in particular. Look at them, Birdie. Look how different they are."

Birdie looked again. They were different, she supposed, though to her one child's painting looked pretty much like another's. Each featured a blue sky, a black-and-white bird, and rolling ocean waves. One of the paintings was more detailed, it seemed, and one appeared brighter than the others.

Then she saw it. One painting had been initialed with Georgie's customary *G*; the other two were signed with a *B*.

She crinkled a brow.

"You see?" Babette leaned closer and pointed to the *B* in one picture. "I asked Georgie why he put a *B* on this picture, and he said he didn't paint it."

A warning spasm gripped Birdie's throat.

"If he didn't paint it," she forced the words out, "then who did?"

"A boy named Bob." Babette's voice went as flat as Abner's singing. "And the other one was painted by a girl named Brittle-knees. Remember? His imaginary playmates."

Birdie took a deep breath and felt bands of tightness in her chest. "Well," she began, staring at the *B*s at the bottom of each painting, "there's no real harm in having imaginary playmates, is there? I'm no expert on child rearing, but it seems to me that creativity is a healthy thing, especially when a child is the only little boy living on this island—"

Her throat closed; she couldn't go on. But Babette seemed not to notice her reluctance.

"I'm so frightened, Birdie! What if this is a sign of multiple personalities? What will I do if one night he tells me that he's Bob? Or Brittle-knees?" She groaned and pressed her hand to her face. "Merciful heavens, what if my little boy starts to believe he's a girl?"

"Really, Babette." Birdie forced a laugh, though to her ears the noise sounded more like a sob. She glanced at Abner, who had stopped rolling out dough in order to watch.

"Babette, don't carry on like this." She patted the younger woman's free hand. "Your son is many things, but he's not mentally ill. He's a normal little boy, with a healthy imagination and a great sense of fun."

"He's never lied to me like this before." Babette wiped tears from the wells of her eyes. "I mean, sure, he's lied to get out of trouble, but alst I had to do was look at him and he'd break down and confess. But I've been giving him, you know, that look all morning, and he still insists Bob and Brittle-knees painted these pictures."

Glancing at Abner, Birdie patted Babette's hand again. "Does he, um, say anything else about these friends of his?"

"Oh, yeah." Babette's tears began to flow in earnest. "He says they wear pumpkin outfits and live in the lighthouse. And once they spent the night under Cap'n Gribbon's boat, until a tall man with long white hair rescued them. And they came from over the sea, they don't have a mommy, and their favorite food is Werther's Originals." She lifted her teary eyes. "Honestly, Birdie, I don't know what to do. I don't want to punish my boy for lying, but I don't see what other choice I have. If he keeps telling these whoppers—"

"Maybe they're not whoppers." Birdie pressed her lips together, then forced a smile. "I mean—if they're real to him, maybe they're . . . really real." She shrugged. "After all, dear, when you were a child, didn't you believe in moonlight and magic and the monster under your bed? No matter what anyone told you, you still knew—"

Snorting, Babette gave Birdie a look of utter disbelief. "Surely you're not saying I should promote belief in monsters and fairy tales."

Birdie shrugged. "I'm saying that maybe you're making a tempest in a teapot over something that isn't really hurtful. And maybe one day you'll discover that these children were real . . . at least real to Georgie."

Babette pulled a tissue from her pocket, then blew her nose. "I don't know"—she dabbed at the end of her nose with the tissue—"but this boy is breaking my heart. I constantly worry about parenting him, about doing the right thing. If I'm this worried when he's almost six, what am I going to do when he's sixteen?"

Birdie gave her a smile. "Honey, I think you grow into the job."

*   *   *

The sun had come out from behind the clouds by the time Birdie, Bea, and Abner finished lunch in the sisters' living quarters. While Bea and Abner speculated about the reasons for Stanley Bidderman's sudden reappearance, Birdie stood and put away the casserole. She had no more than a passing interest in Stanley Bidderman, who was still abed at the B&B and still unable to obtain an audience with his estranged wife.

Birdie was thinking about taking a drive up to the lighthouse . . . even though the town was also buzzing about her frequent trips to the end of the island. The other day she'd caught Abner checking the tires on the golf cart—he said she'd been putting so many miles on the vehicle that he worried for her safety.

After stacking her dishes in the sink, Bea moved to her desk in the keeping room to begin answering the latest stack of angel mail. Standing, Abner tied his apron behind his back and gave Birdie a sly smile.

"Goin' out this afternoon?" His dark eyes glinted with humor. "I can handle the baking, so you don't need to worry about a thing."

Though she'd been about to walk to the coatrack, Birdie halted in midstep. "Where would I be going?"

Abner grinned. "Well, I figure Cap'n Gribbon must be running low on rye bread by now. And I have some snicker doodles that will go to waste if nobody eats 'em. Seems to me the captain might find some use for a dozen snicker doodles."

A thousand questions whirled in Birdie's brain as she stared at him. There he went again, smiling like he knew Salt's secret. Was the baker a mind reader, or had she let something slip?

"Well,"—she reached out and took her coat from the rack—"maybe I will drive on up to the lighthouse and see how the captain's getting on. So if you want to put together a care package for him, that'd be right nice. I'm sure he'd appreciate it."

Winking at her, Abner whirled and moved toward the bakery, humming an off-key rendition of "Silent Night."

After slipping into her coat, Birdie stepped into the hall bathroom, then ran her fingers through her silver hair. She pulled a protective lipstick from the medicine cabinet and ran it over her lips, then paused and stared at her reflection.

What was she doing? She was too old to be thinking about impressing a man, and too inexperienced to be thinking about children. Her work at the Ogunquit library had exposed her to young ones, but she'd done little more than read to them and remind them to shush when they grew too excited. She didn't know a thing about comforting kids with skinned knees . . . or healing broken young hearts. And those children at the lighthouse had to be hurting inside, the poor things. Salt was a good man, but he'd taken them away from their father. Sure, he had reason, but was even a bad daddy better than no daddy at all?

She pressed her fingertips to the mirror and shivered at the chill of the glass. Bea thought Birdie was infatuated with Salt, and maybe she was, a little, but she was far more concerned about Bobby and Brittany. Those kids had never known a mother, if Salt's story could be trusted, and their exile up at Puffin Cove couldn't be good for them, especially at Christmas.

But what could she do? She'd tried to

convince Salt that the townsfolk could be trusted, but he didn't believe her. She'd begged him to let her involve Bea, whose heart was tender, but he'd insisted that the postmistress encountered too many people on a daily basis and therefore couldn't keep a secret. She'd tried to make a case for involving the pastor and his wife, or Babette and Charles, but to each entreaty Salt turned a deaf ear.

He was, she decided, like an offshore lighthouse, built to stand alone in a sea of trouble. Through her reading she'd learned that off-shore lighthouses had to be extra-tough in order to withstand the pounding sea, underwater quakes, and even iceberg collisions. Trouble was, once built, the sea isolated them from everyone and everything.

An out-of-tune rendition of "O Come All Ye Faithful" snapped her out of her reverie. An instant later she heard a short rap at the bathroom door. "Um, excuse me, Birdie, but I've put the care package on your kitchen table. It's all ready for you."

"Coming." She cleared the thickness from her throat, then buttoned her coat. She'd run up to the point and check on the kids, leave them some bakery goodies, and ask if Salt needed anything from the mercantile. Then she'd come back home and try to focus on something useful like coming up with something she could bake that didn't require nutmeg. Or maybe she'd help Bea answer some of the angel mail . . . or she could organize her underwear drawer. Something, anything, was better than worrying about Salt and the kids.

She stood her collar around her throat, then pulled her gloves from her pocket and glanced down the hall. Abner stood in the doorway that led to the bakery, and a shadow of concern darkened his eyes.

He smiled at her as if she were a small child. "You be careful up there, Miss Birdie."

"Oh, Abner"—she yanked on her gloves—"the wind's not that bad."

"I wasn't referring to the wind."

Before she could look up to search his face, the man had turned the corner and disappeared.

The wind had picked up by the time Birdie rolled up to the lighthouse, and she was surprised to see Salt standing outside the small outbuilding that housed the generator. His serious eyes were intent upon the road, and his expression softened only a little when she unzipped the vinyl covering of her cart and waved hello.

The rising wind came whooshing past her, lifting her hair and whipping her coat around her frame as she walked toward him. "How be you?" she called, looking around for the children.

"Nicely," he answered, glancing down the road as if he expected her to bring an entire parade of townspeople into his sacred territory.

"It's just me, Salt," she said, stuffing her hands into her coat pockets as she walked forward. She gave him a smile, then inclined her head toward the lighthouse. "Are the children inside?"

He shook his head, then jerked his thumb toward the old dory he kept on the beach. "They're under there. When we heard you comin', I told 'em to scoot out of sight."

"Why, they'll catch their death under there." Leaving him to his tinkering, Birdie walked toward the boat. "Bobby? Brittany? You can come out; it's only me."

In an instant, two hooded heads appeared and two smiles flashed in her direction.

"I've brought some goodies for you." She pointed toward the cart. "Abner's been busy baking, and he gave me a package of cookies and candy for you."

Brittany scrambled out from under the boat, her sweet face a combination of rose and pearl and wet sand. "Can we look?"

"You may look, and you may have a cookie," Birdie said. "After that, you'll have to ask your grandfather. I wouldn't want to spoil your supper."

As the children sprinted toward the golf cart, Birdie turned back to Salt. He had finished with the generator, apparently, for he'd closed the door and was wiping his bare hands on a grease-stained towel.

"Salt," Birdie began, moving toward him, "can we go inside? I really need to talk to you about Christmas."

Salt shook his head. "I don't want to leave the kids out alone. Yesterday they stayed out longer than an hour, and for a few minutes I couldn't find 'em. I nearly went out of my head with worry."

Birdie drew a deep breath. He wasn't going to make this easy.

"Salt, I really wish you'd let me tell the other townspeople about the children. They could help, especially with Christmas. I'm sure you're going to want to do something special for the kids, but they've already missed the town party—"

"Don't need anything. I'm managin' fine, with your help." He gave her a grudging nod. "And I wasn't planning on doing much for Christmas. We'll just keep quiet and stay out of sight. No sense in getting the kids all riled up about things they can't have."

"Why can't they share in our holiday?" She brushed the windblown bangs out of her eyes. "Maybe you've forgotten, Salt, but Christmas means everything to children. You don't have to give them a stack of presents, but a gift and a festive dinner might be nice—and I'd even be willing to cook the dinner. And the Christmas Eve service— why, that's what Christmas is all about."

He shook his head without looking at her. "We don't need all that stuff. We're doing fine on our own."

"Not quite." Birdie lifted her chin. "This morning I spoke to Babette Graham, who's convinced her son is either a liar or developing multiple personalities. Seems Georgie was with Bobby and Brittany yesterday, and the three of them painted pictures. Georgie went home and showed his mom the paint-ings—" She shrugged. "Well, you get the idea. Quite frankly, your secret is causing Babette a lot of grief, and I don't like being caught in the middle."

His brow wrinkled. "I never intended for you to be involved at all."

"I know, but sometimes—well, sometimes the Lord leads us to places we never ex-pected to be. I never thought I'd be spending hours thinking about two children who mean nothing—I mean, who aren't mine by blood relation." She softened her voice. "Because, you see, they have come to mean a great deal to me. I only want what's best for those kids, and I think the town could give them a lot more than you and I could. Why, Dana Klackenbush is wonderful with children, and she could teach them. And Olympia de Cuvier's Tallu-lah would love to play with the kids—"

"That mangy mutt is up here all the time," Salt interrupted. "So is that dog with the smashed-in face."

"Butch." Birdie supplied the name. "He's the Klackenbushes' bulldog." She hesitated. "Did the children . . . did they like playing with the dogs?"

Salt snorted. "Whaddya think, woman? I had to chase the durn dogs away before I could get the kids back in the lighthouse, and it colder than a clam digger's hands out."

Birdie crossed her arms. "You see? Those kids need someone to play with. There's a whole town down there that'd be willing to keep company with those children, but you've got to let them in on the secret. There's no shame in asking for help, none at all. And it's what you need to do, especially with Christmas only four days away."

Salt set his jaw, bristling the whiskers on his cheek. "I can handle things." He turned and lifted a hand to the side of his mouth. "Bob! Brittany! You two come here and say good-bye to Miss Birdie. She doesn't have time for any more than a dooryard visit today."

Birdie lowered her gaze, lest he see the hot tears that had filled her eyes.

Salt blew out his cheeks as the children came forward with cookies in their hands and a sizable bakery bag tucked beneath Bobby's arm.

"Do you hafta go?" Brittany asked, her face screwing up into a question mark.

"Apparently I do." Birdie's voice had gone as cold as the wind. She smiled though and bent to pat Brittany's cheek. "But I'm sure I'll be back before too long. After all, Christmas is right around the corner."

Determined to ignore her, Salt rested a hand on his hip. "Miss Birdie brought me a bit of bad news from town. Seems that Georgie Graham's in a peck of trouble with his folks for playing with you two. So from now on, you'll have to stay away from that boy. If you see him comin', you get on inside the lighthouse and stay put until he leaves."

"But, Grandfather!" The genuine alarm in Bobby's voice caught Salt by surprise. The child had never argued or voiced a disagreement with any of Salt's rules.

He gave Bobby a stern glance. "You don't want that boy getting in trouble, do you?"

He shifted his gaze from Bobby to Brittany. Sadly, these kids knew what trouble meant, and though Georgie would probably never experience the tortures and neglect these two had known, still, it wouldn't hurt to stress a point.

Lifting his gaze, he saw Birdie staring at

him, her lips pressed together and her eyes glowing with rebuke.

He looked away. "That settles it, then. No more playing with Georgie."

Brittany's eyes welled with tears. "Did we do something wrong? We said we were sorry for staying out too long yesterday."

Unable to stand the sight of the girl's distress, Salt turned and fumbled with the padlock on the door. You had to be firm with children, just like you had to be firm with men.

He heard an audible sniff from Birdie, then the crunch of boots upon gravel as she walked away. Then he heard her call. "Come here, kids, and give me a hug before I take off. What would you like me to bring when I come again? More molasses cookies? Maybe some gingerbread?"

Salt turned in time to see her bend and hug each child. He blew out his cheeks, then walked toward the shore, unable to suppress the troubling notion that he had somehow failed.

Despite all he'd done for those children, he could count on one finger how many times they'd hugged *him*.

*   *   *

Taking Brittany's hand, Bobby stepped back as Miss Birdie zipped the cover to her cart, then waved and drove away. He watched her round the corner and disappear past the dunes, then he turned and saw the grandfather standing alone by the rocky shore.

Something had happened between the grandfather and Miss Birdie, something Bad, but no one had yelled or slapped or cried. Bad things at his daddy's house had always included yelling and slapping and crying, so for a moment he'd thought he had misunderstood . . . but he knew Bad well enough to recognize it.

So. Bad things could happen on this island, too. Only they sounded different. So maybe Bad things had been happening all along, and he'd been too much of a numbhead to realize it.

"Bobby?" Britt tilted her head to look up at him. "Did he mean we can never play with Georgie again?"

"I don't know," Bobby answered, his gaze fastened to the grandfather's back, "but we shouldn't now, that's for sure."

Brittany considered a moment. "But I like Georgie. I want to marry him."

Bobby shrugged. "Well, then, I suppose

you can. And maybe we can still play with him."

His sister's eyes went round. "You mean—"

"Why do we have to obey him?" Bobby nodded toward the grandfather. "I mean, how do we know he's really our grandfather? Daddy never said anything about him. And he took us for no reason; he came and put us in his boat. Maybe we're kidnapped."

He glanced down at his sister and felt a rush of relief when he saw that the word had registered. She'd watched enough TV to know that being kidnapped was big-time Bad Stuff.

"We're kidnapped?" She squeezed his hand. "So who's going to rescue us?"

"Nobody. 'Cause nobody knows we're here." Bobby pulled her toward the road. "Come on, let's walk."

He set out across the salt marsh at a quick pace, much faster than his grandfather could move, and fast enough to make Britt pant after a few steps. They walked fast and far, taking care to keep the sand dunes between them and the houses of Heavenly Daze.

"Maybe we will keep playing with Georgie," he said, his breath misting in the frosty air. "Maybe we'll run away and go back to Daddy."

Brittany stopped in her tracks. "But where is Daddy?"

"We came over in the boat, didn't we?" Bobby jerked on her hand and reestablished his pace. "We'll take the boat and go back. When we get to the other side, we'll call the police. They'll know how to take us back to Daddy."

"Do you really want to go back?" Britt's brows settled in a straight line above her eyes. "There'd be no more cookies. No more Froot Loops. And no more dogs, unless you count the big one that growls at us every time we walk past the neighbor's door."

"At least we'd be with Daddy." Bobby stopped and faced his sister, suddenly unable to explain what he was feeling. How could he make a girl understand? Daddy was loud, and messy, and he drank and stank and hit them, but at least they knew him. Bobby knew what he had to do at Daddy's place—he had to clean up the messes, keep quiet while Daddy slept, bring in the mail, and not answer the phone. He knew how to carry the empty bottles in a sack without letting them chink together, because the chinking sound always woke Daddy, and if he woke when he'd been drinking, he'd be mean and growly and as dangerous as a bear.

But at the grandfather's house, he never knew what a day would bring. The grandfather wanted to do most of the work, and he wanted them to play, but sometimes he didn't want them to play, and sometimes he seemed terribly afraid of something.

On those nights, when the grandfather sat in the fire-lit darkness and stared up at the twirling light overhead, terror gripped Bobby, too.

Bobby tried to explain. "I know Daddy," he said simply, searching Brittany's eyes. "I don't know the grandfather, and he's . . . well, he's not like Daddy. But he was mean to Miss Birdie back there—"

Britt's eyes widened. "How was he mean?"

"I don't know how to 'splain it. I heard it, that's all. Miss Birdie was mad when she left, and I don't know if she'll come back."

Brittany rubbed her nose. "She said she'd come back. She said she'd bring us more cookies."

"Grownups don't always mean what they say. And they don't keep their promises."

Britt didn't answer but turned toward the sea, where the waves crashed against the shore in a steady rhythm. "Okay," she said finally, her voice flat. "If we find a way, let's go home. I don't want to be kidnapped."

CHAPTER TWENTY

"Are you lucky or what!"

In Portland, Melanie poked her head around the doorframe of Annie's office and grinned.

Annie looked up from her work. "Why am I lucky?"

"There's another storm coming in!" Melanie danced into the room and dropped into the guest chair. "Last weekend you spent a couple of days holed up in a bed and breakfast, right? But the ferry couldn't run in the storm."

Annie thought about the cranberries shriveling in the trunk of her car. "Right. So?"

"Chances are that the ferry won't run at Christmas, either. I mean, that storm's not likely to turn tail and head for Europe in the next four days, is it?"

"That'd be a neat trick."

"You see? Through no fault of your own, you won't be able to get to your aunt's house for Christmas." A dimple winked in Melanie's cheek. "But flights will still be operating out of Logan."

Slowly Melanie's point registered with Annie. "Flights will operate . . . but the ferry won't." Her eyes met Melanie's.

Melanie grinned. "I always knew you were a bright girl."

"I don't know." Annie bit her lip. Did she dare make other plans? She could always leave tonight or early tomorrow for Heavenly Daze, and she could probably beat the storm. But she'd planned on doing her Christmas shopping this weekend in Portland and leaving for the island on Monday.

If, however, a storm was coming . . . the ferry might not be running on Monday. And if she couldn't get to the island, why should she sit around all week and do nothing?

"How can you not know what to do?" Melanie asked. "The choice is clear—you can either stay in your lonely apartment and mope through the holiday, or you can go on the cruise with me and have a bodaciously good time." Melanie sprang from the chair and leaned on Annie's desk. "It's a miracle,

Annie. A gift! Your aunt can't blame you for not being home if you can't get there. Come on, wake up and boogie!" With one hand on her hip and the other in the air, Melanie began to shimmy from side to side. "Learn to do the cha-cha, or maybe the rumba. It'll be a blast."

She snatched a silk rose from a vase on the desk, then clamped the stem between her teeth and began to snap her fingers.

Leaning back in her chair, Annie pressed her fingertips together and smiled. Melanie was right. Aunt Olympia couldn't complain about Annie neglecting her if weather kept her from the island.

She tucked her finger beneath the desk drawer pull and gave a little tug. The tickets lay inside, unopened and as yet unrefunded. Maybe she'd kept them because she'd been hoping that something would come up and she'd be able to go. And now—bless Mother Nature's heart! With Christmas right around the corner, another storm had whipped up the northeast Atlantic and would keep her away from Heavenly Daze.

The choice was simple. Christmas, the departure date, was still four days away. She'd have to do her Christmas shopping, pack, and buy a few cruise clothes, but she could do it! By this time next week she would be lathered in Coppertone and basking by Caribbean waters. She'd be inhaling the sights and scents and sounds of sun, surf, and fine cuisine—a far cry from the dry turkey and fat-free pumpkin pie she'd find at Frenchman's Fairest.

"So." Melanie's theatrics slowed. "You'll go?"

Annie nodded. "I'll call Aunt Olympia. If she agrees I can't get there, then yeah." Her grin widened. "Yes. I'm going!"

Melanie squealed, running around the desk and throwing her arms around Annie's neck. "Perfect! We'll have a super good time!"

Annie patted Melanie's arm. They would have great fun, and she wouldn't have to feel one bit guilty. If the Lord hadn't wanted her to go on this cruise, he would have made it possible for her to reach the island.

Still, guilt niggled at her. But it always raised its head when she thought of Olympia, and persistent habits were hard to squash.

When Melanie pulled away, Annie caught her gaze. "What about Mr. Right? Are you okay about leaving him behind?"

With a toss of her hand, Melanie gave Annie the best gift yet. "Mr. Right hasn't called since the office party. I think he's moved to greener pastures."

"I'm sorry."

"Aw, don't be. It was only one date, and I think I read too much into it. As always."

"Any girl would have been tempted to do what you did. He was an awfully sharp guy." Annie felt another nip of guilt, but this time it had nothing to do with Olympia.

When Melanie left, she reached for the phone and dialed Frenchman's Fairest. The old butler answered.

"Caleb? Is Aunt Olympia there?"

A moment later her aunt came on the line. "Oh, Annie, so good to hear from you. I was just telling Caleb that I was glad for your sake that Vernie's order finally arrived. I was sick about you being stranded in Ogunquit with all that stuff."

"It was no big deal—and I had time to catch up on my reading." Annie cleared her throat, then took a deep breath. "Aunt Olympia, it's like this—I have some things I have to do in Portland this weekend, so I won't be able to leave for Heavenly Daze until Monday at the earliest. And I've just heard there's another storm brewing. If that's true, well . . . I may not be able to get to Frenchman's Fairest for Christmas."

Her news resulted in a lengthy silence on the other end of the line.

"You know I would come if I could."

Olympia drew an audible breath. "I know you would, Annie."

"Caleb will be with you—and Birdie and Bea and Cleta and Vernie and the Wickams." Olympia's neighbors were like family, and yet Annie knew their company couldn't make up for her absence, especially this year. Her blood thickened with guilt.

"Annie, I've been thinking."

"Yes?"

"If the storm moves in, why don't you go on that cruise? I know you want to. There's no reason for you to stay in Portland if you can't come home."

Annie felt her pulse quicken. "You wouldn't mind?"

"I would rather have you here with Caleb and me, but some things can't be helped. I only hope there's still room on the boat."

Catching her breath, Annie blinked back tears of gratitude. "I'm pretty sure there is."

"Then go on the cruise, dear. And have a wonderful time."

"Well," Annie stammered, unable to believe her ears. "We still have four days till Christmas. If the storm doesn't hit, I'll try to come home, of course."

"That's not likely, Annie. But thank you."

They chatted for a few more minutes, then Annie realized the shadows in her office were lengthening. Time to go home and start planning.

"I need to go, Aunt Olympia. If I don't see you on Christmas, I'll call you from the airport, okay?"

"That's fine, Annie. Have a merry Christmas, and try not to miss us too much."

As if she'd be thinking of snow-swept Heavenly Daze when she was on a Caribbean cruise! Annie hung up, then stood and lifted her hands in delight. The Lord was good! Life was good! Christmas was good! She was going on the cruise with Aunt Olympia's blessing!

Again, the gremlin of guilt niggled at Annie's heart, but she ignored it. She'd be a fool to look a gift horse in the mouth.

*   *   *

Safe and warm in her bed, Birdie slapped her feather pillow and tried to get comfortable. She'd put in a full day, working in the bakery and making that trip out to the lighthouse. She ought to be bone tired, but the thought of Salt Gribbon chafed against her heart like a new shoe against a blister.

She rolled onto her side and flipped her pillow, then buried her head in the softness. "Sleep, Birdie," she mumbled into the pillowcase. "Just close your eyes and forget about that ornery old rascal. He's more stubborn than a child, but he's a good man at heart. The kids will be okay with him. He loves them, doesn't he?"

She flipped again and lay flat on her back, staring at the swirls in the ceiling plaster. Shoot, she didn't know a thing about young ones, but she knew they needed more than Salt was willing to give. Why not let them play with Georgie? Why not let Babette and Dana and the Wickams in on the secret? Heaven knew the town could use a few more sprinkles of children's laughter, and if Pastor Wickam asked the townsfolk to keep Salt's secret, they would. Not one of them would spill the beans, not even Olympia. And now, in winter, there were very few visitors to the island, so it wasn't like anyone would see the kids and recognize their faces on a milk carton.

She turned onto her other side and slid her hands beneath her pillow. Salt was going to defeat those kids by keeping them cooped up all winter. They'd found a little joy in playing with Georgie; Babette's paintings had proven that. And though Birdie'd never had a kid, she'd been a kid, and she knew kids needed to play. They needed structure and discipline, but they also needed fun and hugs and daily doses of laughter.

Opening her eyes, she stared at the slit of light beneath the door. Bea must still be awake. She'd left her sister in the keeping room, where Bea was working on yet another stack of angel letters. They'd hoped the mail would eventually taper off, but that silly urban legend about angels on Heavenly Daze was apparently as hard to kill as a computer virus.

She propped herself up, then swung her legs out of the covers and stood. Pulling her robe from the foot of the bed, she padded to the door, grateful for the thick woolen socks covering her cold feet.

A moment later she stood shivering by

the fire, her arms crossed. Bea sat in the ladder back chair by the desk, one hand in her lap, the other on the desktop. Braced by the chair, her head was tilted back and her mouth open as she snored softly.

Birdie reached out and tapped her sister's shoulder. "Bea—you're snoring."

Bea's eyes opened and her mouth closed simultaneously, as if they were operating on the same switch. She blinked, then lowered her chin and gave Birdie a cool stare. "I don't snore."

"You do, too. I could hear you from my bedroom."

Birdie sank into her easy chair, suddenly grateful for her sister's company. She nodded toward the letter on the desk. "That one must have stumped you."

Bea looked down at the page. "It did. I don't know what to say."

"Another sick child?" Since the e-mail about angels working miracles on Heavenly Daze had begun circulating on the Internet, the townspeople had been inundated with letters asking for money, toys, and impossible things like cures for paralysis and leukemia. Bea had taken it as a personal challenge to answer as many letters as she

could, and the townspeople helped whenever possible. But for the difficult letters,
they could only promise to pray.

"Not a sick child." Bea picked up the letter. "A sick father."

"Cancer?"

Bea shook her head. "Alcoholism. He's
lost his two kids, he says, and he can't seem
to get his life straightened out. He's afraid
he's lost them forever."

Birdie tucked her legs beneath her. "Lost
his children? To social services?"

"He doesn't say." Bea shook her head.
"So tragic, and so close to home. The return
address is Wells. Imagine such a tragedy
happening just over the water."

Birdie felt a sudden electric tingle in the
pit of her stomach. "Does he give a name?"

Dropping the page back to her desk, Bea
sighed. "Not a last name—ashamed of himself, I reckon. He just signed the letter
'Patrick.'"

Patrick—in Wells. A man who'd lost two
children. And Salt having a son named
Patrick in Wells and two children hidden up
at the lighthouse.

"I don't quite know what to say," Bea
went on, picking up her pen. "I can promise

to put his name on the prayer list at church, but I don't have the authority to speak to the folks at social services. If they took his kids, I'm sure it was for their own protection."

"I know what to do." Birdie caught her sister's gaze and held it. "Invite him to Heavenly Daze . . . for the Christmas Eve service."

Bea's forehead knit in bewilderment. "Invite him to what?"

"To church. To Heavenly Daze."

Bea laughed. "You think an alcoholic in Wells is going to come all the way out here for our tiny Christmas Eve service? That's crazy."

"Maybe." Birdie felt a smile lift the corners of her mouth. "But an invitation couldn't hurt, could it?"

"I reckon not." Bea shook her head a moment, then uncapped her pen and began to write. "Um—how's he supposed to get here? The ferry won't be running that late at night if it's running at all. Storm coming, remember. And if by some miracle the guy takes us up on this invitation, he'll be stuck on the island for Christmas."

Birdie shrugged. "Maybe Floyd and Cleta will take him in at the B&B."

Bea frowned. "And maybe pigs can fly.

You think the Lansdowns are going to take in a stranger on Christmas Eve? They'll want to spend that night with Barbara and Russell, with family."

"If a body can't find hospitality on this island on Christmas Eve," Birdie said, standing, "then we've forgotten what that first Christmas was all about."

Birdie's lips parted as if she would argue the point, then she clamped her mouth shut and bent over the page, her pen driving furiously across the paper.

Smiling, Birdie rubbed her sister's shoulder, then padded back to bed. She had no idea if the invitation would result in anything, but wasn't Christmas supposed to be a time of miracles?

CHAPTER TWENTY-ONE

"Come on, kids." Salt thumped two cereal bowls to the kitchen table, then stood in silent disbelief. Neither Bobby nor Brittany moved; they both sat as immobile as statues before the TV. Some silly cartoon about mutant aliens blared from that noise box, but the kids acted as though it were the most fascinating thing on earth.

"Bob, Brittany." He tried the direct approach. "Come on and eat before your cereal gets soggy."

Still no response. Bobby sat hunched and cross-legged, his hands limp in his lap, while Brittany lay on her stomach, her legs bent at the knee and her feet in the air. Every once in a while her legs swung lazily down and up again, but either she hadn't heard his call or she was ignoring him.

Salt lifted a brow. Could they be ignoring him?

He walked around the table and stood between them, then bent to switch off the TV.

"Hey!" Bobby said, a note of resentment in his voice.

Salt pressed the power button, then crossed his arms. "To the table with both of you." He lowered his voice to the no-nonsense tone that had always motivated his sailors. "I won't tolerate back talk, so get up there and eat."

The growl seemed to work. The children rose and went to the table, though they spooned cereal into their mouths with a great deal less enthusiasm than they had exhibited a few mornings before.

"What is wrong with you two?" Salt asked, coming closer. "The other day you loved Froot Loops."

"I want a doughnut." Brittany propped her head on her hand. "Miss Birdie makes the best doughnuts I ever ate."

"Miss Birdie's not here, and neither are her doughnuts." Salt tried to keep his voice calm and steady. He couldn't lose his temper, especially after yesterday. The kids had been in a pink stink for the rest of the day, and a good night's sleep apparently had done little to improve their mood.

Maybe they needed some encouragement. He glanced around the house, aware
of how little he had to offer in the way of en-
tertainment. When they'd first arrived, they'd
been thrilled to play on the beach or walk
with him up the spiral staircase to the
lantern room and watch him clean the windows and polish the lens. They'd listened
intently to his stories about seafaring and life
as a longliner, but lately his work didn't ap-
pear to interest them at all.

But if it was pastry they wanted . . . He
gestured to the bakery bags Birdie had
brought. "There's food," he said, his desire
to please them overriding Birdie's opinion
that children shouldn't eat cookies for
breakfast.

Bobby shook his head. "No doughnuts."

"I tell you what." he moved toward the
counter and the nearly empty box of Froot
Loops. "I have to go into town this morning
to pick up a few things. While I'm there, I'll
pop over to the bakery and see if Birdie's
got any fresh doughnuts or fritters. Maybe
she'll even have some Christmas cookies."

Brittany's nose crinkled. "I don't think I'd
want to eat a cookie with Christmas on it."

"Why"—Salt bent to her eye level—

"Christmas isn't on the cookies. It's—well, have you never had a Christmas cookie?"

Brittany looked at Bobby, who shook his head. Her suspicions apparently confirmed, she shook her head, too.

Salt straightened, a sad realization beginning to bloom in his chest. Birdie had been right about a lot of things, and she'd been right about Christmas. These kids had never had a proper one, and if they stayed hidden away up here, they wouldn't have one this year, either. He'd made no plans for the holiday other than thinking he'd pick up a toy for each child when he next visited Ogunquit.

"Then we shall have to remedy that oversight." Salt moved toward the door, where his coat and hat and scarf hung from pegs in the wall. "Bob, don't forget to latch the door after I go. Brittany, be a good girl and put your bowls in the sink. Both of you stay in the house until I get back. Then we'll see what sort of goodies Birdie is baking today, okay?"

They watched wordlessly as Salt dressed for the weather, and neither said a word as he went out the door. He waited on the stoop, uncertain, then nodded as he heard the click of the door latch.

Despite their recent moodiness, they were good children. And everything would be fine once he returned with something good to tickle their tummies and restore their faith in him.

After fastening the latch, Bobby turned to the steel staircase, took a deep breath, and began to climb.

"Bobby!" Britt called, looking up at him from the kitchen table. "You know you're not allowed to go up there alone!"

"I'm being careful," Bobby said, climbing higher. "I only want to look out the window. When I see him pass the dunes, I'll know the coast is clear."

Up and up he went, both hands clinging to the chilly iron railing, his eyes focused on the rising metal stairs before him. Halfway to the lantern room, at the point where the air began to feel warm and still, he came to the small window that overlooked the island. Lunging from the safety of the railing to the solidity of the wall, he pressed his hands to the window sill, stood on tiptoe, and looked down to see the grandfather walking toward town.

Bobby felt his mouth twitch. The grandfather walked with his hands in his pockets and his shoulders hunched forward. The wind pushed at him, flapping his coat, and Bobby felt sad as he watched. The grandfather wasn't mean, exactly, even if he was a kidnapper. But he wasn't their daddy, so they had to go home. Daddy needed them. The grandfather didn't.

Leaning against the window sill, his breath misting the glass, Bobby watched the grandfather pass the dunes, then saw him approach the brick building for the fire truck and jail. "If you're bad, they'll put you in the jail," Georgie had told them as they painted puffin pictures on the sidewalk. "I've never been inside, but once I saw a drunk man they locked up. He was from away, and he broke a lot of bottles in Miss Vernie's store before Mr. Floyd and my daddy got a hold of him."

Bobby lowered his chin to his hands. The grandfather had said something about their daddy coming to get them one day, but if their daddy came here, they'd put him in the jail 'cause he was drunk almost all the time. They'd put the grandfather in the jail, too, if they knew he was a kidnapper. That had to be why he and Brittany were supposed to be a secret.

Once the lanky figure had moved a bit farther down the road, Bobby turned and began to make his way down the stairs. "It's okay," he called, carefully minding the steps. Going down seemed scarier than going up, because he could see how far away the floor was. "Get dressed, Britt. Wear your snowsuit . . . and you'd better take Miranda. We won't be coming back."

Brittany's mouth twisted in a knot. "Are you sure we can get home?"

Bobby nodded and raised his voice to be heard above the metallic thunk-thunk of his steps on the stairs. "When we get to shore, we'll go straight to the cops. We'll probably be home in time for supper."

Stepping off the staircase, he moved to the kitchen. The white bag of bakery goodies sat on the table, and he opened it to peer inside. There were still several gingerbread men, half a loaf of rye bread, and several sweet brioches.

"We'd better eat all of this before we go," he told his sister. "We may not get lunch."

So he and Britt stuffed themselves until they couldn't hold another bite, then they dressed in their snowsuits. Bobby helped Brittany put on her mittens, then tied the string under her jacket hood. She helped him, too, then picked up her doll and held Miranda tight in the crook of her elbow.

"Okay." Bobby grabbed his encyclopedia from where he'd hidden it in his bedroll, tucked it under his arm, then took a final look around the lighthouse. The grandfather was probably tired of taking care of them, so it was time they went home. Daddy would be worried; he might even be angry they'd stayed gone so long. But a whipping, Bobby figured, wasn't as bad as being kidnapped and hidden away for the rest of their lives.

Lifting the latch on the door, he drew a deep breath and said, "Let's go."

A half-hour later, Bobby sat on the rocks near the boat, his chin propped on his fist. His careful plan had failed, and he didn't know what to do next. After watching Gabe lift the old dory with one hand, he'd figured he could lift the boat, too. But he couldn't. He and Britt had tried lifting it from the right side, the left side, the back, and the front, and nothing worked. They could rock it from side to side, but not even repeated rocking could flip the boat over.

Not only were they kidnapped, they were stuck.

"Hey, guys!" Georgie Graham's voice rang out, startling Bobby. Georgie ran forward, his white tennis shoes shining beneath a pair of bright red sweatpants. He carried his backpack again, and for a minute Bobby wondered if he'd packed some sort of tool that could flip a boat.

"We're not a-sposed to play with you anymore," Brittany announced, grinning at Georgie from beneath her hood. "But I still want to marry you."

Georgie shrugged at the news. "Yeah, I know. I got in trouble, too. I showed your pictures to my mom and she started crying."

"It's because we're kidnapped." Bobby spread his hands. "We were going to escape, but we can't lift the boat."

"Not even both of us," Britt added. "We tried rocking it."

Turning, Georgie dropped his backpack on the sand next to Bobby's encyclopedia. "Aw, that's nothin'. I'll bet I could lift that boat." He placed his hands on his hips. "I'm strong. My mom says so."

"Really?" Brittany ran to his side. "Can I watch?"

Bobby stood, and the three of them walked to the side of the boat. Spreading his legs, Georgie rubbed his mittens together, then squatted with his rear only an inch from the wet sand.

He grunted. "I saw them do this on the Olympics," he explained, putting his hands beneath the edge of the boat. "One, two, three, lift!"

Britt started clapping as the boat began to move, but not even Georgie could get it to flip over. He kept holding it, though, grunting as he shifted his feet into different positions. "Is it moving?"

"Not anymore." Brittany's voice sounded empty.

Bobby stepped forward. "Let me help."

"No! I can do it!"

"You're not doing it, so let me help," Bobby insisted.

"I can help, too!" Britt grabbed the boat, and the three of them grunted and strained and lifted, but the boat didn't budge.

"Maybe we should all do it like the Olympic people," Bobby suggested.

"Good idea," Georgie said. "Because my arms are getting tired."

They lowered the boat, then Bobby stepped back while Georgie flexed his arms.

Bobby shifted his gaze to the sea. "Going to be a good day for the trip."

Georgie stopped flexing. "Where you going?"

"Home." Brittany stepped into his field of vision and pointed to her doll, safely seated on a rock. "I'm taking Miranda."

Georgie crinkled his nose. "Where's home?"

Pointing across the water, Bobby said, "Right over there. The grandfather brought us over in this boat, so we know how to get back. We're going home to our daddy so we won't be kidnapped anymore."

Georgie whistled softly. "Cool."

"It's a secret," Britt added. "We're ex-scaping."

"I can help," Georgie said. "I can go with you and help row the boat."

Bobby shook his head. "You have to stay here. We're not even supposed to be talking to you."

"But I'm strong!" Georgie flexed again,

but Bobby couldn't see anything under the boy's bulky jacket.

"You can't go." He squatted next to the boat. "Are you ready? Let's try together."

"But I want to go!"

"If we don't get this thing turned over, none of us is going anywhere."

Reluctantly, Georgie squatted and gripped the boat. Brittany ducked down next to him, then gave his arm an affectionate squeeze.

Bobby placed his hands on the rim. "Pull after three," he called. "One, two, three, go!"

They did, each of them standing as they lifted, and this time the old boat didn't even protest. It flipped over as easily as a turtle, rolling onto the sand and rocking into place.

Georgie grinned. "Cool!"

Bobby picked up the oars that had been stored under the boat and dropped them into the bow. "Now we push," he said, his hands falling to his hips. "Should slide pretty easy, I think."

His prediction proved true. With all three children pushing, the boat moved across the damp sand as easily as if she rode on water. When the stern splashed into the waves, Bobby called a halt, then nodded to his sister. "Onto the bench thwart with you," he said, repeating the words the grandfather had said that afternoon so many weeks ago. "We'll keep you dry as we shove off."

Like a pampered princess, Britt climbed in and moved toward the bench at the back, holding Miranda tightly in her arms. Carefully she brushed sand from the seat, then perched on the edge and flashed Georgie a bright smile. "Ready!"

Bobby turned to Georgie. "Thanks. I think I can take it from here."

Georgie crossed his arms. "I want to go. I can help."

"No, you can't." Bobby spoke in the firm tone the grandfather had used when he made them turn off the television.

A mischievous light lit Georgie's eyes. "If you don't let me go, I'll run down the road and tell everybody you're gone. And then they'll send other boats out after you, and you'll be in the worst trouble ever."

Bobby frowned as he considered Georgie's comment. This goofy kid was no dummy, and he could help. Besides, he had a mother and a father, so if he had trouble getting back to the island, his parents would come get him. Probably.

"Okay, you can go, but you've got to get in now, with her." Bobby nodded toward his sister. "I'm not going to have you wet and complaining all the way over."

"Okay." Grinning, Georgie threw himself over the side of the boat, moved to the middle seat and picked up the oars.

"You'll have to leave one of the paddles for me," Bobby called as he began to push. The wet sand seemed to have gripped the bottom, but each incoming wave seemed to lift and release it for a moment before the wet sand claimed it again. Bobby waited until a particularly good-sized wave rolled in, then pushed with all his might and waded into the cold surf. The boat rose and fell on the waves, finally free of the sand.

"Here!" Georgie held out his hand. "Come on, get in!"

"Just a minute." As the cold water nipped at his ankles, Bobby turned to watch the sea. He'd spent days studying the waves on the island. Here at the north point, the waves came in at an angle to the beach, so if he could catch the current, the swells should carry him away from the shore and toward home . . .

He gave the boat one final push, propelling it northward, then took Georgie's hand and pitched himself forward. For an awkward moment he hung over the edge like a hooked fish, then Brittany grabbed his coat with both hands and pulled him in.

"Yeah!" Georgie crowed, splashing in the water with his oar.

Bobby glared at him. For an island kid, Georgie knew nothing about rowing. Bobby had never done it, but he'd watched the grandfather.

"Let me have that." He took the oar from Georgie, then sat with his back to the stern and placed his oar through the hole in the side of the boat. "You have to sit here." He pointed to the empty place next to him. "And I have to put my oar through this other hole, and then we have to row together. Okay?"

Georgie nodded happily, then took his seat and held the oar. He splashed it once, spraying Britt and making her squeal, until Bobby gave him a stern look. "You have to wait until I'm ready."

Georgie lowered his head, but he waited until Bobby had threaded his oar through the ring.

"Okay." Bobby checked both oars' positions. "Now we pull together. Ready?"

And then, as Brittany lifted her face to the sun and sang to her doll, the two boys began to row.

"Why, look what the wind blew in!"

Caught by the note of surprise in Abner's voice, Birdie looked up, then felt her heart do a double thump. Captain Salt Gribbon stood in her store, one hand palm up on the counter, the other in his pocket. For a moment, standing there with his hand outstretched, he looked like a beggar asking for alms . . . or a man begging for forgiveness.

"I'll take care of this customer, Abner," she said, rising from her chair at the work desk. She walked toward him, taking care to keep her expression composed. "Can I help you, Cap'n Gribbon?"

He stared at her like a fellow faced with a hard sum in arithmetic. "Ayuh," he finally said. "I need more bread."

She lifted a brow. "Ate all that rye already? I didn't know you had such an appetite."

A flush rose from his collar, coloring his face with red blotches. "A man's got a right to buy what he pleases, doesn't he?"

"Ayuh." She walked to the display case. "That he does."

He followed her movements as she slipped on a pair of plastic gloves. "And I was wonderin' if you might be willing to do me a favor."

"A favor?" Her voice sounded like chilled steel even in her own ears.

"I need to go over to Ogunquit." He glanced at Abner back at the work counter, then lowered his voice. "Before the storm rolls in, I need you to come out to the light-house for a while so I can go over on the ferry. I'll only be gone a few hours, but I need to pick up a few things for Christmas."

Though every nerve in Birdie's body rebelled against the thought of doing Salt Gribbon a favor, her heart warmed at his words. So the old man was willing to let the kids celebrate Christmas! She couldn't have been more surprised if he'd confessed a belief in Santa Claus.

"My, um, company needs to have somethin' on Christmas morning," he said, speaking out of the corner of his mouth. "I can't have those kids waking up and finding nothing in my house for 'em. And I can't buy anything at the mercantile without Vernie Bidderman getting all suspicious." He looked directly at her then, and when he spoke again, she heard a note of apology in his voice. "Will you come?"

Torn between her pride and her desire to help, Birdie closed her eyes. Yesterday he'd been downright snippy, sending her away with scarcely a thank-you and reacting to her pleas with another hardening of his heart. But this was softness, wasn't it? He might not be able to reach out to the town yet, but at least he was reaching out to her.

"Abner." She glanced over her shoulder. "Can you cover things here if I go up to the lighthouse for a few hours?"

"Sure." Abner flashed an Aquafresh smile. "Everything's under control."

She met Salt's eye. "Let me get my coat," she said, pulling off her plastic gloves. "And we're driving up there in my golf cart. If you think I'm walking all that way in this cold, you've got another think coming, Salt Gribbon."

"Fine." He nodded, and as she walked to

the back to fetch her coat and hat, she heard him ask Abner for a dozen frosted Christmas cookies.

Imagine!

CHAPTER TWENTY-TWO

Salt said little on the drive up to the lighthouse, though he groaned when Birdie hit potholes and threw his hands over his eyes when she headed straight toward a boulder, then jerked the wheel at the last minute.

"You've got to do it like that," she remarked coolly, not looking at him. "It's the only way you can avoid that big rut in the road."

"Why pay that one any special favors?" Salt demanded, peering through his gloved fingers. "You managed to hit all the others."

She gave him a sarcastic smile, then rounded the corner at Puffin Cove. The red-and-white lighthouse gleamed in the bright light of early afternoon, while beyond the point the sea roiled with whitecaps.

Leaving Salt to unzip himself out of the cart, she set her shoulders and marched toward the front door of the lighthouse. "I'll fix the kids a bit of supper if you're delayed," she called, shivering as the wind chafed her cheeks. "They'll probably want lunch, too, seein' as how you've been gone all morning and the little dears have been left to scrounge for themselves."

Salt mumbled something in reply, but the wind caught his answer and carried it away. She rapped lightly on the lighthouse door, then tried the knob, expecting the door to be latched from within. It wasn't.

Strange. The kids knew Salt expected them to batten down and wait whenever he went into town. She opened the door and stepped inside, scanning the round room, then glanced up at the spiraling staircase. No sign of the children on the stairs, in the room or—she crossed to the bathroom, opened the door, and found it empty.

She hurried to the doorway. "Salt? The kids aren't here."

And in that moment she saw a sight she would carry with her until her dying day. Salt stood on the beach in water to his ankles, his hands pressed to his face. The sand where he stood had been marred with a long scrape, and the dory that always rested upside down on the shore was . . . gone.

*   *   *

With blood pounding thickly in his ears, Salt pulled his hands away from his eyes, hoping to find that the world had somehow righted itself while he closed himself off. But the beach was still empty, the sand still marked with tiny footprints and a long scrape. And despite the fervency of his whispered prayer, his boat had not materialized.

Birdie stood at his side now, tugging on his sleeve. "Salt," she was saying, fear radiating from her like a halo, "those kids couldn't have taken the boat—could they? Why, there's no way they could manage it without help."

Salt's heart was hammering; he could feel each thump like a punch in his chest. "Of course not, they couldn't take it." He looked down at the sand and followed the long abrasion to the place where it began—the spot where his boat had rested only a few hours before. Footprints sprinkled the beach here, but there wasn't an adult-sized print among them.

"We have to get help." Birdie's voice had risen to a fevered pitch. She was breathing in quick gasps, and her face had gone the color of paper, even with the biting wind. "You don't—you can't handle this one alone. You don't have a boat; you don't have anything."

He turned and moved past her, striding toward the lighthouse, but for what? Every muscle in him yearned to do something, to push or pull and labor, but what could he do? Something in him wanted to race to the switching panel and manually activate the light, but what good would that accomplish?

Pausing in the doorway, he pressed his hands to the jambs, straining against the wood. His grandkids were out on a rough sea with a storm approaching. The waves would soon be high enough to warrant a small craft warning, and not even independent Bobby would know how to handle a dory in waves higher than three or four feet.

From the beach, Birdie let out an anguished scream. Salt ran toward her, fearing that she'd seen something in the waves, but she was pointing to something on the sand.

"What is it?" he panted, running up. Then

394 Lori Copeland and Angela Hunt

he saw what she'd seen—Bobby's encyclopedia and a blue backpack.

She knelt and placed her hand on the
bag. "This belongs to Georgie Graham. He
carries it all the time."

Without a word, Salt turned to the footprints. In the sand, written plainly for anyone
to interpret, he read the tale of three children. Three distinct sets of footprints
cluttered the beach, one small, one
medium-sized, and one with the word Nike
emblazoned along the instep.

Fire blazed in Birdie's eyes when she
looked at him again. "Georgie Graham is
with them." Abruptly she turned on her heel
and strode toward the golf cart.

Salt ran after her. "Where are you going?"

She whirled to face him. "Charles and
Babette need to know their son is in danger. And after I go to their house, I'm going
to get Floyd to call the Coast Guard. And
then I'm going to tell the pastor, so he and
Edith can call everyone and get the town
praying. And after that—" Her voice broke
as her gaze drifted toward the sea. "After
that, I'm going down to the docks to wait, I
suppose. And I'm going to pray that noth-

ing happens to those children—because if it does, Salt Gribbon, the fault will rest on your head."

Her words stung like a whip, yet he knew he deserved every lash. She lifted her chin as if she expected him to argue, but he pointed toward the cart. "Let's go," he said, moving toward the passenger side. "We've no time to waste."

Birdie slid behind the wheel. Salt had barely managed to tumble onto the bench beside her before she pressed on the accelerator and spun around, slamming him against the support rail. He clung to the pole, however, knowing that anything he endured now was a small price to pay for his mistakes.

The cart flew up the road, spewing snow and gravel and slush in its wake. Birdie flew over the potholes, jarring Salt's bones and setting his teeth to rattling in his head, but he bit down and closed his eyes.

He hadn't meant it to end like this. He'd only intended the best for those children. And Birdie had been right all along.

Why hadn't he asked for help sooner? Why did he have to ruin every young life he touched? He'd ruined Patrick's life by being gone too much, and now he'd hurt these children by being around too much. Why couldn't he get it right?

If the authorities took the kids away—please, God, if he could find 'em—they'd have every right to place the children in a proper home. He'd blown his chance to make a good home for them, to reconcile his past and redeem his own failures.

But now he had to save their lives. He would find Russell Higgs at the dock and borrow his lobster boat. They'd go out and comb the channel between the island and the mainland. If they didn't find the kids there, they'd go farther to search. But he wouldn't quit, no matter how bad a squall blew in.

Birdie slowed as they passed the Lobster Pot, then stopped outside the gallery. "I'm going in to speak to the Grahams," she said, turning to give him a stern look. "We'll call the Coast Guard. You take this cart and drive on down to the B&B. Russell should be home; if he's not, try the docks. I'm pretty sure I saw his boat tied up there this morning."

Salt nodded and let her go, then slid

over on the seat and gripped the steering wheel. The pitch of the electric motor rose when he pressed on the accelerator, and he drove as fast as the vehicle would allow until he reached the Baskahegan Bed and Breakfast. Electric candles glowed in the decorated windows, and he gulped in the scent of evergreen as he raced up the path and the porch steps.

He pounded on the door, then went to the wide bay window and pressed his hands to the glass, peering into the darkness. Nothing moved in the fancy parlor beyond, but a fire crackled in the fireplace and he could hear the strains of Christmas music.

A moment later the door opened. Floyd Lansdown stood in the foyer, his cardigan sweater buttoned at the waist and a notebook beneath his arm.

"I need a boat." Salt crossed the wooden porch in two steps. "Is your lobsterman home?"

"Russell?" Floyd took a step out the door and looked toward the docks. "He's working on his boat. The engine's out of her, I think; he's doin' maintenance and repairs."

Salt sprang off the porch, jumping over a

snow-dusted bank of boxwoods, and ignored Floyd's urgent cry: "Is this an
emergency? Should I get the fire truck?"

For an instant Salt debated whether or
not he should even bother with the golf cart,
for the dock lay just beyond Frenchman's
Fairest on the hill. But his bones were aching
from his leap and his muscles were tense
with panic. He jumped into the cart and
floored the accelerator, arriving at the dock a
moment later. The ferry was nowhere in
sight, but Russell Higgs's lobster boat, the
Barbara Jean, bobbed alongside the dock.

Salt set off at a sprint, each cold snatch of
air searing the back of his throat. His steps
pounded the boards of the dock, sounding
for all the world like gunshots.

Heavens, he was too old for this! Why
had he ever thought a seventy-year-old man
could care for a couple of young 'uns?

"Higgs!" he bellowed, his voice an octave
higher than usual. "Are you there?"

Russell Higgs, clad in a hat, earmuffs, and
flannel jacket, thrust his head out of the
cabin. His eyes went wide and his thin
mouth opened slightly when Salt leaned on
the railing and panted: "Need your boat.

Kids out on the water, and the wind's bawlin' up something fierce."

Russell blinked several times in rapid succession. "Cap'n, I'd be glad to help, but—" He spread his hands, gesturing to the deck. Following his gaze, Salt felt his heart leap uncomfortably into the back of his throat. Russell's engine—most of it, anyway—lay in carefully arranged pieces on the wooden floor.

Salt clung harder to the railing as his knees buckled under him. The dock was pounding again, this time with faster footsteps. Without looking, he knew that Birdie, Babette, and Charles Graham were rushing toward him.

If God was merciful, they'd drown him here and now.

Out on the ocean, Bobby squinted and searched the horizon for a sign of the shore. It was hard to see anything through the milky stuff the grandfather had called sea smoke. He said it was a fog that rose whenever the air grew colder than the water, and not even the wind could blow it all away.

The thick white smoke blanketed the sea around them. Some of it had gotten into the boat as well, clammy tendrils that brushed his face and drifted between Brittany and Georgie, huddling at the stern.

Georgie had stopped rowing long ago, claiming that his muscles were worn out. Even Olympic weightlifters, he said, needed to rest.

"Bobby?" Britt's voice trembled. "Are we there yet?"

Bobby dropped both oars into the water and pulled again, but the boat only shifted a tiny bit to the right.

"Gonna be a little while longer," he said, keeping his eyes on the blue horizon. Brittany crouched on the bench with her doll, shivering visibly. They'd lost sight of Heavenly Daze and the lighthouse, and now Bobby wasn't sure where they were. He expected to see home at any time and couldn't understand why the trip was taking so long. It hadn't taken this long for the grandfather to row them over . . . or maybe he hadn't noticed how long they'd traveled.

He pulled at the oars again and felt the

boat shift. One thing was sure—it hadn't been this cold when they crossed over with the grandfather.

They were moving, though, and that was good. The waves kept pushing at the boat, sending it faster and farther than he and Georgie could ever drive it with the oars. So if they were patient, and waited a little longer . . .

"I'm hungry." Georgie squirmed on his seat. "I had crackers in my backpack. Has anyone seen my backpack?"

"You didn't put it in the boat." Britt's teeth were chattering like one of those wind-up toy skulls.

"Rats. I like those crackers." Georgie slumped, then looked at Bobby. "You got any food?"

Bobby shook his head. "We ate before."

He'd remembered to eat, but in the rush of launching the boat, he'd forgotten his encyclopedia. Apparently Brittany was the only one who'd remembered to bring anything. She still clung to Miranda, and every once in a while she'd hug the doll and whisper, "Just a little bit longer."

Releasing the oars, Bobby tucked his

cold hands into his armpits and tried to think about the woodstove back in the lighthouse. Some nights, while the wind howled outside and the stars shone so bright you knew it was frosty outside, the stove would fill the place with such heat that he'd wake up sweating. Amazing, really, that such a little thing could make a person feel so warm.

"Bobby?" Britt was looking at him again. "Is it going to get dark soon?"

The question made goose bumps rise on his goose bumps. He felt a sudden anger at Brittany for even thinking such a question, because some things couldn't hurt you as long as you didn't think about them. But now she'd gone and talked about dark, which meant it would surely come.

He looked past Britt to the horizon where the sun had slipped low behind the clouds. His shadow on the water had grown longer, and soon, he knew, it would be swallowed by the night.

"We'll be fine," he said, hunkering down into his coat. "We'll be there soon."

*   *   *

On the dock, Salt paced back and forth, his hands in his pockets, his eyes glaring at the dark, hungry ocean, empty under the moon. For four hours the Coast Guard had been patrolling the waters between Heavenly Daze and the mainland, and they'd promised to radio as soon as they found anything.

At the dock, Russell Higgs worked frantically to piece his engine back together. Salt would have offered to help, but Russell was a regular old woman when it came to his boat and Salt didn't want to get in his way.

From where he stood, he could see Birdie, the Grahams, and Floyd Lansdown holed up in the tiny shack that served as the ferry office. Floyd kept the radio transmitter at his mouth, most likely talking to the Coast Guard, while Birdie hovered by his shoulder. The Grahams kept a vigil at the window, staring out at the empty water. Birdie had invited Salt to share their shelter, but he'd refused. She had managed to get him to accept a cup of coffee, but he felt guilty drinking it—why should he be enjoying the comfort of a hot beverage when three kids were out on the cold and windy sea because he'd been an unreasonable old mule?

He knew the Grahams blamed him for everything, and Birdie probably did, too. The Coast Guard guys undoubtedly had a few questions about how three children had managed to access a boat and take off without adult supervision, and Salt knew he deserved whatever censure they wanted to toss his way. Shoot, if they wanted him to pay for the search and rescue mission, he'd sell everything he owned to make things right again.

He'd give his soul to see those children safe and sound.

He turned and looked toward the mainland, where the sun was lowering. The Coast Guard had surely finished crisscrossing the waters on the west of the island; soon they'd have to turn their attention toward the open sea.

Salt clung to a crusty piling and looked toward the east, where the ocean stretched out in a cold expanse that ended on European shores. Like every islander, he knew the prevailing winds came from the southwest. The children had launched their boat from the leeward side of the island, so if they hadn't been fortunate enough to immediately drift west, they'd have been blown out to sea. The boat was seaworthy, he had no worries about their vessel, but how long could three young children survive freezing temperatures in treacherous wind-tossed waters?

Salt lifted his eyes to the crystal-clear sky. "God Almighty," he whispered, tears stinging his eyes, "if you can forgive an old fool for years of neglect, will you listen to me now? The children are upon your sea, Lord, but they're not prepared for the night. Help us, Lord. Please."

Gavriel received the summons the instant Salt began to pray. "Yes, Father." He smiled. "I rejoice to do your will."

In a microsecond the angelic captain materialized, moving from invisibility to visibility, from supernatural form to mortal. His wings retracted and folded into flesh, his stature shrank to a scale more in keeping with man, God's lower creation. As the pulsing subatomic particles of his being transformed, strength rippled through his frame, flushing his golden skin with the blushing tones of blood and earth.

Moving with the confidence of an angelic warrior, he left the church and walked down to the beach where his escorts waited.

Birdie felt her apprehension rise as the sun lowered. When it finally disappeared behind a dark cloud bank, she stood and went to the window, not wanting the others to read the apprehension in her face. She could not conceal her panic; it shook her until she feared her teeth would chatter.

In the dim glow of a streetlight she saw Salt on the dock, a thin figure clinging to a post as though it alone kept him upright. He had to be chilled to the marrow, but he wouldn't come inside . . . and, deep within, she knew why. He couldn't face the Grahams, and he didn't want to face her. But no one could have foreseen or prevented this.

"I can't believe Georgie did this," Babette was whimpering, her fingers clawing at a piece of clotted tissue. She dabbed the end of her nose, then smiled weakly when Birdie pulled another tissue from the box on the ferry captain's desk. "He knows he's not supposed to wander far from home. Why would he think he could jump into a boat and go out to sea?"

"Maybe he didn't realize the danger," Birdie said, keeping her gaze on the man outside. "Maybe he thought of it as an adventure. Boys will be boys, you know." She bit her lip, realizing that Babette might think it strange to hear a spinster give child-rearing advice. "Or so I've heard."

"I'm going to hug the breath out of him, then I'm going to spank him," Charles proclaimed, crumpling an empty foam cup in his fist. "Then I'm going to confine him to his room for a year. No playing outside, no wandering all over the island—"

"Charles, you can't mean that." Babette rebuked him gently. "This is the safest place in the world for a kid—well, one who obeys his parents' rules. Georgie knew he wasn't supposed to climb on the rocks or go near the lighthouse."

Charles ran his hand through his hair. "I reckon we forgot to tell him it's not okay to take a neighbor's boat, launch out, and row away." Charles turned to embrace his weeping wife. "I'm sorry to sound sarcastic, honey. I just want our boy back."

As Babette wept, Birdie kept her gaze focused out the window, not wanting to intrude on the couple's private grief. Across the island, she saw lights burning in all the houses of Heavenly Daze, but the lights of the church fairly glowed with brilliance. Pastor Wickam had called an emergency prayer meeting, and as far as she knew, every single islander had reported to pray. Bea was there now with Abner, as were Vernie and Elezar, Olympia and Caleb, Zuriel, the Klackenbushes and Yakov, Cleta, Barbara, and Micah, as well as Edith and Winslow Wickam. A few minutes ago, Floyd had abandoned the radio and walked to the church. Birdie had thanked him for his help, assuring him that time spent in prayer was every bit as useful as time spent aiding the Coast Guard. Dr. Marc was trudging toward the church now, eager to pray for Georgie and two children he didn't even know.

Or did he? Birdie's thoughts drifted again to the stranger who had sheltered the kids on that cold night when Salt was sick. Could Dr. Marc have been the kind man who took them in? Such kindness was part of his nature, and he was tall and hand-some, which fit Bobby's description. Maybe the boy had invented the part about the long white hair. After all, his sister was given to wild stories . . .

She jumped as a foghorn shattered the stillness.

"What's that?" Charles leaped up and peered through the windows of the ferry shack.

Birdie opened the door and looked out into the night. A large boat with a star-span-gled flag was pulling up to the dock.

"Must be the Coast Guard." She buttoned her coat. "I'm going to go out and see what they've found."

Babette and Charles followed right be-hind her. "We're coming, too."

The three of them covered the distance between the shed and the dock in long strides. As they drew nearer, Birdie noticed how the Coast Guard cutter shone in the moonlight. The color was a dazzling white she'd never seen before; it almost seemed to shimmer against the inky night waters. Odd, too, that the boat bore no seals, no numbers, no markings of any kind.

A uniformed man on deck was tossing a mooring line—a pristine cream-colored cord—to Salt, who caught it effortlessly. Another man, who wore a white pea coat over a uniform as bright as the gleaming boat, stood on deck with his hands behind his back. He nodded gravely as she and the Grahams approached, and a moment later a gangplank extended from the deck to the dock.

"Please." The captain stepped forward, his smile beckoning her through the darkness. "Come aboard. We understand there's a rescue to be performed, and there isn't much time."

No one needed to be asked twice. The Grahams walked straightway up the gangway, Charles tenderly shielding Babette. Birdie followed behind and turned at the end, noticing that Salt seemed to hesitate.

"Salt?"

He shook his head. "I can't. It's all my fault."

"Captain Gribbon?" The man in white spoke now, his manner dignified and respectful. "Sir, my commanding officer has charged me with finding you. It would be our privilege to have your help in this mission."

Something in the man's tone or manner seemed to energize Salt. He lifted his head, and for an instant the mantle of defeat seemed to fall from his shoulders. After giving a brusque nod, he trudged up the gangplank, inclined his head toward the captain, then took Birdie's elbow and led her away from the opening at the rail.

When they were aboard, one of the sailors ran down the gangway, cast off the ropes, and returned to the deck. Within minutes, the ship had pulled away from the dock and headed out to sea.

Though the captain had invited her into the cabin where she'd be shielded from the cold wind and sea spray, Birdie found a place to sit on the deck. If Salt wouldn't go inside, she wouldn't, either.

He stood alone near the bow, one arm wrapped around a post. Though the strong wind had been freezing on the dock, once the boat began to move the wind increased to a great roaring current of frigid air, a torrent so biting Birdie had to turn and lower her head in order to catch a breath. The cold slapped at her like an icy hand determined to buffet her into submission.

The wind was unbelievably brutal, yet Salt stood silent in its assault, either bent on punishing himself or bitterly reliving his sea days. Birdie nearly deserted her post, then decided she would keep Salt company no matter what his motivation. If she were to help him, she'd have to understand him, and how could she understand a man like this unless she experienced what he did? She would stay with him, her heart keeping pace with the ship on its flight through the darkness.

They cruised at a steady pace, riding the waves toward the rising moon, and despite her discomfort Birdie found herself marveling at the beauty and power of the churning sea. A person could get lost out here. This was a world apart, populated by animals and a breed of men she'd been around all her life but had never really understood.

Salt moved to the bow and placed his hands upon the railing, his eyes scanning the sea as the ship slapped down the peaks of the waves. With each dip of the boat a spray of water rained over him, but he seemed not to care that he'd soon be covered in an icy glaze.

What sort of man was this?

Fortunately, the rising moon brightened the night, and after a few moments someone turned on a searchlight that swept the ocean in wide arcs. Then the captain cut the engine, and the empty air filled with dread as the boat floated silently on the choppy sea.

Birdie swallowed as doubts rose in her mind. Why had they stopped? She turned, and through the cabin window saw that Charles Graham had apparently wondered the same thing. He was speaking to the captain, his face a study in worry, his hands rising and falling like the wings of a frantic, wounded bird.

And then she heard the treble sounds of children calling, "Heeeeeeeeeey!"

On her feet in an instant, she rushed to Salt's side. In front and to the right of the ship bobbed the dory, populated with three bundled children. The searchlight found and held them, and in its bright beam Birdie saw Bobby, Brittany, and Georgie, alive and well. Bobby was standing in the boat, holding an oar over his head.

"Thank God," she whispered, closing her eyes.

A masculine voice rang out through a bullhorn. "Hello, children! Sit still; we'll send a raft to pick you up."

When Birdie opened her eyes, she saw that Georgie and Brittany were jumping up and down, clapping their hands, and causing the boat to rock. As a wave lifted the boat the kids squealed and gripped the edge, but as soon as the wave relaxed, so did the children. Georgie was leaning over the side now, reaching out and causing the dory to list—

"Sit down!" called the man on the bullhorn. "You must sit still."

But either the children couldn't hear above the wind or they weren't of a mind to obey, because now Bobby was jumping, too, waving the oar above his head.

"They can't hear," Birdie whispered. The wind was blowing toward the big boat, carrying the children's voices but working against the man with the bullhorn.

"I've got to get to them," Salt roared in Birdie's ear. "If a wave catches 'em off balance like that, they'll spill."

"Children!" the bullhorn voice called again. "Sit down!"

Birdie clung to the railing, grateful for its stability on the shifting sea, but her heart froze when she heard a splash.

CHAPTER TWENTY-THREE

Got to get to the kids. Got to keep them from tipping the boat. The thoughts rose in Salt's head like the air bubbles thundering past his ears. The briny water filled his nose, the familiar tang carrying him back to places and years long gone. Reflexively he curved his body to rise toward the silvery moon.

He held his breath until his head broke the surface, then he began to swim in what should have been long, sure strokes. As a seasoned sailor he swam like a fish, so why did his arms and legs feel like lead?

The cold. The villainous cold had attacked his limbs, as it would soon attack his lungs and incapacitate every cell in his body. In his urgency to reach the children, he'd underestimated its power on his aging body.

Stroke. He lowered his head and thrust out an arm, forced it past his benumbed body, but he could see nothing but darkness.

Was he horizontal? Was he still swimming toward the dory?

Stroke. He pulled with the other arm, forced it to sweep back to his side, commanded it to push against the water that felt like stinging alcohol on his skin. He tried to move his other arm, found that he couldn't, and had the presence of mind to turn and float on his back.

An old sailor's trick—the best way to conserve energy. Fill the lungs and float, curling into a ball if you had to, and wait for drowning or hypothermia to overpower you.

"Where'd the old man go?" Charles asked. He and Babette stood at the railing with Birdie now, and she could feel their fear. The searchlight operator hadn't taken the beam off the kids for fear of frightening them, so Salt was swimming in darkness.

Moving with quick, powerful steps, the captain joined them at the rail. Birdie stepped back to ask him a question and frowned when she noticed a white ponytail at the back of his cap. Since when did the Coast Guard allow their members to wear long hair?

She brushed the question aside. The man could have hair down to his knees for all she cared. "Captain," she touched his arm, "please, how do we get them on board?"

"We get Cap'n Gribbon first," the officer said, accepting the life preserver another sailor handed him. "The children are dry as long as they're in the boat, but a man can't survive in these waters for long."

"The old fool," Charles muttered. "What was he thinking?"

As a rush of defensiveness fired Birdie's blood, she swiveled to face Georgie's father. "The children couldn't hear the bullhorn above the wind. He was afraid they'd fall in."

"Salt Gribbon," the captain called, leaning over the bow railing with the life preserver in his hand. "Do you hear me?"

By some miracle, Salt heard. "Aye," came the weak response.

"I'm going to throw you a life preserver."

"No." Salt's wind-borne voice had a haunted quality, but Birdie recognized the stubbornness in it.

"Salt Gribbon, you obey this man!" she yelled into the darkness, leaning over the railing as far as she dared. "For once in your life, don't argue!"

The wind whispered his response: "Get . . . kids . . . first."

"We can't do that, Cap'n." The skipper of the rescue ship lifted his head toward the children, and one of the sailors handed him the bullhorn. "Kids?" the captain called. "We're going to have to take the light off you for a moment."

The children must have heard, for Brittany began to wail. "Nooooooooo!"

The captain looked at Birdie. "Please, Miss Wester," he asked, his eyes at once gentle and powerful. "Will you talk to them?"

Trembling, Birdie took the bullhorn from his hand and leaned over the railing. "Listen, Brittany, we're going to come out and get you in a minute. But first, we've got to use the light to find your grandfather. Do you understand?"

"I don't wanna be in the dark!"

Birdie clutched the railing, her heart torn. She didn't want to plunge the children into darkness, either, but if Salt were to be saved—

Birdie watched, amazed, as Bobby lowered the oar he'd been holding and put his arm around Brittany, then looked up into the light. "It's okay," he called, his voice distinct and strong for one so young. "We'll be fine. Please save our grandfather."

The captain didn't hesitate. "Move the light!" he called. Immediately the searchlight shifted from the dory and moved unerringly toward an object floating off the right bow—Salt Gribbon.

The captain expertly drew back his hand and tossed the life preserver, which fell within inches of Salt's limp arms. But the stubborn lighthouse keeper did not move.

"Salt!" Birdie screamed, hysteria rising in her chest. "You take that line and you take it now!" She knew what he was doing, but this was not the time nor the place to punish himself for the children's mishap.

Finding courage from some place deep inside herself, Birdie snatched the bullhorn she'd returned to the captain. "The children are all right," she called. "They're waiting for you to reach out. Catch the line, Salt. Your grandchildren want you safe."

And then, while the group at the bow watched, Salt's fingertips appeared against the stark whiteness of the bobbing life preserver. Charles, Babette, and the captain yelled encouragement as he looped his arm through the circle, then the skipper gave the order to pull him in.

As a pair of sailors lowered a rubber raft to go fetch the children, Birdie waited by the railing until Salt was brought aboard and taken to the cabin. She turned her back as a couple of the sailors stripped off Salt's wet clothes and wrapped him in a large towel, then they laid him on a cot and covered him in layers of blankets.

When he had been safely tucked in, she sat beside him and ran her fingers over the soft beard on his cheek. His bleary eyes met hers, and his mouth moved for a moment before sound crossed his lips. "I'm sorry," he said.

"I'm not," she answered, placing her hand full against his face. A moment later the cabin door opened and Bobby, Brittany, and Georgie swarmed into the room, accompanied by Babette and Charles, the captain, and a pair of smiling sailors.

"Were you scared?" Babette kept asking, her arms around her son. "We were so worried!"

"We weren't scared at all," Georgie said, puffing out his chest. "Brittle-knees said that as long as we held up the assistants of God, we'd be okay."

Babette looked at Birdie, a confused expression on her face.

"The assistants of God?" Birdie asked, looking from Brittany to Bobby. "I'm afraid I don't understand."

Bobby grinned as he looked at the tall, white-haired skipper. "I remembered," he said simply, "when Moses held up the big stick and won the battle. God told him to hold it up, and when he got tired, his friends helped him."

"We helped hold it," Georgie said, flexing his muscles. "We held up that oar for hours!"

Birdie looked at Salt, who closed his eyes. "Thank God," he said simply, reaching out for Bobby's hand.

"Everybody warm up," the captain said, walking to the wheel. He glanced at Salt. "Sir, we've tied your boat to the stern and will haul her in for you. Everybody is safe and sound, so our mission is accomplished."

"God bless the Coast Guard," Babette whispered, wrapping her arms around her shivering son.

Shifting her gaze from Babette, Birdie saw the white-haired captain smile.

*   *   *

Drifting on a tide of fatigue, Salt floated in and out of consciousness, weighted by a weariness that seemed to drag body and soul into the depths of darkness. In clearer moments he felt himself being lifted, then heard a hum of voices that faded to a silent echo. Some still-functioning part of his brain registered soft sheets, a warm bed, and the faint scent of lilacs.

But none of that mattered. The children were safe, his secret had been revealed, and soon the world would know that he'd stolen his grandchildren and proven himself an unfit guardian. Soon bureaucrats from the State of Maine's Social Services Department would descend upon Heavenly Daze and take the children away.

"You worry too much, Salt Gribbon."

The voice, powerful and unfamiliar, jerked him from the benumbing darkness. Opening his eyes, Salt turned his head and saw that he was not alone. A man sat in a chair across from the bed—a man dressed all in white, with snowy hair spilling over his shoulders. His eyes were the most piercing shade of blue—

Salt sat up and stared, tongue-tied, when he recognized the fellow. Why had the Coast Guard captain come into his bedroom?

"It's not your bedroom," the man said, his voice calm and matter-of-fact. "You're in a guest room at the Baskahegan B&B. The lavender room, Cleta calls it. Rather charming, don't you think?"

Nonplussed, Salt could do little but nod. This had to be a dream. No one could read a man's thoughts.

"It's no dream . . . well, not like any dream you've ever had. Consider this a visualization, if you like. A special gift from the Father."

Salt felt his mouth go dry. "Whose father?"

"Your Father, the Almighty God." The man stood, then held out his hand. "Come with me, friend. Don't worry—the Lord will supply the strength you need. You have only to trust."

Salt clutched at the blanket. What was this, some deranged version of *A Christmas Carol*? Whatever it was, he didn't need it. He was no Ebenezer Scrooge. He was a fair man, an independent man, a man who wanted only to be left alone to do what duty demanded—

A faint smile played at the corners of the stranger's mouth. "God knows who and what you are."

Salt blinked several times in rapid succession, hoping the man would disappear and prove to be a figment of his imagination. But the image persisted.

"Who—who are you?"

The seaman's smile deepened. "I am a messenger from the Most High God."

"Not a Coast Guard captain, then. And not a ghost like the Spirit of Christmas Past."

"I am a captain. I am called Gavriel, but you can call me Gabe."

As the name registered with his dizzied senses, the being who called himself Gabe stood and gripped the back of Salt's shirt— an odd flannel pajama top at least two sizes too big and decorated with little red fire trucks. Before Salt could protest the strange clothing and the even stranger situation, the room filled with bright light and a whooshing sound. Cleta Lansdown's curtains and doilies and bed ruffles flapped and fluttered in an invisible wind, then the double windows blew open and Gavriel carried Salt out into the night.

Salt blinked in stupefaction as the ground flew away from his feet. Together they rose above the island, its outline dimming and eventually becoming lost in a diorama of lights from the coastlands below.

"Is this dangerous?" Salt gazed around in wonder. "I mean—can't I get radiated or something up here?"

Gabe smiled. "You'll be fine," he said, his voice reaching Salt's ear despite the sound of rushing wind. "Your body absorbs radiation all the time, both from the world and from your own body. Your cells can usually repair any damage, though. In fact, without the natural background radiation the Lord designed for this planet, your cellular repair mechanisms would become dormant, making you much more vulnerable to sudden bursts of radiation."

Salt swallowed the information with a simple "Oh."

"Every second, every human on earth is penetrated by more than one hundred cosmic rays," Gabe went on, apparently warming to his subject. "In the same second, more than 50,000 gamma rays from your surroundings zip through you at the speed of light, while thousands of potassium atoms and two or three uranium atoms within your body release more radiation. With every breath, you take in several radioactive atoms that decay in your lungs."

Salt forced a laugh. "Reckon it's a miracle I've lived to threescore and ten, heh?"

"Every day is a miracle, Captain. But life is not the miracle I'm to show you tonight."

Salt squirmed in his pajama top. "I can't fall, can I?" He dared not look down, but he couldn't help but see that they now flew over a glittering array of lights. Boston? Washington, D.C.?

"You cannot fall. You are held in the palm of God's own hand."

Salt didn't feel terribly *held* by anyone or anything, but he kept his mouth shut. Up and up they flew until the rushing wind grew silent and they moved through utter sound-lessness. Holding his breath, Salt wondered if they had crossed into outer space, but the blackness was like that of the sea at night, the stars like the reflection of a million tiny organisms that spun and glowed in the deepest compartments of Davy Jones's locker . . .

That's all this is, a dream springing from my subconscious—

But suddenly the angel roared upward in a blaze of brilliance so stunning that Salt threw up his arms and still his eyes burned behind his fists and his closed eyelids. He could feel light pressuring his eyes and knew he couldn't open them without blinding pain. Even behind his fists and lids, his pupils must be mere pinpricks, so intense was the light—

"Humble yourself," Gabe said, his voice now a reverent whisper. "You are about to behold the throne room of God."

Still hiding behind his hands, Salt whimpered. "I'm in heaven?"

"No. You're being allowed a glimpse; the things you see are only a shadow of the glory that exists in the third heaven. Your mortal body could not survive the journey into that realm."

And suddenly the blinding pressure eased. Lowering his clenched fists, Salt saw that they were moving through an atmosphere the color of a Maine sky on a summer's day. Bright lights winked through this firmament, and as each light approached Salt caught a glimpse of a face and smile, then the dazzling creatures passed with no more sound than a sigh.

He and Gavriel flew on, toward a gleaming temple with pillars that radiated in a soft golden glow. Through a courtyard they moved, over a sea of those intelligent, brilliant lights.

"What are they?"

"The spirits of those who await the resurrection," Gabe replied.

On the wings of this celestial morning they descended into a chamber dominated by a throne so impressive in its brightness that Salt's weakened eyes ached to look at it. A man sat upon the throne, and at their approach his eyes lifted—

Salt covered his face with his hands. "Is that—"

"Yes," Gabe answered. "The Ancient of Days, the Alpha and the Omega. He who was, and is, and is to come. He who is holy."

Salt cringed, knowing that he reeked of grief and guilt. The ravages of his life on earth clung to him like smoke from his woodstove, permeating his clothing and pores and even his soul. "You've brought me here to die," he cried, tears stinging his eyes. "I know what the Good Book says. No man can see God and live."

"That's right, for God is a spirit, and only

those with spirit eyes can see spiritual beings," Gabe answered, his voice but a breath in Salt's ear. "The souls you see as lights below—they see him, they know him. But until you are incorporated in spirit, Salt Gribbon, you must see him as he is."

Salt raised his arms, determined to flee from the sight. "I can't!"

What had he done to merit this supernatural interrogation? He had done wrong, he knew it, but he was willing to pay for his pride and stubbornness. Let them come and take the children; let them take everything he owned. He had been wrong; he did not deserve to live. He was guilty, guilty, and he knew it. He had been willing to die in the sea; he was willing to die now.

So why was he here? As a child he'd been taught to honor and obey God, except the preacher in his small church had always pronounced the word GOHD, as if it must be spoken in an affected and holy whisper. GOHD, the preacher had frequently intoned, did not suffer fools. He watched over all; he kept accurate accounts, He knew when every single person sinned and fell short of his holy standard. Therefore every man had to fear GOHD, and tremble before him, lest he be cast aside in the final reckoning . . .

"Salt." This voice was new, but it resonated through every fiber of Salt's being. It was the voice of knowledge, love, and justice.

"Salt, do you not know who I am, even after all the time I have been with you?"

Lowering his hands an inch, Salt peeked over his fingertips. The One on the throne had risen and seemed to be speaking to him alone.

But I can see you!

The Lord smiled. "Anyone who has seen me has seen the Father. I am in the Father and the Father is in me."

Gabe whispered in Salt's ear: "The Word became human and lived on earth among us. He was full of unfailing love and faithfulness. And now you see his glory, the glory of the only Son of the Father."

Salt felt his spirit wavering before the steadfast concentration of those loving eyes.

Why have you brought me here?

"Because I long for your companionship."

The words were spoken without rancor, but they fell with the weight of stones in still water, spreading ripples of guilt and conviction. Salt bowed his head, unable to face the loving rebuke in those eyes.

"Because God's children are made of mortal flesh and blood," Gabe whispered, "Jesus also became flesh and blood by being born in human form. For only as a human being could he die, and only by dying could he break the power of the Devil, who had the power of death. Only in this way could he deliver those who have lived all their lives as slaves to the fear of dying."

Salt felt a trembling arise from some place at the center of his soul.

"Do you not see?" The angel's voice softened. "It was necessary for Jesus to be in every respect like you, his brothers and sisters, so he could be your merciful and faithful High Priest before God. He then could offer a sacrifice that would take away the sins of the people. Since he himself has gone through suffering and temptation, he is able to help you when you are being tempted—or when you're afraid. He endured it all for you, Salt—so you wouldn't have to endure pain alone."

Like a careening vehicle, the truth

crashed into Salt full force, wrenching a soft cry of despair from his battered heart.

What a fool he'd been. Self-reliant and stubborn, he had scorned Birdie's help, refused the town's assistance, and ignored this Savior who stood ready and willing to give grace and comfort and fellowship. Oh, he'd muttered perfunctory prayers every night when the children first arrived, but he'd addressed them to the great and powerful GOHD, never really believing that he would be interested in Salt's situation. And then, as time passed and Salt's little family settled into a routine, he had convinced himself that he hadn't needed GOHD after all. He alone had made things work.

But all he'd done was make a mess of the situation. And he'd known that he could never be the permanent answer for Bobby and Brittany, for his mortal life span was already far spent . . .

Forgive me, Lord.

"I will." His voice, low and passionate, commanded the glittering chamber. "As you forgive those who have wronged you."

Salt gulped hard as hot tears streamed down his cheeks.

Oh, the shame of his life! He'd been so judgmental, so hard-hearted! He had given up on a wayward son and steeled himself against the pain he'd caused. He had taken two wounded and impressionable children and subjected them to a solitary existence more suited to a misanthropic hermit than youngsters on the threshold of life.

"Forgive me," he whispered, turning to bury his face in the softness of the flannel pajama sleeves. He tasted the salt of tears on his lips, and when he opened his eyes again, he was back in the lavender bedroom, propped on two lilac-scented pillows and covered with a pristine white counterpane.

CHAPTER TWENTY-FOUR

On Sunday morning, Birdie ate a day-old doughnut for breakfast, then placed two phone calls. In the first, Babette announced that Bobby and Brittany were still sleeping. Georgie's first official sleepover had ended, Babette assured Birdie, far sooner than Georgie had anticipated. At eight she had bundled the three children in warm bed-clothes and placed them in front of an animated video with a huge bowl of pop-corn. In less than ten minutes, all three kids were fast asleep.

A call to the B&B revealed that Salt still slept, too. Cleta said the lightkeeper hadn't moved, but Dr. Marc had come by just after sunup and found Salt sleeping soundly with a steady pulse.

Birdie had been glad to hear that Salt would fully recover from his misadventure, but she knew she wouldn't be able to rest until she saw him herself. So at eight-thirty she bundled herself in hat, coat, and gloves, then walked the short distance to the Baskahegan Bed and Breakfast.

Floyd answered the door and let her in with no comment other than a knowing smile. As Birdie shed her coat and hat in the foyer, Micah thrust his head out of the kitchen and asked if she wanted a cup of coffee or cider.

"In a minute, maybe," she called, pulling off her gloves. "After I check on Cap'n Gribbon."

"First door on the left at the top of the stairs," Cleta called from the kitchen. "He was snoring like a walrus last time I walked by."

Birdie climbed the stairs with more energy than she'd felt in days.

Salt didn't answer when she rapped at the door, which was probably a good sign. She turned the knob and let herself in, then stood in silence for a moment at the foot of the bed.

What a man he was. Stubborn and mule-headed, for certain, but loyal, hardworking, and responsible. As a husband he'd be the type to show his love in actions, not words, but Birdie figured she could learn to live with that.

Once he realized he needed a wife.

She sank to the edge of the mattress and ran her hand over the soft bedspread. Salt lay flat on his back, his chin jutting above the covers, the collar of Floyd's pajamas framing his strong face.

She pressed her hand to the spot just above his heart. At her touch, his eyelids fluttered open. "Wh–What?"

"It's me, Salt." She smiled as his gaze lowered and met hers. "How be you this morning?"

He closed his eyes for a moment, then groaned. "Nicely, I reckon. But my toes are still cold."

"That's okay. I expect they'll warm up soon enough."

He struggled to push himself up into a sitting position. "What about the kids?"

"They're staying with the Grahams. Babette said Georgie was thrilled to have friends sleep over, but they conked out ten minutes after she got 'em into their jammies."

His mouth twisted in something not quite

a smile. "That's good. I expect they can stay there . . . until they have to go. If Babette will keep 'em."

Birdie shook her head. "Why would they have to leave you?"

"Oh, Birdie." Lines of concentration deepened along his brows and under his eyes. "I was wrong to take 'em in the first place—I should have gotten some help for my boy. Or I should have taken him in. But instead I wrote him off and took those kids, thinking I could do with them what I never did with my own son—be a father, I mean. I was always gone when Patrick needed me, and last summer I took his children and left him alone, just like I've always done."

He turned slightly, gazing out the window with chilling intensity for a long moment. "Last night I learned something—I was never meant to live alone. I thought I had God's help, I thought I knew him, but I only knew the figurehead." His squint tightened, and Birdie saw thought working in his eyes. "Last night I met Jesus. And I realized that I've been the most hardheaded man on the planet."

Birdie felt her throat tighten as his blue eyes brimmed with tears. Something had happened to Salt, and though she didn't understand it, she felt a thrill shiver through her senses. God worked miracles all the time, even on the little island of Heavenly Daze.

"Salt." She reached out and took his hand, then held it gently between both her own. "Do you know what I read the other day?"

Looking away, he shook his head as if he could dislodge the tears from his eyes.

Continuing, she kept her voice light. "I read a quote by George Bernard Shaw. He said, 'I can think of no other edifice constructed by man as altruistic as a lighthouse. They were built only to serve. They weren't built for any other purpose.'"

Salt looked at her again. "What does that have to do with—"

"You're a lighthouse. Yes, you're hardheaded, and yes, you make mistakes because you're human. But God created you with a mile-wide streak of responsibility, and your intentions were good. You wanted to serve those children, and you've done a good job with them."

"But my son—"

"You can start tomorrow with your son.

Don't dwell on the past, Salt; look toward the future. Let your light shine."

He gave her a quick, denying glance. "That sounds real nice, Birdie, but it's too late. Lighthouses are a relic of the past. They've got these newfangled things now, aerobeacons and navigational buoys. With that GPS system, nobody really needs a lighthouse anymore . . . just like nobody needs an old mule like me."

"I know two children who'd disagree with you—three, if you count Georgie. He thinks you're a real hero."

He snorted softly. "I'm nobody's hero."

"You're mine." Birdie lowered her voice. "Last night I saw your light shining out, and I saw you risk much for those you loved—and yes, Salt, you can love deeply, I saw it as plain as the sun in heaven. And I knew then how much I loved you, Salt Gribbon."

And then, carried away by the realization that the moment would never come again, Birdie leaned forward and kissed Old Man Gribbon smack on the lips.

*   *   *

Downstairs in the kitchen, Floyd sat at the table staring at Cleta.

Cleta glared back.

Stanley sat between the warring couple, slumped over a bowl of oatmeal.

Across from him, Vernie focused on the refrigerator.

Six days had passed since she'd found Stanley hidden away in her friends' house. Though after that discovery she'd stomped out and vowed never to return, time and Elezar's gentle prodding had softened her heart. Last night she'd finally agreed to one round of peace talks before worship.

She reckoned it was the least she could do, it bein' a Sunday and her calling herself a Christian. Especially since Floyd had convinced her that Stanley Bidderman was a dying man. She didn't feel so good herself these days.

Now she sat at the Lansdowns' kitchen table listening to the clock tick away long minutes. Though sharp eyes dominated the unspoken conversation, for the moment a weak truce kept the peace.

"I think," Floyd broke the strained silence,

"we should leave the room, Cleta, and let Stanley and Vernie talk."

Vernie crossed her arms and looked away. "I don't want to talk to that worm, but I will. I want you all to know that I'm here under distress."

"That's duress," Floyd corrected.

"That, too."

Cleta wearily dropped her chin into her hand. "He's not going to budge until you hear him out, Vernie." Her unspoken meaning was clear—get him out of my house, please!

Floyd tapped Vernie's arm. "Hear him out. If you don't like what he says—"

"You'll ask him to leave?" She sniffed. "You should have never brought him here in the first place."

Lifting a feeble hand, Floyd closed his eyes. "Just let the man talk," he said, his teeth clenched.

Chair legs scraped the floor as Floyd and Cleta got up. Giving Vernie's shoulder a re-assuring squeeze, Cleta said, "I'll be right outside the door if you need me." She bent closer. "Don't forget that there are other fish in the sea—there's always Eugene Fleming."

Vernie snorted.

A veil of silence enveloped the kitchen as the door closed. For a moment Vernie stared at her hands, unwilling to give Stanley a moment's satisfaction. Her head throbbed and she felt as hot as a blast furnace. Was she coming down with the flu, too? Cleta had developed a fever three days ago and still looked a little streak-ed.

When the silence stretched to an uncomfortable thinness, Stanley lifted his head. He'd aged. Of course, he was probably thinking the same about her. His once-youthful features had weathered. Lines creased his cheeks—what had put them there? Age alone, or age plus regret?

She looked away, pretending to study the photographs on the refrigerator. "Say what you've come to say, Stanley, so you can go in peace."

Stanley's eyes shone with remorse. "I know I hurt you badly, Vernie. I hurt myself even worse, and I'm sorry for it."

She refused to meet his gaze. "You should have shot me, Stanley. It would have hurt less."

He stiffened. "I'm here to ask your forgiveness."

"It's too late for that."

"You're wrong, Vernie. I can see you haven't changed a lick, but that's okay. I'm not responsible for your reactions, just my actions. So I'm here to ask for forgiveness, and I'm telling you it's not too late for us to make things right."

Vernie crossed her legs, struggling to digest the apology and the man who had so forcefully delivered it. This wasn't the man she'd known—that fellow would have tucked his tail and run back to his hiding place after she hung up on him the first time. Then again . . . a pending appointment with heaven might motivate even Stanley to get serious about settling his eternal affairs.

She slowly lifted her gaze. "How long do you have?"

He frowned. "I'm not sure. Cleta wants me out, but Floyd said—"

"Good grief, Stanley, do you think we're thick as planks? You're dying, aren't you? You're only here to make amends before you meet the Lord."

Surprise crossed his wan features. "I'm not dying, at least, I don't think I am. I was perfectly fine before I came down with this flu."

Vernie tapped her fingernail on the plastic place mat. He wasn't dying? He wasn't terminal and he obviously still had all his marbles. So he had changed. A lot.

Stiffly, she looked straight at him. "Why, Stanley?"

To his credit, Stanley didn't avoid the question. "Because I didn't feel you needed me."

A simple, forthright reply. Vernie suspected he had rehearsed his answer. "I didn't feel you needed me," he repeated, his voice softer now. "A man needs to feel wanted and important; I felt like an intruder in my own home. I felt you didn't love or need me."

The words stung. When had she ever made him feel like an intruder? Why, he should have felt like a king in his castle, pampered in every way! She had always seen to their business, looked after things, made decisions, managed the mercantile, and ordered stock. She had downright coddled him. Why, she didn't even complain about the bowling he loved so much though she knew his time could be better spent.

She had worried about bills and mortgages and food on the table while he stood in the background, rarely offering an opinion on anything more important than the color of a new bowling ball. He couldn't decide on something as simple as supper.

"What do you want for supper, Stanley?"

"Whatever you want."

"Chicken?"

"That's fine."

"Or maybe beef?"

"That's fine."

How she had longed for him to thump his chest and yell, "Forget the beef and chicken. I want a can of hot tamales!"

But noooooooo, Stanley never said anything. At first she got tired of being in charge, then she got used to it. But now he had the nerve to accuse her of indifference?

Stanley's voice broke into her reflection. "You asked why I came here, and I've told you. I don't expect you to understand."

Closing his eyes, he began again: "Leaving you was the worst mistake of my life. I knew it within a few weeks, but by then I knew coming back would only make things worse. You never seemed to need me, and nothing I did was ever good enough. You got bent out of shape no matter whether I agreed or disagreed. So, that night, I just decided to miss the ferry. I spent the night at a hotel, and the next morning I decided to go to Wells. Before I knew it, I was running, leaving the one commitment I'd managed to make in my life. I knew it was wrong, and I knew running wouldn't change anything. But then I couldn't face you, so I stayed away."

Somehow, Vernie found her voice. "What made you . . . why did you decide to call?"

Shaking his head, he looked up. "A commercial on television—one of those Hallmark things, I think. I saw a couple about our age, welcoming home the kids for Christmas, and I suddenly realized that we could have had twenty Christmases like that one, but I'd messed it up. So I decided to come home and apologize. See if you could find it in your heart to forgive me."

Pushing back from the table, he got up. "I can see in your face that forgiveness isn't exactly what you had in mind. So, if you'll excuse me, I've said what I came to say. I reckon I'll go up and pack my things, get out of Cleta's way."

Vernie pressed her hand to her mouth as he left the room.

Dazed, she sat in the quiet kitchen with her thoughts.

And Stanley's words.

Stanley's apology.

And Stanley's accusation.

Throughout morning worship and all afternoon Vernie replayed Stanley's words in her mind. *"I decided to come home . . . and see if you could find it in your heart to forgive me."*

Could she forgive? On one level it'd be easy. It'd be easy as pie to say, "Yes, because I'm a Christian, I forgive you, but get out of my sight and stay out, Stanley Bidderman." She could find sweet justice in that, and nobody on the island could blame her for booting Stanley off Heavenly Daze for good.

But . . . was that the kind of forgiveness Christ expected of her? It wasn't what he gave. Every time she goofed up, the savior welcomed her back with loving arms and sweet acceptance. He loved her, blunders and all, and when he forgave, he forgot.

So why couldn't she forgive Stanley?

Because he'd cost her years of physical and mental suffering. Because he'd ravaged her emotions and left her numb and too tired to care about love. Because he'd taken the best years of her life, years in which she could have had the whole Hallmark commercial . . .

So he'd hurt her . . . but hadn't she committed her share of hurts? She'd hurt him, too, though she'd never understood how until this morning. She'd taken over Stanley's life, interpreting his sweet nature as incompetence, mistaking his patience as weakness. She'd stolen his masculinity, his leadership, his role as a husband. She'd worn the pants in the family, sure, but she'd stepped into them first.

She should have waited for Stanley.

She pulled down her Bible, ran her finger over the verses where the Lord told his disciples they should forgive not seven times, but "seventy times seven." In the margin, she had written, "Forgiveness is my choice to personally bear the consequences of your choice, and never again hold you responsible for what you did to hurt me."

The words cut through her soul like a knife.

When had she written that? Probably years before Pastor Wickam came to town, since he tended to major on the minor prophets. Pastor Claude might have preached this sermon, and she might have written this even while Stanley sat by her side in the Heavenly Daze Church . . .

Funny, how lessons were never really learned until you put them into practice.

That evening she climbed the Lansdowns' attic staircase. Pausing at Stanley's bedroom door, she called, "Stan?"

She heard shuffling sounds, then, "Ayuh?"

"Can I come in?"

After a long pause, Stanley opened the door.

Feeling feverish, Vernie walked in and reached out for the bedpost. She probably shouldn't have come, but flu or no flu, she had to speak to her husband before he left.

Grasping the bedpost, she closed her eyes as her head swam. She'd be in bed tomorrow, too, most likely, and Elezar would have to play nurse and run the mercantile . . .

"What's wrong, Vernie?" Concern tinged Stanley's voice.

Chuckling softly, Vernie opened her eyes and saw the open suitcase, the clothes piled on the bed. He was leaving, so this couldn't be postponed, not even if she fainted.

"Are you okay?" Stanley reached out to support her. The touch seemed familiar, even after all these years.

"Stan?"

"I'm here, Vernie."

She looked up, meeting his troubled gaze. "You know how you said I didn't need you?"

His eyes softened. "Ayuh."

She drew a long shuddering breath, chills assaulting her fevered body. "Well, right now I couldn't need you more."

CHAPTER TWENTY-FIVE

On the afternoon of the twenty-fourth, Annie dropped her last pair of new shorts and summer blouses into her suitcase. Outside her window, snow fell in heavy sheets while the radio played holiday music as a prelude to Christmas Eve. She kept one ear alert for weather reports as she packed. The promised storm was on its way.

The D. J. segued out of "I'll Be Home for Christmas" with a weather bulletin, so Annie leaned forward to turn up the volume. "A few flights have been delayed, but most airlines are still operating. Snow totals estimated to be between eight and ten inches before this system passes. Well, folks, we're usually begging for a white Christmas, but this year we're gonna get a doozy!"

Annie's thoughts drifted to Frenchman's Fairest. Caleb would be in the kitchen, probably stuffing the turkey and making his famous fat-free pumpkin pie. Olympia would be wrapping the old butler's gift, tying a candy cane into the ribbon. Caleb loved peppermints.

Annie's gifts for Caleb and her aunt sat on her pillow, wrapped and ready to be delivered the moment she returned from the cruise. Neither Olympia nor Caleb would mind the delay, and a little festivity after the holiday would only extend the season . . . wouldn't it?

Melanie had already called twice to remind her that their group was meeting at the airport gate. The flight left Portland at 6 P.M., then they'd change planes in Boston and fly through the darkness to Miami. By this time tomorrow, Annie would be sitting on the deck of the *Glorious* sipping a tall glass of tropical fruit punch decorated with a tiny umbrella.

So why wasn't she doing handsprings?

She tossed a bottle of suntan lotion into her bag, then sat down on the side of the bed and stared at the suitcase.

"Go on the cruise, dear. And have a wonderful time."

Throwing her head back, Annie shut her eyes. "Don't do this! Keep packing."

She pulled herself off the bed, then moved to the closet and added another pair of dress slacks. "The ferry isn't running," she reminded herself. "You couldn't get there if you wanted to."

Pulling her favorite pajamas from beneath her pillow, she tossed them in the suitcase.

Just think—dozens of single men, unlimited food, dancing under the stars.

Her gaze fell upon the framed picture on her nightstand—a photo of Caleb and Olympia, snapped in happier days. Staring at the picture, she could almost smell Caleb's turkey and dressing, see the joy on his face when he gave her his Christmas present . . .

She turned away.

"Snorkeling," she muttered. "Swimming with the manta rays. Shopping—lots of wonderful shopping!"

She bent to rummage through her sock drawer, and Dr. Marc's face flitted through her mind. *"You are coming to my Christmas Eve party, aren't you? You and Alex would hit it off."*

"Sorry." Annie thrust an extra pair of hose into her bag. "Can't get there—tried, honest. Can't make it."

She straightened and ticked off her list on her fingertips—clothes for dining, dancing, playing, swimming. Underwear, socks, pajamas, toothbrush. Makeup, of course. Hairbrush. Shoes, lots of shoes.

Done. She glanced at the bedside clock and smiled. Packed and ready with hours to spare. Time enough to call . . . Her eyes traveled to the phone.

No. No sense asking for trouble.

She closed the lid on her suitcase, picked it up . . . and set it back down.

She was a sentimental fool cursed with a devilishly good memory. Aunt Olympia hadn't remembered Crazy Odell, but Annie couldn't forget him. And she couldn't go on a cruise without at least trying to reach Heavenly Daze. It'd been years since she'd heard anything of Crazy Odell, so it would serve her right if the man had developed a sudden attack of good sense and preferred the warmth of his own home and hearth on Christmas Eve. The only thing Annie knew for certain was she had to try to be with Olympia this Christmas before she could think of herself.

She slipped into her coat, then walked to the phone. "Melanie? Don't freak out on me, but I've got to do something before I leave." She explained her dilemma. "If I'm not at the gate by flight time, leave without me. If I can't get to Heavenly Daze, I'll keep driving and meet you in Boston."

A moment later she packed a smaller bag, flipped off the lights, and locked the door. She carried both suitcases and her Christmas gifts to the car, then stowed them in the trunk.

And as she turned the key, one thought flashed across her brain: She should seriously consider getting professional help.

Perkins Cove was deserted and sheeted with snow when Annie arrived just before six, and, as she'd suspected, the ferry was moored to the dock and Captain Stroble's office sat empty. A laminated sign in the window advised that the ferry would not run until adverse weather conditions abated.

Annie drew a deep breath and turned toward the row of small houses lining the street leading to the Cove. She had expected this obstacle. Now, if only Crazy Odell were still alive . . . and reckless.

Odell proved to be not only alive, but also

thriving. Ninety-two, he told her when she knocked on his cottage door, and still kicking.

Even more surprising, the old man remembered Annie. "Olympia's niece, right?" he said, pulling on his gloves. "Lost your parents in that plane crash back in '82?"

"That's me," she said, shivering. "And I'd be happy to pay you thirty dollars if you can get me out to the island."

He cackled a laugh and tugged on another glove. "Keep your money, child, and Merry Christmas. I can get you there as long as you don't mind being scared out of your britches. I only ask one thing."

Annie lowered her head as he glanced furtively left and right. "Don't tell my granddaughter. She'll have my hide."

Because she valued her britches, Annie wavered, then Odell assured her the passage would be cold, wet, and safe.

"Old Sally's seen worse," he said, referring to his thirty-foot lobster boat. The wooden vessel had to be fifty years old, had peeling paint and a deck heaped with lobster traps, but Odell assured her the boat would get her to Heavenly Daze. "Why, last week I took Stanley Bidderman across without any trouble."

"Stanley Bidderman?" Annie frowned. "I thought he was dead."

The old man chuckled and winked. "Might be now. Vernie's bound to have torn into him, and I ain't seen him come back across."

Annie waited in her car while Odell rowed out to get the boat. *The Sally* rocked in the harbor, dusted with snow and looking anything but eager for the trip.

When she saw Odell climb aboard the vessel, Annie dragged her small suitcase from the trunk, along with a shopping bag containing Caleb's and Olympia's Christmas gifts, Vernie's cat food, two clanking bags of nutmeg tins, and five five-pound bags of sugar. She'd ditched the no-longer-fresh cranberries in Portland.

She tucked her scarf around her neck and chin, pulled her knitted cap low on her head, and picked up her burdens. Balancing her load between two hands, she started toward the dock, wading through snow up to her ankles.

While she picked her way through the slippery parking lot, another car pulled in and braked. A moment later a man got out, clothed in a heavy coat, hat, gloves, and sensible snow boots. Annie squinted, not recognizing the car or the figure. This could be Odell's granddaughter's husband, come to fetch the old lobsterman home.

No. The stranger moved to his trunk and retrieved a suit bag and small duffel. He slung the suit bag over his shoulder, then strode toward the ferry.

"Hello, there!" Annie called. "The ferry isn't running!"

The man halted in midstep. "What? I need to reach Heavenly Daze tonight!"

Annie pointed toward the crowded harbor. "I've found a boat to take me across. You're welcome to share, if you don't mind riding with Crazy Odell."

Odell wouldn't mind the extra passenger, and Annie knew she'd feel safer with a younger man aboard. She didn't relish the prospect of *The Sally* going down and ninety-two-year-old Odell trying to save her. Or vice versa.

Walking with a long and easy stride, the stranger approached. "Thanks. I had an emergency, so I arrived later than I'd planned. I had hoped to catch the six o'clock ferry."

Annie stood stock still as the voice reverberated in her ears. She knew that voice. She squinted into the growing darkness, trying to decipher the man's features.

"A. J.?" The name slipped out like a wish.

He came closer. "Could that be Annie?"

Stunned, Annie shook her head. If this was a dream, she didn't want to wake up.

"You're not Annie?" Was that disappointment in his tone?

She burst into laughter. "No, I am. I mean, yes, it's me." She dropped her bags as a pair of strong arms swept her into a friendly embrace.

"What are you doing here?" A. J. asked, his eyes snapping joyfully.

She breathed in the scent of his crisp, clean, and oh-so-familiar aftershave. "I live here—when I'm not in Portland, that is. What are you doing here?"

His hold tightened possessively around her waist. It was the most pleasant sensation Annie had experienced in—well, ever.

"Trying to get to Dad's for Christmas." A. J. paused, his eyes sobering. "Oh, no."

Stepping back, he held her at arm's length, his eyes slowly perusing her.

Annie frowned. "What?"

A small smile played at the corner of his

mouth. "You wouldn't be tomatoes-in-winter Annie, would you?"

She groaned as something clicked in her brain. "Oh, no. You aren't Mr. Great Catch from New York . . . are you?"

His smile deepened. "Guilty as charged, I'm afraid, if you believe my father."

"Me, too. I'm Tomato Annie."

And as she stood there, with A. J.'s hands lightly holding hers, Annie thought that God had just given her the best and most unexpected Christmas surprise ever. She might have given up a Caribbean cruise, but she'd received her own Mr. Perfect on a cold, snowy Christmas Eve.

Thank you, God.

Reluctantly dropping A. J.'s hands, she smiled up at him in the light of a street lamp. "Dr. Marc told me his son was named Alex."

"Alexander James," he said, slipping his hands into his coat pockets. "My friends call me A. J. My patients call me Dr. Hayes. Dad is the only one who calls me Alex."

While they stood there, relishing the pleasant surprise, a taxi pulled into the parking lot. A figure got out of the backseat and bent to count out change for the driver. A moment later Annie saw that the passenger was a man, hatless and gloveless in the cold. He jogged toward them and yelled out a greeting. "Is the ferry running?"

"Not tonight."

Annie was aware that A. J.'s arm had slipped around her waist, a perfectly wonderful feeling. She leaned closer to his protective warmth, fitting snugly under his arm.

When the man came closer, Annie pointed to the harbor. "The ferry won't run in this weather, but Crazy Odell's about to pull up and take us aboard. You're welcome to come along . . . if you're up to battling rough water."

The man shoved his hands in his pockets, glanced toward the sea, then gave Annie an abrupt nod. "Yes, I'm up to it. Thank you." He seemed to think a moment, then extended his hand. "Patrick Gribbon."

"Annie Cuvier." She shook the man's hand and found it cold and trembling. "And this is Dr. Alex Hayes." She smiled up at A. J., realizing that his name slid off her lips like rich, sweet molasses.

A. J. shook Patrick's hand. "Merry Christmas."

Patrick lifted his shoulders and hunched inside his coat, then turned his gaze toward the black horizon where Heavenly Daze lay just out of sight. "Do you believe in miracles?" he asked, glancing back at Annie for a brief instant.

"I do, Patrick." Annie smiled up at A. J. "Of course I do."

A moment passed, then Patrick nodded. "I wasn't sure I did . . . until a moment ago."

As an air horn echoed in the harbor, the trio moved toward the dock. Though *The Sally* plowed through the waters more like an arthritic Tyrannosaurus rex than a cruise ship, Annie thought it the most beautiful boat in the world.

CHAPTER TWENTY-SIX

"Oh come, all ye faithful . . ."

Salt turned in the pew to watch the children enter through the back of the church. Edith Wickam had done a wonderful job of outfitting Bobby, Brittany, and Georgie in short white baptismal robes accented by floppy red neck bows. As each child carried a candle down the center aisle, accompanied by the strains of the beloved carol, Salt felt the joy of the season echo in his heart for the first time in years.

Beside him, Birdie slipped her hand into his and squeezed. He squeezed back, then felt a sudden burst of gratitude for the lowered lights in the sanctuary. Oh, how Olympia's and Vernie's tongues would clack if they caught him blushing while holding Birdie Wester's hand!

With all the reverence due a nativity scene, the children walked to the candelabra at the front of the church and fitted their candles into the holder, then slipped to their places on the front pew. Charles and Babette drew Georgie to a spot between them, not quite willing to let him wriggle out of their grasp.

Outside, the rising wind howled and whistled through the belfry, but in the sanctuary all was cozy and warm.

Salt glanced around at the assembled villagers—100 percent attendance, if he figured correctly. Bea played at the piano, her face lit by candlelight, while Olympia de Cuvier and Caleb Smith sat on the front pew, with Tallulah occupying her mistress's lap. The Grahams, Brittany, and Bobby filled the other seats, and across the aisle Edith Wickam sat with Buddy Franklin. The Lansdowns and Higgses occupied another pew, followed by Dr. Marc and the Klackenbushes. Vernie sat on their right, accompanied by Stanley Bidderman, who kept solicitously handing her tissues for her sniffles. At the rear of the church, an entire pew was filled with Smiths—Abner, Micah, Yakov, Zuriel, and Elezar.

Salt settled back against the pew, struggling against the snugness of a sports coat he hadn't worn in ten years. Birdie had declared that he looked right handsome, and the praise had warmed him more than he wanted to admit.

Winslow Wickam stood from his seat on the platform and walked to the pulpit. "Brothers and sisters, fellow citizens of Heavenly Daze," he said, his round face beaming a smile over the congregation, "we are gathered here tonight to celebrate a most miraculous birthday. For without it, we would be forever lost on this planet, helpless in our sins. But God had mercy upon us."

Winslow opened his Bible and began to read:

In the beginning the Word already existed. He was with God, and he was God. He was in the beginning with God. He created everything there is. Nothing exists that he didn't make. Life itself was in him, and this life gives light to everyone. The light shines through the darkness, and the darkness can never extinguish it. . . .

But although the world was made through him, the world didn't recognize him when he came. Even in his own land and among his own people, he was not accepted. But to all who believed him and accepted him, he gave the right to become children of God. They are reborn! This is not a physical birth resulting from human passion or plan—this rebirth comes from God.

So the Word became human and lived here on earth among us. He was full of unfailing love and faithfulness. And we have seen his glory, the glory of the only Son of the Father.

Salt felt his soul expand as the minister read of the light and the glory and the One who had come. He had seen that light! He had beheld that glory! And he, who did not deserve it, had seen the One who came, the one he'd met as a child and neglected for so many years.

"Jesus was born so you and I might be reborn," Winslow said, closing his Bible. "Without the miracle of Christmas, there would be no mercy at Calvary. Without the miracle of the virgin birth, there would be no miracle of a spiritual birth for you or me. We owe our blessed hope to the Child in the manger."

As Winslow bowed his head, the double doors at the back of the sanctuary swung open, sending a blast of Arctic air into the comfortable room. The candles sputtered and went out, but Bea had the presence of mind to lean over and flip the switch near the piano.

Light flooded the church, revealing three bewildered strangers in the aisle.

"Alex?"

"Annie?"

Dr. Marc sprang from the pew to embrace his son, while Olympia and Caleb rose to welcome Annie. And slowly, Salt stood and stepped into the aisle, ignoring the hubbub of greetings.

The third man, a stranger to Heavenly Daze, lifted his head and met Salt's gaze head-on.

"Dad—I've come to ask your forgiveness . . . and the forgiveness of my kids."

"Patrick." The word slipped from Salt's tongue of its own accord. Reflexively, he took a half-step back toward the front pew where Bobby and Brittany sat transfixed.

"Dad?" As Patrick took a shaky step forward, silence fell over the sanctuary. Olympia and Annie stood frozen in an over-the-pew embrace, and Dr. Marc released his son.

"Patrick." Salt said the name again, and

this time his voice trembled. He extended his hand. "Welcome home, son."

Then he ran forward on legs that trembled more violently than they had when he was lost and cold in the water, and suddenly Patrick was in his arms and his son's tears were wetting his shirt, then Bobby and Brittany were hugging his legs, all four of them swirling in a tumultuous embrace as the church smiled and the residents of Heavenly Daze lifted their hands in spontaneous applause and joyous laughter.

And Salt Gribbon's heart swelled with emotions he'd thought he'd never feel again.

EPILOGUE

*So distinctly I remember it was in a
   cold December,
And every village member came
   rejoicing to my door . . .*

Gavriel here, hoping you've enjoyed another sneak peek at the happenings in Heavenly Daze. The month's end found us with many changes on our little island—Stanley Bidderman vacated the B&B's attic room in favor of Vernie Bidderman's guest room. Vernie took to her bed with the flu on Christmas Day, and Stanley proved to be a most compassionate and caring nurse. Now she doesn't object so much to "sweetums," and there's talk they might actually renew their marriage vows in the spring . . .

A bit of a brouhaha erupted when Annie and Bea invited Vernie to the bakery for a surprise intervention . . . and the town learned that it had been vanilla syrup, not schnapps, that Vernie had been hiding beneath the counter. After being offended, Vernie softened when she realized that her neighbors cared enough to confront her with what they feared was a self-destructive habit.

Romance hit our humans hard this Christmas. Annie and A. J. hardly spent a minute apart during the holiday, and even when A. J. was called back to New York for a medical emergency, his pager kept flashing with Annie's special message: 703870. Apparently, to a love-struck mortal, those numbers look somewhat like "tomato."

On the thirty-first, as the second hand was sweeping in a new year, Birdie Wester convinced Captain Gribbon that the lighthouse needed more than the occasional woman's touch . . . as did he. Wedding bells may be ringing soon, because mortal life is a fleeting thing.

Patrick Gribbon and his children shared a sweet time of fellowship with Salt at the lighthouse, and Patrick has agreed to seek help for his alcoholism. Salt will continue to keep Bobby and Brittany, and Birdie is delighted to help.

The folks at Frenchman's Fairest enjoyed a truly blessed holiday. Olympia found Annie's gift of a cashmere sweater delightful. Caleb especially liked the Humphrey Bogart video Annie bought him, a movie called *We're No Angels*. I hear it's a comedy, but the title alone is enough to make me chuckle.

But amid all the renewed relationships and tinsel and wrapping, one of the best gifts to grace the island crept quietly onto the scene. Shortly before lunch on Christmas day, as Annie went out to the carriage house to call Dr. Marc and A. J. in for Christmas dinner, she discovered it on the ground, dusted with snow: a perfect, ruby-red tomato.

Sometimes miracles bloom in the most unlikely places.

Until we meet again,

—Gavriel

BIRDIE WESTER'S NUTMEG SHORTBREAD

Though these cookies bake for nearly an hour, not much preparation is required.

Yields eight triangles and stores well in tins. Makes great gifts!
11/3 cups flour
1 teaspoon nutmeg
1/4 pound cold butter, cut into 1/4 inch cubes
6 tablespoons sugar
1 large egg yolk (Birdie saves the egg white for meringue.)

Heat the oven to 325 degrees. Grease an eight-inch round cake or pie pan.

In a medium bowl, whisk together the flour and 3/4 teaspoon of the nutmeg. With your fingers, rub in the butter completely until the mixture is the texture of a sandy beach. Stir in 5 tablespoons of the sugar.

Stir in the egg yolk. Press the mixture together to make a dry, crumbly dough and put it on a work surface. Knead the dough several times until it holds together.

Press the dough into the prepared pan. Make sure it is smooth and level. With a small, sharp knife, mark eight wedges halfway into the dough. With a fork, prick the dough every half-inch.

In a small bowl, combine the remaining 1 tablespoon sugar and 1/4 teaspoon nutmeg, then sprinkle it on the dough. Bake the shortbread until golden, 50–55 minutes.

Let the shortbread cool slightly in the pan set on a rack, then cut into wedges. Leave it in the pan until completely cooled.

Invite a few friends over for coffee and enjoy!

IF YOU WANT TO
KNOW MORE ABOUT . . .

- The birth of Jesus Christ: Luke 2

- Gabe's story about the preexistence of Jesus Christ: John 1:1–12

- The story about Moses' staff and the battle against Amalek: Exodus 17:10–12

- How cooperation can sustain people in times of weakness: Exodus 17:12

- Angels as servants and messengers: Genesis 24:7; Exodus 23:20; Hebrews 1:14

- Angels are as "swift as the wind" and "servants made of flaming fire": Hebrews 1:7

- Angels' special care for children: Matthew 18:10

- Angels as protectors: Psalm 91:11–12

- The heavenly throne room: 2 Chronicles 18:18; Psalm 89:14; Psalm 11:4; Revelation 4:1–6

- Angels' limited knowledge: Matthew 24:36

- Angels eagerly watching humans: 1 Peter 1:12

- The third, or highest, heaven: 2 Corinthians 12:2; Deuteronomy 10:14; 1 Kings 8:27; Psalm 115:16

For the latest news from Heavenly Daze, visit

www.heavenlydazeME.com